Before the race was the deluge, and before the deluge another race, whose nature it is not for mankind to understand.

There was a war between this race, which was a great one, and another. The other was spawned in mighty machines by some accident of a science before our aboriginal conception of its complexities. And the machines, servants of the people, became the people's masters, and great were the battles that followed. . . .

—From "Killdozer!" by Theodore Sturgeon

"And the machines...became the people's masters..." is a notion at the heart of many all-time favorite science fiction stories: the fear of technology gone wrong. Here are stories of far-future battles, of fearsome weapons and great courage, drawn from the best-known authors in the field. From famous award-winners like Alfred Bester's "Fondly Fahrenheit" to newer stories like David Drake's "Under the Hammer," MACHINES THAT KILL will thrill every reader who loves action and adventure.

MACHINES THAT KILL

Edited by
Fred Saberhagen and
Martin Harry Greenberg

ACE SCIENCE FICTION BOOKS
NEW YORK

MACHINES THAT KILL

An Ace Science Fiction Book/published by arrangement with
the editors

PRINTING HISTORY
Ace Original/December 1984

ISBN: 0-441-51358-1

Ace Science Fiction Books are published by The Berkley Publishing Group,
200 Madison Avenue, New York, New York 10016.
PRINTED IN THE UNITED STATES OF AMERICA

ACKNOWLEDGMENTS

Contents

KILLDOZER!

Theodore Sturgeon

Before the race was the deluge, and before the deluge another race, whose nature it is not for mankind to understand. Not unearthly, not alien, for this was their earth and their home.

There was a war between this race, which was a great one, and another. The other was truly alien, a sentient cloudform, an intelligent grouping of tangible electrons. It was spawned in mighty machines by some accident of a science before our aboriginal conception of its complexities. And the machines, servants of the people, became the people's masters, and great were the battles that followed. The electron-beings had the power to warp the delicate balances of atom-structure, and their life-medium was metal, which they permeated and used to their own ends. Each weapon the people developed was possessed and turned against them, until a time when the remnants of that vast civilization found a defense—

An insulator. The terminal product or by-product of all energy research—neutronium.

In its shelter they developed a weapon. What it was we shall never know, and our race will live—or we shall know, and our race will perish as theirs perished. For, to destroy the

1

enemy, it got out of hand and its measureless power destroyed them with it, and their cities, and their possessed machines. The very earth dissolved in flame, the crust writhed and shook and the ocean boiled. Nothing escaped it, nothing that we know as life, and nothing of the pseudolife that had evolved within the mysterious force-fields of their incomprehensible machines, save one hardy mutant.

Mutant it was, and ironically this one alone could have been killed by the first simple measures used against its kind—but it was past time for simple expediences. It was an organized electron-field possessing intelligence and mobility and a will to destroy, and little else. Stunned by the holocaust, it drifted over the grumbling globe, and in a lull in the violence of the forces gone wild on Earth, sank to the steaming ground in its half-conscious exhaustion. There it found shelter—shelter built by and for its dead enemies. An envelope of neutronium. It drifted in, and its consciousness at last fell to its lowest ebb. And there it lay while the neutronium, with its strange constant flux, its interminable striving for perfect balance, extended itself and closed the opening. And thereafter in the turbulent eons that followed, the envelope tossed like a gray bubble on the surface of the roiling sphere, for no substance on Earth would have it or combine with it.

The ages came and went, and chemical action and reaction did their mysterious work, and once again there was life and evolution. And a tribe found the mass of neutronium, which is not a substance but a static force, and were awed by its aura of indescribable chill, and they worshiped it and built a temple around it and made sacrifices to it. And ice and fire and the seas came and went, and the land rose and fell as the years went by, until the ruined temple was on a knoll, and the knoll was an island. Islanders came and went, lived and built and died, and races forgot. So now, somewhere in the Pacific to the west of the archipelago called Islas Revillagigeda, there was an uninhabited island. And one day—

Chub Horton and Tom Jaeger stood watching the *Sprite* and her squat tow of three cargo lighters dwindle over the glassy sea. The big ocean-going towboat and her charges seemed to be moving out of focus rather than traveling away. Chub spat cleanly around the cigar that grew out of the corner of his mouth.

"That's that for three weeks. How's it feel to be a guinea pig?"

"We'll get it done." Tom had little crinkles all around the outer ends of his eyes. He was a head taller than Chub and rangy, and not so tough, and he was a real operator. Choosing him as a foreman for the experiment had been wise, for he was competent and he commanded respect. The theory of airfield construction that they were testing appealed vastly to him, for here were no officers-in-charge, no government inspectors, no timekeeping or reports. The government had allowed the company a temporary land grant, and the idea was to put production-line techniques into the layout and grading of the project. There were six operators and two mechanics and more than a million dollars' worth of the best equipment that money could buy. Government acceptance was to be on a partially completed basis, and contingent on government standards. The theory obviated both gold-bricking and graft, and neatly sidestepped the manpower shortage. "When that blacktopping crew gets here, I reckon we'll be ready for 'em," said Tom.

He turned and scanned the island with an operator's vision and saw it as it was, and in all the stages it would pass through, and as it would look when they had finished, with four thousand feet of clean-draining runway, hard-packed shoulders, four acres of plane-park, the access road and the short taxiway. He saw the lay of each lift that the power shovel would cut as it brought down the marl bluff, and the ruins on top of it that would give them stone to haul down the salt-flat to the little swamp at the other end, there to be walked in by the dozers.

"We got time to walk the shovel up there to the bluff before dark."

They walked down the beach toward the outcropping where the equipment stood surrounded by crates and drums of supplies. The three tractors were ticking over quietly, the two-cycle diesel chuckling through their mufflers and the big D-7 whacking away in metronomic compression knock on every easy revolution. The Dumptors were lined up and silent, for they would not be ready to work until the shovel was ready to load them. They looked like a mechanical interpretation of Dr. Doolittle's "Pushme-pullyou," the fantastic animal with two front ends. They had two large driving wheels and two small steerable wheels. The motor and the driver's seat were side by side over the front—or smaller—wheels; but the driver faced the dump body between the big rear wheels, exactly the opposite of the way he would sit in a dump truck. Hence, in traveling from shovel to dumping-ground, the operator drove backwards, looking over his shoulder, and in dumping he backed the machine up but he himself traveled forward—quite a trick for fourteen hours a day! The shovel squatted in the midst of all the others, its great hulk looming over them, humped there with its boom low and its iron chin on the ground, like some great tired dinosaur.

Rivera, the Puerto Rican mechanic, looked up grinning as Tom and Chub approached, and stuck a bleeder wrench into the top pocket of his coveralls.

"She says 'Sigalo,'" he said, his white teeth flashlighting out of the smear of grease across his mouth. "She says she wan' to get dirt on dis paint." He kicked the blade of the Seven with his heel.

Tom sent the grin back—always a surprising thing in his grave face.

"That Seven'll do that, and she'll take a good deal off her bitin' edge along with the paint before we're through. Get in the saddle, Goony. Build a ramp off the rocks down to the flat there, and blade us off some humps from here to the bluff yonder. We're walking the dipper up there."

The Puerto Rican was in the seat before Tom had finished, and with a roar the Seven spun in its length and moved back along the outcropping to the inland edge. Rivera dropped his blade and the sandy marl curled and piled up in front of the dozer, loading the blade and running off in two even rolls at the ends. He shoved the load toward the rocky edge, the Seven revving down as it took the load, *blat blat blatting* and pulling like a supercharged ox as it fired slowly enough for them to count the revolutions.

"She's a hunk of machine," said Tom.

"A hunk of operator, too," gruffed Chub, and added, "for a mechanic."

"The boy's all right," said Kelly. He was standing there with them, watching the Puerto Rican operate the dozer, as if he had been there all along, which was the way Kelly always arrived places. He was tall, slim, with green eyes too long and an easy stretch to the way he moved, like an attenuated cat. He said, "Never thought I'd see the day when equipment was shipped set up ready to run like this. Guess no one ever thought of it before."

"There's times when heavy equipment has to be unloaded in a hurry these days," Tom said. "If they can do it with tanks, they can do it with construction equipment. We're doin' it to build something instead, is all. Kelly, crank up the shovel. It's oiled. We're walking it over to the bluff."

Kelly swung up into the cab of the big dipper-stick and, diddling the governor control, pulled up the starting handle. The Murphy diesel snorted and settled down into a thudding idle. Kelly got into the saddle, set up the throttle a little, and began to boom up.

"I still can't get over it," said Chub. "Not more'n a year ago we'd a had two hundred men on a job like this."

Tom smiled. "Yeah, and the first thing we'd have done would be to build an office building, and then quarters. Me, I'll take this way. No timekeepers, no equipment-use reports, no progress and yardage summaries, no nothin' but eight men, a million bucks worth of equipment, an' three weeks. A shovel an' a mess of tool crates'll keep the rain off us, an' army field rations'll keep our bellies full. We'll get it done, we'll get out and we'll get paid."

Rivera finished the ramp, turned the Seven around and climbed it, walking the new fill down. At the top he dropped his blade, floated it, and backed down the ramp, smoothing out the rolls. At a wave from Tom he started out across the shore, angling up toward the bluff, beating out the humps and carrying fill into the hollows. As he worked, he sang, feeling the beat of the mighty motor, the micrometric obedience of that vast implacable machine.

"Why doesn't that monkey stick to his grease guns?"

Tom turned and took the chewed end of a match stick out of his mouth. He said nothing, because he had for some time been trying to make a habit of saying nothing to Joe Dennis. Dennis was an ex-accountant, drafted out of an office at the last gasp of a defunct project in the West Indies. He had become an operator because they needed operators badly. He had been released with alacrity from the office because of his propensity for small office politics. It was a game he still played, and completely aside from his boiled-looking red face and his slightly womanish walk, he was out of place in the field; for boot-licking and back-stabbing accomplish even less out in the field than they do in an office. Tom, trying so hard to keep his mind on his work, had to admit to himself that of all Dennis' annoying traits the worst was that he was as good a pan operator as could be found anywhere, and no one could deny it.

Dennis certainly didn't.

"I've seen the day when anyone catching one of those goonies so much as sitting on a machine during lunch, would kick his fanny," Dennis groused. "Now they give 'em a man's work and a man's pay."

"*Doin'* a man's work, ain't he?" Tom said.

"He's a Puerto Rican!"

Tom turned and looked at him levelly. "Where was it you said *you* come from," he mused. "Oh yeah. Georgia."

"What do you mean by that?"

Tom was already striding away. "Tell you as soon as I have to," he flung back over his shoulder. Dennis went back to watching the Seven.

Tom glanced at the ramp and then waved Kelly on. Kelly set his house-brake so the shovel could not swing, put her into travel gear, and shoved the swing lever forward. With a crackling of drive chains and a massive scrunching of compacting coral sand, the shovel's great flat pads carried her over and down the ramp. As she tipped over the peak of the ramp the heavy manganese steel bucket-door gaped open and closed, like a hungry mouth, slamming up against the bucket until suddenly it latched shut and was quiet. The big Murphy diesel crooned hollowly under compression as the machine ran downgrade and then the sensitive governor took hold and it took up its belly-beating thud.

Peebles was standing by one of the door-pan combines, sucking on his pipe and looking out to sea. He was grizzled and heavy, and from under the bushiest gray brows looked the calmest gray eyes Tom had ever seen. Peebles had never gotten angry at a machine—a rare trait in a born mechanic—and in fifty-odd years he had learned it was even less use getting angry at a man. Because no matter what, you could always fix what was wrong with a machine. He said around his pipestem:

"Hope you'll give me back my boy, there."

Tom's lips quirked in a little grin. There had been an understanding between old Peebles and himself ever since they

had met. It was one of those things which exists unspoken—
they knew little about each other because they had never found
it necessary to make small talk to keep their friendship extant.
It was enough to know that each could expect the best from
the other, without persuasion.

"Rivera?" Tom asked. "I'll chase him back as soon as he
finishes that service road for the dipper-stick. Why—got anything on?"

"Not much. Want to get that arc welder drained and flushed
and set up a grounded table in case you guys tear anything
up." He paused. "Besides, the kid's filling his head up with
too many things at once. Mechanicing is one thing; operating
is something else."

"Hasn't got in his way much so far, has it?"

"Nope. Don't aim t' let it, either. 'Less you need him."

Tom swung up on the pan tractor. "I don't need him that
bad, Peeby. If you want some help in the meantime, get Dennis."

Peebles said nothing. He spat. He didn't say anything at
all.

"What's the matter with Dennis?" Tom wanted to know.

"Look yonder," said Peebles, waving his pipestem. Out on
the beach Dennis was talking to Chub, in Dennis' indefatigable
style, standing beside Chub, one hand on Chub's shoulder. As
they watched they saw Dennis call his side-kick, Al Knowles.

"Dennis talks too much," said Peebles. "That most generally
don't amount to much, but that Dennis, he sometimes says too
much. Ain't got what it takes to run a show, and knows it.
Makes up for by messin' in between folks."

"He's harmless," said Tom.

Still looking up the beach, Peebles said slowly:

"Is, so far."

Tom started to say something, then shrugged. "I'll send you
Rivera," he said, and opened the throttle. Like a huge electric
dynamo, the two-cycle motor whined to a crescendo. Tom lifted
the dozer with a small lever by his right thigh and raised the
pan with the long control sprouting out from behind his shoulder. He moved off, setting the rear gate of the scraper so that
anything the blade bit would run off to the side instead of
loading into the pan. He slapped the tractor into sixth gear and
whined up to and around the crawling shovel, cutting neatly
in under the boom and running on ahead with his scraper blade

just touching the ground, dragging to a fine grade the service road Rivera had cut.

Dennis was saying, "It's that little Hitler stuff. Why should I take that kind of talk? 'You come from Georgia,' he says. What is he—a Yankee or something?"

"A crackah f'm Macon," chortled Al Knowles, who came from Georgia, too. He was tall and stringy and round-shouldered. All of his skill was in his hands and feet, brains being a commodity he had lived without all his life until he had met Dennis and used him as a reasonable facsimile thereof.

"Tom didn't mean nothing by it," said Chub.

"No, he didn't mean nothin'. Only that we do what he says the way he says it, specially if he finds a way we don't like it. *You* wouldn't do like that, Chub. Al, think Chub would carry on thataway?"

"Sure wouldn't," said Al, feeling it expected of him.

"Nuts," said Chub, pleased and uncomfortable, and thinking, what have I got against Tom?—not knowing, not liking Tom as well as he had. "Tom's the man here, Dennis. We got a job to do—let's skit and git. Man can take anything for a lousy six weeks."

"Oh, sho'," said Al.

"Man can take just so much," Dennis said. "What they put a man like that on top for, Chub? What's the matter with you? Don't you know grading and drainage as good as Tom? Can Tom stake out a side hill like you can?"

"Sure, sure, but what's the difference, long as we get a field built? An' anyhow, hell with bein' the boss-man. Who gets the blame if things don't run right, anyway?"

Dennis stepped back, taking his hand off Chub's shoulder, and stuck an elbow in Al's ribs.

"You see that, Al? Now there's a smart man. That's the thing Uncle Tom didn't bargain for. Chub, you can count on Al and me to do just that little thing."

"Do just what little thing?" asked Chub, genuinely puzzled.

"Like you said. If the job goes wrong, the boss gets blamed. So if the boss don't behave, the job goes wrong."

"Uh-huh," agreed Al with the conviction of mental simplicity.

Chub double-took this extraordinary logical process and

grasped wildly at anger as the conversation slid out from under him. "I didn't say any such thing! This job is goin' to get done, no matter what! Hitler ain't hangin' no iron cross on me or anybody else around here if I can help it."

"That's the ol' fight," feinted Dennis. "We'll show that guy what we think of his kind of sabotage."

"You talk too much," said Chub and escaped with the remnants of coherence. Every time he talked with Dennis he walked away feeling as if he had an unwanted membership card stuck in his pocket that he couldn't throw away with a clear conscience.

Rivera ran his road up under the bluff, swung the Seven around, punched out the master clutch and throttled down, idling. Tom was making his pass with the pan, and as he approached, Rivera slipped out of the seat and behind the tractor, laying a sensitive hand on the final drive casing and sprocket bushings, checking for overheating. Tom pulled alongside and beckoned him up on the pan tractor.

"Que pase, Goony? Anything wrong?"

Rivera shook his head and grinned. "Nothing wrong. She is perfect, that *'De Siete.'* She—".

"That what? 'Daisy Etta'?"

"De siete. In Spanish, D-7. It means something in English?"

"Got you wrong," smiled Tom. "But Daisy Etta is a girl's name in English, all the same."

He shifted the pan tractor into neutral and engaged the clutch, and jumped off the machine. Rivera followed. They climbed aboard the Seven, Tom at the controls.

Rivera said "Daisy Etta," and grinned so widely that a soft little chuckling noise came from behind his back teeth. He reached out his hand, crooked his little finger around one of the tall steering clutch levers, and pulled it all the way back. Tom laughed outright.

"You got something there," he said. "The easiest runnin' cat ever built. Hydraulic steerin' clutches and brakes that'll bring you to a dead stop if you spit on 'em. Forward an' reverse lever so's you got all your speeds front and backwards. A little different from the old jobs. They had no booster springs, eighten years ago; a sixty-pound pull to get a steerin' clutch back. Cuttin' a side-hill with an angle-dozer really was a job in them days. You try it sometime, dozin' with one hand, holdin' her nose out o' the bank with the other, ten hours a day. And what'd it get you? Eighty cents an hour an'"—Tom took his cigarette and butted the fiery end out against the horny palm of his hand—"these."

"*Santa Maria!*"

"Want to talk to you, Goony. Want to look over the bluff, too, at that stone up there. It'll take Kelly pret' near an hour to get this far and sumped in, anyhow."

They started up the slope, Tom feeling the ground under the four-foot brush, taking her up in a zigzag course like a hairpin road on a mountainside. Though the Seven carried a muffler on the exhaust stack that stuck up out of the hood before them, the blat of four big cylinders hauling fourteen tons of steel upgrade could outshout any man's conversation, so they sat without talking, Tom driving, Rivera watching his hands flick over the controls.

The bluff started in a low ridge running almost the length of the little island, like a lopsided backbone. Toward the center it rose abruptly, sent a wing out toward the rocky outcropping at the beach where their equipment had been unloaded, and then rose again to a small, almost square plateau area, half a mile square. It was humpy and rough until they could see all of it, when they realized how incredibly level it was, under the brush and ruins that covered it. In the center—and exactly in the center they realized suddenly—was a low, overgrown mound. Tom threw out the clutch and revved her down.

"Survey report said there was stone up here," Tom said, vaulting out of the seat. "Let's walk around some."

They walked toward the knoll, Tom's eyes casting about as he went. He stooped down into the heavy, short grass and scooped up a piece of stone, blue-gray, hard and brittle.

"Rivera—look at this. This is what the report was talking about. See—more of it. All in small pieces, though. We need big stuff for the bog if we can get it."

"Good stone?" asked Rivera.

"Yes, boy—but it don't belong here. Th' whole island's sand and marl and sandstone on the outcrop down yonder. This here's a bluestone, like diamond clay. Harder'n blazes. I never saw this stuff on a marl hill before. Or near one. Anyhow, root around and see if there is any big stuff."

They walked on. Rivera suddenly dipped down and pulled grass aside.

"Tom—here's a beeg one."

Tom came over and looked down at the corner of stone sticking up out of the topsoil. "Yeh. Goony, get your girlfriend over here and we'll root it out."

Rivera sprinted back to the idling dozer and climbed aboard. He brought the machine over to where Tom waited, stopped, stood up and peered over the front of the machine to locate the stone, then sat down and shifted gears. Before he could move the machine Tom was on the fender beside him, checking him with a hand on his arm.

"No, boy—no. Not third. First. And half throttle. That's it. Don't try to bash a rock out of the ground. Go on up to it easy; set your blade against it, lift it out, don't boot it out. Take it with the middle of your blade, not the corner—get the load on both hydraulic cylinders. Who told you to do like that?"

"No one tol' me, Tom. I see a man do it, I do it."

"Yeah? Who was it?"

"Dennis, but—"

"Listen, Goony, if you want to learn anything from Dennis, watch him while he's on a pan. He dozes like he talks. That reminds me—what I wanted to talk to you about. You ever have any trouble with him?"

Rivera spread his hands. "How I have trouble when he never talk to me?"

"Well, that's all right then. You keep it that way. Dennis is O.K., I guess, but you better keep away from him."

He went on to tell the boy then about what Peebles had said concerning being an operator and a mechanic at the same time. Rivera's lean dark face fell, and his hand strayed to the blade control, touching it lightly, feeling the composition grip and the machined locknuts that held it. When Tom had quite finished he said:

"O.K., Tom—if you want, you break 'em, I feex 'em. But if you wan' help some time, I run *Daisy Etta* for you, no?"

"Sure, kid, sure. But don't forget, no man can do everything."

"You can do everything," said the boy.

Tom leaped off the machine and Rivera shifted into first and crept up to the stone, setting the blade gently against it.

Taking the load, the mighty engine audibly bunched its muscles; Rivera opened the throttle a little and the machine set solidly against the stone, the tracks slipping, digging into the ground, piling loose earth up behind. Tom raised a fist, thumb up, and the boy began lifting his blade. The Seven lowered her snout like an ox pulling through mud; the front of the tracks buried themselves deeper and the blade slipped upward an inch on the rock, as if it were on a ratchet. The stone shifted, and suddenly heaved itself up out of the earth that covered it, bulging the sod aside like a ship's slow bow wave. And the blade lost its grip and slipped over the stone. Rivera slapped out the master clutch within an ace of letting the mass of it poke through his radiator core. Reversing, he set the blade against it again and rolled it at last into daylight.

Tom stood staring at it, scratching the back of his neck. Rivera got off the machine and stood beside him. For a long time they said nothing.

The stone was roughly rectangular, shaped like a brick with one end cut at about a thirty-degree angle. And on the angled face was a square-cut ridge, like the tongue on a piece of milled lumber. The stone was about 3 × 2 × 2 feet, and must have weighed six or seven hundred pounds.

"Now that," said Tom, bug-eyed, "didn't grow *here,* and if it did it never grew that way."

"Una piedra de una casa," said Rivera softly. "Tom, there was a building here, no?"

Tom turned suddenly to look at the knoll.

"There is a building here—or what's left of it. Lord on'y knows how old—"

They stood there in the slowly dwindling light, staring at the knoll; and there came upon them a feeling of oppression, as if there were no wind and no sound anywhere. And yet there was a wind, and behind them *Daisy Etta* whacked away with her muttering idle, and nothing had changed and—was that it? That nothing had changed? That nothing would change, or could, here?

Tom opened his mouth twice to speak, and couldn't, or didn't want to—he didn't know which. Rivera slumped down suddenly on his hunkers, back erect, and his eyes wide.

It grew very cold. "It's cold," Tom said, and his voice sounded harsh to him. And the wind blew warm on them, the earth was warm under Rivera's knees. The cold was not a lack of heat, but a lack of something else—warmth, but the specific warmth of life-force, perhaps. The feeling of oppression grew, as if their recognition of the strangeness of the place had started it, and their increasing sensitivity to it made it grow.

Rivera said something, quietly, in Spanish.

"What are you looking at?" asked Tom.

Rivera started violently, threw up an arm, as if to ward off the crash of Tom's voice.

"I . . . there is nothin' to see, Tom. I feel this way wance before. I dunno—" He shook his head, his eyes wide and blank. "An' after, there was being wan hell of a thunderstorm—" His voice petered out.

Tom took his shoulder and hauled him roughly to his feet. "Goony! You slap-happy?"

The boy smiled, almost gently. The down on his upper lip held little spheres of sweat. "I ain' nothin', Tom. I'm jus' scare like hell."

"You scare yourself right back up there on that cat and git to work," Tom roared. More quietly then he said, "I know there's something—wrong—here, Goony, but that ain't goin' to get us a runway built. Anyhow, I know what to do about a dawg 'at gits gun-shy. Ought to be able to do as much fer you. Git along to th' mound now and see if it ain't a cache o' big stone for us. We got a swamp down there to fill."

Rivera hesitated, started to speak, swallowed and then walked slowly over to the Seven. Tom stood watching him, closing his mind to the impalpable pressure of something, somewhere near, making his guts cold.

The bulldozer nosed over to the mound, grunting, reminding Tom suddenly that the machine's Spanish slang name was *puerco*—pig, boar. Rivera angled into the edge of the mound with the cutting corner of the blade. Dirt and brush curled up, fell away from the mound and loaded from the bank side, out along the moldboard. The boy finished his pass along the mound, carried the load past it and wasted it out on the flat, turned around and started back again.

Ten minutes later Rivera struck stone, the manganese steel screaming along it, a puff of gray dust spouting from the cutting corner. Tom knelt and examined it after the machine had passed. It was the same kind of stone they had found out on the flat—

and shaped the same way. But here it was a wall, the angled faces of the block ends obviously tongued and grooved together.

Cold, cold as—

Tom took one deep breath and wiped sweat out of his eyes. "I don't care," he whispered, "I got to have that stone. I got to fill me a swamp." He stood back and motioned to Rivera to blade into a chipped crevice in the buried wall.

The Seven swung into the wall and stopped while Rivera shifted into first, throttled down and lowered his blade. Tom looked up into his face. The boy's lips were white. He eased in the master clutch, the blade dipped and the corner swung neatly into the crevice.

The dozer blatted protestingly and began to crab sideways, pivoting on the end of the blade. Tom jumped out of the way, ran around behind the machine, which was almost parallel with the wall now, and stood in the clear, one hand ready to signal, his eyes on the straining blade. And then everything happened at once.

With a toothy snap the block started and came free, pivoting outward from its square end, bringing with it its neighbor. The block above them dropped, and the whole mound seemed to settle. And *something* whoosed out of the black hole where the rocks had been. Something like a fog, but not a fog that could be seen, something huge that could not be measured. With it came a gust of that cold which was not cold, and the smell of ozone, and the prickling crackle of a mighty static discharge.

Tom was fifty feet from the wall before he knew he had moved. He stopped and saw the Seven suddenly buck like a wild stallion, once, and Rivera turning over twice in the air. Tom shouted some meaningless syllable and tore over to the boy, where he sprawled in the rough grass, lifted him in his arms, and ran. Only then did he realize that he was running from the machine.

It was like a mad thing. Its moldboard rose and fell. It curved away from the mound, howling governor gone wild, controls flailing. The blade dug repeatedly into the earth, gouging it up in great dips through which the tractor plunged, clanking and bellowing furiously. It raced away in a great irregular arc, turned and came snorting back to the mound, where it beat at the buried wall, slewed and scraped and roared.

Tom reached the edge of the plateau sobbing for breath, and kneeling, laid the boy gently down on the grass.

"Goony, boy . . . hey—"

The long silken eyelashes fluttered, lifted. Something wrenched in Tom as he saw the eyes, rolled right back so that only the whites showed. Rivera drew a long quivering breath which caught suddenly. He coughed twice, threw his head from side to side so violently that Tom took it between his hands and steadied it.

"*Ay . . . Maria madre . . . que ha me pasado,* Tom—w'at has happen to me?"

"Fell off the Seven, stupid. You . . . how you feel?"

Rivera scrabbled at the ground, got his elbows half under him, then sank back weakly. "Feel O.K. Headache like hell. W-w'at happen to my feets?"

"Feet? They hurt?"

"No hurt—" The young face went gray, the lips tightened with effort. "No, nothin', Tom."

"You can't move 'em?"

Rivera shook his head, still trying. Tom stood up. "You take it easy. I'll go get Kelly. Be right back."

He walked away quickly and when Rivera called to him he did not turn around. Tom had seen a man with a broken back before.

At the edge of the little plateau Tom stopped, listening. In the deepening twilight he could see the bulldozer standing by the mound. The motor was running; she had not stalled herself. But what stopped Tom was that she wasn't idling, but revving up and down as if an impatient hand were on the throttle—*hroom hroooom,* running up and up far faster than even a broken governor should permit, then coasting down to near silence, broken by the explosive punctuation of sharp and irregular firing. Then it would run up and up again, almost screaming, sustaining an r.p.m. that threatened every moving part, shaking the great machine like some deadly ague.

Tom walked swiftly toward the Seven, a puzzled and grim frown on his weatherbeaten face. Governors break down occasionally, and once in a while you will have a motor tear itself to pieces, revving up out of control. But it will either do that or it will rev down and quit. If an operator is fool enough to

leave his machine with the master clutch engaged, the machine
will take off and run the way the Seven had—but it will not
run unless the blade corner catches in something unresisting,
and then the chances are very strong that it will stall. But in
any case, it was past reason for any machine to act this way,
revving up and down, running, turning, lifting and dropping
the blade.

The motor slowed as he approached, and at last settled down
into something like a steady and regular idle. Tom had the
sudden crazy impression that it was watching him. He shrugged
off the feeling, walked up and laid a hand on the fender.

The Seven reacted like a wild stallion. The big diesel roared,
and Tom distinctly saw the master clutch lever snap back over
center. He leaped clear, expecting the machine to jolt forward,
but apparently it was in a reverse gear, for it shot backward,
one track locked, and the near end of the blade swung in a
swift vicious arc, breezing a bare fraction of an inch past his
hip as he danced back out of the way.

And as if it had bounced off a wall, the tractor had shifted
and was bearing down on him, the twelve-foot blade rising,
the two big headlights looming over him on their bowlegged
supports, looking like the protruding eyes of some mighty toad.
Tom had no choice but to leap straight up and grasp the top
of the blade in his two hands, leaning back hard to brace his
feet against the curved moldboard. The blade dropped and sank
into the soft topsoil, digging a deep little swale in the ground.
The earth loading on the moldboard rose and churned around
Tom's legs; he stepped wildly, keeping them clear of the rolling
drag of it. Up came the blade then, leaving a four-foot pile at
the edge of the pit; down and up the tractor raced as the tracks
went into it; up and up as they climbed the pile of dirt. A quick
balance and overbalance as the machine lurched up and over
like a motorcycle taking a jump off a ramp, and then a spine-
shaking crash as fourteen tons of metal smashed blade-first into
the ground.

Part of the leather from Tom's tough palms stayed with the
blade as he was flung off. He went head over heels backwards,
but had his feet gathered and sprang as they touched the ground;
for he knew that no machine could bury its blade like that and
get out easily. He leaped to the top of the blade, got one hand
on the radiator cap, vaulted. Perversely, the cap broke from

its hinge and came away in his hand, in that split instant when only that hand rested on anything. Off balance, he landed on his shoulder with his legs flailing the air, his body sliding off the hood's smooth shoulder toward the track now churning the earth beneath. He made a wild grab at the air intake pipe, barely had it in his fingers when the dozer freed itself and shot backwards up and over the hump. Again that breathless flight pivoting over the top, and the clanking crash as the machine landed, this time almost flat on its tracks.

The jolt tore Tom's hand away, and as he slid back over the hood the crook of his elbow caught the exhaust stack, the dull red metal biting into his flesh. He grunted and clamped the arm around it. His momentum carried him around it, and his feet crashed into the steering clutch levers. Hooking one with his instep, he doubled his legs and whipped himself back, scrabbling at the smooth warm metal, crawling frantically backward until he finally fell heavily into the seat.

"Now," he gritted through a red wall of pain, "you're gonna git operated." And he kicked out the master clutch.

The motor wailed, with the load taken off so suddenly. Tom grasped the throttle, his thumb clamped down on the ratchet release, and he shoved the lever forward to shut off the fuel.

It wouldn't shut off; it went down to a slow idle, but it wouldn't shut off.

"There's one thing you can't do without," he muttered, "compression."

He stood up and leaned around the dash, reaching for the compression-release lever. As he came up out of the seat, the engine revved up again. He turned to the throttle, which had snapped back into the "open" position. As his hand touched it the master clutch lever snapped in and the howling machine lurched forward with a jerk that snapped his head on his shoulders and threw him heavily back into the seat. He snatched at the hydraulic blade control and threw it to "float" position; and then as the falling moldboard touched the ground, into "power down." The cutting edge bit into the ground and the engine began to labor. Holding the blade control, he pushed the throttle forward with his other hand. One of the steering clutch levers whipped back and struck him agonizingly on the kneecap. He involuntarily let go of the blade control and the moldboard began to rise. The engine began to turn faster and he realized that it was not responding to the throttle. Cursing, he leaped to his feet; the suddenly flailing levers struck him three times in the groin before he could get between them.

Blind with pain, Tom clung gasping to the dash. The oil-pressure gauge fell off the dash to his right, with a tinkling of broken glass, and from its broken quarter-inch line scalding oil drenched him. The shock of it snapped back his wavering consciousness. Ignoring the blows of the left steering clutch and the master clutch which had started the same mad punching, he bent over the left end of the dash and grasped the compression lever. The tractor rushed forward and spun sickeningly, and Tom knew he was thrown. But as he felt himself leave the decking his hand punched the compression lever down. The great valves at the cylinder heads opened and locked open; atomized fuel and superheated air chattered out, and as Tom's head and shoulders struck the ground the great wild machine rolled to a stop, stood silently except for the grumble of water boiling in the cooling system.

Minutes later Tom raised his head and groaned. He rolled over and sat up, his chin on his knees, washed by wave after wave of pain. As they gradually subsided, he crawled to the machine and pulled himself to his feet, hand over hand on the track. And groggily he began to cripple the tractor, at least for the night.

He opened the cock under the fuel tank, left the warm yellow fluid gushing out on the ground. He opened the drain on the reservoir by the injection pump. He found a piece of wire in the crank box and with it tied down the compression release lever. He crawled up on the machine, wrenched the hood and ball jar off the air intake precleaner, pulled off his shirt and stuffed it down the pipe. He pushed the throttle all the way forward and locked it with the locking pin. And he shut off the fuel on the main line from the tank to the pump.

Then he climbed heavily to the ground and slogged back to the edge of the plateau where he had left Rivera.

They didn't know Tom was hurt until an hour and a half later—there had been too much to do—rigging a stretcher for the Puerto Rican, building him a shelter, an engine crate with an Army pup tent for a roof. They brought out the first-aid kit and the medical books and did what they could—tied and splinted and dosed with an opiate. Tom was a mass of bruises, and his right arm, where it had hooked the exhaust stack, was a flayed mass. They fixed him up then, old Peebles handling the sulfa powder and bandages like a trained nurse. And only then was there talk.

"I've seen a man thrown off a pan," said Dennis, as they sat around the coffee urn munching C rations. "Sittin' up on the armrest on a cat, looking backwards. Cat hit a rock and bucked. Threw him off on the track. Stretched him out ten feet long." He in-whistled some coffee to dilute the mouthful of food he had been talking around, and masticated noisily. "Man's a fool to set up there on one side of his butt even on a pan. Can't see why th' goony was doin' it on a dozer."

"He wasn't," said Tom.

Kelly rubbed his pointed jaw. "He set flat on th' seat an' was th'owed?"

"That's right."

After an unbelieving silence Dennis said, "What was he doin'—drivin' over sixty?"

Tom looked around the circle of faces lit up by the artificial brilliance of a pressure lantern, and wondered what the reaction would be if he told it all just as it was. He had to say something, and it didn't look as if it could be the truth.

"He was workin'," he said finally. "Bucking stone out of the wall on an old building up on the mesa there. One turned loose an' as it did the governor must've gone haywire. She bucked like a loco hoss and ran off."

"Run off?"

Tom opened his mouth and closed it again, and just nodded.

Dennis said, "Well, reckon that's what happens when you put a mechanic to operatin'."

"That had nothin' to do with it," Tom snapped.

Peebles spoke up quickly. "Tom—what about the Seven? Broke up any?"

"Some," said Tom. "Better look at the steering clutches. An' she was hot."

"Head's cracked," said Harris, a burly young man with shoulders like a buffalo and a famous thirst.

"How do you know?"

"Saw it when Al and me went up with the stretcher to get the kid while you all were building the shelter. Hot water runnin' down the side of the block."

"You mean you walked all the way out to the mound to look at that tractor while the kid was lyin' there? I told you where he was!"

"Out to the mound!" Al Knowles's bulging eyes teetered out of their sockets. "We found that cat stalled twenty feet away from where the kid was!"

"What!"

"That's right, Tom," said Harris. "What's eatin' you? Where'd you leave it?"

"I told you...by the mound...the ol' building we cut into."

"Leave the startin' motor runnin'?"

"Starting motor?" Tom's mind caught the picture of the small, two-cylinder gasoline engine bolted to the side of the big diesel's crankcase, coupled through a Bendix gear and clutch to the flywheel of the diesel to crank it. He remembered his last glance at the still machine, silent but for the sound of water boiling. "Hell no!"

Al and Harris exchanged a glance. "I guess you were sort of slap-happy at the time, Tom," Harris said, not unkindly. "When we were halfway up the hill we heard it, and you know you can't mistake that racket. Sounded like it was under a load."

Tom beat softly at his temples with his clenched fists. "I left that machine dead," he said quietly. "I got compression off her and tied down the lever. I even stuffed my shirt in the intake. I drained the tank. But...I didn't touch the starting motor."

Peebles wanted to know why he had gone to all that trouble. Tom just looked vaguely at him and shook his head. "I shoulda pulled the wires. I never thought about the starting motor," he whispered. Then, "Harris—you say you found the starting motor running when you got to the top?"

"No—she was stalled. And hot—awmighty hot. I'd say the startin' motor was seized up tight. That must be it, Tom. You left the startin' motor runnin' and somehow engaged the clutch an' Bendix." His voice lost conviction as he said it— it takes seventeen separate motions to start a tractor of this type. "Anyhow, she was in gear an' crawled along on the little motor."

"I done that once," said Chub. "Broke a con rod on an Eight, on a highway job. Walked her about three-quarters of a mile on the startin' motor that way. Only I had to stop every hundred yards and let her cool down some."

Not without sarcasm, Dennis said, "Seems to me like the Seven was out to get th' goony. Made one pass at him and then went back to finish the job."

Al Knowles haw-hawed extravagantly.

Tom stood up, shaking his head, and went off among the crates to the hospital they had jury-rigged for the kid.

A dim light was burning inside, and Rivera lay very still, with his eyes closed. Tom leaned in the doorway—the open end of the engine crate—and watched him for a moment. Behind him he could hear the murmur of the crew's voices; the night was otherwise windless and still. Rivera's face was the peculiar color that olive skin takes when drained of blood. Tom looked at his chest and for a panicky moment thought he could discern no movement there. He entered and put a hand over the boy's heart. Rivera shivered, his eyes flew open, and he drew a sudden breath which caught raggedly at the back of his throat. "Tom . . . Tom!" he cried weakly.

"O.K., Goony . . . *qué pasa?*"

"She comeen back . . . Tom!"

"Who?"

"*El de siete.*"

Daisy Etta—"She ain't comin' back, kiddo. You're off the mesa now. Keep your chin up, fella."

Rivera's dark, doped eyes stared up at him without expression. Tom moved back and the eyes continued to stare. They weren't seeing anything. "Go to sleep," he whispered. The eyes closed instantly.

Kelly was saying that nobody ever got hurt on a construction job unless somebody was dumb. "An' most times you don't realize how dumb what you're doin' is until somebody does get hurt."

"The dumb part was gettin' a kid, an' not even an operator at that, up on a machine," said Dennis in his smuggest voice.

"I heard you try to sing that song before," said old Peebles quietly. "I hate to have to point out anything like this to a man because it don't do any good to make comparisons. But I've worked with that fella Rivera for a long time now, an' I've seen 'em as good but doggone few better. As far as you're concerned, you're O.K. on a pan, but the kid could give you cards and spades and still make you look like a cost accountant on a dozer."

Dennis half rose and mouthed something filthy. He looked at Al Knowles for backing and got it. He looked around the circle and got none. Peebles lounged back, sucking on his pipe, watching from under those bristling brows. Dennis subsided, running now on another track.

"So what does that prove? The better you say he is, the less reason he had to fall off a cat and get himself hurt."

"I haven't got the thing straight yet," said Chub, in a voice whose tone indicated "I hate to admit it, but—"

About this time Tom returned, like a sleepwalker, standing with the brilliant pressure lantern between him and Dennis. Dennis rambled right on, not knowing he was anywhere near: "There's something you never will find out. That Puerto Rican is a pretty husky kid. Could be Tom said somethin' he didn't like an' he tried to put a knife in Tom's back. They all do, y'know. Tom didn't get all that bashin' around just stoppin' a machine. They must've went round an' round for a while an' the goony wound up with a busted back. Tom sets the dozer to walk him down while he lies there and comes on down here and tries to tell us—" His voice fluttered to a stop as Tom loomed over him.

Tom grabbed the pan operator up by the slack of his shirt front with his uninjured arm and shook him like an empty burlap bag.

"Skunk," he growled. "I oughta lower th' boom on you." He set Dennis on his feet and backhanded his face with the edge of his forearm. Dennis went down—cowered down, rather then fell. "Aw, Tom, I was just talkin'. Just a joke, Tom, I was just—"

"Yellow, too," snarled Tom, stepping forward, raising a solid Texan boot. Peebles barked "Tom!" and the foot came back to the ground.

"Out o' my sight," rumbled the foreman. "Git!"

Dennis got. Al Knowles said vaguely, "Naow, Tom, y'all cain't—"

"You, y'wall-eyed string bean!" Tom raved, his voice harsh

and strained. "Go 'long with yer Siamese twin!"

"O.K., O.K.," said Al, white-faced, and disappeared into the dark after Dennis.

"Nuts to this," said Chub. "I'm turnin' in." He went to a crate and hauled out a mosquito-hooded sleeping bag and went off without another word. Harris and Kelly, who were both on their feet, sat down again. Old Peebles hadn't moved.

Tom stood staring out into the dark, his arms straight at his sides, his fists knotted.

"Sit down," said Peebles gently. Tom turned and stared at him.

"Sit down. I can't change that dressing 'less you do." He pointed at the bandage around Tom's elbow. It was red, a widening stain, the tattered tissues having parted as the big Georgian bunched his infuriated muscles. He sat down.

"Talkin' about dumbness," said Harris calmly, as Peebles went to work, "I was about to say that I got the record. I done the dumbest thing anybody ever did on a machine. You can't top it."

"I could," said Kelly. "Runnin' a crane dragline once. Put her in boom gear and started to boom her up. Had an eighty-five-foot stick on her. Machine was standing on wooden mats in th' middle of a swamp. Heard the motor miss and got out of the saddle to look at the filer-glass. Messed around back there longer than I figured, and the boom went straight up in the air and fell backwards over the cab. Th' jolt tilted my mats an' she slid backwards slowly and stately as you please, butt-first into the mud. Buried up to the eyeballs, she was." He laughed quietly. "Looked like a ditching machine!"

"I still say I done the dumbest thing ever, bar none," said Harris. "It was on a river job, widening a channel. I come back to work from a three-day binge, still rum-dumb. Got up on a dozer an' was workin' around on the edge of a twenty-foot cliff. Down at the foot of the cliff was a big hickory tree, an' growin' right along the edge was a great big limb. I got the dopey idea I should break it off. I put one track on the limb and the other on the cliff edge and run out away from the truck. I was about halfway out, an' the branch saggin' some, before I thought what would happen if it broke. Just about then it did break. You know hickory—if it breaks at all it breaks alto-gether. So down we go into thirty feet of water—me an' the cat. I got out from under somehow. When all them bubbles stopped comin' up I swum around lookin' down at it. I was still peddlin' around when the superintendent came rushin' up. He wants to know what's up. I yell at him, 'Look down there, the way that water is movin' an' shiftin', looks like the cat is workin' down there.' He pursed his lips and *tsk tsked*. My, that man said some nasty things to me."

"Where'd you get your next job?" Kelly exploded.

"Oh, he didn't fire me," said Harris soberly. "Said he couldn't afford to fire a man as dumb as that. Said he wanted me around to look at whenever he felt bad."

Tom said, "Thanks, you guys. That's as good a way as any of sayin' that everybody makes mistakes." He stood up, examining the new dressing, turning his arm in front of the lantern. "You all can think what you please, but I don't recollect there was any dumbness went on on that mesa this evenin'. That's finished with, anyway. Do I have to say that Dennis's idea about it is all wet?"

Harris said one foul word that completely disposed of Dennis and anything he might say.

Peebles said, "It'll be all right. Dennis an' his pop-eyed friend'll hang together, but they don't amount to anything. Chub'll do whatever he's argued into."

"So you got 'em all lined up, hey?" Tom shrugged. "In the meantime, are we going to get an airfield built?"

"We'll get it built," Peebles said. "Only—Tom, I got no right to give you any advice, but go easy on the rough stuff after this. It does a lot of harm."

"I will if I can," said Tom gruffly. They broke up and turned in.

Peebles was right. It did do harm. It made Dennis use the word "murder" when they found, in the morning, that Rivera had died during the night.

The work progressed in spite of everything that had happened. With equipment like that, it's hard to slow things down. Kelly bit two cubic yards out of the bluff with every swing of the big shovel, and Dumptors are the fastest short-haul earth movers yet devised. Dennis kept the service road clean for them with his pan, and Tom and Chub spelled each other on the bulldozer they had detached from its pan to make up for the lack of the Seven, spending their alternate periods with transit and stakes. Peebles was rod-man for the surveys, and in between times worked on setting up his field shop, keeping the water cooler and battery chargers running, and lining up his forge and welding tables. The operators fueled and serviced their own equipment, and there was little delay. Rocks and marl came out of the growing cavity in the side of the central mesa—a whole third of it had to come out—were spun down to the edge of the swamp, which lay across the lower end of the projected runway, in the hornet-howling dump-tractors, their big driving wheels churned up vast clouds of dust, and were dumped and spread and walked in by the whining two-cycle dozer. When muck began to pile up in front of the fill, it was blasted out of the way with carefully placed charges of sixty percent dynamite and the crates filled with rocks, stone from the ruins, and surfaced with easily compacting marl, run out of a clean deposit by the pan.

And when he had his shop set up, Peebles went up the hill to get the Seven. When he got to it he just stood there for a moment scratching his head, and then, shaking his head, he ambled back down the hill and went for Tom.

"Been looking at the Seven," he said, when he had flagged the moaning two-cycle and Tom had climbed off.

"What'd you find?"

Peebles held out an arm. "A list as long as that." He shook his head. "Tom, what really happened up there?"

"Governor went haywire and she run away," Tom said promptly, deadpan.

"Yeah, but—" For a long moment he held Tom's gaze. Then he sighed. "O.K., Tom. Anyhow, I can't do a thing up there. We'll have to bring her back and I'll have to have this tractor to tow her down. And first I have to have some help— the track idler adjustment bolt's busted and the right track is off the track rollers."

"Oh-h-h. So that's why she couldn't get to the kid, running on the starting motor. Track would hardly turn, hey?"

"It's a miracle she ran as far as she did. That track is really jammed up. Riding right up on the roller flanges. And that ain't the half of it. The head's gone, like Harris said, and Lord only knows what I'll find when I open her up."

"Why bother?"

"What?"

"We can get along without that dozer," said Tom suddenly. "Leave her where she is. There's lots more for you to do."

"But what for?"

"Well, there's no call to go to all that trouble."

Peebles scratched the side of his nose and said, "I got a new head, track master pins—even a spare starting motor. I got tools to make what I don't stock." He pointed at the long row of dumps left by the hurtling dump-tractors while they had been talking. "You got a pan tied up because you're using this machine to doze with, and you can't tell me you can't use another one. You're gonna have to shut down one or two o' those Dumptors if you go on like this."

"I had all that figured out as soon as I opened my mouth," Tom said sullenly. "Let's go."

They climbed on the tractor and took off, stopping for a moment at the beach outcropping to pick up a cable and some tools.

Daisy Etta sat at the edge of the mesa, glowering out of her stilted headlights at the soft sward which still bore the impression of a young body and the tramplings of the stretcher-bearers. Her general aspect was woebegone—there were scratches on her olive-drab paint and the bright metal of the scratches was already dulled red by the earliest powder-rust. And though the ground was level, she was not, for her right track was off its lower rollers, and she stood slightly canted, like a man who has had a broken hip. And whatever passed for consciousness within her mulled over that paradox of the bulldozer that every operator must go through while he is learning his own machine.

It is the most difficult thing of all for the beginner to understand, that paradox. A bulldozer is a crawling powerhouse, a behemoth of noise and toughness, the nearest thing to the famous irresistible force. The beginner, awed and with the pictures of unconquerable Army tanks printed on his mind from the newsreels, taken all in his stride and with a sense of limitless power treats all obstacles alike, not knowing the fragility of a cast-iron radiator core, the mortality of tempered manganese, the friability of overheated babbitt, and most of all, the ease with which a tractor can bury itself in mud. Climbing off to stare at a machine which he has reduced in twenty seconds to a useless hulk, or which was running a half-minute before on ground where it now has its tracks out of sight, he has that sense of guilty disappointment which overcomes any man on having made an error in judgment.

So, as she stood, *Daisy Etta* was broken and useless. These soft persistent bipeds had built her, and if they were like any other race that built machines, they could care for them. The ability to reverse the tension of a spring, or twist a control rod, or reduce to zero the friction in a nut and lock-washer, was not enough to repair the crack in a cylinder head nor bearings welded to a crankshaft in an overheated starting motor. There had been a lesson to learn. It had been learned. *Daisy Etta* would be repaired, and the next time—well, at least she would know her own weaknesses.

Tom swung the two-cycle machine and edged in next to the Seven, with the edge of his blade all but touching *Daisy Etta*'s push-beam. They got off and Peebles bent over the drum-tight right track.

"Watch yourself," said Tom.

"Watch what?"

"Oh—nothin', I guess." He circled the machine, trained eyes probing over frame and fittings. He stepped forward suddenly and grasped the fuel-tank drain cock. It was closed. He opened it; golden oil gushed out. He shut it off, climbed up on the machine and opened the fuel cap on top of the tank. He pulled out the bayonet gauge, wiped it in the crook of his knee, dipped and withdrew it.

The tank was more than three quarters full.

"What's the matter?" asked Peebles, staring curiously at Tom's drawn face.

"Peeby, I opened the cock to drain this tank. I left it with oil runnin' out on the ground. She shut herself off."

"Now, Tom, you're lettin' this thing get you down. You just thought you did. I've seen a main-line valve shut itself off when it's worn bad, but only 'cause the fuel pump pulls it shut when the motor's runnin'. But not a gravity drain."

"Main-line valve?" Tom pulled the seat up and looked. One glance was enough to show him that this one was open.

"She opened this one, too."

"O.K.—O.K. Don't look at me like that!" Peebles was

as near to exasperation as he could possibly get. "What difference does it make?"

Tom did not answer. He was not the type of man who, when faced with something beyond his understanding, would begin to doubt his own sanity. His was a dogged insistence that what he saw and sensed was what had actually happened. In him was none of the fainting fear of madness that another, more sensitive, man might feel. He doubted neither himself nor his evidence, and so could free his mind for searching out the consuming "why" of a problem. He knew instinctively that to share "unbelievable" happenings with anyone else, even if they had really occurred, was to put even further obstacles in his way. So he kept his clamlike silence and stubbornly, watchfully investigated.

The slipped track was so tightly drawn up on the roller flanges that there could be no question of pulling the master pin and opening the track up. It would have to be worked back in place—a very delicate operation, for a little force applied in the wrong direction would be enough to run the track off altogether. To complicate things, the blade of the Seven was down on the ground and would have to be lifted before the machine could be maneuvered, and its hydraulic hoist was useless without the motor.

Peebles unhooked twenty feet of half-inch cable from the rear of the smaller dozer, scratched a hole in the ground under the Seven's blade, and pushed the eye of the cable through. Climbing over the moldboard, he slipped the eye on to the big towing hook bolted to the underside of the bellyguard. The other end of the cable he threw out on the ground in front of the machine. Tom mounted the other dozer and swung into place, ready to tow. Peebles hooked the cable onto Tom's drawbar, hopped up on the Seven. He put her in neutral, disengaged the master clutch, and put the blade control over into "float" position, then raised an arm.

Tom perched upon the armrest of his machine, looking backwards, moved slowly, taking up the slack in the cable. It straightened and grew taut, and as it did it forced the Seven's blade upward. Peebles waved for slack and put the blade control into "hold." The cable bellied downward away from the blade.

"Hydraulic system's O.K., anyhow," called Peebles, as Tom throttled down. "Move over and take a strain to the right, sharp as you can without fouling the cable on the track. We'll see if we can walk this track back on."

Tom backed up, cut sharply to the right, and drew the cable out almost at right angles to the other machine. Peebles held the right track of the Seven with the brake and released both steering clutches. The left track now could turn free, the right not at all. Tom was running at a quarter throttle in his lowest gear, so that his machine barely crept along, taking the strain. The Seven shook gently and began to pivot on the taut right track, unbelievable foot-pounds of energy coming to bear on the front of the track where it rode high up on the idler wheel. Peebles released the right brake with his foot and applied it again in a series of skilled, deft jerks. The track would move a few inches and stop again, force being applied forward and sideways alternately, urging the track persuasively back in place. Then, a little jolt and she was in, riding true on the five truck rollers, the two track carrier rollers, the driving sprocket and the idler.

Peebles got off and stuck his head in between the sprocket and the rear carrier, squinting down and sideways to see if there were any broken flanges or roller bushes. Tom came over and pulled him out by the seat of his trousers. "Time enough for that when you get her in the shop," he said, masking his nervousness. "Reckon she'll roll?"

"She'll roll. I never saw a track in that condition come back that easy. By gosh, it's as if she was tryin' to help!"

"They'll do it sometimes," said Tom stiffly. "You better take the tow-tractor, Peeby. I'll stay with this'n."

"Anything you say."

And cautiously they took the steep slope down, Tom barely holding the brakes, giving the other machine a straight pull all the way. And so they brought *Daisy Etta* down to Peebles's outdoor shop, where they pulled her cylinder head off, took off her starting motor, pulled out a burned clutch facing, had her quite helpless—

And put her together again.

"I tell you it was outright, cold-blooded murder," said Dennis hotly. "An' here we are takin' orders from a guy like that. What are we goin' to do about it?" They were standing by the cooler—Dennis had run his machine there to waylay Chub.

Chub Horton's cigar went down and up like a semaphore with a short circuit. "We'll skip it. The blacktopping crew will be here in another two weeks or so, an' we can make a report. Besides, I don't know what happened up there any more than you do. In the meantime we got a runway to build."

"You don't know what happened up there? Chub, you're a smart man. Smart enough to run this job better than Tom Jaeger even if he wasn't crazy. And you're surely smart enough not to believe all that cock and bull about that tractor runnin' out from under that grease-monkey. Listen—" he leaned forward and tapped Chub's chest. "He said it was the governor. I saw that governor myself an' heard ol' Peebles say there wasn't a thing wrong with it. Th' throttle control rod had slipped off its yoke, yeah—but you know what a tractor will do when the throttle control goes out. It'll idle or stall. It won't run away, whatever."

"Well, maybe so, but—"

"But nothin'! A guy that'll commit murder ain't sane. If he did it once, he can do it again and I ain't fixin' to let that happen to me."

Two things crossed Chub's steady but not too bright mind at this. One was that Dennis, whom he did not like but could not shake, was trying to force him into something that he did not want to do. The other was that under all of his swift talk Dennis was scared spitless.

"What do you want to do—call up the sheriff?"

Dennis ha-ha-ed appreciatively—one of the reasons he was so hard to shake. "I'll tell you what we can do. As long as we have you here, he isn't the only man who knows the work. If we stop takin' orders from him, you can give 'em as good or better. An' there won't be anything he can do about it."

"Doggone it, Dennis," said Chub, with sudden exasperation. "What do you think you're doin'—handin' me over the keys to the kingdom or something? What do you want to see me bossin' around here for?" He stood up. "Suppose we did what you said? Would it get the field built any quicker? Would it get me any more money in my pay envelope? What do you think I want—glory? I passed up a chance to run for councilman once. You think I'd raise a finger to get a bunch of mugs to do what I say—when they do it anyway?"

"Aw, Chub—I wouldn't cause trouble just for the fun of it. That's not what I mean at all. But unless we do something about that guy we ain't safe. Can't you get that through your head?"

"Listen, windy. If a man keeps busy enough he can't get into no trouble. That goes for Tom—you might keep that in mind. But it goes for you, too. Get back up on that rig an' get back to the marl pit." Dennis, completely taken by surprise, turned to his machine.

"It's a pity you can't move earth with your mouth," said Chub, as he walked off. "They could have left you to do this job singlehanded."

Chub walked slowly toward the outcropping, switching at beach pebbles with a grade stake and swearing to himself. He was essentially a simple man and believed in the simplest possible approach to everything. He liked a job where he could do everything required and where nothing turned up to complicate things. He had been in the grading business for a long time as an operator and survey party boss, and he was remarkable for one thing—he had always held aloof from the cliques and internecine politics that are the breath of life to most construction men. He was disturbed and troubled at the back-stabbing that went on around him on various jobs. If it was blunt, he was disgusted, and subtlety simply left him floundering and bewildered. He was stupid enough so that his basic honesty manifested itself in his speech and actions, and he had learned that complete honesty in dealing with men above and below him was almost invariably painful to all concerned, but he had not the wit to act otherwise, and did not try to. If he had a bad tooth, he had it pulled out as soon as he could. If he got a raw deal from a superintendent over him, that superintendent would get told exactly what the trouble was, and if he didn't like it, there were other jobs. And if the pulling and hauling of cliques got in his hair, he had always said so and left. Or he had sounded off and stayed; his completely selfish reaction to things that got in the way of his work had earned him a lot of regard from men he had worked under. And so, in this instance, he had no hesitation about choosing a course of action. Only—how did you go about asking a man if he was a murderer?

He found the foreman with an enormous wrench in his hand, tightening up the new track adjustment bolt they had installed in the Seven.

"Hey, Chub! Glad you turned up. Let's get a piece of pipe

over the end of this thing and really bear down." Chub went for the pipe, and they fitted it over the handle of the four-foot wrench and hauled until the sweat ran down their backs, Tom checking the track clearance occasionally with a crowbar. He finally called it good enough and they stood there in the sun gasping for breath.

"Tom," panted Chub, "did you kill that Puerto Rican?"

Tom's head came up as if someone had burned the back of his neck with a cigarette.

"Because," said Chub, "if you did you can't go on runnin' this job."

Tom said, "That's a lousy thing to kid about."

"You know I ain't kiddin'. Well, did you?"

"No!" Tom sat down on a keg, wiped his face with a bandanna. "What's got into you?"

"I just wanted to know. Some of the boys are worried about it."

Tom's eyes narrowed. "Some of the boys, huh? I think I get it. Listen to me, Chub. Rivera was killed by that thing there." He thumbed over his shoulder at the Seven, which was standing ready now, awaiting only the building of a broken cutting corner on the blade. Peebles was winding up the welding machine as he spoke. "If you mean, did I put him up on the machine before he was thrown, the answer is yes. That much I killed him, and don't think I don't feel it. I had a hunch something was wrong up there, but I couldn't put my finger on it and I certainly didn't think anybody was going to get hurt."

"Well, what was wrong?"

"I still don't know." Tom stood up. "I'm tired of beatin' around the bush, Chub, and I don't much care any more what anybody thinks. There's somethin' wrong with that Seven, something that wasn't built into her. They don't make tractors better'n that one, but whatever it was happened up there on the mesa has queered this one. Now go ahead and think what you like, and dream up any story you want to tell the boys. In the meantime you can pass the word—nobody runs that machine but me, understand? Nobody!"

"Tom—"

Tom's patience broke. "That's all I'm going to say about it! If anybody else gets hurt, it's going to be me, understand? What more do you want?"

He strode off, boiling. Chub stared after him, and after a long moment reached up and took the cigar from his lips. Only then did he realize that he had bitten it in two; half the butt was still inside his mouth. He spat and stood there, shaking his head.

"How's she going, Peeby?"

Peebles looked up from the welding machine. "Hi, Chub, have her ready for you in twenty minutes." He gauged the distance between the welding machine and the big tractor. "I should have forty feet of cable," he said, looking at the festoons of arc and ground cables that hung from the storage hooks in the back of the welder. "Don't want to get a tractor over here to move the thing, and don't feel like cranking up the Seven just to get it close enough." He separated the arc cable and threw it aside, walked to the tractor, paying the ground cable off his arm. He threw out the last of his slack and grasped the ground clamp when he was eight feet from the machine. Taking it in his left hand, he pulled hard, reaching out with his right to grasp the moldboard of the Seven, trying to get it far enough to clamp on to the machine.

Chub stood there watching him, chewing on his cigar, absentmindedly diddling with the controls on the arc-welder. He pressed the starter button, and the six-cylinder motor responded with a purr. He spun the work-selector dials idly, threw the arc generator switch—

A bolt of incredible energy, thin, searing, blue-white, left the rod-holder at his feet, stretched itself *fifty feet* across to Peebles, whose fingers had just touched the moldboard of the tractor. Peebles's head and shoulders were surrounded for a second by a violet nimbus, and then he folded over and dropped. A circuit breaker clacked behind the control board of the welder, but too late. The Seven rolled slowly backward, without firing, on level ground, until it brought up against a road-roller.

Chub's cigar was gone, and he didn't notice. He had the knuckles of his right hand in his mouth, and his teeth sunk into the pudgy flesh. His eyes protruded; he crouched there and quivered, literally frightened out of his mind. For old Peebles was almost burned in two.

They buried him next to Rivera. There wasn't much talk afterwards; the old man had been a lot closer to all of them than they had realized until now. Harris, for once in his rum-dumb, lighthearted life, was quiet and serious, and Kelly's walk seemed to lose some of its lightness. Hour after hour Dennis's flabby mouth worked, and he bit at his lower lip until it was swollen and tender. Al Knowles seemed more or less unaffected, as was to be expected from a man who had something less than the brains of a chicken. Chub Horton had snapped out of it after a couple of hours and was very nearly himself again. And in Tom Jaeger swirled a black, furious anger at this unknowable curse that had struck the camp.

And they kept working. There was nothing else to do. The shovel kept up its rhythmic swing and dig, swing and dump, and the Dumptors screamed back and forth between it and the little that there was left of the swamp. The upper end of the runway was grassed off; Chub and Tom set grade stakes and Dennis began the long job of cutting and filling the humpy surface with his pan. Harris manned the other and followed him, a cut behind. The shape of the runway emerged from the land, and then that of the paralleling taxiway; and three days went by. The horror of Peebles's death wore off enough so that they could talk about it, and very little of the talk helped anybody. Tom took his spells at everything, changing over with Kelly to give him a rest from the shovel, making a few rounds with a pan, putting in hours on a Dumptor. His arm was healing slowly but clean, and he worked grimly in spite of it, taking a perverse sort of pleasure from the pain of it. Every man on the job watched his machine with the solicitude of a mother with her firstborn; a serious breakdown would have been disastrous without a highly skilled mechanic.

The only concession that Tom allowed himself in regard to Peebles's death was to corner Kelly one afternoon and ask him about the welding machine. Part of Kelly's rather patchy past had been spent in a technical college, where he had studied electrical engineering and women. He had learned a little of the former and enough of the latter to get him thrown out on his ear. So, on the off-chance that he might know something about the freak arc, Tom put it to him.

Kelly pulled off his high-gauntlet gloves and batted sandflies with them. "What sort of an arc was that? Boy, you got me there. Did you ever hear of a welding machine doing like that before?"

"I did not. A welding machine just don't have that sort o' push. I saw a man get a full jolt from a 400-amp welder once, an' although it sat him down it didn't hurt him any."

"It's not amperage that kills people," said Kelly, "it's voltage. Voltage is the pressure behind a current, you know. Take an amount of water, call it amperage. If I throw it in your face, it won't hurt you. If I put it through a small hose you'll feel it. But if I pump it through the tiny holes on a diesel injector nozzle at about twelve hundred pounds, it'll draw blood. But a welding arc generator just is not wound to build up that kind of voltage. I can't see where any short circuit anywhere through the armature or field windings could do such a thing."

"From what Chub said, he had been foolin' around with the work selector. I don't think anyone touched the dials after it happened. The selector dial was run all the way over to the low-current application segment, and the current control was around the halfway mark. That's not enough juice to get you a good bead with a quarter-inch rod, let alone kill somebody— or roll a tractor back thirty feet on level ground."

"Or jump fifty feet," said Kelly. "It would take thousands of volts to generate an arc like that."

"Is it possible that something in the Seven could have pulled that arc? I mean, suppose the arc wasn't driven over, but was drawn over? I tell you, she was hot for four hours after that."

Kelly shook his head. "Never heard of any such thing. Look, just to have something to call them, we call direct current terminals positive and negative, and just because it works in theory we say that current flows from negative to positive. There couldn't be any more positive attraction in one electrode than there is negative drive in the other; see what I mean?"

"There couldn't be some freak condition that would cause a sort of oversize positive field? I mean one that would suck out the negative flow all in a heap, make it smash through under a lot of pressure like the water you were talking about through an injector nozzle?"

"No, Tom. It just don't work that way, far as anyone knows. I dunno, though—there are some things about static electricity that nobody understands. All I can say is that what happened couldn't happen and if it did it couldn't have killed Peebles. And you know the answer to that."

Tom glanced away at the upper end of the runway, where

the two graves were. There was bitterness and turbulent anger
naked there for a moment, and he turned and walked away
without another word. And when he went back to have another
look at the welding machine, *Daisy Etta* was gone.

Al Knowles and Harris squatted together near the water
cooler.

"Bad," said Harris.

"Nevah saw anythin' like it," said Al. "Ol' Tom come back
f'm the shop theah jus' *raisin'* Cain. 'Weah's 'at Seven gone?
Weah's 'at Seven?' I never heered sech cah'ins on."

"Dennis did take it, huh?"

"Sho' did."

Harris said, "He came spoutin' around to me a while back,
Dennis did. Chub'd told him Tom said for everybody to stay
off that machine. Dennis was mad as a wet hen. Said Tom was
carryin' that kind o' business too far. Said there was probably
somethin' about the Seven Tom didn't want us to find out.
Might incriminate him. Dennis is ready to say Tom killed the
kid."

"Reckon he did, Harris?"

Harris shook his head. "I've known Tom too long to think
that. If he won't tell us what really happened up on the mesa,
he has a reason for it. How'd Dennis come to take the dozer?"

"Blew a front tire on his pan. Came back heah to git anothah
rig—maybe a Dumptor. Saw th' Seven standin' theah ready to
go. Stood theah lookin' at it and cussin' Tom. Said he was
tired of bashin' his kidneys t'pieces on them othah rigs an'
bedamned if he wouldn't take suthin' that rode good fo' a
change. I tol' him ol' Tom'd raise th' roof when he found him
on it. He had a couple mo' things t'say 'bout Tom then."

"I didn't think he had the guts to take the rig."

"Aw, he talked himself blind mad."

They looked up as Chub Horton trotted up, panting. "Hey,
you guys, come on. We better get up there to Dennis."

"What's wrong?" asked Harris, climbing to his feet.

Tom passed me a minute ago lookin' like the wrath o' God
and hightailin' it for the swamp fill. I asked him what was the
matter and he hollered that Dennis had took the Seven. Said
he was always talkin' about murder, and he'd get his fill of it
foolin' around that machine." Chub went wall-eyed, licked his
lips beside his cigar.

"Oh-oh," said Harris quietly. "That's the wrong kind o' talk for just now."

"You don't suppose he—"

"Come on!"

They saw Tom before they were halfway there. He was walking slowly, with his head down. Harris shouted. Tom raised his face, stopped, stood there waiting with a peculiarly slumped stance.

"Where's Dennis?" barked Chub.

Tom waited until they were almost up to him and then weakly raised an arm and thumbed over his shoulder. His face was green.

"Tom—is he—"

Tom nodded, and swayed a little. His granite jaw was slack.

"Al, stay with him. He's sick. Harris, let's go."

Tom was sick, then and there. Very. Al stood gaping at him, fascinated.

Chub and Harris found Dennis. All of twelve square feet of him, ground and churned and rolled out into a torn-up patch of earth. *Daisy Etta* was gone.

Back at the outcropping, they sat with Tom while Al Knowles took a Dumptor and roared away to get Kelly.

"You saw him?" he said dully after a time.

Harris said, "Yeh."

The screaming Dumptor and a mountainous cloud of dust arrived, Kelly driving, Al holding on with a death-grip to the dump-bed guards. Kelly flung himself off, ran to Tom. "Tom—what is all this? Dennis dead? And you . . . you—"

Tom's head came up slowly, the slackness going out of his long face, a light suddenly coming into his eyes. Until this moment it had not crossed his mind what these men might think.

"I—What?"

"Al says you killed him."

Tom's eyes flicked at Al Knowles, and Al winced as if the glance had been a quirt.

Harris said, "What about it, Tom?"

"Nothing about it. He was killed by that Seven. You saw that for yourself."

"I stuck with you all along," said Harris slowly. "I took everything you said and believed it."

"This is too strong for you?" Tom asked.

Harris nodded. "Too strong, Tom."

Tom looked at the grim circle of faces and laughed suddenly. He stood up, put his back against a tall crate. "What do you plan to do about it?"

There was a silence. "You think I went up there and knocked that windbag off the machine and ran over him?" More silence. "Listen. I went up there and saw what you saw. He was dead before I got there. That's not good enough either?" He paused and licked his lips. "So after I killed him, I got up on the tractor and drove it far enough away so you couldn't see or hear it when you got there. And then I sprouted wings and flew back so's I was halfway here when you met me—*ten minutes* after I spoke to Chub on my way up!"

Kelly said vaguely, "Tractor?"

"Well," said Tom harshly to Harris, "was the tractor there when you and Chub went up and saw Dennis?"

"No—"

Chub smacked his thigh suddenly. "You could've drove it into the swamp, Tom."

Tom said angrily, "I'm wastin' my time. You guys got it all figured out. Why ask me anything at all?"

"Aw, take it easy," said Kelly. "We just want the facts. Just what did happen? You met Chub and told him that Dennis would get all the murderin' he could take if he messed around that machine. That right?"

"That's right."

"Then what?"

"Then the machine murdered him."

Chub, with remarkable patience, asked, "What did you mean the day Peebles was killed when you said that something had queered the Seven up there on the mesa?"

Tom said furiously, "I meant what I said. You guys are set to crucify me for this and I can't stop you. Well, listen. Something's got into that Seven. I don't know what it is and I don't think I ever will know. I thought that after she smashed herself up that it was finished with. I had an idea that when we had her torn down and helpless we should have left her that way. I was dead right but it's too late now. She's killed Rivera and she's killed Dennis and she sure had something to do with killing Peebles. And my idea is that she won't stop as long as there's a human being alive on this island."

"Whaddaya know!" said Chub.

"Sure, Tom, sure," said Kelly quietly. "That tractor is out to get us. But don't worry; we'll catch it and tear it down. Just don't you worry about it any more; it'll be all right."

"That's right, Tom," said Harris. "You just take it easy around camp for a couple of days till you feel better. Chub and the rest of us will handle things for you. You had too much sun."

"You're a swell bunch of fellows," gritted Tom, with the deepest sarcasm. "You want to live," he shouted, "git out there and throw that maverick bulldozer!"

"That maverick bulldozer is at the bottom of the swamp where you put it," growled Chub. His head lowered and he started to move it. "Sure we want to live. The best way to do that is to put you where you can't kill anybody else. *Get him!*"

He leaped. Tom straightened him with his left and crossed with his right. Chub went down, tripping Harris. Al Knowles scuttled to a toolbox and dipped out a fourteen-inch crescent wrench. He circled around, keeping out of trouble, trying to look useful. Tom loosened a haymaker at Kelly, whose head seemed to withdraw like a turtle's; it whistled over, throwing Tom badly off balance. Harris, still on his knees, tackled Tom's legs; Chub hit him in the small of the back with a meaty shoulder, and Tom went flat on his face. Al Knowles, holding the wrench in both hands, swept it up and back like a baseball bat; at the top of its swing Kelly reached over, snatched it out of his hands and tapped Tom delicately behind the ear with it. Tom went limp.

It was late, but nobody seemed to feel like sleeping. They sat around the pressure lantern, talking idly. Chub and Kelly played an inconsequential game of casino, forgetting to pick up their points; Harris paced up and down like a man in a cell, and Al Knowles was squinched up close to the light, his eyes wide and watching, watching—

"I need a drink," said Harris.

"Tens," said one of the casino players.

Al Knowles said, "We shoulda killed him. We oughta kill him now."

"There's been too much killin' already," said Chub. "Shut

up, you." And to Kelly, "With big casino," sweeping up cards.

Kelly caught his wrist and grinned. "Big casino's the ten of diamonds, not the ten of hearts. Remember?"

"Oh."

"How long before the blacktopping crew will be here?" quavered Al Knowles.

"Twelve days," said Harris. "And they better bring some likker."

"Hey, you guys."

They fell silent.

"Hey!"

"It's Tom," said Kelly. "Building sixes, Chub."

"I'm gonna go kick his ribs in," said Knowles, not moving.

"I heard that," said the voice from the darkness. "If I wasn't hogtied—"

"We know what you'd do," said Chub. "How much proof do you think we need?"

"Chub, you don't have to do any more to him!" It was Kelly, flinging his cards down and getting up. "Tom, you want water?"

"Yes."

"Siddown, siddown," said Chub.

"Let him lie there and bleed," Al Knowles said.

"Nuts!" Kelly went and filled a cup and brought it to Tom. The big Georgian was tied thoroughly, wrists together, taut rope between elbows and elbows behind his back, so that his hands were immovable over his solar plexus. His knees and ankles were bound as well, although Knowles' little idea of a short rope between ankles and throat hadn't been used.

"Thanks, Kelly." Tom drank greedily, Kelly holding his head. "Goes good." he drank more. "What hit me?"

"One of the boys. 'Bout the time you said the cat was haunted."

"Oh, yeah." Tom rolled his head and blinked with pain.

"Any sense asking you if you blame us?"

"Kelly, does somebody else have to be killed before you guys wake up?"

"None of us figure there will be any more killin'—now."

The rest of the men drifted up. "He willing to talk sense?" Chub wanted to know.

Al Knowles laughed, "Hyuk! Hyuk! Don't he look dangerous now!"

Harris said suddenly, "Al, I'm gonna hafta tape your mouth with the skin off your neck."

"Am I the kind of guy that makes up ghost stories?"

"Never have that I know of, Tom." Harris kneeled down beside him. "Never killed anyone before, either."

"Oh, get away from me. Get away," said Tom tiredly.

"Get up and make us," jeered Al.

Harris got up and backhanded him across the mouth. Al squeaked, took three steps backward and tripped over a drum of grease. "I told you," said Harris almost plaintively. "I *told* you, Al."

Tom stopped the bumble of comment. "Shut up!" he hissed. "SHUT UP!" he roared.

They shut.

"Chub," said Tom, rapidly, "what did you say I did with that Seven?"

"Buried it in the swamp."

"Yeh. Listen."

"Listen at what?"

"Be quiet and listen!"

So they listened. It was another still, windless night, with a thin crescent of moon showing nothing true in the black and muffled silver landscape. The smallest whisper of surf drifted up from the beach, and from far off to the right, where the swamp was, a scandalized frog croaked protest at the manhandling of his mudhole. But the sound that crept down, freezing their bones, came from the bluff behind their camp.

It was the unmistakable staccato of a starting engine.

"The Seven!"

"'At's right, Chub," said Tom.

"Wh-who's crankin' her up?"

"Are we all here?"

"All but Peebles and Dennis and Rivera," said Tom.

"It's Dennis's ghost," moaned Al.

Chub snapped, "Shut up, lamebrain."

"She's shifted to diesel," said Kelly, listening.

"She'll be here in a minute," said Tom. "Y'know, fellas, we can't all be crazy, but you're about to have a time convincin' yourselves of it."

"You like this, doncha?"

"Some ways. Rivera used to call that machine *Daisy Etta*, 'cause she's *de siete* in Spig. *Daisy Etta*, she wants her a man."

"Tom," said Harris, "I wish you'd stop that chatterin'. You make me nervous."

"I got to do somethin'. I can't run," Tom drawled.

"We're going to have a look," said Chub. "If there's nobody on that cat, we'll turn you loose."

"Mighty white of you. Reckon you'll get back before she does?"

"We'll be back. Harris, come with me. We'll get one of the pan tractors. They can outrun a Seven. Kelly, take Al and get the other one."

"Dennis's machine has a flat tire on the pan," said Al's quavering voice.

"Pull the pin and cut the cables, then! Git!" Kelly and Al Knowles ran off.

"Good huntin', Chub."

Chub went to him, bent over. "I think I'm goin' to have to apologize to you, Tom."

"No you ain't. I'd a done the same. Get along now, if you think you got to. But hurry back."

"I got to. An' I'll hurry back."

Harris said, "Don't go 'way, boy." Tom returned the grin, and they were gone. But they didn't hurry back. They didn't come back at all.

It was Kelly who came pounding back, with Al Knowles on his heels, a half hour later. "Al—gimme your knife."

He went to work on the ropes. His face was drawn.

"I could see some of it," whispered Tom. "Chub and Harris?"

Kelly nodded. "There wasn't nobody on the Seven like you said." He said it as if there were nothing else in his mind, as if the most rigid self-control was keeping him from saying it over and over.

"I could see the lights," said Tom. "A tractor angling up the hill. Pretty soon another, crossing it, lighting up the whole slope."

"We heard it idling up there somewhere," Kelly said. "Olive-drab paint—couldn't see it."

"I saw the pan tractor turn over—oh, four, five times down the hill. It stopped, lights still burning. Then something hit it and rolled it again. That sure blacked it out. What turned it over first?"

"The Seven. Hanging up there just at the brow of the bluff. Waited until Chub and Harris were about to pass, sixty, seventy feet below. Tipped over the edge and rolled down on them with her clutches out. Must've been going thirty miles an hour when she hit. Broadside. They never had a chance. Followed the pan as it rolled down the hill and when it stopped booted it again."

"Want me to rub yo' ankles?" asked Al.

"You! Get outa my sight!"

"Aw, Tom—" whimpered Al.

"Skip it, Tom," said Kelly. "There ain't enough of us left to carry on that way. Al, you mind your manners from here on out, hear?"

"Ah jes' wanted to tell y'all. I knew you weren't lyin' 'bout Dennis, Tom, if only I'd stopped to think. I recollect when Dennis, he'd take that tractuh out . . . 'membah, Kelly? . . . He went an' got the crank and walked around to th' side of th' machine and stuck it in th' hole. It was barely in theah befo' the startin' engine kicked off. 'Whadda ya know!' he says t'me. 'She started by here'f! I nevah pulled that handle!' And I said, 'She sho' rarin' t'go!'"

"You pick a fine time to 'recollec'' something," gritted Tom. "C'mon—let's get out of here."

"Where to?"

"What do you know that a Seven can't move or get up on?"

"That's a large order. A big rock, maybe."

"Aint' nothing that big around here," said Tom.

Kelly thought a minute, then snapped his fingers. "Up on the top of my last cut with the shovel," he said. "It's fourteen feet if it's an inch. I was pullin' out small rock an' topsoil, and Chub told me to drop back and dip out marl from a pocket there. I sumped in back of the original cut and took out a whole mess o' marl. That left a big neck of earth sticking thirty feet or so out of the cliff. The narrowest part is only about four feet wide. If *Daisy Etta* tries to get us from the top, she'll straddle the neck and hang herself. If she tries to get us from below, she can't get traction to climb; it's too loose and too steep."

"And what happens if she builds herself a ramp?"

"We'll be gone from there."

"Let's go."

Al agitated for the choice of a Dumptor because of its speed, but was howled down. Tom wanted something that could not get a flat tire and that would need something really powerful to turn it over. They took the two-cycle pan tractor with the bulldozer blade that had been Dennis's machine and crept out into the darkness.

It was nearly six hours later that *Daisy Etta* came and woke them up. Night was receding before a paleness in the east, and a fresh ocean breeze had sprung up. Kelly had taken the first lookout and Al the second, letting Tom rest the night out. And Tom was far too tired to argue the arrangement. Al had immediately fallen asleep on his watch, but fear had such a sure, cold hold on his vitals that the first faint growl of the big diesel engine snapped him erect. He tottered on the edge of the tall neck of earth that they slept on and squeaked as he scrabbled to get his balance.

"What's giving?" asked Kelly, instantly wide awake.

"It's coming," blubbered Al. "Oh my, oh my—"

Kelly stood up and stared into the fresh, dark dawn. The motor boomed hollowly, in a peculiar way heard twice at the same time as it was thrown to them and echoed back by the bluffs under and around them.

"It's coming and what are we goin' to do?" chanted Al. "What is going to happen?"

"My head is going to fall off," said Tom sleepily. He rolled to a sitting position, holding the brutalized member between his hands. "If that egg behind my ear hatches, it'll come out a full-sized jack-hammer." He looked at Kelly. "Where is she?"

"Don't rightly know," said Kelly. "Somewhere down around the camp."

"Probably pickin' up our scent."

"Figure it can do that?"

"I figure it can do anything," said Tom. "Al, stop your moanin'."

The sun slipped its scarlet edge into the thin slot between sea and sky, and rosy light gave each rock and tree a shape and a shadow. Kelly's gaze swept back and forth, back and forth, until, minutes later, he saw movement.

"There she is!"

"Where?"

"Down by the grease rack."

Tom rose and stared. "What's she doin'?"

After an interval Kelly said, "She's workin'. Diggin' a swale in front of the fuel drums."

"You don't say. Don't tell me she's goin' to give herself a grease job."

"She don't need it. She was completely greased and new oil put in the crankcase after we set her up. But she might need fuel."

"Not more'n half a tank."

"Well, maybe she figures she's got a lot of work to do today." As Kelly said this Al began to blubber. They ignored him.

The fuel drums were piled in a pyramid at the edge of the camp, in forty-four-gallon drums piled on their sides. The Seven was moving back and forth in front of them, close up, making pass after pass, gouging earth up and wasting it out past the pile. She soon had a huge pit scooped out, about fourteen feet wide, six feet deep and thirty feet long, right at the very edge of the pile of drums.

"What you reckon she's playin' at?"

"Search me. She seems to want fuel, but I don't . . . look at that! She's stopped in the hole; she's pivoting, smashing the top corner of the moldboard into one of the drums on the bottom!"

Tom scraped the stubble on his jaw with his nails. "An' you wonder how much that critter can do! Why, she's got the whole thing figured out. She knows if she tried to punch a hole in a fuel drum that she'd only kick it around. If she did knock a hole in it, how's she going to lift it? She's not equipped to handle hose, so . . . see? Look at her now! She just gets herself lower than the bottom drum on the pile, and punches a hole. She can do that then, with the whole weight of the pile holding it down. Then she backs her tank under the stream of fuel runnin' out!"

"How'd she get the cap off?"

Tom snorted and told them how the radiator cap had come off its hinges as he vaulted over the hood the day Rivera was hurt.

"You know," he said after a moment's thought, "if she knew as much then as she does now, I'd be snoozin' beside Rivera and Peebles. She just didn't know her way around then. She ran herself like she'd never run before. She's learned plenty since."

"She has," said Kelly, "and here's where she uses it on us.

She's headed this way."

She was. Straight out across the roughed-out runway she came, grinding along over the dew-sprinkled earth, yesterday's dust swirling up from under her tracks. Crossing the shoulder line, she took the rougher ground skillfully, angling up over the occasional swags in the earth, by-passing stones, riding free and fast and easily. It was the first time Tom had actually seen her clearly running without an operator, and his flesh crept as he watched. The machine was unnatural, her outline somehow unreal and dreamlike purely through the lack of the small silhouette of a man in the saddle. She looked hulked, compact, dangerous.

"What are we gonna do?" wailed Al Knowles.

"We're gonna sit and wait," said Kelly, "and you're gonna shut your trap. We won't know for five minutes yet whether she's going to go after us from down below or from up here."

"If you want to leave," said Tom gently, "go right ahead." Al sat down.

Kelly looked down at his beloved power shovel, sitting squat and unlovely in the cut below them and away to their right. "How do you reckon she'd stand up against the dipper stick?"

"If it ever came to a rough-and-tumble," said Tom, "I'd say it would be just too bad for *Daisy Etta*. But she wouldn't fight. There's no way you could get the shovel within punchin' range; *Daisy*'d just stand there and laugh at you."

"I can't see her now," whined Al.

Tom looked. "She's taken the bluff. She's going to try it from up here. I move we sit tight and see if she's foolish enough to try to walk out here over that narrow neck. If she does, she'll drop on her belly with one truck on each side. Probably turn herself over trying to dig out."

The wait then was interminable. Back over the hill they could hear the laboring motor; twice they heard the machine stop momentarily to shift gears. Once they looked at each other hopefully as the sound rose to a series of bellowing roars, as if she ᵂᵉre backing and filling; then they realized that she was trying to take some particularly steep part of the bank and having trouble getting traction. But she made it; the motor revved up as she made the brow of the hill, and she shifted into fourth gear and came lumbering out into the open. She lurched up to the edge of the cut, stopped, throttled down, dropped her blade on the ground and stood there idling. Al Knowles backed away to the very edge of the tongue of earth they stood on, his eyes practically on stalks.

"O.K.—put up or shut up," Kelly called across harshly.

"She's looking the situation over," said Tom. "That narrow pathway don't fool her a bit."

Daisy Etta's blade began to rise, and stopped just clear of the ground. She shifted without clashing her gears, began to back slowly, still at little more than an idle.

"She's gonna jump!" screamed Al. "I'm gettin' out of here!"

"Stay here, you fool," shouted Kelly. "She can't get us as long as we're up here! If you go down, she'll hunt you down like a rabbit."

The blast of the Seven's motor was the last straw for Al. He squeaked and hopped over the edge, scrambling and sliding down the almost sheer face of the cut. He hit the bottom running.

Daisy Etta lowered her blade and raised her snout and growled forward, the blade loading. Six, seven, seven and a half cubic yards of dirt piled up in front of her as she neared the edge. The loaded blade bit into the narrow pathway that led out to their perch. It was almost all soft, white, crumbly marl, and the great machine sank nose down into it, the monstrous overload of topsoil spilling down on each side.

"She's going to bury herself!" shouted Kelly.

"No—wait." Tom caught his arm. "She's trying to turn—she made it! She made it! She's ramping herself down to the flat!"

"She is—and she's cut us off from the bluff!"

The bulldozer, blade raised as high as it could possibly go, the hydraulic rod gleaming clean in the early light, freed herself of the last of her tremendous load, spun around and headed back upward, sinking her blade again. She made one more pass between them and the bluff, making a cut now far too wide for them to jump, particularly to the crumbly footing at the bluff's edge. Once down again, she turned to face their haven, now an isolated pillar of marl, and revved down, waiting.

"I never thought of this," said Kelly guiltily. "I knew we'd be safe from her ramping up, and I never thought she'd try it the other way!"

"Skip it. In the meantime, here we sit. What happens—do

we wait up here until she idles out of fuel, or do we starve to death?"

"Oh, this won't be a siege, Tom. That thing's too much of a killer. Where's Al? I wonder if he's got guts enough to make a pass near here with our tractor and draw her off?"

"He had just guts enough to take our tractor and head out," said Tom. "Didn't you know?"

"He took our—*what?*" Kelly looked out toward where they had left their machine the night before. It was gone. "Why that dirty little yellow rat!"

"No sense cussin'," said Tom steadily, interrupting what he knew was the beginning of some really flowery language. "What else could you expect?"

Daisy Etta decided, apparently, how to go about removing their splendid isolation. She uttered the snort of a too-quick throttle, and moved into their peak with a corner of her blade, cutting out a huge swipe, undercutting the material over it so that it fell on her side and track as she passed. Eight inches disappeared from that side of their little plateau.

"Oh-oh. That won't do a-tall," said Tom.

"Fixin' to dig us down," said Kelly grimly. "Take her about twenty minutes. Tom, I say leave."

"It won't be healthy. You just got no idea how fast that thing can move now. Don't forget, she's a good deal more than she was when she had a man runnin' her. She can shift from high to reverse to fifth speed forward like that"—he snapped his fingers—"and she can pivot faster'n you can blink and throw that blade just where she wants it."

The tractor passed under them, bellowing, and their little table was suddenly a foot shorter.

"Awright," said Kelly. "So what do you want to do? Stay here and let her dig the ground out from under our feet?"

"I'm just warning you," said Tom. "Now listen. We'll wait until she's taking a load. It'll take her a second to get rid of it when she knows we're gone. We'll split—she can't get both of us. You head out in the open, try to circle the curve of the bluff and get where you can climb it. Then come back over here to the cut. A man can scramble off a fourteen-foot cut faster'n any tractor ever built. I'll cut in close to the cut, down at the bottom. If she takes after you, I'll get clear all right. If she takes after me, I'll try to make the shovel and at least give her a run for her money. I can play hide an' seek in an' around and under that dipper-stick all day if she wants to play."

"Why me out in the open?"

"Don't you think those long laigs o' yours can outrun her in that distance?"

"Reckon they got to," grinned Kelly. "O.K., Tom."

They waited tensely. *Daisy Etta* backed close by, started another pass. As the motor blatted under the load, Tom said, "Now!" and they jumped. Kelly, catlike as always, landed on his feet. Tom, whose knees and ankles were black and blue with rope bruises, took two staggering steps and fell. Kelly scooped him to his feet as the dozer's steel prow came around the bank. Instantly she was in fifth gear and howling down at them. Kelly flung himself to the left and Tom to the right, and they pounded away, Kelly out toward the runway, Tom straight for the shovel. *Daisy Etta* let them diverge for a moment, keeping her course, trying to pursue both; then she evidently sized Tom up as the slower, for she swung toward him. The instant's hesitation was all Tom needed to get the little lead necessary. He tore up to the shovel, his legs going like pistons, and dived down between the shovel's tracks.

As he hit the ground, the big manganese-steel moldboard hit the right track of the shovel, and the impact set all forty-seven tons of the great machine quivering. But Tom did not stop. He scrabbled his way under the rig, stood up behind it, leaped and caught the sill of the rear window, clapped his other hand on it, drew himself up and tumbled inside. Here he was safe for the moment; the huge tracks themselves were higher than the Seven's blade could rise, and the floor of the cab was a good sixteen inches higher than the top of the track. Tom went to the cab door and peeped outside. The tractor had drawn off and was idling.

"Study away," gritted Tom, and went to the big Murphy diesel. He unhurriedly checked the oil with the bayonet gauge, replaced it, took the governor cut-out rod from its rack and inserted it in the governor casing. He set the master throttle at the halfway mark, pulled up the starter-handle, twitched the cut-out. The motor spat a wad of blue smoke out of its hooded exhaust and caught. Tom put the rod back, studied the fuel-flow glass and pressure gauges, and then went to the door and looked out again. The Seven had not moved, but it was revving up and down in that uneven fashion it had shown up on the mesa. Tom had the extraordinary idea that it was gathering itself to spring. He slipped into the saddle, threw the master clutch. The big gears that half-filled the cab obediently began to turn. He kicked the brake locks loose with his heels, let his feet rest lightly on the pedals as they rose.

Then he reached over his head and snapped back the throttle. As the Murphy picked up he grasped both hoist and swing levers and pulled them back. The engine howled; the two-yard bucket came up off the ground with a sudden jolt as the cold friction grabbed it. The big machine swung hard to the right; Tom snapped his hoist lever forward and checked the bucket's rise with his foot on the brake. He shoved the crowd lever forward; the bucket ran out to the end of its reach, and the heel of the bucket wiped across the Seven's hood, taking with it the exhaust stack, muffler and all, and the pre-cleaner on the air intake. Tom cursed. He had figured on the machine's leaping backward. If it had, he would have smashed the cast-iron radiator core. But she had stood still, making a split-second decision.

Now she moved, though, and quickly. With that incredibly fast shifting, she leaped backwards and pivoted out of range before Tom could check the shovel's mad swing. The heavy swing-friction blocks smoked acridly as the machine slowed, stopped and swung back. Tom checked her as he was facing the Seven, hoisted his bucket a few feet, and rehauled, bringing it about halfway back, ready for anything. The four great dipper-teeth gleamed in the sun. Tom ran a practiced eye over cables, boom and dipper-stick, liking the black polish of crater compound on the sliding parts, the easy tension of well-greased cables and links. The huge machine stood strong, ready and profoundly subservient for all its brute power.

Tom looked searchingly at the Seven's ruined engine hood. The gaping end of the broken air-intake pipe stared back at him. "Aha!" he said. "A few cupfuls of nice dry marl down there'll give you something to chew on."

Keeping a wary eye on the tractor, he swung into the bank, dropped his bucket and plunged it into the marl. He crowded it deep, and the Murphy yelled for help but kept on pushing. At the peak of the load a terrific jar rocked him in the saddle. He looked back over his shoulder through the door and saw the Seven backing off again. She had run up and delivered a terrific punch to the counterweight at the back of the cab. Tom grinned tightly. She'd have to do better than that. There was nothing back there but eight or ten tons of solid steel. And he didn't much care at the moment whether or not she scratched his paint.

He swung back again, white marl running away on both sides of the heaped bucket. The shovel rode perfectly now, for a shovel is counterweighted to balance true when standing level with the bucket loaded. The hoist and swing frictions and the brake linings had heated and dried themselves of the night's condensation moisture, and she answered the controls in a way that delighted the operator in him. He handled the swing lever lightly, back to swing to the right, forward to swing to the left, following the slow dance the Seven had started to do, stepping warily back and forth like a fighter looking for an opening. Tom kept the bucket between himself and the tractor, knowing that she could not hurl a tool that was built to smash hard rock for twenty hours a day and like it.

Daisy Etta bellowed and rushed in. Tom snapped the hoist lever back hard, and the bucket rose, letting the tractor run underneath. Tom punched the bucket trip, and the great steel jaw opened, cascading marl down on the broken hood. The tractor's fan blew it back in a huge billowing cloud. The instant that it took Tom to check and dump was enough, however, for the tractor to dance back out of the way, for when he tried to drop it on the machine to smash the coiled injector tubes on top of the engine block, she was gone.

The dust cleared away, and the tractor moved in again, feinted to the left, then swung her blade at the bucket, which was just clear of the ground. Tom swung to meet her, her feint having gotten her in a little closer than he liked, and bucket met blade with a shower of sparks and a clank that could be heard for half a mile. She had come in with her blade high, and Tom let out a wordless shout as he saw the A-frame brace behind the blade had caught between two of his dipper-teeth. He snatched at his hoist lever and the bucket came up, lifting with it the whole front end of the bulldozer.

Daisy Etta plunged up and down and her tracks dug violently into the earth as she raised and lowered her blade, trying to shake herself free. Tom rehauled, trying to bring the tractor in

closer, for the boom was set too low to attempt to lift such a
dead weight. As it was, the shovel's off track was trying its
best to get off the ground. But the crowd and rehaul frictions
could not handle her alone; they began to heat and slip.

Tom hoisted a little; the shovel's off track came up a foot
off the ground. Tom cursed and let the bucket drop, and in an
instant the dozer was free and running clear. Tom swung wildly
at her, missed. The dozer came into a long curve; Tom swung
to meet her again, took a vicious swipe at her which she took
on her blade. But this time she did not withdraw after being
hit, but bored right in, carrying the bucket before her. Before
Tom realized what she was doing, his bucket was around in
front of the tracks and between them, on the ground. It was
as swift and skillful a maneuver as could be imagined, and it
left the shovel without the ability to swing as long as *Daisy
Etta* could hold the bucket trapped between the tracks.

Tom crowded furiously, but that succeeded only in lifting
the boom higher in the air, since there is nothing to hold a
boom down but its own weight. Hoisting did nothing but make
his frictions smoke and rev the engine down dangerously close
to the stalling point.

Tom swore again and reached down to the cluster of small
levers at his left. These were the gears. On this type of shovel,
the swing lever controls everything except crowd and hoist.
With the swing lever, the operator, having selected his gear,
controls the travel—that is, power to the tracks—in forward
and reverse; booming up and booming down; and swinging.
The machine can do only one of these things at a time. If she
is in travel gear, she cannot swing. If she is in swing gear, she
cannot boom up or down. Not once in years of operating would
this inability bother an operator; now, however, nothing was
normal.

Tom pushed the swing gear control down and pulled up on
the travel. The clutches involved were jaw clutches, not frictions, so that he had to throttle down to an idle before he could
make the castellations mesh. As the Murphy revved down,
Daisy Etta took it as a signal that something could be done
about it, and she shoved furiously into the bucket. But Tom
had all controls in neutral and all she succeeded in doing was
to dig herself in, her sharp new cleats spinning deep into the
dirt.

Tom set his throttle up again and shoved the swing lever forward. There was a vast crackling of drive chains; and the big tracks started to turn.

Daisy Etta had sharp cleats; her pads were twenty inches wide and her tracks were fourteen feet long, and there were fourteen tons of steel on them. The shovel's big flat pads were three feet wide and twenty feet long, and forty-seven tons aboard. There was simply no comparison. The Murphy bellowed the fact that the work was hard, but gave no indication of stalling. *Daisy Etta* performed the incredible feat of shifting into a forward gear while she was moving backwards, but it did her no good. Round and round her tracks went, trying to drive her forward, gouging deep; and slowly and surely she was forced backward toward the cut wall by the shovel.

Tom heard a sound that was not part of a straining machine; he looked out and saw Kelly up on top of the cut, smoking, swinging his feet over the edge, making punching motions with his hands as if he had a ringside seat at a big fight—which he certainly had.

Tom now offered the dozer little choice. If she did not turn aside before him, she would be borne back against the bank and her fuel tank crushed. There was every possibility that, having her pinned there, Tom would have time to raise his bucket over her and smash her to pieces. And if she turned before she was forced against the bank, she would have to free Tom's bucket. This she had to do.

The Murphy gave him warning, but not enough. It crooned as the load came off, and Tom knew then that the dozer was shifting into a reverse gear. He whipped the hoist lever back, and the bucket rose as the dozer backed away from him. He crowded it out and let it come smashing down—and missed. For the tractor danced aside—and while he was in travel gear he could not swing to follow it. *Daisy Etta* charged then, put one track on the bank and went over almost on her beam-ends, throwing one end of her blade high in the air. So totally unexpected was it that Tom was quite unprepared. The tractor flung itself on the bucket, and the cutting edge of the blade dropped between the dipper teeth. This time there was the whole weight of the tractor to hold it there. There would be no way for her to free herself—but at the same time she had trapped the bucket so far out from the center pin of the shovel that

Tom couldn't hoist without overbalancing and turning the monster over.

Daisy Etta ground away in reverse, dragging the bucket out until it was checked by the bumper-blocks. Then she began to crab sideways, up against the bank and when Tom tried tentatively to rehaul, she shifted and came right with him, burying one whole end of her blade deep into the bank.

Stalemate. She had hung herself up on the bucket, and she had immobilized it. Tom tried to rehaul, but the tractor's anchorage in the bank was too solid. He tried to swing, to hoist. All the overworked frictions could possibly give out was smoke. Tom grunted and throttled to an idle, leaned out the window. *Daisy Etta* was idling too, loudly without her muffler, the stackless exhaust giving out an ugly flat sound. But after the roar of the two great motors the partial silence was deafening.

Kelly called down, "Double knockout, hey?"

"Looks like it. What say we see if we can't get close enough to her to quiet her down some?"

Kelly shrugged. "I dunno. If she's really stopped herself, it's the first time. I respect that rig, Tom. She wouldn't have got herself into that spot if she didn't have an ace up her sleeve."

"Look at her, man! Suppose she was a civilized bulldozer and you had to get her out of there. She can't raise her blade high enough to free it from those dipper-teeth, y'know. Think you'd be able to do it?"

"It might take several seconds," Kelly drawled. "She's sure high and dry."

"O.K., let's spike her guns."

"Like what?"

"Like taking a bar and prying out her tubing." He referred to the coiled brass tubing that carried the fuel, under pressure, from the pump to the injectors. There were many feet of it, running from the pump reservoir, stacked in expansion coils over the cylinder head.

As he spoke *Daisy Etta*'s idle burst into that maniac revving up and down characteristic of her.

"What do you know!" Tom called above the racket. "Eavesdropping!"

Kelly slid down the cut, stood up on the track of the shovel and poked his head in the window. "Well, you want to get a bar and try?"

"Let's go!"

Tom went to the toolbox and pulled out the pinch bar that Kelly used to replace cables on his machine, and swung to the ground. They approached the tractor warily. She revved up as they came near, began to shudder. The front end rose and dropped and the tracks began to turn as she tried to twist out of the vise her blade had dropped into.

"Take it easy, sister," said Tom. "You'll just bury yourself. Set still and take it, now, like a good girl. You got it comin'."

"Be careful," said Kelly. Tom hefted the bar and laid a hand on the fender.

The tractor literally shivered, and from the rubber hose connection at the top of the radiator, a blinding stream of hot water shot out. It fanned and caught them both full in the face. They staggered back, cursing.

"You O.K. Tom?" Kelly gasped a moment later. He had got most of it across the mouth and cheek. Tom was on his knees, his shirt tail out, blotting at his face.

"My eyes...oh, my eyes—"

"Let's see!" Kelly dropped down beside him and took him by the wrists, gently removing Tom's hands from his face. He whistled. "Come on," he gritted. He helped Tom up and led him away a few feet. "Stay here," he said hoarsely. He turned, walked back toward the dozer, picking up the pinchbar. "You dirty——!" he yelled, and flung it like a javelin at the tube coils. It was a little high. It struck the ruined hood, made a deep dent in the metal. The dent promptly inverted with a loud *thung-g-g!* and flung the bar back at him. He ducked; it whistled over his head and caught Tom in the calves of his legs. He went down like a poled ox, but staggered to his feet again.

"Come on!" Kelly snarled, and taking Tom's arm, hustled him around the turn of the cut. "Sit down! I'll be right back."

"Where you going? Kelly—be careful!"

"Careful and how!"

Kelly's long legs ate up the distance back to the shovel. He swung into the cab, reached back over the motor and set up the master throttle all the way. Stepping up behind the saddle, he opened the running throttle and the Murphy howled. Then he hauled back on the hoist lever until it knuckled in, turned and leaped off the machine in one supple motion.

The hoist drum turned and took up slack; the cable straightened as it took the strain. The bucket stirred under the dead weight of the bulldozer that rested on it; and slowly, then, the great flat tracks began to lift their rear ends off the ground. The great obedient mass of machinery teetered forward on the tips of her tracks, the Murphy revved down and under the incredible load, but it kept the strain. A strand of the two-part hoist cable broke and whipped around, singing; and then she was balanced—over-balanced—

And the shovel had hauled herself right over and had fallen with an earth-shaking crash. The boom, eight tons of solid steel, clanged down onto the blade of the bulldozer, and lay there, crushing it down tightly onto the imprisoning row of dipper-teeth.

Daisy Etta sat there, not trying to move now, racing her motor impotently. Kelly strutted past her, thumbing his nose, and went back to Tom.

"Kelly! I thought you were never coming back! What happened?"

"Shovel pulled herself over on her nose."

"Good boy! Fall on the tractor?"

"Nup. But the boom's laying across the top of her blade. Caught like a rat in a trap."

"Better watch out the rat don't chew its leg off to get out," said Tom, drily. "Still runnin', is she?"

"Yep. But we'll fix that in a hurry."

"Sure. Sure. How?"

"How? I dunno. Dynamite, maybe. How's the optics?"

Tom opened one a trifle and grunted. "Rough. I can see a little, though. My eyelids are parboiled, mostly. Dynamite, you say? Well—"

Tom sat back against the bank and stretched out his legs. "I tell you, Kelly, I been too blessed busy these last few hours to think much, but there's one thing that keeps comin' back to me—somethin' I was mullin' over long before the rest of you guys knew anything was up at all, except that Rivera had got hurt in some way I wouldn't tell you all about. But I don't reckon you'll call me crazy if I open my mouth now and let it all run out?"

"From now on," Kelly said fervently, "nobody's crazy. After this I'll believe anything."

"O.K. Well, about that tractor. What do you suppose has got into her?"

"Search me. I dunno."

"No—don't say that. I just got an idea we can't stop at 'I dunno.' We got to figure all the angles on this thing before we know just what to do about it. Let's just get this thing lined up. When did it start? On the mesa. How? Rivera was opening an old building with the Seven. This thing came out of there. Now here's what I'm getting at. We can dope these things out about it: It's intelligent. It can only get into a machine and not into a man. It—"

"What about that? How do you know it can't?"

"Because it had the chance to and didn't. I was standing right by the opening when it kited out. Rivera was upon the machine at the time. It didn't directly harm either of us. It got into the tractor, and the tractor did. By the same token, it can't hurt a man when it's out of a machine, but that's all it wants to do when it's in one. O.K.?"

"To get on: once it's in one machine it can't get out again. We know that because it had plenty of chances and didn't take them. That scuffle with the dipper-stick, f'r instance. My face woulda been plenty red if it had taken over the shovel—and you can bet it would have if it could."

"I got you so far. But what are we going to do about it?"

"That's the thing. You see, I don't think it's enough to wreck the tractor. We might burn it, blast it, take whatever it was that got into it up on the mesa."

"That makes sense. But I don't see what else we can do than just break up the dozer. We haven't got a line on actually what the thing is."

"I think we have. Remember I asked you all those screwy questions about the arc that killed Peebles. Well, when that happened, I recollected a flock of other things. One—when it got out of that hole up there, I smelled that smell that you notice when you're welding; sometimes when lightning strikes real close."

"Ozone," said Kelly.

"Yeah—ozone. Then, it likes metal, not flesh. But most of all, there was that arc. Now, that was absolutely screwy. You know as well as I do—better—that an arc generator simply don't have the push to do a thing like that. It can't kill a man, and it can't throw an arc no fifty feet. But it did. An' that's why I asked you if there could be something—a field, or some such—that could *suck* current out of a generator, all at once, faster than it could flow. Because this thing's electrical; it fits all around."

"Electronic," said Kelly doubtfully, thoughtfully.

"I wouldn't know. Now then. When Peebles was killed, a funny thing happened. Remember what Chub said? The Seven moved back—straight back, about thirty feet, until it bumped into a roadroller that was standing behind it. It did that with no fuel in the starting engine—without even using the starting engine, for that matter—and with the compression valves locked open!

"Kelly, that thing in the dozer can't do much, when you come right down to it. It couldn't fix itself up after the joyride on the mesa. It can't make the machine do too much more than the machine can do ordinarily. What it actually can do, seems to me, is to make a spring push instead of pull, like the control levers, and make a fitting slip when it's supposed to hold, like the ratchet on the throttle lever. It can turn a shaft, like the way it cranks its own starting motor. But if it was so all-fired high-powered, it wouldn't have to use the starting motor! The absolute biggest job it's done so far, seems to me, was when it walked back from that welding machine when Peebles got his. Now, why did it do that just then?"

"Reckon it didn't like the brimstone smell, like it says in the Good Book," said Kelly sourly.

"That's pretty close, seems to me. Look, Kelly—this thing *feels* things. I mean, it can get sore. If it couldn't it never woulda kept driving in at the shovel like that. It can think. But if it can do all those things, then it cán be *scared!*"

"Scared? Why should it be scared?"

"Listen. Something went on in that thing when the arc hit it. What's that I read in a magazine once about heat—something about molecules runnin' around with their heads cut off when they got hot?"

"Molecules do. They go into rapid motion when heat is applied. But—"

"But nothin'. That machine was hot for four hours after that. But she was hot in a funny way. Not just around the place where the arc hit, like as if it was a welding arc. But hot all over—from the moldboard to the fuel-tank cap. Hot everywhere. And just as hot behind the final drive housings as she was at the top of the blade where the poor guy put his hand.

"And look at this." Tom was getting excited, as his words crystallized his ideas. "She was scared—scared enough to back off from that welder, putting everything she could into it, to get back from that welding machine. And after that, she was sick. I say that because in the whole time she's had that what-ever-ya-call-it in her, she's never been near men without trying to kill them, except for those two days after the arc hit her. She had juice enough to start herself when Dennis came around with the crank, but she still needed someone to run her till she got her strength back."

"But why didn't she turn and smash up the welder when Dennis took her?"

"One of two things. She didn't have the strength, or she didn't have the guts. She was scared, maybe, and wanted out of there, away from that thing."

"But she had all night to go back for it!"

"Still scared. Or . . . oh, *that's* it! She had other things to do first. Her main idea is to kill men—there's no other way you can figure it. It's what she was built to do. Not the tractor—they don't build 'em sweeter'n that machine; but the thing that's runnin' it."

"What *is* that thing?" Kelly mused. "Coming out of that old building—temple—what have you—how old is it? How long was it there? What kept it in there?"

"What kept it in there was some funny gray stuff that lined the inside of the buildin'," said Tom. "It was like rock, an' it was like smoke.

"It was a color that scared you to look at it, and it gave Rivera and me the creeps when we got near it. Don't ask me what it was. I went up there to look at it, and it's gone. Gone from the building, anyhow. There was a little lump of it on the ground. I don't know whether that was a hunk of it, or all of it rolled up into a ball. I get the creeps again thinkin' about it."

Kelly stood up. "Well, the heck with it. We been beatin' our gums up here too long anyhow. There's just enough sense in what you say to make me want to try something nonsensical, if you see what I mean. If that welder can sweat the Ol' Nick out of that tractor, I'm on. Especially from fifty feet away. There should be a Dumptor around here somewhere; let's move from here. Can you navigate now?"

"Reckon so, a little." Tom rose and together they followed the cut until they came on the Dumptor. They climbed on, cranked it up and headed toward camp.

About halfway there Kelly looked back, gasped, and putting his mouth close to Tom's ear, bellowed against the scream of the motor. "Tom! 'Member what you said about the rat in the trap biting off a leg?"

Tom nodded.

"Well, *Daisy* did too! She's left her blade an' pushbeams an' she's followin' us in!"

They howled into the camp, gasping against the dust that followed when they pulled up by the welder.

Kelly said, "You cast around and see if you can find a drawpin to hook that rig up to the Dumptor with. I'm goin' after some water an' chow!"

Tom grinned. Imagine old Kelly forgetting that a Dumptor had no drawbar! He groped around to a toolbox, peering out of the narrow slit beneath swollen lids, felt behind it and located a shackle. He climbed up on the Dumptor, turned it around and backed up to the welding machine. He passed the shackle through the ring at the end of the steering tongue of the welder, screwed in the pin and dropped the shackle over the front towing hook of the Dumptor. A Dumptor being what it is, having no real front and no real rear, and direct reversing gears in all speeds, it was no trouble to drive it "backwards" for a change.

Kelly came pounding back, out of breath. "Fix it? Good. Shackle? No drawbar! *Daisy*'s closin' up fast; I say let's take the beach. We'll be concealed until we have a good lead out o' this pocket, and the going's pretty fair, long as we don't bury this jalopy in the sand."

"Good," said Tom as they climbed on and he accepted an open tin of K. "Only go easy; bump around too much and the welder'll slip off the hook. An' I somehow don't want to lose it just now."

They took off, zooming up the beach. A quarter of a mile up, they sighted the Seven across the flat. It immediately turned and took a course that would intercept them.

"Here she comes," shouted Kelly, and stepped down hard on the accelerator. Tom leaned over the back of the seat, keeping his eye on their tow. "Hey! Take it easy! Watch it!

"Hey!"

But it was too late. The tongue of the welding machine responded to that one bump too many. The shackle jumped up off the hook, the welder lurched wildly, slewed hard to the left. The tongue dropped to the sand and dug in; the machine rolled up on it and snapped it off, finally stopped, leaning crazily askew. By a miracle it did not quite turn over.

Kelly tramped on the brakes and both their heads did their utmost to snap off their shoulders. They leaped off and ran back to the welder. It was intact, but towing it was now out of the question.

"If there's going to be a showdown, it's gotta be here."

The beach here was about thirty yards wide, the sand almost level, and undercut banks of sawgrass forming the landward edge in a series of little hummocks and headlands. While Tom stayed with the machine, testing starter and generator contacts, Kelly walked up one of the little mounds, stood up on it and scanned the beach back the way he had come. Suddenly he began to shout and wave his arms.

"What's got into you?"

"It's Al!" Kelly called back. "With the pan tractor!"

Tom dropped what he was doing, and came to stand beside Kelly. "Where's the Seven? I can't see."

"Turned on the beach and followin' our track. Al! Al! You little skunk, c'mere!"

Tom could now dimly make out the pan tractor cutting across directly toward them and the beach.

"He don't see *Daisy Etta*," remarked Kelly disgustedly, "or he'd sure be headin' the other way."

Fifty yards away Al pulled up and throttled down. Kelly shouted and waved to him. Al stood up on the machine, cupped his hands around his mouth. "Where's the Seven?"

"Never mind that! Come here with that tractor!"

Al stayed where he was. Kelly cursed and started out after him.

"You stay away from me," he said when Kelly was closer.

"I ain't got time for you now," said Kelly. "Bring that tractor down to the beach."

"Where's that *Daisy Etta?*" Al's voice was oddly strained.

"Right behind us." Kelly thumbed over his shoulder. "On the beach."

Al's bulging eyes clicked wide almost audibly. He turned

on his heel and jumped off the machine and started to run. Kelly uttered a wordless syllable that was somehow more obscene than anything else he had ever uttered, and vaulted into the seat of the machine. "Hey!" he bellowed after Al's rapidly diminishing figure. "You're runnin' right into her." Al appeared not to hear, but went pelting down the beach.

Kelly put her into fifth gear and poured on the throttle. As the tractor began to move he whacked out the master clutch, snatched the overdrive lever back to put her into sixth, rammed the clutch in again, all so fast that she did not have time to stop rolling. Bucking and jumping over the rough ground, the fast machine whined for the beach.

Tom was fumbling back to the welder, his ears telling him better than his eyes how close the Seven was—for she was certainly no nightingale, particularly without her exhaust stack. Kelly reached the machine as he did.

"Get behind it," snapped Tom. "I'll jam the tierod with the shackle, and you see if you can't bunt her up into that pocket between these two hummocks. Only take it easy—you don't want to tear up that generator. Where's Al?"

"Dont' ask me. He run down the beach to meet *Daisy*."

"He *what?*"

The whine of the two-cycle drowned out Kelly's answer, if any. He got behind the welder and set his blade against it. Then in a low gear, slipping his clutch in a little, he slowly nudged the machine toward the place Tom had indicated. It was a little hollow in between two projecting banks. The surf and the high-tide mark dipped inland here to match it; the water was only a few feet away.

Tom raised his arm and Kelly stopped. From the other side of the projecting shelf, out of their sight now, came the flat roar of the Seven's exhuast. Kelly sprang off the tractor and went to help Tom, who was furiously throwing out coils of cable from the rack back of the welder. "What's the game?"

"We got to ground that Seven some way," panted Tom. He threw the last bit of cable out to clear it of kinks and turned to the panel. "How was it—about sixty volts and the amperage on 'special application'?" He spun the dials, pressed the starter button. The motor responded instantly. Kelly scooped up ground clamp and rod holder and tapped them together. The solenoid governor picked up the load and the motor hummed as a good live spark took the jump.

"Good," said Tom, switching off the generator. "Come on, Lieutenant General Electric, figure me out a way to ground that maverick."

Kelly tightened his lips, shook his head. "I dunno—unless somebody actually clamps this thing on her."

"No, boy, can't do that. If one of us gets killed—"

Kelly tossed the ground clamp idly, his lithe body taut. "Don't give me that, Tom. You know I'm elected because you can't see good enough yet to handle it. You know you'd do it if you could. You—"

He stopped short, for the steadily increasing roar of the approaching Seven had stopped, was blatting away now in that extraordinary irregular throtting that *Daisy Etta* affected.

"Now, what's got into her?"

Kelly broke away and scrambled up the bank. "Tom!" he gasped. "Tom—come up here!"

Tom followed, and they lay side by side, peering out over the top of the escarpment at the remarkable tableau.

Daisy Etta was standing on the beach, near the water, not moving. Before her, twenty or thirty feet away, stood Al Knowles, his arms out in front of him, talking a blue streak. *Daisy* made far too much racket for them to hear what he was saying.

"Do you reckon he's got guts enough to stall her off for us?" said Tom.

"If he has, it's the queerest thing that's happened yet on this old island," Kelly breathed, "an' that's saying something."

The Seven revved up till she shook, and then throttled back. She ran down so low then that they thought she had shut herself down, but she caught on the last two revolutions and began to idle quietly. And then they could hear.

Al's voice was high, hysterical. "—I come t' he'p you, I come t' he'p you, don' kill me, I'll he'p you—" He took a step forward; the dozer snorted and he fell to his knees. "I'll wash you an' grease you and change yo' ile," he said in a high singsong.

"The guy's not human," said Kelly wonderingly.

"He ain't housebroke either," Tom chuckled.

"—lemme he'p you. I'll fix you when you break down. I'll he'p you kill those other guys—"

"She don't need any help!" said Tom.

"The louse," growled Kelly. "The rotten little double-

crossing polecat!" He stood up. "Hey, you Al! Come out o'
that. I mean now! If she don't get you I will, if you don't
move."

Al was crying now. "Shut up!" he screamed. "I know who's
bawss hereabouts, an' so do you!" He pointed at the tractor.
"She'll kill us all off'n we don't do what she wants!" He turned
back to the machine. "I'll k-kill 'em fo' you. I'll wash you
and shine you up and f-fix yo' hood. I'll put yo' blade back
on. . . ."

Tom reached out and caught Kelly's leg as the tall man
started out, blind mad. "Git back here," he barked. "What you
want to do—get killed for the privilege of pinnin' his ears
back?"

Kelly subsided and came back, threw himself down beside
Tom, put his face in his hands. He was quivering with rage.

"Don't take on so," Tom said. "The man's plumb loco. You
can't argue with him any more'n you can with *Daisy,* there.
If he's got to get his, *Daisy*'ll give it to him."

"Aw, Tom, it ain't that. I know he ain't worth it, but I can't
sit up here and watch him get himself killed. I can't, Tom."

Tom thumped him on the shoulder, because there was simply no words to be said. Suddenly he stiffened, snapped his
fingers.

"There's our ground," he said urgently, pointing seaward.
"The water—the wet beach where the surf runs. If we can get
our ground clamp out there and her somewhere near it—"

"Ground the pan tractor. Run it out into the water. It ought
to reach—partway, anyhow."

"That's it—c'mon."

They slid down the bank, snatched up the ground clamp,
attached it to the frame of the pan tractor.

"I'll take it," said Tom, and as Kelly opened his mouth,
Tom shoved him back against the welding machine. "No time
to argue," he snapped, swung on to the machine, slapped her
in gear and was off. Kelly took a step toward the tractor, and
then his quick eye saw a bight of the ground cable about to
foul a wheel of the welder. He stooped and threw it off, spread
out the rest of it so it would pay off clear. Tom, with the
incredible single-mindedness of the trained operator, watched
only the black line of the trailing cable on the sand behind him.
When it straightened, he stopped. The front of the tracks were

sloshing in the gentle surf. He climbed off the side away from the Seven and tried to see. There was movement, and the growl of her motor now running at a bit more than idle, but he could not distinguish much.

Kelly picked up the rod-holder and went to peer around the head of the protruding bank. Al was on his feet, still crooning hysterically, sidling over toward *Daisy Etta*. Kelly ducked back, threw the switch on the arc generator, climbed the bank and crawled along through the sawgrass paralleling the beach until the holder in his hand tugged and he knew he had reached the end of the cable. He looked out at the beach; measured carefully with his eye the arc he would travel if he left his position and, keeping the cable taut, went out on the beach. At no point would he come within seventy feet of the possessed machine, let alone fifty. She had to be drawn in closer. And she had to be maneuvered out to the wet sand, or in the water—

Al Knowles, encouraged by the machine's apparent decision not to move, approached, though warily, and still running off at the mouth. "—we'll kill'em off an' then we'll keep it a secret and th' bahges'll come an' take us offen th' island and we'll go to anothah job an' kill us lots mo' . . . an' when yo' tracks git dry an' squeak we'll wet 'em up with blood, and you'll be rightly king o' th' hill . . . look yondah, look yondah, *Daisy Etta*, see them theah, by the otheh tractuh, theah they are, kill 'em, *Daisy*, kill 'em, *Daisy*, an' lemme he'p . . . heah me. *Daisy*, heah me, say you heah me—" and the motor roared in response. Al laid a timid hand on the radiator guard, leaning far over to do it, and the tractor still stood there grumbling but not moving. Al stepped back, motioned with his arm, began to walk off slowly toward the pan tractor, looking backwards as he did so like a man training a dog. "C'mon, c'mon, theah's one theah, le's *kill'm, kill'm, kill'm*. . . ."

And with a snort the tractor revved up and followed.

Kelly licked his lips without effect because his tongue was dry, too. The madman passed him, walking straight up the center of the beach, and the tractor, now no longer a bulldozer, followed him; and there the sand was bone dry, sundried, dried to powder. As the tractor passed him, Kelly got up on all fours, went over the edge of the bank onto the beach, crouched there.

Al crooned, "I love ya, honey, I love ya, 'deed I do—"

• • •

Kelly ran crouching, like a man under machine-gun fire, making himself as small as possible and feeling as big as a barn door. The torn-up sand where the tractor had passed was under his feet now; he stopped, afraid to get much closer, afraid that a weakened, badly grounded arc might leap from the holder in his hand and serve only to alarm and infuriate the thing in the tractor. And just then Al saw him.

"There!" he screamed; and the tractor pulled up short. "Behind you! Get'm, *Daisy! Kill'm, kill'm, kill'm.*"

Kelly stood up almost wearily, fury and frustration too much to be borne. "In the water," he yelled, because it was what his whole being wanted. "Get'er in the water! Wet her tracks, Al!"

"Kill' m, kill' m—"

As the tractor started to turn, there was a commotion over by the pan tractor. It was Tom, jumping, shouting, waving his arms, swearing. He ran out from behind his machine, straight at the Seven. *Daisy Etta*'s motor roared and she swung to meet him, Al barely dancing back out of the way. Tom cut sharply, sand spouting under his pumping feet, and ran straight into the water. He went out to about waist deep, suddenly disappeared. He surfaced, spluttering, still trying to shout. Kelly took a better grip on his rod holder and rushed.

Daisy Etta, in following Tom's crazy rush, had swung in beside the pan tractor, not fifteen feet away; and she, too, was now in the surf. Kelly closed up the distance as fast as his long legs would let him; and as he approached to within that crucial fifty feet, Al Knowles hit him.

Al was frothing at the mouth, gibbering. The two men hit full tilt; Al's head caught Kelly in the midriff as he missed a straightarm, and the breath went out of him in one great *whoosh!* Kelly went down like tall timber, the whole world turned to one swirling red-gray haze. Al flung himself on the bigger man, clawing, smacking, too berserk to ball his fists.

"Ah'm go' to kill you," he gurgled. "She'll git one, I'll git t'other, an' then she'll know—"

Kelly covered his face with his arms, and as some wind was sucked at last into his laboring lungs, he flung them upward and sat up in one mighty surge. Al was hurled upward and to one side, and as he hit the ground Kelly reached out a long arm, and twisted his fingers into the man's coarse hair, raised him up, and came across with his other fist in a punch that would have killed him had it landed square. But Al managed to jerk to one side enough so that it only amputated a cheek. He fell and lay still. Kelly scrambled madly around in the sand for his welding-rod holder, found it and began to run again. He couldn't see Tom at all now, and the Seven was standing in the surf, moving slowly from side to side, backing out, ravening. Kelly held the rod-clamp and its trailing cable blindly before him and ran straight at the machine. And then it came— that thin, soundless bolt of energy. But this time it had its full force, for poor old Peebles's body had not been the ground that this swirling water offered. *Daisy Etta* literally leaped backwards toward him, and the water around her tracks spouted upward in hot steam. The sound of her engine ran up and up, broke, took on the rhythmic, uneven beat of a swing drummer. She threw herself from side to side like a cat with a bag over its head. Kelly stepped a little closer, hoping for another bolt to come from the clamp in his hand, but there was none, for—

"The circuit breaker!" cried Kelly.

He threw the holder up on the deck plate of the Seven in front of the seat, and ran across the little beach to the welder. He reached behind the switchboard, got his thumb on the contact hinge and jammed it down.

Daisy Etta leaped again, and then again, and suddenly her motor stopped. Heat in turbulent waves blurred the air over her. The little gas tank for the starting motor went out with a cannon's roar, and the big fuel tank, still holding thirty-odd gallons of diesel oil, followed. It puffed itself open rather than exploded, and threw a great curtain of flame over the ground behind the machine. Motor or no motor, then, Kelly distinctly saw the tractor shudder convulsively. There was a crawling movement of the whole frame, a slight wave of motion away from the fuel tank, approaching the front of the machine, and moving upward from the tracks. It culminated in the crown of the radiator core, just in front of the radiator cap; and suddenly an area of six or seven square inches literally *blurred* around the edges. For a second, then, it was normal, and finally it slumped molten, and liquid metal ran down the sides, throwing out little sparks as it encountered what was left of the charred paint. And only then was Kelly conscious of agony in his left hand. He looked down. The welding machine's generator had stopped, through the motor was still turning, having smashed the friable coupling on its drive shaft. Smoke poured from the generator, which had become little more than a heap of slag.

Kelly did not scream, though, until he looked and saw what
had happened to his hand—

When he could see straight again, he called for Tom, and
there was no answer. At last he saw something out in the water,
and plunged in after it. The splash of cold salt water on his
left hand he hardly felt, for the numbness of shock had set in.
He grabbed at Tom's shirt with his good hand, and then the
ground seemed to pull itself out from under his feet. That was
it, then—a deep hole right off the beach. The Seven had run
right to the edge of it, had kept Tom there out of his depth
and—

He flailed wildly, struck out for the beach, so near and so
hard to get to. He gulped a stinging lungful of brine, and only
the lovely shock of his knee striking solid beach kept him from
giving up to the luxury of choking to death. Sobbing with effort,
he dragged Tom's dead weight inshore and clear of the surf.
It was then that he became conscious of a child's shrill weeping;
for a mad moment he thought it was himself, and then he
looked and saw it was Al Knowles. He left Tom and went over
to the broken creature.

"Get up, you," he snarled. The weeping only got louder.
Kelly rolled him over on his back—he was quite unresisting—
and belted him back and forth across the mouth until Al began
to choke. Then he hauled him to his feet and led him over to
Tom.

"Kneel down, scum. Put one of your knees between his
knees." Al stood still. Kelly hit him again and he did as he
was told.

"Put your hands on his lower ribs. There. O.K. Lean, you
rat. Now sit back." He sat down, holding his left wrist in his
right hand, letting the blood drop from the ruined hand. "Lean.
Hold it—sit back. Lean. Sit. Lean. Sit."

Soon Tom sighed and began to vomit weakly, and after that
he was all right.

This is the story of *Daisy Etta,* the bulldozer that went mad
and had a life of its own, and not the story of the flat-top
Marokuru of the Imperial Japanese Navy, which has been told
elsewhere. But there is a connection. You will remember how
the *Marokuru* was cut off from its base by the concentrated

attack on Truk, how it slipped far to the south and east and was sunk nearer to our shores than any other Jap warship in the whole course of the war. And you will remember how a squadron of five planes, having been separated by three vertical miles of water from their flight deck, turned east with their bombloads and droned away for a suicide mission. You read that they bombed a minor airfield in the outside of Panama's far-flung defenses, and all hands crashed in the best sacrificial fashion.

Well, that was no airfield, no matter what it might have looked like from the air. It was simply a roughly graded runway, white marl against brown scrub-grass.

The planes came two days after the death of *Daisy Etta,* as Tom and Kelly sat in the shadow of the pile of fuel drums, down in the coolness of the swag that *Daisy* had dug there to fuel herself. They were poring over paper and pencil, trying to complete the impossible task of making a written statement of what had happened on the island, and why they and their company had failed to complete their contract. They had found Chub and Harris, and had buried them next to the other three. Al Knowles was tied up in the camp, because they had heard him raving in his sleep, and it seemed he could not believe that *Daisy* was dead and he still wanted to go around killing operators for her. They knew that there must be an investigation, and they knew just how far their story would go; and having escaped a monster like *Daisy Etta,* life was far too sweet for them to want to be shot for sabotage. And murder.

The first stick of bombs struck three hundred yards behind them at the edge of the camp, and at the same instant a plane whistled low over their heads, and that was the first they knew about it. They ran to Al Knowles and untied his feet and the three of them headed for the bush. They found refuge, strangely enough, inside the mound where *Daisy Etta* had first met her possessor.

"Bless their black little hearts," said Kelly as he and Tom stood on the bluff and looked at the flaming wreckage of a camp and five medium bombers below them. And he took the statement they had been sweating out and tore it across.

"But what about him?" said Tom, pointing at Al Knowles, who was sitting on the ground, playing with his fingers. "He'll still spill the whole thing, no matter if we do try to blame it all on the bombing."

"What's the matter with that?" said Kelly.

Tom thought a minute, then grinned. "Why, nothing! That's just the sort of thing they'll expect from him!"

ALPHA RALPHA BOULEVARD

Cordwainer Smith

We were drunk with happiness in those early years. Everybody was, especially the young people. These were the first years of the Rediscovery of Man, when the Instrumentality dug deep in the treasury, reconstructing the old cultures, the old languages and even the old troubles. The nightmare of perfection had taken our forefathers to the edge of suicide. Now under the leadership of the Lord Jestocost and the Lady Alice More, the ancient civilizations were rising like great land masses out of the sea of the past.

I myself was the first man to put a postage stamp on a letter, after sixteen thousand years. I took Virginia to hear the first piano recital. We watched at the eye-machine when cholera was released in Tasmania, and we saw the Tasmanians dancing in the streets, now that they did not have to be protected any more. Everywhere, things became exciting. Everywhere, men and women worked with a wild will to build a more imperfect world.

I myself went into a hospital and came out French. Of course I remembered my early life; I remembered it, but it did not matter. Virginia was French, too, and we had the years of our future lying ahead of us like ripe fruit hanging in an orchard of perpetual summers. We had no idea when we would die. Formerly, I would be able to go to bed and think, "The government has given me four hundred years. Three hundred and seventy-four years from now, they will stop the stroon injections and I will then die." Now I knew anything could happen. The safety devices had been turned off. The diseases ran free. With luck and hope and love, I might live a thousand years. Or I might die tomorrow. I was free.

We reveled in every moment of the day.

Virginia and I bought the first French newspaper to appear since the Most Ancient World fell. We found delight in the news, even in the advertisements. Some parts of the culture were hard to reconstruct. It was difficult to talk about foods of which only the names survived, but the homunculi and the machines, working tirelessly in Downdeep-downdeep, kept the surface of the world filled with enough novelties to fill anyone's heart with hope. We knew that all of this was make-believe, and yet it was not. We knew that when the diseases had killed the statistically correct number of people, they would be turned off; when the accident rate rose too high, it would stop without our knowing why. We knew that over us all, the Instrumentality watched. We had confidence that the Lord Jestocost and the Lady Alice More would play with us as friends and not use us as victims of a game.

Take, for example, Virginia. She had been called Menerima, which represented the coded sounds of her birth number. She was small, verging on chubby; she was compact; her head was covered with tight brown curls; her eyes were a brown so deep and so rich that it took sunlight, with her squinting against it, to bring forth the treasures of her irises. I had known her well, but never known her. I had seen her often, but never seen her with my heart, until we met just outside the hospital after becoming French.

I was pleased to see an old friend and started to speak in the Old Common Tongue, but the words jammed, and as I tried to speak it was not Menerima any longer, but someone of ancient beauty, rare and strange—someone who had wandered into these latter days from the treasure worlds of time past. All I could do was to stammer:

"What do you call yourself now?" And I said it in ancient French.

She answered in the same language, "Je m'appelle Virginia."

Looking at her and falling in love was a single process. There was something strong, something wild in her, wrapped and hidden by the tenderness and youth of her girlish body. It was as though destiny spoke to me out of the certain brown eyes, eyes which questioned me surely and wonderingly, just as we both questioned the fresh new world which lay about us.

"May I?" said I, offering her my arm, as I had learned in the hours of hypnopedia. She took my arm and we walked away from the hospital.

I hummed a tune which had come into my mind, along with the ancient French language.

She tugged gently on my arm and smiled up at me.

"What is it," she asked, "or don't you know?"

The words came soft and unbidden to my lips and I sang it very quietly, muting my voice in her curly hair, half-singing, half-whispering the popular song which had poured into my mind with all the other things which the Rediscovery of Man had given me:

> "She wasn't the woman I went to seek.
> I met her by the merest chance.
> She did not speak the French of France,
> But the surded French of Martinique.
>
> "She wasn't rich. She wasn't chic.
> She had a most entrancing glance,
> And that was all...."

Suddenly I ran out of words. "I seem to have forgotten the rest of it. It's called 'Macouba' and it has something to do with a wonderful island which the ancient French called Martinique."

"I know where that is," she cried. She had been given the same memories that I had. "You can see it from Earthport!"

This was a sudden return to the world we had known. Earthport stood on its single pedestal, twelve miles high, at the eastern edge of the small continent. At the top of it, the lords worked amid machines which had no meaning any more. There the ships whispered their way in from the stars. I had seen pictures of it, but I had never been there. As a matter of fact, I had never known anyone who had actually been up to Earth-port. Why should we have gone? We might not have been welcome, and we could always see it just as well through the pictures on the eye-machine. For Menerima—familiar, dully pleasant, dear little Menerima—to have gone there was uncanny. It made me think that in the Old Perfect World things had not been as plain or forthright as they seemed.

Virginia, the new Menerima, tried to speak in the Old Common Tongue, but she gave up and used French instead:

"My aunt," she said, meaning a kindred lady, since no one had had aunts for thousands of years, "was a Believer. She took me to the Abba-dingo. To get holiness and luck."

The old me was a little shocked; the French me was disquieted by the fact that this girl had done something unusual even before mankind itself turned to the unusual. The Abba-dingo was a long obsolete computer set partway up the column of Earthport. The homunculi treated it as a god, and occasionally people went to it. To do so was tedious and vulgar.

Or had been. Till all things became new again.

Keeping the annoyance out of my voice, I asked her, "What was it like?"

She laughed lightly, yet there was a trill to her laughter which gave me a shiver. If the old Menerima had had secrets, what might the new Virginia do? I almost hated the fate which made me love her, which made me feel that the touch of her hand on my arm was a link between me and time-forever.

She smiled at me instead of answering my question. The surfaceway was under repair; we followed a ramp down to the level of the top underground, where it was legal for true persons and hominids and homunculi to walk.

I did not like the feeling; I had never gone more than twenty minutes' trip from my birthplace. This ramp looked safe enough. There were few hominids around these days, men from the stars who (though of true human stock) had been changed to fit the conditions of a thousand worlds. The homunculi were morally repulsive, though many of them look like very handsome people; bred from animals into the shape of men, they took over the tedious chores of working with machines where no real man would wish to go. It was whispered that some of them had even bred with actual people, and I would not want my Virginia to be exposed to the presence of such a creature.

She had been holding my arm. When we walked down the ramp to the busy passage, I slipped my arm free and put it over her shoulders, drawing her closer to me. It was light enough, bright enough to be clearer than the daylight which we had left behind, but it was strange and full of danger. In the old days, I would have turned around and gone home rather than to expose myself to the presence of such dreadful beings. At this time, in this moment, I could not bear to part from my newfound love, and I was afraid that if I went back to my own apartment in the tower, she might go to hers. Anyhow, being French gave a spice to danger.

Actually, the people in the traffic looked commonplace enough. There were many busy machines, some in human forms and some not. I did not see a single hominid. Other people, whom I knew to be homunculi because they yielded the right of way to us, looked no different from the real human beings on the surface. A brilliantly beautiful girl gave me a look which I did not like—saucy, intelligent, provocative beyond all limits of flirtation. I suspected her of being a dog by origin. Among the hominids, d'persons are the ones most apt to take liberties. They even have a dogman philosopher who once produced a tape arguing that since dogs are the most ancient of men's allies, they have the right to be closer to man than any other form of life. When I saw the tape, I thought it amusing that a dog should be bred into the form of a Socrates; here, in the top underground, I was not so sure at all. What would I do if one of them became insolent? Kill him? That meant a brush with the law and a talk with the subcommissioners of the Instrumentality.

Virginia noticed none of this.

She had not answered my question, but was asking me questions about the top underground instead. I had been there only once before, when I was small, but it was flattering to have her wondering, husky voice murmuring in my ear.

Then it happened.

At first I thought he was a man, foreshortened by some trick of the underground light. When he came closer, I saw that it was not. He must have been five feet across the shoulders. Ugly red scars on his forehead showed where the horns had been dug out of his skull. He was a homunculus, obviously derived from cattle stock. Frankly, I had never known that they left them that ill-formed.

And he was drunk.

As he came closer I could pick up the buzz of his mind. ". . . they're not people, they're not hominids, and they're not us—what are they doing here? The words they think confuse me." He had never telepathed French before.

This was bad. For him to talk was common enough, but only a few of the homunculi were telepathic—those with special jobs, such as in the Downdeep-downdeep, where only telepathy could relay instructions.

Virginia clung to me.

Thought I, in clear Common Tongue: "True men are we. You must let us pass."

There was no answer, but a roar. I do not know where he got drunk, or on what, but he did not get my message.

I could see his thoughts forming up into panic, helplessness, hate. Then he charged, almost dancing toward us, as though he could crush our bodies.

My mind focused and I threw the stop order at him.

It did not work.

Horror-stricken, I realized that I had thought French at him.

Virginia screamed.

The bull-man was upon us.

At the last moment he swerved, passed us blindly, and let out a roar which filled the enormous passage. He had raced beyond us.

Still holding Virginia, I turned around to see what had made him pass us.

What I beheld was odd in the extreme.

Our figures ran down the corridor away from us—my black purple cloak flying in the still air as my image ran, Virginia's golden dress swimming out behind her as she ran with me. The images were perfect and the bull-man pursued them.

I stared around in bewilderment. We had been told that the safeguards no longer protected us.

A girl stood quietly next to the wall. I had almost mistaken her for a statue. Then she spoke.

"Come no closer. I am a cat. It was easy enough to fool him. You had better get back to the surface.

"Thank you," I said, "thank you. What is your name?"

"Does it matter?" said the girl. "I'm not a person."

A little offended, I insisted, "I just wanted to thank you." As I spoke to her I saw that she was as beautiful and as bright as a flame. Her skin was clear, the color of cream, and her hair—finer than any human hair could possibly be—was the wild golden orange of a Persian cat.

"I'm C'mell," said the girl, "And I work at Earthport."

That stopped both Virginia and me. Cat-people were below us and should be shunned, but Earthport was above us and had to be respected. Which was C'mell?

She smiled, and her smile was better suited for my eyes than for Virginia's. It spoke a whole world of voluptuous knowledge. I knew she wasn't trying to do anything to me; the rest of her manner showed that. Perhaps it was the only smile she knew.

"Don't worry," she said, "about the formalities. You'd better take these steps here. I hear him coming back."

I spun around, looking for the drunken bull-man. He was not to be seen.

"Go up here," urged C'mell. "They are emergency steps and you will be back on the surface. I can keep him from following. Was that French you were speaking?"

"Yes," said I. "How did you . . . ?"

"Get along," she said. "Sorry I asked. Hurry!"

I entered the small door. A spiral staircase went to the surface. It was below our dignity as true people to use steps, but with C'mell urging me, there was nothing else I could do. I nodded goodbye to C'mell and drew Virginia after me up the stairs.

At the surface we stopped.

Virginia gasped, "Wasn't it horrible?"

"We're safe now," said I.

"It's not safety," she said. "It's the dirtiness of it. Imagine having to talk to her!"

Virginia meant that C'mell was worse than the drunken bull-man. She sensed my reserve because she said, "The sad thing is, you'll see her again . . ."

"What! How do you know that?"

"I don't know it," said Virginia. "I guess it. But I guess good, very good. After all, I went to the Abba-dingo."

"I asked you, darling, to tell me what happened there."

She shook her head mutely and began walking down the streetway. I had no choice but to follow her. It made me a little irritable.

I asked again, more crossly, "What was it like?"

With hurt, girlish dignity she said, "Nothing, nothing. It was a long climb. The old woman made me go with her. It turned out that the machine was not talking that day, anyhow, so we got permission to drop down a shaft and to come back on the rolling road. It was just a wasted day."

She had been talking straight ahead, not to me, as though the memory were a little ugly.

Then she turned her face to me. The brown eyes looked into my eyes as though she were searching for my soul. (*Soul.* There's a word we have in French, and there is nothing quite like it in the Old Common Tongue.) She brightened and pleaded with me:

"Let's not be dull on the new day. Let's be good to the new us, Paul. Let's do something really French, if that's what we are to be."

"A café," I cried. "We need a café. And I know where one is."

"Where?"

"Two undergrounds over. Where the machines come out and where you can see the homunculi peering over the edge." The thought of homunculi peering out struck the new-me as funny, though the old-me had taken them as much for granted as clouds or windows or tables. Of course homunculi had feelings; they weren't exactly people, since they were bred from animals, but they looked just about like people, and they could talk. It took a Frenchman like the new-me to realize that those things were picturesque. More than picturesque: romantic.

Evidently Virginia thought the same, for she said, "But they're *nette*, just adorable. And what is the café called?"

"The Greasy Cat," said I.

The Greasy Cat. How was I to know that this led to a nightmare between high waters and to the winds which cried? How was I to suppose that this had anything to do with Alpha Ralpha Boulevard?

No force in the world could have taken me there if I had known.

●   ●   ●

Other new-French people had gotten to the café before us.

A waiter with a big brown moustache took our order. I looked closely at him to see if he might be a licensed homunculus, allowed to work among people because his services were indispensable; but he was not. He was pure machine, though his voice rang out with old-Parisian heartiness, and the designers had even built into him the nervous old habit of mopping the back of his hand against his big moustache, and had fixed him so that little beads of sweat showed high upon his brow, just below the hairline.

"Mademoiselle? M'sieur? Beer? Coffee? Red wine next month. The sun will shine in the quarter after the hour and after the half hour. At twenty minutes to the hour it will rain for five minutes so that you can enjoy these umbrellas. I am a native of Alsace. You may speak French or German to me."

"Anything," said Virginia. "You decide, Paul."

"Beer, please," said I. "Blond beer for both of us."

"But certainly, m'sieur," said the waiter.

He left, waving his cloth wildly over his arm.

Virginia puckered up her eyes against the sun and said, "I wish it would rain now. I've never seen real rain."

"Be patient, honey."

She turned earnestly to me. "What is 'German,' Paul?"

"Another language, another culture. I read they will bring it to life next year. But don't you like being French?"

"I like it fine," she said. "Much better than being a number. But Paul. . . ." And then she stopped, her eyes blurred with perplexity.

"Yes, darling?"

"Paul," she said, and the statement of my name was a cry of hope from some depth of her mind beyond new-me, beyond old-me, beyond even the contrivances of the lords who molded us. I reached for her hand.

Said I, "You can tell me, darling."

"Paul," she said, and it was almost weeping, "Paul, why does it all happen so fast? This is our first day, and we both feel that we may spend the rest of our lives together. There's something about marriage, whatever that is, and we're supposed to find a priest, and I don't understand that, either. Paul, Paul, Paul, why does it happen so fast? I want to love you. I do love you. But I don't want to be *made* to love you. I want it to be to the real me," and as she spoke, tears poured from her eyes though her voice remained steady enough.

Then it was that I said the wrong thing.

"You don't have to worry, honey. I'm sure that the lords of the Instrumentality have programmed everything well."

At that, she burst into tears, loudly and uncontrollably. I had never seen an adult weep before. It was strange and frightening.

A man from the next table came over and stood beside me, but I did not so much as glance at him.

"Darling," said I, reasonably, "darling, we can work it out. . . ."

"Paul, let me leave you, so that I may be yours. Let me go away for a few days or a few weeks or a few years. Then, if—if—if I *do* come back, you'll know it's me and not some program ordered by a machine. For God's sake, Paul—for God's sake!" In a different voice she said, "What is God, Paul? They gave us the words to speak, but I do not know what they mean."

The man beside me spoke. "I can take you to God," he said.

"Who are you?" said I. "And who asked you to interfere?" This was not the kind of language that we had ever used when speaking the Old Common Tongue—when they had given us a new language they had built in temperament as well.

The stranger kept his politeness—he was as French as we but he kept his temper well.

"My name," he said, "is Maximilien Macht, and I used to be a Believer."

Virginia's eyes lit up. She wiped her face absentmindedly while staring at the man. He was tall, lean, sunburned. (How could he have gotten sunburned so soon?) He had reddish hair and a moustache almost like that of the robot waiter.

"You asked about God, mademoiselle," said the stranger. "God is where he has always been—around us, near us, in us."

This was strange talk from a man who looked worldly. I rose to my feet to bid him good-by. Virginia guessed what I was doing and she said, "that's nice of you, Paul. Give him a chair."

There was warmth in her voice.

The machine waiter came back with two conical beakers

made of glass. They had a golden fluid in them with a cap of foam on top. I had never seen or heard of beer before, but I knew exactly how it would taste. I put imaginary money on the tray, received imaginary change, paid the waiter an imaginary tip. The Instrumentality had not yet figured out how to have separate kinds of money for all the new cultures, and of course you could not use real money to pay for food or drink. Food and drink are free.

The machine wiped his moustache, used his serviette (checked red and white) to dab the sweat off his brow and then looked inquiringly at Monsieur Macht.

"M'sieur, you will sit here?"

"Indeed," said Macht.

"Shall I serve you here?"

"But why not?" said Macht. "If these good people permit."

"Very well," said the machine, wiping his moustache with the back of his hand. He fled to the dark recesses of the bar.

All this time Virginia had not taken her eyes off Macht.

"You are a Believer?" she asked. "You are still a Believer, when you have been made French like us? How do you know you're you? Why do I love Paul? Are the lords and their machines controlling everything in us? I want to be *me*. Do you know how to be *me?*"

"Not you, mademoiselle," said Macht, "that would be too great an honor. But I am learning how to be myself. You see," he added, turning to me, "I have been French for two weeks now, and I know how much of me is myself, and how much has been added by this new process of giving us language and danger again."

The waiter came back with a small beaker. It stood on a stem, so that it looked like an evil little miniature of Earthport. The fluid it contained was milky white.

Macht lifted his glass to us. "Your health!"

Virginia stared at him as if she were going to cry again. When he and I sipped, she blew her nose and put her handkerchief away. It was the first time I had ever seen a person perform that act of blowing the nose, but it seemed to go well with our new culture.

Macht smiled at both of us, as if he were going to begin a speech. The sun came out, right on time. It gave him a halo and made him look like a devil or a saint.

But it was Virginia who spoke first.

"You have been there?"

Macht raised his eyebrows a little, frowned and said, "Yes," very quietly.

"Did you get a word?" she persisted.

"Yes." He looked glum and a little troubled.

"What did it say?"

For answer, he shook his head at her, as if there were things which should never be mentioned in public.

I wanted to break in, to find out what this was all about.

Virginia went on, heeding me not at all: "But it did say something!"

"Yes," said Macht.

"Was it important?"

"Mademoiselle, let us not talk about it."

"We must," she cried. "It's life or death." Her hands were clenched so tightly together that her knuckles showed white. Her beer stood in front of her, untouched, growing warm in the sunlight.

"Very well," said Macht, "you may ask. . . . I cannot guarantee to answer."

I controlled myself no longer. "What's all this about?"

Virginia looked at me with scorn, but even her scorn was the scorn of a lover, not the cold remoteness of the past. "Please, Paul, you wouldn't know. Wait a while. What did it say to you, M'sieur Macht?"

"That I, Maximilien Macht, would live or die with a brown-haired girl who was already betrothed." He smiled wryly. "And I do not even quite know what 'betrothed' means."

"We'll find out," said Virginia. "When did it say this?"

"Who is 'it'?" I shouted at them. "For God's sake, what is this all about?"

Macht looked at me and dropped his voice when he spoke: "The Abba-dingo." To her he said, "Last week."

Virginia turned white. "So it does work, it does, it does. Paul, darling, it said nothing to me. But it said to my aunt something which I can't ever forget!"

I held her arm firmly and tenderly and tried to look into her eyes, but she looked away. Said I, "What did it say?"

"Paul and Virginia."

"So what?" said I.

I scarcely knew her. Her lips were tense and compressed. She was not angry. It was something different, worse. She was in the grip of tension. I suppose we had not seen that for thousands of years, either. "Paul, seize this simple fact, if you can grasp it. The machine gave that woman our names—but it gave them to her twelve years ago."

Macht stood up so suddenly that his chair fell over, and the waiter began running toward us.

"That settles it," he said. "We're all going back."

"Going where?" I said.

"To the Abba-dingo."

"But why now?" said I; and, "Will it work?" said Virginia, both at the same time.

"It always works," said Macht, "if you go on the northern side."

"How do you get there?" said Virginia.

Macht frowned sadly. "There's only one way. By Alpha Ralpha Boulevard." Virginia stood up. And so did I.

Then, as I rose, I remembered. Alpha Ralpha Boulevard. It was a ruined street hanging in the sky, faint as a vapor trail. It had been a processional highway once, where conquerors came down and tribute went up. But it was ruined, lost in the clouds, closed to mankind for a hundred centuries.

"I know it," said I. "It's ruined."

Macht said nothing, but he stared at me as if I were an outsider. . . .

Virginia, very quiet and white of countenance, said, "Come along."

"But why?" said I. "Why?"

"You fool," she said. "If we don't have a god, at least we have a machine. This is the only thing left on or off the world which the Instrumentality doesn't understand. Maybe it tells the future. Maybe it's an un-machine. It certainly comes from a different time. Can't you see it, darling? If it says we're us, we're *us*."

"And if it doesn't?"

"Then we're not." Her face was sullen with grief.

"What do you mean?"

"If we're not us," she said, "we're just toys, dolls, puppets that the lords have written on. You're not you and I'm not me. But if the Abba-dingo, which knew the names Paul and Virginia

twelve years before it happened—if the Abba-dingo says that
we are us, I don't care if it's a predicting machine or a god or
a devil or a what. I don't care, but I'll have the truth."

What could I have answered to that? Macht led, she followed
and I walked third in single file. We left the sunlight of The
Greasy Cat; just as we left, a light rain began to fall. The
waiter, looking momentarily like the machine that he was,
stared straight ahead. We crossed the lip of the underground
and went down to the fast expressway.

When we came out, we were in a region of fine homes. All
were in ruins. The trees had thrust their way into the buildings.
Flowers rioted across the lawn, through the open doors, and
blazed in the roofless rooms. Who needed a house in the open,
when the population of Earth had dropped so that the cities
were commodious and empty?

Once I thought I saw a family of homunculi, including little
ones, peering at me as we trudged along the soft gravel road.
Maybe the faces I had seen at the edge of the house were
fantasies.

Macht said nothing.

Virginia and I held hands as we walked beside him. I could
have been happy at this odd excursion, but her hand was tightly
clenched in mine. She bit her lower lip from time to time. I
knew it mattered to her—she was on a pilgrimage. (A pilgrimage was an ancient walk to some powerful place, very
good for body and soul.) I didn't mind going along. In fact,
they could not have kept me from coming, once she and Macht
decided to leave the café. But I didn't have to take it seriously.
Did I?

What did Macht want?

Who was Macht? What thoughts had that mind learned in
two short weeks? How had he preceded us into a new world
of danger and adventure? I did not trust him. For the first time
in my life I felt alone. Always, always, up to now, I had only
to think about the Instrumentality and some protector leaped
fully armed into my mind. Telepathy guarded against all dangers, healed all hurts, carried each of us forward to the one
hundred and forty-six thousand and ninety-seven days which
had been allotted us. Now it was different. I did not know this
man, and it was on him that I relied, not on the powers which
had shielded and protected us.

We turned from the ruined road into an immense boulevard. The pavement was so smooth and unbroken that nothing grew on it, save where the wind and dust had deposited random little pockets of earth.

Macht stopped.

"This is it," he said. "Alpha Ralpha Boulevard."

We fell silent and looked at the causeway of forgotten empires.

To our left the boulevard disappeared in a gentle curve. It led far north of the city in which I had been reared. I knew that there was another city to the north, but I had forgotten its name. Why should I have remembered it? It was sure to be just like my own.

But to the right. . . .

To the right the boulevard rose sharply, like a ramp. It disappeared into the clouds. Just at the edge of the cloud line there was a hint of disaster. I could not see for sure, but it looked to me as though the whole boulevard had been sheared off by unimaginable forces. Somewhere beyond the clouds there stood the Abba-dingo, the place where all questions were answered. . . .

Or so they thought.

Virginia cuddled close to me.

"Let's turn back," said I. "We are city people. We don't know anything about ruins."

"You can if you want to," said Macht. "I was just trying to do you a favor."

We both looked at Virginia.

She looked up at me with those brown eyes. From the eyes there came a plea older than woman or man, older than the human race. I knew what she was going to say before she said it. She was going to say that she *had* to know.

Macht was idly crushing some soft rocks near his foot.

At last Virginia spoke up: "Paul, I don't want danger for its own sake. But I meant what I said back there. Isn't there a chance that we were *told* to love each other? What sort of a life would it be if our happiness, our own selves, depended on a thread in a machine or on a mechanical voice which spoke to us when we were asleep and learning French? It may be fun to go back to the old world. I guess it is. I know that you give me a kind of happiness which I never even suspected before this day. If it's really us, we have something wonderful, and we ought to know it. But if it isn't . . ." She burst into sobs.

I wanted to say, "If it isn't, it will seem just the same," but the ominous sulky face of Macht looked at me over Virginia's shoulder as I drew her to me. There was nothing to say.

I held her close.

From beneath Macht's foot there flowed a trickle of blood. The dust drank it up.

"Macht," said I, "are you hurt?"

Virginia turned around, too.

Macht raised his eyebrows at me and said with unconcern, "No. Why?"

"The blood. At your feet."

He glanced down. "Oh, those," he said, "they're nothing. Just the eggs of some kind of an un-bird which does not even fly."

"Stop it!" I shouted telepathically, using the Old Common Tongue. I did not even try to think in our new-learned French.

He stepped back a pace in surprise.

Out of nothing there came to me a message: thankyou thankyou goodgreat gohomeplease thankyou goodgreat goaway man-bad manbad manbad. . . . Somewhere an animal or bird was warning me against Macht. I thought a casual *thanks* to it and turned my attention to Macht.

He and I stared at each other. Was this what *culture* was? Were we now men? Did freedom always include the freedom to mistrust, to fear, to hate?

I liked him not at all. The words of forgotten crimes came into my mind: assassination, murder, abduction, insanity, rape, robbery. . . .

We had known none of these things and yet I felt them all.

He spoke evenly to me. We had both been careful to guard our minds against being read telepathically, so that our only means of communication were empathy and French. "It's your idea," he said, most untruthfully, "or at least your lady's. . . ."

"Has lying already come into the world," said I, "so that we walk into the clouds for no reason at all?"

"There is a reason," said Macht.

I pushed Virginia gently aside and capped my mind so tightly that the antitelepathy felt like a headache.

"Macht," said I, and I myself could hear the snarl of an animal in my own voice, "tell me why you have brought us here or I will kill you."

He did not retreat. He faced me, ready for a fight. He said, "Kill? You mean, to make me dead?" but his words did not carry conviction. Neither one of us knew how to fight, but he readied for defense and I for attack.

Underneath my thought shield an animal thought crept in: goodman goodman take him by the neck no-air he-aaah no-air he-aaah like broken egg. . . .

I took the advice without worrying where it came from. It was simple. I walked over to Macht, reached my hands around his throat and squeezed. He tried to push my hands away. Then he tried to kick me. All I did was hang onto his throat. If I had been a lord or a go-captain, I might have known about fighting. But I did not, and neither did he.

It ended when a sudden weight dragged at my hands.

Out of surprise, I let go.

Macht had become unconscious. Was that *dead?*

It could not have been, because he sat up. Virginia ran to him. He rubbed his throat and said with a rough voice:

"You should not have done that."

This gave me courage. "Tell me," I spat at him, "tell me why you wanted us to come, or I will do it again."

Macht grinned weakly. He leaned his head against Virginia's arm. "It's fear," he said. "Fear."

"Fear?" I knew the word—*peur*—but not the meaning. Was it some kind of disquiet or animal alarm?

I had been thinking with my mind open; he thought back *yes.*

"But why do you like it?" I asked.

It is delicious, he thought. *It makes me sick and thrilly and alive. It is like strong medicine, almost as good as stroon. I went there before. High up, I had much fear. It was wonderful and bad and good, all at the same time. I lived a thousand years in a single hour. I wanted more of it, but I thought it would be even more exciting with other people.*

"Now I will kill you," said I in French. "You are very— very. . . ." I had to look for the word. "You are very evil."

"No," said Virginia, "let him talk."

He thought at me, not bothering with words. *This is what the lords of the Instrumentality never let us have. Fear. Reality. We were born in a stupor and we died in a dream. Even the underpeople, the animals, had more life than we did. The machines did not have fear. That's what we were. Machines who thought they were men. And now we are free.*

He saw the edge of raw red anger in my mind, and he changed the subject. *I did not lie to you. This is the way to the Abba-dingo. I have been there. It works. On this side, it always works.*

"It works," cried Virginia. "You see he says so. It works! He is telling the truth. Oh, Paul, do let's go on!"

"All right," said I, "we'll go."

I helped him rise. He looked embarrassed, like a man who has shown something of which he is ashamed.

We walked onto the surface of the indestructible boulevard. It was comfortable to the feet.

At the bottom of my mind the little unseen bird or animal babbled its thoughts at me: goodman goodman make him dead take water take water. . . .

I paid no attention as I walked forward with her and him, Virginia between us. I paid no attention.

I wish I had.

We walked for a long time.

The process was new to us. There was something exhilarating in knowing that no one guarded us, that the air was free air, moving without benefit of weather machines. We saw many birds, and when I thought at them I found their minds startled and opaque; they were natural birds, the like of which I had never seen before. Virginia asked me their names, and I outrageously applied all the bird names which we had learned in French without knowing whether they were historically right or not.

Maximilien Macht cheered up, too, and he even sang us a song, rather off key, to the effect that we would take the high road and he the low one, but he would be in Scotland before us. It did not make sense, but the lilt was pleasant. Whenever he got a certain distance ahead of Virginia and me, I made up variations on "Macouba" and sang-whispered the phrases into her pretty ear:

> *"She wasn't the woman I went to seek.*
> *I met her by the merest chance.*
> *She did not speak the French of France,*
> *But the surded French of Martinique."*

We were happy in adventure and freedom until we became hungry. Then our troubles began.

Virginia stepped up to a lamp post, struck it lightly with her fist and said, 'Feed me." The post should either have opened, serving us a dinner, or else told us where, within the next few hundred yards, food was to be had. It did neither. It did nothing. It must have been broken.

With that, we began to make a game of hitting every single post.

Alpha Ralpha Boulevard had risen about half a kilometer above the surrounding countryside. The wild birds wheeled below us. There was less dust on the pavement, and fewer patches of weeds. The immense road, with no pylons below it, curved like an unsupported ribbon into the clouds.

We wearied of beating posts and there was neither food nor water.

Virginia became fretful: "It won't do any good to go back now. Food is even farther the other way. I do wish you'd brought something."

How should I have thought to carry food? Who ever carries food? Why would they carry it, when it is everywhere? My darling was unreasonable, but she was my darling and I loved her all the more for the sweet imperfections of her temper.

Macht kept tapping pillars, partly to keep out of our fight, and obtained an unexpected result.

At one moment I saw him leaning over to give the pillar of a large lamp the usual hearty but guarded *whop*—in the next instant he yelped like a dog and was sliding uphill at a high rate of speed. I heard him shout something, but could not make out the words, before he disappeared into the clouds ahead.

Virginia looked at me. "Do you want to go back now? Macht is gone. We can say that I got tired."

"Are you serious?"

"Of course, darling."

I laughed, a little angrily. She had insisted that we come, and now she was ready to turn around and give it up, just to please me.

"Never mind," said I. "It can't be far now. Let's go on."

"Paul...." She stood close to me. Her brown eyes were troubled, as though she were trying to see all the way into my mind through my eyes. I thought to her, *Do you want to take this way?*

"No," she said in French. "I want to say things one at a time. Paul, I do want to go to the Abba-dingo. I need to go. It's the biggest need in my life. But at the same time I don't want to go. There is something wrong up there. I would rather have you on the wrong terms than not have you at all. Something could happen."

Edgily, I demanded, "Are you getting this 'fear' that Macht was talking about?"

"Oh, no, Paul, not at all. This feeling isn't exciting. It feels like something broken in a machine. . . ."

"Listen!" I interrupted her.

From far ahead, from within the clouds, there came a sound like an animal wailing. There were words in it. It must have been Macht. I thought I heard "Take care." When I sought him with my mind, the distance made circles and I got dizzy.

"Let's follow, darling," said I.

"Yes, Paul," said she, and in her voice there was an unfathomble mixture of happiness, resignation and despair. . . .

Before we moved on, I looked carefully at her. She *was* my girl. The sky had turned yellow and the lights were not yet on. In the yellow rich sky her brown curls were tinted with gold, her brown eyes approached the black in their irises, her young and fate-haunted face seemed more meaningful than any other human face I had ever seen.

"You *are* mine," I said.

"Yes, Paul," she answered me and then smiled brightly. *"You* said it! That is doubly nice."

A bird on the railing looked sharply at us and then left. Perhaps he did not approve of human nonsense, so flung himself downward into dark air. I saw him catch himself, far below, and ride lazily on his wings.

"We're not as free as birds, darling," I told Virginia, "but we are freer than people have been for a hundred centuries."

For answer she hugged my arm and smiled at me.

"And now," I added, "to follow Macht. Put your arms around me and hold me tight. I'll try hitting that post. If we don't get dinner we may get a ride."

I felt her take hold tightly and then I struck the post.

Which post? An instant later the posts were sailing by us in a blur. The ground beneath our feet seemed steady, but we were moving at a fast rate. Even in the service underground I had never seen a roadway as fast as this. Virginia's dress was blowing so hard that it made snapping sounds like the snap of fingers. In no time at all we were in the cloud and out of it again.

A new world surrounded us. The clouds lay below and above. Here and there blue sky shone through. We were steady. The ancient engineers must have devised the walkway cleverly. We rode up, up, up without getting dizzy.

Another cloud.

Then things happened so fast that the telling of them takes longer than the event.

Something dark rushed at me from up ahead. A violent blow hit me in the chest. Only much later did I realize that this was Macht's arm trying to grab me before we went over the edge. Then we went into another cloud. Before I could even speak to Virginia a second blow struck me. The pain was terrible. I had never felt anything like that in all my life. For some reason, Virginia had fallen over me and beyond me. She was pulling at my hands.

I tried to tell her to stop pulling me because it hurt, but I had no breath. Rather than argue, I tried to do what she wanted. I struggled toward her. Only then did I realize that there was nothing below my feet—no bridge, no jetway, nothing.

I was on the edge of the boulevard, the broken edge of the upper side. There was nothing below me except for some looped cables and, far underneath them, a tiny ribbon which was either a river or a road.

We had jumped blindly across the great gap and I had fallen just far enough to catch the upper edge of the roadway on my chest.

It did not matter, the pain.

In a moment, the doctor-robot would be there to repair me.

A look at Virginia's face reminded me there was no doctor-robot, no world, no Instrumentality, nothing but wind and pain. She was crying. It took a moment for me to hear what she was saying.

"I did it, I did it, darling, are you dead?"

Neither one of us was sure what "dead" meant, because people always went away at their appointed time, but we knew that it meant a cessation of life. I tried to tell her that I was living, but she fluttered over me and kept dragging me farther from the edge of the drop.

I used my hands to push myself into a sitting position.

She knelt beside me and covered my face with kisses.

At last I was able to gasp, "Where's Macht?"

She looked back. "I don't see him."

I tried to look too. Rather than have me struggle, she said, "You stay quiet. I'll look again."

Bravely she walked to the edge of the sheared-off boulevard. She looked over toward the lower side of the gap, peering through the clouds which drifted past us as rapidly as smoke sucked by a ventilator. Then she cried out:

"I see him. He looks so funny. Like an insect in the museum. He is crawling across on the cables."

Struggling to my hands and knees, I neared her and looked too. There he was, a dot moving along a thread with the birds soaring by beneath him. It looked very unsafe. Perhaps he was getting all the "fear" that he needed to keep himself happy. I did not want that "fear," whatever it was. I wanted food, water and a doctor-robot.

None of these was here.

I struggled to my feet. Virginia tried to help me but I was standing before she could do more than touch my sleeve.

"Let's go on."

"On?" she said.

"On to the Abba-dingo. There may be friendly machines up there. Here there is nothing but cold and wind, and the lights have not yet gone on."

She frowned. "But Macht . . . ?"

"It will be hours before he gets here. We can come back."

She obeyed.

Once again we went to the left of the boulevard. I told her to squeeze my waist while I struck the pillars, one by one. Surely there must have been a reactivating device for the passengers on the road.

The fourth time, it worked.

Once again the wind whipped our clothing as we raced upward on Alpha Ralpha Boulevard.

We almost fell as the road veered to the left. I caught my balance, only to have it veer the other way.

And then we stopped.

This was the Abba-dingo.

A walkway littered with white objects—knobs and rods and imperfectly formed balls about the size of my head.

Virginia stood beside me, silent.

About the size of my head? I kicked one of the objects aside and then knew, knew for sure, what it was. It was people. The inside parts. I had never seen such things before. And that, that on the ground, must once have been a hand. There were hundreds of such things along the wall.

"Come, Virginia," said I, keeping my voice even, and my thoughts hidden.

She followed without saying a word. She was curious about the things on the ground, but she did not seem to recognize them.

For my part, I was watching the wall.

At last I found them—the little doors of Abba-dingo.

One said, METEOROLOGICAL. It was not Old Common Tongue, nor was it French, but it was so close that I knew it had something to do with the behavior of air. I put my hand against the panel of the door. The panel became translucent and ancient writing showed through. There were numbers which meant nothing, words which meant nothing, and then: "Typhoon coming."

My French had not taught me what a "coming" was, but "typhoon" was plainly *typhon*, a major air disturbance. Thought I, let the weather machines take care of the matter. It had nothing to do with us.

"That's no help," said I.

"What does it mean?" she said.

"The air will be disturbed."

"Oh," said she. "That couldn't matter to us, could it?"

"Of course not."

I tried the next panel, which said FOOD. When my hand touched the little door, there was an aching creak inside the wall, as though the whole tower retched. The door opened a little bit and a horrible odor came out of it. Then the door closed again.

The third door said HELP and when I touched it nothing happened. Perhaps it was some kind of tax-collecting device from the ancient days. It yielded nothing to my touch. The fourth door was larger and already partly open at the bottom. At the top, the name of the door was PREDICTIONS. Plain enough, that one was, to anyone who knew Old French. The name at the bottom was more mysterious: PUT PAPER HERE it said, and I could not guess what it meant.

I tried telepathy. Nothing happened. The wind whistled past

us. Some of the calcium balls and knobs rolled on the pavement. I tried again, trying my utmost for the imprint of long-departed thoughts. A scream entered my mind, a thin long scream which did not sound much like people. That was all.

Perhaps it did upset me. I did not feel "fear," but I was worried about Virginia.

She was staring at the ground.

"Paul," she said, "isn't that a man's coat on the ground among those funny things?"

Once I had seen an ancient X-ray in the museum, so I knew that the coat still surrounded the material which had provided the inner structure of the man. There was no ball there, so that I was quite sure he was *dead*. How could that have happened in the old days? Why did the Instrumentality let it happen? But then, the Instrumentality had always forbidden this side of the tower. Perhaps the violators had met their own punishment in some way I could not fathom.

"Look, Paul," said Virginia. "I can put my hand in."

Before I could stop her, she had thrust her hand into the flat open slot which said PUT PAPER HERE.

She screamed.

Her hand was caught.

I tried to pull at her arm, but it did not move. She began gasping with pain. Suddenly her hand came free.

Clear words were cut into the living skin. I tore my cloak off and wrapped her hand.

As she sobbed beside me I unbandaged her hand. As I did so she saw the words on her skin.

The words said, in clear French, "You will love Paul all your life."

Virginia let me bandage her hand with my cloak and then she lifted her face to be kissed. "It was worth it," she said, "it was worth all the trouble, Paul. Let's see if we can get down. Now I know."

I kissed her again and said, reassuringly, "You do know, don't you?"

"Of course," she smiled through her tears. "The Instrumentality could not have contrived this. What a clever old machine! Is it a god or a devil, Paul?"

I had not studied those words at that time, so I patted her instead of answering. We turned to leave.

At the last minute I realized that I had not tried PREDICTIONS myself.

"Just a moment, darling. Let me tear a little piece off the bandage."

She waited patiently. I tore a piece the size of my hand, and then I picked up one of the ex-person units on the ground. It may have been the front of an arm. I returned to push the cloth into the slot, but when I turned to the door, an enormous bird was sitting there.

I used my hand to push the bird aside, and he cawed at me. He even seemed to threaten me with his cries and his sharp beak. I could not dislodge him.

Then I tried telepathy. *I am a true man. Go away!*

The bird's dim mind flashed back at me nothing but *no-no-no-no-no!*

With that I struck him so hard with my fist that he fluttered to the ground. He righted himself amid the white litter on the pavement and then, opening his wings, he let the wind carry him away.

I pushed in the scrap of cloth, counted to twenty in my mind and pulled the scrap out.

The words were plain but they meant nothing: "You will love Virginia twenty-one more minutes."

Her happy voice, reassured by the prediction but still unsteady from the pain in her written-on hand, came to me as though it were far away. "What does it say, darling?"

Accidentally on purpose, I let the wind take the scrap. It fluttered away like a bird. Virginia saw it go.

"Oh," she cried disappointedly, "we've lost it! What did it say?"

"Just what yours did."

"But what words, Paul? How did it say it?"

With love and heartbreak and perhaps a little "fear," I lied to her and whispered gently,

"It said, 'Paul will always love Virginia.'"

She smiled at me radiantly. Her stocky, full figure stood firmly and happily against the wind. Once again she was the chubby, pretty Menerima whom I had noticed in our block when we both were children. And she was more than that. She was my newfound love in our newfound world. She was my mademoiselle from Martinique. The message was foolish. We had seen from the food slot that the machine was broken.

"There's no food or water here," said I. Actually, there was a puddle of water near the railing, but it had been blown over the human structural elements on the ground, and I had no heart to drink it.

Virginia was so happy that, despite her wounded hand, her lack of water and her lack of food, she walked vigorously and cheerfully.

Thought I to myself, "Twenty-one minutes. About six hours have passed. If we stay here we face unknown dangers."

Vigorously we walked downward, down Alpha Ralpha Boulevard. We had met the Abba-dingo and were still "alive." I did not think that I was "dead," but the words had been meaningless so long that it was hard to think them.

The ramp was so steep going down that we pranced like horses. The wind blew into our faces with incredible force. That's what it was, *wind*, but I looked up the word *vent* only after it was all over.

We never did see the whole tower—just the wall at which the ancient jetway had deposited us. The rest of the tower was hidden by clouds which fluttered like torn rags as they raced past the heavy material.

The sky was red on one side and a dirty yellow on the other.

Big drops of water began to strike at us.

"The weather machines are broken," I shouted at Virginia.

She tried to shout back at me but the wind carried her words away. I repeated what I had said about the weather machines. She nodded happily and warmly, though the wind was by now whipping her hair past her face and the pieces of water which fell from up above were spotting her flame golden gown. It did not matter. She clung to my arm. Her happy face smiled at me as we stamped downward, bracing ourselves against the decline in the ramp. Her brown eyes were full of confidence and life. She saw me looking at her and she kissed me on the upper arm without losing step. She was my own girl, forever, and she knew it.

The water-from-above, which I later knew was actual "rain," came in increasing volume. Suddenly it included birds. A large bird flapped his way vigorously against the whistling air and managed to stand still in front of my face, though his airspeed was many leagues per hour. He cawed in my face and then was carried away by the wind. No sooner had that one gone than another bird struck me in the body. I looked down at it but it too was carried away by the racing current of air. All I got was a telepathic echo from its bright blank mind: *no-no-no-no!*

No what? thought I. A bird's advice is not much to go upon.

Virginia grabbed my arm and stopped.

I too stopped.

The broken edge of Alpha Ralpha Boulevard was just ahead. Ugly yellow clouds swam through the break like poisonous fish hastening on an inexplicable errand.

Virginia was shouting.

I could not hear her, so I leaned down. That way her mouth could almost touch my ear.

"Where's Macht?" she shouted.

Carefully I took her to the left side of the road, where the railing gave us some protection against the heavy racing air and against the water commingled with it. By now neither of us could see very far. I made her drop to her knees. I got down beside her. The falling water pelted our backs. The light around us had turned to a dark dirty yellow.

We could still see, but we could not see much.

I was willing to sit in the shelter of the railing, but she nudged me. She wanted us to do something about Macht. What anyone could do, that was beyond me. If he had found shelter, he was safe, but if he was out on those cables, the wild pushing air would soon carry him off and then there would be no more Maximilien Macht. He would be "dead" and his interior parts would bleach somewhere on the open ground.

Virginia insisted.

We crept to the edge.

A bird swept in, true as a bullet, aiming for my face. I flinched. A wing touched me. It stung against my cheek like fire. I did not know that feathers were so tough. The birds must all have damaged mental mechanisms, thought I, if they hit people on Alpha Ralpha. That is not the right way to behave toward true people.

At last we reached the edge, crawling on our bellies. I tried to dig the fingernails of my left hand into the stonelike material of the railing, but it was flat, and there was nothing much to hold to, save for the ornamental fluting. My right arm was around Virginia. It hurt me badly to crawl forward that way because my body was still damaged from the blow against the edge of the road, on the way coming up. When I hesitated, Virginia thrust herself forward.

We saw nothing.

The gloom was around us.

The wind and the water beat at us like fists.

Her gown pulled at her like a dog worrying its master. I wanted to get her back into the shelter of the railing where we could wait for the air disturbance to end.

Abruptly, light shone all around us. It was wild electricity, which the ancients called *lightning*. Later I found that it occurs quite frequently in the areas beyond the reach of the weather machines.

The bright quick light showed us a white face staring at us. He hung on the cables below us. His mouth was open, so he must have been shouting. I shall never know whether the expression on his face showed "fear" or great happiness. It was full of excitement. The bright light went out and I thought that I heard the echo of a call. I reached for his mind telepathically and there was nothing there. Just some dim, obstinate bird thinking at me, *no-no-no-no-no!*

Virginia tightened in my arms. She squirmed around. I shouted at her in French. She could not hear.

Then I called with my mind.

Someone else was there.

Virginia's mind blazed at me, full of revulsion. "The cat girl. She is going to *touch* me!"

She twisted. My right arm was suddenly empty. I saw the gleam of a golden gown flash over the edge, even in the dim light. I reached with my mind, and I caught her cry: "Paul, Paul, I love you. Paul . . . help me!"

The thoughts faded as her body dropped.

The someone else was C'mell, whom we had first met in the corridor.

"I came to get you both," she thought at me; "not that the birds cared about her."

"What have the birds got to do with it?"

"You saved them. You saved their young, when the red-topped man was killing them all. All of us have been worried about what you true people would do to us when you were

free. We found out. Some of you are bad and kill other kinds
of life. Others of you are good and protect life."

Thought I, is that all there is to *good* and *bad?*

Perhaps I should not have left myself off guard. People did
not have to understand fighting, but the homunculi did. They
were bred amid battle and they served through troubles. C'mell,
cat-girl that she was, caught me on the chin with a pistonlike
fist. She had no anesthesia, and the only way—cat or no cat—
that she could carry me across the cables in the "typhoon" was
to have me unconscious and relaxed.

I awakened in my own room. I felt very well indeed. The
doctor-robot was there. Said he: "You've had a shock. I've
already reached a subcommissioner of the Instrumentality, and
I can erase the memories of the last full day if you want me
to."

His expression was pleasant.

Where was the racing wind? The air falling like stone around
us? The water driving where no weather machines controlled
it? Where was the golden gown and the wild fear-hungry face
of Maximilien Macht?

I thought these things, but the doctor-robot, not being telepathic, caught none of it. I stared hard at him.

"Where," I cried, "is my own true love?"

Robots cannot sneer, but this one attempted to do so. "The
naked cat-girl with the blazing hair? She left to get some clothing."

I stared at him.

His fuddy-duddy little machine mind cooked up its own
nasty little thoughts: "I must say, sir, you 'free people' change
very fast indeed. . . ."

Who argues with a machine? It wasn't worth answering
him.

But that other machine? Twenty-one minutes. How could
that work out? How could it have known? I did not want to
argue with that other machine either. It must have been a very
powerful leftover machine—perhaps something once used in
ancient wars. I had no intention of finding out. Some people
might call it a god. I call it nothing. I do not need "fear" and
I do not propose to go back to Alpha Ralpha Boulevard again.

But hear, O heart of mine!—how can you ever visit the
café again?

C'mell came in and the doctor-robot left.

HUNTING MACHINE

Carol Emshwiller

It sensed Ruthie McAlister's rapid heartbeat, just as it sensed any other animal's. The palms of her hands were damp, and it felt that, too—it also felt the breathing, in and out. And it heard her nervous giggle.

She was watching her husband, Joe, as he leaned over the control unit of the thing that sensed heartbeats—the gray-green thing they called the hound, or Rover, or sometimes the bitch.

"Hey," she said. "I guess it's okay, huh?"

Joe turned a screw with his thumbnail and pulled out the wire attached to it. "Gimme a bobby pin."

Ruthie reached to the back of her head. "I mean it's not dangerous, is it?"

"Naw."

"I don't just mean about *it*." She nodded at the gray-green thing. "I mean, I know you're good at fixing things like this, like the time you got beer for nothing out of the beer vendor and, golly, I guess we haven't paid for a TV show for years. I mean, I *know* you can fix things right, only won't they know when we bring it back to be checked out?"

100

"Look, these wardens are country boys, and besides, I can put this thing back so *nobody* knows."

The gray-green thing squatted on its six legs where Joe could lean over it; it sensed that Ruthie's heartbeat had slowed almost to normal, and it heard her sigh.

"I guess you're pretty good at this, huh, Joe?" She wiped her damp hands on her green tunic. "That's the weight dial, isn't it?" she asked, watching him turn the top one.

He nodded. "Fifteen hundred pounds," he said slowly.

"Oo, was he really and truly that big?"

"Bigger." And now the thing felt Joe's heart and breathing surge.

They had been landed day before yesterday, with their geodesic tent, pneumatic form beds, automatic camping stove and pocket air tables, pocket TV set, four disposable hunting costumes apiece (one for each day), and two folding guns with power settings.

In addition, there was the bug-scat, go-snake, sun-stop and the gray-green hunter, sealed by the warden and set for three birds, two deer and one black bear. They had only the bear to go; now, Joe McAlister had unsealed the controls, released the governor and changed the setting to brown bear, 1,500 pounds.

"I don't care," he said, "I want that bear."

"Do you think he'll still be there tomorrow?"

Joe patted one of the long jointed legs of the thing. "If he's not, ol' bitch here will find him for us."

Next day was clear and cool, and Joe breathed big, expanding breaths and patted his beginning paunch. "Yes, sir," he said, "this is the day for something big—something really big, that'll put up a real fight."

He watched the red of the sunrise fade out of the sky while Ruthie turned on the stove and then got out her makeup kit. She put sun-stop on her face, then powdered it with a tan powder. She blackened her eyelids and purpled her lips; after that, she opened the stove and took out two disposable plates with eggs and bacon.

They sat in the automatic blowup chairs, at the automatic blowup table. Joe said that there was nothing like north air to give you an appetite, and Ruthie said she bet they were sweltering back in the city. Then she giggled.

Joe leaned back in his chair and sipped his coffee. "Shooting deer is just like shooting a cow," he said. "No fight to 'em at all. Even when ol' hound here goads 'em, they just want to run off. But this bear's going to be different. Of course bears are shy too, but ol' hound knows what to do about that."

"They say it's getting to be so there aren't many of the big kind left."

"Yes, but one more won't hurt. Think of a skin and head that size in our living room. I guess anybody that came there would sure sit up and take notice."

"It won't match the curtains," his wife said.

"I think what I'll do is pack the skin up tight and leave it somewhere up here, till the warden checks us through. Then, maybe a couple of days later, I'll come back and get it."

"Good idea." Ruthie had finished her coffee and was perfuming herself with bug-scat.

"Well, I guess we'd better get started." They hung their folded-up guns on their belts. They put their dehydrated, self-heating lunch in their pockets. They slung on their cold-unit canteens. They each took a packet containing chair, table and sunshade; then Joe fastened on the little mike that controlled the hunter. It fit on his shoulder where he could turn his head to the side and talk into it.

"All right, houn' dog," he said, shoulder hunched and head tilted, "get a move on, boy. Back to that spot where we saw him yesterday. You can pick up the scent from there."

The hunting machine ran on ahead of them. It went faster than anything it might have to hunt. Two miles, three miles—Joe and Ruthie were left behind. They followed the beam it sent back to them, walking and talking and helping each other over the rough spots.

About eleven o'clock, Joe stopped, took off his red hunting hat and mopped his balding forehead with the new bandanna he'd bought at Hunter's Outfitters in New York. It was then he got the signal. *Sighted, sighted, sighted....*

Joe leaned over his mike. "Stick on him boy. How far are you? Well, try to move him down this way if you can." He turned to his wife. "Let's see, about three miles ... we'll take a half-hour out for lunch. Maybe we'll get there a couple of hours from now. How's it going, kid?"

"Swell," Ruthie said.

The big bear sat on the rocks by the stream. His front paws were wet almost to the elbows. There were three torn fish heads lying beside him. He ate only the best parts because he was a good fisher; and he looked, now, into the clean cold water for another dark blueback that would pause on its way upstream.

It wasn't a smell that made him turn. He had a keen nose, but the hunting machine was made to have no smell. It was the gray dead lichen's crackle that made him look up. He stood still, looking in the direction of the sound and squinting his small eyes, but it wasn't until it moved that he saw it.

Three-quarters of a ton, he was; but like a bird or a rabbit or a snake, the bear avoided things that were large and strange. He turned back the way he always took, the path to his rubbing tree and to his home. He moved quietly and rapidly, but the thing followed.

He doubled back to the stream again, then, and waded down it on the opposite side from the thing—but still it followed, needing no scent. Once the hunting machine sighted, it never lost its prey.

Heart beat normal, respiration normal, it sensed. Size almost 1,600 pounds.

The bear got out on the bank and turned back, calling out in low growls. He stood up on his hind legs and stretched his full height. Almost two men tall, he stood and gave warning.

The hunting machine waited twenty yards away. The bear looked at it a full minute; then he fell back on all fours and turned south again. He was shy and he wanted no trouble.

Joe and Ruthie kept on walking north at their leisurely pace until just noon. Then they stopped for lunch by the side of the same stream the bear had waded, only lower down. And they used its cold water on their dehydrated meal—beef and onions, mashed potatoes, a lettuce salad that unfolded in the water like Japanese paper flowers. There were coffee tablets that contained a heating unit too and fizzled in the water like firecracker fuses until the water was hot, creamy coffee.

The bear didn't stop to eat. Noon meant nothing to him. Now he moved with more purpose, looking back and squinting his small eyes.

The hunter felt the heart beat faster, the breathing heavy, pace increasing. Direction generally south.

Joe and Ruthie followed the signal until it suddenly changed.

It came faster; that meant they were near.

They stopped and unfolded their guns. "Let's have a cup of coffee first," Ruthie said.

"Okay, Hon." Joe released the chairs which blew themselves up to size. "Good to take a break so we can really enjoy the fight."

Ruthie handed Joe a fizzing cup of coffee. "Don't forget you want ol' Rover to goad some."

"Uh-huh. Bear's not much better than a deer without it. Good you reminded me." He turned and spoke softly into the little mike.

The hunting machine shortened the distance slowly. Fifteen feet, ten, five. The bear heard and turned. Again he rose up, almost two men tall, and roared his warning sound to tell the thing to keep back.

Joe and Ruthie shivered and didn't look at each other. They heard it less with their ears and more with their spines—with an instinct they had forgotten.

Joe shook his shoulder to shake away the feeling of the sound. "I guess the ol' bitch is at him."

"Good dog," Ruthie said. "Get 'im, boy."

The hunter's arm tips drew blood, but only in the safe spots—shoulder scratches at the heavy lump behind his head, thigh punctures. It never touched the veins, or arteries.

The bear swung at the thing with his great paw. His claws screeched down the body section but didn't so much as make a mark on the metal. The blow sent the thing thirty feet away, but it came back every time. The muscles, claws and teeth were nothing to it. It was made to withstand easily more than what one bear could do, and it knew with its built-in knowledge how to make a bear blind-angry.

Saliva came to the bear's mouth and flew out over his chin as he moved his heavy head sideways and back. It splashed, gummy on his cheeks, and made dark, damp streaks across his chest. Only his rage was real to him now, and he screamed a deep rasp of frustration again and again.

Two hundred yards away, Joe said, "Some roar!"

"Uh-huh. If noise means anything, it sounds like he's about ready for a real fight."

They both got up and folded up the chairs and cups. They sighted along their gun barrels to see that they were straight.

"Set 'em at medium," Joe said. "We want to start off slow."

They came to where the bear was, and took up a good position on a high place. Joe called in his mike to the hunter thing. "Stand by, houn' dog, and slip over here to back us up." Then he called to the bear. "Hey, boy. This way, boy. This way."

The gray-green thing moved back and the bear saw the new enemy, two of them. He didn't hesitate; he was ready to charge anything that moved. He was only five feet away when their small guns popped. The force knocked him down, and he rolled out of the way, dazed; he turned again for another charge and came at them, all claws and teeth.

Joe's gun popped again. This time the bear staggered, but still came on. Joe backed up, pushing at his gun dial to raise the power. He bumped into Ruthie behind him and they both fell. Joe's voice was a crazy scream. "Get him."

The hunting machine moved fast. Its sharp forearm came like an uppercut, under the jaw and into the brain.

He lay, looking smaller, somehow, but still big, his ragged fur matted with blood. Fleas were alive on it, and flies already coming. Joe and Ruthie looked down at him and took big breaths.

"You shouldna got behind me," Joe said as soon as he caught his breath. "I coulda kept it going longer if you'da just stayed out of the way."

"You told me to," Ruthie said. "You told me to stay right behind you."

"Well, I didn't mean *that* close."

Ruthie sniffed. "Anyway," she said, "how are you going to get the fur off it?"

"Hmmmph."

"I don't think that moth-eaten thing will make much of a rug. It's pretty dirty, too, and probably full of germs."

Joe walked around the bear and turned its head sideways with his toe. "Be a big messy job, all right, skinning it. Up to the elbows in blood and gut, I guess."

"I didn't expect it to be like *this* at all," Ruthie said. "Why don't you just forget it? You had your fun."

Joe stood, looking at the bear's head. He watched a fly land on its eye and then walk down to a damp nostril.

"Well, come *on*." Ruthie took her small pack. "I want to

get back in time to take a bath before supper."

"Okay." Joe leaned over his mike. "Come on ol' Rover, ol' hound dog. You did fine."

AUTO-DA-FÉ

Roger Zelazny

Still do I remember the hot sun upon the sands of the Plaza del Autos, the cries of the soft-drink hawkers, the tiers of humanity stacked across from me on the sunny side of the arena, sunglasses like cavities in their gleaming faces.

Still do I remember the smells and the colors: the reds and the blues and the yellows, the ever-present tang of petroleum fumes upon the air.

Still do I remember that day, that day with its sun in the middle of the sky and the sign of Aries, burning in the blooming of the year. I recall the mincing steps of the pumpers, heads thrown back, arms waving, the white dazzles of their teeth framed with smiling lips, cloths like colorful tails protruding from the rear pockets of their coveralls; and the horns—I remember the blare of a thousand horns over the loudspeakers, on and off, off and on, over and over, and again, and then one shimmering, final note, sustained, to break the ear and the heart with its infinite power, its pathos.

Then there was silence.

I see it now as I did on that day so long ago. . . .

He entered the arena, and the cry that went up shook blue heaven upon its pillars of white marble.

"¡Viva! ¡El mechador! ¡Viva! ¡El mechador!"

I remember his face, dark and sad and wise.

Long of jaw and nose was he, and his laughter was as the roaring of the wind, and his movements were as the music of the theramin and the drum. His coveralls were blue and silk and tight and stitched with thread of gold and broidered all about with black braid. His jacket was beaded and there were flashing scales upon his breast, his shoulders, his back.

His lips curled into the smile of a man who has known much glory and has hold upon the power that will bring him into more.

He moved, turning in a circle, not shielding his eyes against the sun.

He was above the sun. He was Manolo Stillete Dos Muertos, the mightiest *mechador* the world had ever seen, black boots upon his feet, pistons in his thighs, fingers with the discretion of micrometers, halo of dark locks about his head and the angel of death in his right arm, there, in the center of the grease-stained circle of truth.

He waved, and a cry went up once more.

"Manolo! Manolo! Dos Muertos! Dos Muertos!"

After two years' absence from the ring, he had chosen this, the anniversary of his death and retirement, to return—for there was gasoline and methyl in his blood and his heart was a burnished pump ringed 'bout with desire and courage. He had died twice within the ring, and twice had the medics restored him. After his second death, he had retired, and some said that it was because he had known fear. This could not be true.

He waved his hand and his name rolled back upon him.

The horns sounded once more: three long blasts.

Then again there was silence, and a pumper wearing red and yellow brought him the cape, removed his jacket.

The tinfoil backing of the cape flashed in the sun as Dos Muertos swirled it.

Then there came the final, beeping notes.

The big door rolled upward and back into the wall.

He draped his cape over his arm and faced the gateway.

The light above was red and from within the darkness there came the sound of an engine.

The light turned yellow, then green, and there was the sound of cautiously engaged gears.

The car moved slowly into the ring, paused, crept forward, paused again.

It was a red Pontiac, its hood stripped away, its engine like a nest of snakes, coiling and engendering behind the circular shimmer of its invisible fan. The wings of its aerial spun round and round, then fixed upon Manolo and his cape.

He had chosen a heavy one for his first, slow on turning, to give him a chance to limber up.

The drums of its brain, which had never before recorded a man, were spinning.

Then the consciousness of its kind swept over it, and it moved forward.

Manolo swirled his cape and kicked its fender as it roared past.

The door of the great garage closed.

When it reached the opposite side of the ring the car stopped, parked.

Cries of disgust, booing and hissing arose from the crowd.

Still, the Pontiac remained parked.

Two pumpers, bearing buckets, emerged from behind the fence and threw mud upon its windshield.

It roared then and pursued the nearest, banging into the fence. Then it turned suddenly, sighted Dos Muertos, and charged.

His *verónica* transformed him into a statue with a skirt of silver. The enthusiasm of the crowd was mighty.

It turned and charged once more, and I wondered at Manolo's skill, for it would seem that his buttons had scraped cherry paint from the side panels.

Then it paused, spun its wheels, ran in a circle about the ring.

The crowd roared as it moved past him and recircled.

Then it stopped again, perhaps fifty feet away.

Manolo turned his back upon it and waved to the crowd.

—Again, the cheering and the calling of his name.

He gestured to someone behind the fence.

A pumper emerged and bore to him, upon a velvet cushion, his chrome-plated monkey wrench.

He turned then again to the Pontiac and strode toward it.

It stood there shivering and he knocked off its radiator cap.

A jet of steaming water shot into the air and the crowd bellowed. Then he struck the front of the radiator and banged upon each fender.

He turned his back upon it again and stood there.

When he heard the engagement of the gears he turned once more, and with one clean pass it was by him, but not before he had banged twice upon the trunk with his wrench.

It moved to the other end of the ring and parked.

Manolo raised his hand to the pumper behind the fence.

The man with the cushion emerged and bore to him the long-handled screwdriver and the short cape. He took the monkey wrench away with him, as well as the long cape.

Another silence came over the Plaza del Autos.

The Pontiac, as if sensing all this, turned once more and blew its horn twice. Then it charged.

There were dark spots upon the sand from where its radiator had leaked water. Its exhaust arose like a ghost behind it. It bore down upon him at a terrible speed.

Dos Muertos raised the cape before him and rested the blade of the screwdriver upon his left forearm.

When it seemed he would surely be run down, his hand shot forward, so fast the eye could barely follow it, and he stepped to the side as the engine began to cough.

Still the Pontiac continued on with a deadly momentum, turned sharply without braking, rolled over, slid into the fence, and began to burn. Its engine coughed and died.

The Plaza shook with the cheering. They awarded Dos Muertos both headlights and the tailpipe. He held them high and moved in slow promenade about the perimeter of the ring. The horns sounded. A lady threw him a plastic flower and he sent for a pumper to bear her the tailpipe and to ask her to dine with him. The crowd cheered more loudly, for he was known to be a great layer of women, and it was not such an unusual thing in the days of my youth as it is now.

The next was a blue Chevrolet, and he played with it as a child plays with a kitten, tormenting it into striking, then stopping it forever. He received both headlights. The sky had clouded over by then and there was a tentative mumbling of thunder.

The third was a black Jaguar XKE, which calls for the highest skill possible and makes for a very brief moment of truth. There was blood as well as gasoline upon the sand before he dispatched it, for its side mirror extended farther than one would think, and there was a red furrow across his rib cage before he had done with it. But he tore out its ignition system with such grace and artistry that the crowd boiled over into the ring, and the guards were called forth to beat them with clubs and herd them with cattle prods back into their seats.

Surely, after all of this, none could say that Dos Muertos had ever known fear.

A cool breeze arose, and I bought a soft drink and waited for the last.

His final car sped forth while the light was still yellow. It was a mustard-colored Ford convertible. As it went past him the first time, it blew its horn and turned on its windshield wipers. Everyone cheered, for they could see it had spirit.

Then it came to a dead halt, shifted into reverse, and backed toward him at about forty miles an hour.

He got out of the way, sacrificing grace to expediency, and it braked sharply, shifted into low gear, and sped forward again.

He waved the cape and it was torn from his hands. If he had not thrown himself over backward, he would have been struck.

Then someone cried: "It's out of alignment!"

But he got to his feet, recovered his cape, and faced it once more.

They still tell of those five passes that followed. Never has there been such a flirting with bumper and grill! Never in all of the Earth has there been such an encounter between *mechador* and machine! The convertible roared like ten centuries of streamlined death, and the spirit of St. Detroit sat in its driver's seat, grinning, while Dos Muertos faced it with his tinfoil cape, cowed it and called for his wrench. It nursed its overheated engine and rolled its windows up and down, up and down, clearing its muffler the while with lavatory noises and much black smoke.

By then it was raining, softly, gently, and the thunder still came about us. I finished my soft drink.

Dos Muertos had never used his monkey wrench on the engine before, only upon the body. But this time he threw it. Some experts say he was aiming at the distributor; others say he was trying to break its fuel pump.

The crowd booed him.

Something gooey was dripping from the Ford onto the sand. The red streak brightened on Manolo's stomach. The rain came down.

He did not look at the crowd. He did not take his eyes from the car. He held out his right hand, palm upward, and waited.

A panting pumper placed the screwdriver in his hand and ran back toward the fence.

Manolo moved to the side and waited.

It leaped at him and he struck.

There was more booing.

He had missed the kill.

No one left, though. The Ford swept around him in a tight circle, smoke now emerging from its engine. Manolo rubbed his arm and picked up the screwdriver and cape he had dropped. There was more booing as he did so.

By the time the car was upon him, flames were leaping forth from its engine.

Now some say that he struck and missed again, going off balance. Others say that he began to strike, grew afraid and drew back. Still others say that, perhaps for an instant, he knew a fatal pity for his spirited adversary, and that this had stayed his hand. I say that the smoke was too thick for any of them to say for certain what had happened.

But it swerved and he fell forward, and he was borne upon that engine, blazing like a god's catafalque, to meet with his third death as they crashed into the fence together and went up in flames.

There was much dispute over the final *corrida*, but what remained of the tailpipe and both headlights were buried with what remained of him, beneath the sands of the Plaza, and there was much weeping among the women he had known. I say that he could not have been afraid or known pity, for his strength was as a river of rockets, his thighs were pistons, and the fingers of his hands had the discretion of micrometers; his hair was a black halo and the angel of death rode on his right arm. Such a man, a man who has known truth, is mightier than any machine. Such a man is above anything but the holding of power and the wearing of glory.

Now he is dead though, this one, for the third and final time. He is dead as all the dead who have ever died before the bumper, under the grill, beneath the wheels. It is well that he cannot rise again, for I say that his final car was his apotheosis, and anything else would be anticlimactic. Once I saw a blade of grass growing up between the metal sheets of the world in a place where they had become loose, and I destroyed it because I felt it must be lonesome. Often have I regretted doing this thing, for I took away the glory of its aloneness. Thus does life the machine, I feel, consider man, sternly, then with regret, and the heavens do weep upon him through eyes that grief has opened in the sky.

All the way home I thought of this thing, and the hoofs of my mount clicked upon the floor of the city as I rode through the rain toward evening, that spring.

SECOND VARIETY

Philip K. Dick

The Russian soldier made his way nervously up the ragged side of the hill, holding his gun ready. He glanced around him, licking his dry lips, his face set. From time to time he reached up a gloved hand and wiped perspiration from his neck, pushing down his coat collar.

Eric turned to Corporal Leone. "Want him? Or can I have him?" He adjusted the view sight so the Russian's features squarely filled the glass, the lines cutting across his hard, somber features.

Leone considered. The Russian was close, moving rapidly, almost running. "Don't fire. Wait." Leone tensed. "I don't think we're needed."

The Russian increased his pace, kicking ash and piles of debris out of his way. He reached the top of the hill and stopped, panting, staring around him. The sky was overcast, with drifting clouds of gray particles. Bare trunks of trees jutted up occasionally; the ground was level and bare, rubble-strewn, with the ruins of buildings standing out here and there like yellowing skulls.

The Russian was uneasy. He knew something was wrong.

He started down the hill. Now he was only a few paces from the bunker. Eric was getting fidgety. He played with his pistol, glancing at Leone.

"Don't worry," Leone said. "He won't get here. They'll take care of him."

"Are you sure? He's got damn far."

"They hang around close to the bunker. He's getting into the bad part. Get set!"

The Russian began to hurry, sliding down the hill, his boots sinking into the heaps of gray ash, trying to keep his gun up. He stopped for a moment, lifting his field glasses to his face.

"He's looking right at us," Eric said.

The Russian came on. They could see his eyes, like two blue stones. His mouth was open a little. He needed a shave; his chin was stubbled. On one bony cheek was a square of tape, showing blue at the edge. A fungoid spot. His coat was muddy and torn. One glove was missing. As he ran, his belt counter bounced up and down against him.

Leone touched Eric's arm. "Here one comes."

Across the ground something small and metallic came, flashing in the dull sunlight of midday. A metal sphere. It raced up the hill after the Russian, its treads flying. It was small, one of the baby ones. Its claws were out, two razor projections spinning in a blur of white steel. The Russian heard it. He turned instantly, firing. The sphere dissolved into particles. But already a second had emerged and was following the first. The Russian fired again.

A third sphere leaped up the Russian's leg, clicking and whirring. It jumped to the shoulder. The spinning blades disappeared into the Russian's throat.

Eric relaxed. "Well, that's that. God, those damn things give me the creeps. Sometimes I think we were better off before."

"If we hadn't invented them, they would have." Leone lit a cigarette shakily. "I wonder why a Russian would come all this way alone. I didn't see anyone covering him."

Lieutenant Scott came slipping up the tunnel, into the bunker. "What happened? Something entered the screen."

"An Ivan."

"Just one?"

Eric brought the viewscreen around. Scott peered into it.

Now there were numerous metal spheres crawling over the prostrate body, dull metal globes clicking and whirring, sawing up the Russian into small parts to be carried away.

"What a lot of claws," Scott murmured.

"They come like flies. Not much game for them any more."

Scott pushed the sight away, disgusted. "Like flies. I wonder why he was out there. They know we have claws all around."

A larger robot had joined the smaller spheres. A long blunt tube with projecting eyepieces, it was directing operations. There was not much left of the soldier. What remained was being brought down the hillside by the host of claws.

"Sir," Leone said. "If it's all right, I'd like to go out there and take a look at him."

"Why?"

"Maybe he came with something."

Scott considered. He shrugged. "All right. But be careful."

"I have my tab." Leone patted the metal band at his wrist. "I'll be out of bounds."

He picked up his rifle and stepped carefully up to the mouth of the bunker, making his way between blocks of concrete and steel prongs, twisted and bent. The air was cold at the top. He crossed over the ground toward the remains of the soldier, striding across the soft ash. A wind blew around him, swirling gray particles up in his face. He squinted and pushed on.

The claws retreated as he came close, some of them stiffening into immobility. He touched his tab. The Ivan would have given something for that! Short hard radiation emitted from the tab neutralized the claws, put them out of commission. Even the big robot with its two waving eyestalks retreated respectfully as he approached.

He bent down over the remains of the soldier. The gloved hand was closed tightly. There was something in it. Leone pried the fingers apart. A sealed container, aluminum. Still shiny.

He put it in his pocket and made his way back to the bunker. Behind him the claws came back to life, moving into operation again. The procession resumed, metal spheres moving through the gray ash with their loads. He could hear their treads scrabbling against the ground. He shuddered.

Scott watched intently as he brought the shiny tube out of his pocket. "He had that?"

"In his hand." Leone unscrewed the top. "Maybe you should look at it, sir."

Scott took it. He emptied the contents out in the palm of his hand. A small piece of silk paper, carefully folded. He sat down by the light and unfolded it.

"What's it say, sir?" Eric said. Several officers came up the tunnel. Major Hendricks appeared.

"Major," Scott said. "Look at this."

Hendricks read the slip. "This just come?"

"A single runner. Just now."

"Where is he?" Hendricks asked sharply.

"The claws got him."

Major Hendricks grunted. "Here." He passed it to his companions. "I think this is what we've been waiting for. They certainly took their time about it."

"So they want to talk terms," Scott said. "Are we going along with them?"

"That's not for us to decide." Hendricks sat down. "Where's the communications officer? I want the Moon Base."

Leone pondered as the communications officer raised the outside antenna cautiously, scanning the sky above the bunker for any sign of a watching Russian ship.

"Sir," Scott said to Hendricks. "It's sure strange they suddenly came around. We've been using the claws for almost a year. Now all of a sudden they start to fold."

"Maybe claws have been getting down in their bunkers."

"One of the big ones, the kind with stalks, got into an Ivan bunker last week," Eric said. "It got a whole platoon of them before they got their lid shut."

"How do you know?"

"A buddy told me. The thing came back with—with remains."

"Moon Base, sir," the communications officer said.

On the screen the face of the lunar monitor appeared. His crisp uniform contrasted to the uniforms in the bunker. And he was clean shaven. "Moon Base."

"This is forward command L-Whistle. On Terra. Let me have General Thompson."

The monitor faded. Presently General Thompson's heavy features came into focus. "What is it, Major?"

"Our claws got a single Russian runner with a message. We

don't know whether to act on it—there have been tricks like this in the past."

"What's the message?"

"The Russians want us to send a single officer on policy level over to their lines. For a conference. They don't state the nature of the conference. They say that matters of—" He consulted the slip: "—matters of grave urgency make it advisable that discussion be opened between a representative of the UN forces and themselves."

He held the message up to the screen for the general to scan. Thompson's eyes moved.

"What should we do?" Hendricks said.

"Send a man out."

"You don't think it's a trap?"

"It might be. But the location they give for their forward command is correct. It's worth a try, at any rate."

"I'll send an officer out. And report the results to you as soon as he returns."

"All right, Major." Thompson broke the connection. The screen died. Up above, the antenna came slowly down.

Hendricks rolled up the paper, deep in thought.

"I'll go," Leone said.

"They want somebody at policy level." Hendricks rubbed his jaw. "Policy level. I haven't been outside in months. Maybe I could use a little air."

"Don't you think it's risky?"

Hendricks lifted the view sight and gazed into it. The remains of the Russian were gone. Only a single claw was in sight. It was folding itself back, disappearing into the ash, like a crab. Like some hideous metal crab. . . . "That's the only thing that bothers me." Hendricks rubbed his wrist. "I know I'm safe as long as I have this on me. But there's something about them. I hate the damn things. I wish we'd never invented them. There's something wrong with them. Relentless little—"

"If we hadn't invented them, the Ivans would have."

Hendricks pushed the sight back. "Anyhow, it seems to be winning the war. I guess that's good."

"Sounds like you're getting the same jitters as the Ivans."

Hendricks examined his wristwatch. "I guess I had better get started, if I want to be there before dark."

• • •

He took a deep breath and then stepped out onto the gray rubbled ground. After a minute he lit a cigarette and stood gazing around him. The landscape was dead. Nothing stirred. He could see for miles, endless ash and slag, ruins of buildings. A few trees without leaves or branches, only the trunks. Above him the eternal rolling clouds of gray, drifting between Terra and the sun.

Major Hendricks went on. Off to the right something scuttled, something round and metallic. A claw, going lickety-split after something. Probably after a small animal, a rat. They got rats, too. As a sort of sideline.

He came to the top of the little hill and lifted his field glasses. The Russian lines were a few miles ahead of him. They had a forward command post there. The runner had come from it.

A squat robot with undulating arms passed by him, its arms weaving inquiringly. The robot went on its way, disappearing under some debris. Hendricks watched it go. He had never seen that type before. There were getting to be more and more types he had never seen, new varieties and sizes coming up from the underground factories.

Hendricks put out his cigarette and hurried on. It was interesting, the use of artificial forms in warfare. How had they got started? Necessity. The Soviet Union had gained great initial success, usual with the side that got the war going. Most of North America had been blasted off the map. Retaliation was quick in coming, of course. The sky was full of circling diskbombers long before the war began; they had been up there for years. The disks began sailing down all over Russia within hours after Washington got it.

But that hadn't helped Washington.

The American bloc governments moved to the Moon Base the first year. There was not much else to do. Europe was gone, a slag heap with dark weeds growing from the ashes and bones. Most of North America was useless; nothing could be planted, no one could live. A few million people kept going up in Canada and down in South America. But during the second year Soviet parachutists began to drop, a few at first, then more and more. They wore the first really effective anti-radiation equipment; what was left of American production moved to the Moon along with the governments.

All but the troops. The remaining troops stayed behind as best they could, a few thousand here, a platoon there. No one knew exactly where they were; they stayed where they could, moving around at night, hiding in ruins, in sewers, cellars, with the rats and snakes. It looked as if the Soviet Union had the war almost won. Except for a handful of projectiles fired off from the Moon daily, there was almost no weapon in use against them. They came and went as they pleased. The war, for all practical purposes, was over. Nothing effective opposed them.

And then the first claws appeared. And overnight the complexion of the war changed.

The claws were awkward, at first. Slow. The Ivans knocked them off almost as fast as they crawled out of their underground tunnels. But then they got better, faster and more cunning. Factories, all on Terra, turned them out. Factories a long way underground, behind the Soviet lines, factories that had once made atomic projectiles, now almost forgotten.

The claws got faster, and they got bigger. New types appeared, some with feelers, some that flew. There were a few jumping kinds. The best technicians on the Moon were working on designs, making them more and more intricate, more flexible. They became uncanny; the Ivans were having a lot of trouble with them. Some of the little claws were learning to hide themselves, burrowing down into the ash, lying in wait.

And then they started getting into the Russian bunkers, slipping down when the lids were raised for air and a look around. One claw inside a bunker, a churning sphere of blades and metal—that was enough. And when one got in others followed. With a weapon like that the war couldn't go on much longer.

Maybe it was already over.

Maybe he was going to hear the news. Maybe the Politburo had decided to throw in the sponge. Too bad it had taken so long. Six years. A long time for war like that, the way they had waged it. The automatic retaliation disks, spinning down all over Russia, hundreds of thousands of them. Bacteria crystals. The Soviet guided missiles, whistling through the air. The chain bombs. And now this, the robots, the claws—

The claws weren't like other weapons. They were *alive*, from any practical standpoint, whether the Governments wanted to admit it or not. They were not machines. They were living things, spinning, creeping, shaking themselves up suddenly from the gray ash and darting toward a man, climbing up him, rushing for his throat. And that was what they had been designed to do. Their job.

They did their job well. Especially lately, with the new designs coming up. Now they repaired themselves. They were on their own. Radiation tabs protected the UN troops, but if a man lost his tab he was fair game for the claws, no matter what his uniform. Down below the surface automatic machinery stamped them out. Human beings stayed a long way off. It was too risky; nobody wanted to be around them. They were left to themselves. And they seemed to be doing all right. The new designs were faster, more complex. More efficient.

Apparently they had won the war.

Major Hendricks lit a second cigarette. The landscape depressed him. Nothing but ash and ruins. He seemed to be alone, the only living thing in the whole world. To the right the ruins of a town rose up, a few walls and heaps of debris. He tossed the dead match away, increasing his pace. Suddenly he stopped, jerking up his gun, his body tense. For a minute it looked like—

From behind the shell of a ruined building a figure came, walking slowly toward him, walking hesitantly.

Hendricks blinked. "Stop!"

The boy stopped. Hendricks lowered his gun. The boy stood silently, looking at him. He was small, not very old. Perhaps eight. But it was hard to tell. Most of the kids who remained were stunted. He wore a faded blue sweater, ragged with dirt, and short pants. His hair was long and matted. Brown hair. It hung over his face and around his ears. He held something in his arms.

"What's that you have?" Hendricks said sharply.

The boy held it out. It was a toy, a bear. A teddy bear. The boy's eyes were large, but without expression.

Hendricks relaxed. "I don't want it. Keep it."

The boy hugged the bear again.

"Where do you live?" Hendricks said.

"In there."

"The ruins?"

"Yes."

"Underground?"

"Yes."

"How many are there?"

"How—how many?"

"How many of you. How big's your settlement?"

The boy did not answer.

Hendricks frowned. "You're not all by yourself, are you?"

The boy nodded.

"How do you stay alive?"

"There's food?"

"What kind of food?"

"Different."

Hendricks studied him. "How old are you?"

"Thirteen."

It wasn't possible. Or was it? The boy was thin, stunted. And probably sterile. Radiation exposure, years straight. No wonder he was so small. His arms and legs were like pipe cleaners, knobby and thin. Hendricks touched the boy's arm. His skin was dry and rough; radiation skin. He bent down, looking into the boy's face. There was no expression. Big eyes, big and dark.

"Are you blind?" Hendricks said.

"No. I can see some."

"How do you get away from the claws?"

"The claws?"

"The round things. That run and burrow."

"I don't understand."

Maybe there weren't any claws around. A lot of areas were free. They collected mostly around bunkers, where there were people. The claws had been designed to sense warmth, warmth of living things.

"You're lucky." Hendricks straightened up. "Well? Which way are you going? Back—back there?"

"Can I come with you?"

"With *me?*" Hendricks folded his arms. "I'm going a long way. Miles. I have to hurry." He looked at his watch. "I have to get there by nightfall."

"I want to come."

Hendricks fumbled in his pack. "It isn't worth it. Here." He tossed down the food cans he had with him. "You take these and go back. Okay?"

The boy said nothing.

"I'll be coming back this way. In a day or so. If you're around here when I come back you can come along with me. All right?"

"I want to go with you now."

"It's a long walk."

"I can walk."

Hendricks shifted uneasily. It made too good a target, two people walking along. And the boy would slow him down. But he might not come back this way. And if the boy were really all alone—

"Okay. Come along."

The boy fell in beside him. Hendricks strode along. The boy walked silently, clutching his teddy bear.

"What's your name?" Hendricks said, after a time.

"David Edward Derring."

"David? What—what happened to your mother and father?"

"They died."

"How?"

"In the blast."

"How long ago?"

"Six years."

Hendricks slowed down. "You've been alone six years?"

"No. There were other people for a while. They went away."

"And you've been alone since?"

"Yes."

Hendricks glanced down. The boy was strange, saying very little. Withdrawn. But that was the way they were, the children who had survived. Quiet. Stoic. A strange kind of fatalism gripped them. Nothing came as a surprise. They accepted anything that came along. There was no longer any *normal*, any natural course of things, moral or physical, for them to expect. Custom, habit, all the determining forces of learning were gone; only brute experience remained.

"Am I walking too fast?" Hendricks said.

"No."

"How did you happen to see me?"

"I was waiting."

"Waiting?" Hendricks was puzzled. "What were you waiting for?"

"To catch things."

"What kind of things?"

"Things to eat."

"Oh." Hendricks set his lips grimly. A thirteen-year-old boy, living on rats and gophers and half-rotten canned food. Down in a hole under the ruins of a town. With radiation pools and claws, and Russian dive-mines up above, coasting around the sky.

"Where are we going?" David asked.

"To the Russian lines."

"Russian?"

"The enemy. The people who started the war. They dropped the first radiation bombs. They began all this."

The boy nodded. His face showed no expression.

"I'm an American," Hendricks said.

There was no comment. On they went, the two of them, Hendricks walking a little ahead, David trailing behind him, hugging his dirty teddy bear against his chest.

About four in the afternoon they stopped to eat. Hendricks built a fire in a hollow between some slabs of concrete. He cleared the weeds away and heaped up bits of wood. The Russians' lines were not very far ahead. Around him was what had once been a long valley, acres of fruit trees and grapes. Nothing remained now but a few bleak stumps and the mountains that stretched across the horizon at the far end. And the clouds of rolling ash that blew and drifted with the wind, settling over the weeds and remains of buildings, walls here and there, once in a while what had been a road.

Hendricks made coffee and heated up some boiled mutton and bread. "Here." He handed bread and mutton to David. David squatted by the edge of the fire, his knees knobby and white. He examined the food and then passed it back, shaking his head.

"No."

"No? Don't you want any?"

"No."

Hendricks shrugged. Maybe the boy was a mutant, used to special food. It didn't matter. When he was hungry he would find something to eat. The boy was strange. But there were many strange changes coming over the world. Life was not the same anymore. It would never be the same again. The human race was going to have to realize that.

"Suit yourself," Hendricks said. He ate the bread and mutton

by himself, washing it down with coffee. He ate slowly, finding
the food hard to digest. When he was done he got to his feet
and stamped the fire out.

David rose slowly, watching him with his young-old eyes.

"We're going," Hendricks said.

"All right."

Hendricks walked along, his gun in his arms. They were
close; he was tense, ready for anything. The Russians should
be expecting a runner, an answer to their own runner, but they
were tricky. There was always the possibility of a slip-up. He
scanned the landscape around him. Nothing but slag and ash,
a few hills, charred trees. Concrete walls. But some place ahead
was the first bunker of the Russian lines, the forward command.
Underground, buried deep, with only a periscope showing, a
few gun muzzles. Maybe an antenna.

"Will we be there soon?" David asked.

"Yes. Getting tired?"

"No."

"Why, then?"

David did not answer. He plodded carefully along behind,
picking his way over the ash. His legs and shoes were gray
with dust. His pinched face was streaked, lines of gray ash in
riverlets down the pale white of his skin. There was no color
to his face. Typical of the new children, growing up in cellars
and sewers and underground shelters.

Hendricks slowed down. He lifted his field glasses and
studied the ground ahead of him. Were they there, some place,
waiting for him? Watching him, the way his men had watched
the Russian runner? A chill went up his back. Maybe they were
getting their guns ready, preparing to fire, the way his men
had prepared, made ready to kill.

Hendricks stopped, wiping perspiration from his face.
"Damn." It made him uneasy. But he should be expected. The
situation was different.

He strode over the ash, holding his gun tightly with both
hands. Behind him came David. Hendricks peered around,
tight-lipped. Any second it might happen. A burst of white
light, a blast, carefully aimed from inside a deep concrete
bunker.

He raised his arm and waved it around in a circle.

Nothing moved. To the right a long ridge ran, topped with

dread tree trunks. A few wild vines had grown up around the trees, remains of arbors. And the eternal dark weeds. Hendricks studied the ridge. Was anything up there? Perfect place for a lookout. He approached the ridge warily, David coming silently behind. If it were his command he'd have a sentry up there, watching for troops trying to infiltrate into the command area. Of course, if it were his command there would be the claws around the area for full protection.

He stopped, feet apart, hands on his hips.

"Are we there?" David said.

"Almost."

"Why have we stopped?"

"I don't want to take any chances." Hendricks advanced slowly. Now the ridge lay directly beside him, along his right. Overlooking him. His uneasy feeling increased. If an Ivan were up there he wouldn't have a chance. He waved his arm again. They should be expecting someone in the UN uniform, in response to the note capsule. Unless the whole thing was a trap.

"Keep up with me." He turned toward David. "Don't drop behind."

"With you?"

"Up beside me! We're close. We can't take any chances. Come on."

"I'll be all right." David remained behind him, in the rear, a few paces away, still clutching his teddy bear.

"Have it your way." Hendricks raised his glasses again, suddenly tense. For a moment—had something moved? He scanned the ridge carefully. Everything was silent. Dead. No life up there, only tree trunks and ash. Maybe a few rats. The big black rats that had survived the claws. Mutants—built their own shelters out of saliva and ash. Some kind of plaster. Adaptation. He started forward again.

A tall figure came out on the ridge above him, cloak flapping. Gray-green. A Russian. Behind him a second soldier appeared, another Russian. Both lifted their guns, aiming.

Hendricks froze. He opened his mouth. The soldiers were kneeling, sighting down the side of the slope. A third figure had joined them on the ridge top, a smaller figure in gray-green. A woman. She stood behind the other two.

Hendricks found his voice. "Stop!" He waved up at them frantically. "I'm—"

The two Russians fired. Behind Hendricks there was a faint *pop*. Waves of heat lapped against him, throwing him to the ground. Ash tore at his face, grinding into his eyes and nose. Choking, he pulled himself to his knees. It was all a trap. He was finished. He had come to be killed, like a steer. The soldiers and the woman were coming down the side of the ridge toward him, sliding down through the soft ash. Hendricks was numb. His head throbbed. Awkwardly, he got his rifle up and took aim. It weighed a thousand tons; he could hardly hold it. His nose and cheeks stung. The air was full of the blast smell, a bitter acrid stench.

"Don't fire," the first Russian said, in heavily accented English.

The three of them came up to him, surrounding him. "Put down your rifle, Yank," the other said.

Hendricks was dazed. Everything had happened so fast. He had been caught. And they had blasted the boy. He turned his head. David was gone. What remained of him was strewn across the ground.

The three Russians studied him curiously. Hendricks sat, wiping blood from his nose, picking out bits of ash. He shook his head, trying to clear it. "Why did you do it?" he murmured thickly. "The boy."

"Why?" One of the soldiers helped him roughly to his feet. He turned Hendricks around. "Look."

Hendricks closed his eyes.

"Look!" The two Russians pulled him forward. "See. Hurry up. There isn't much time to spare, Yank!"

Hendricks looked. And gasped.

"See now? Now do you understand?"

From the remains of David a metal wheel rolled. Relays, glinting metal. Parts, wiring. One of the Russians kicked at the heap of remains. Parts popped out, rolling away, wheels and springs and rods. A plastic section fell in, half charred. Hendricks bent shakily down. The front of the head had come off. He could make out the intricate brain, wires and relays, tiny tubes and switches, thousands of minute studs—

"A robot," the soldier holding his arm said. "We watched it tagging you."

"Tagging me?"

"That's their way. They tag along with you. Into the bunker. That's how they get in."

Hendricks blinked, dazed. "But—"

"Come on." They led him toward the ridge. "We can't stay here. It isn't safe. There must be hundreds of them all around here."

The three of them pulled him up the side of the ridge, sliding and slipping on the ash. The woman reached the top and stood waiting for them.

"The forward command," Hendricks muttered. "I came to negotiate with the Soviet—"

"There is no more forward command. *They* got in. We'll explain." They reached the top of the ridge. "We're all that's left. The three of us. The rest were down in the bunker."

"This way. Down this way." The woman unscrewed a lid, a gray manhole cover set in the ground. "Get in."

Hendricks lowered himself. The two soldiers and the woman came behind him, following him down the ladder. The woman closed the lid after them, bolting it tightly into place.

"Good thing we saw you," one of the two soldiers grunted. "It had tagged you about as far as it was going to."

"Give me one of your cigarettes," the woman said. "I haven't had an American cigarette for weeks."

Hendricks pushed the pack to her. She took a cigarette and passed the pack to the two soldiers. In the corner of the small room the lamp gleamed fitfully. The room was low-ceilinged, cramped. The four of them sat around a small wood table. A few dirty dishes were stacked to one side. Behind a ragged curtain a second room was partly visible. Hendricks saw the corner of a coat, some blankets, clothes hung on a hook.

"We were here," the soldier beside him said. He took off his helmet, pushing his blond hair back. "I'm Corporal Rudi Maxer. Polish. Impressed in the Soviet Army two years ago." He held out his hand.

Hendricks hesitated and then shook. "Major Joseph Hendricks."

"Klaus Epstein." The other soldier shook with him, a small dark man with thinning hair. Epstein plucked nervously at his ear. "Austrian. Impressed God knows when. I don't remember. The three of us were here, Rudi and I, with Tasso." He indicated the woman. "That's how we escaped. All the rest were down in the bunker."

"And—and *they* got in?"

Epstein lit a cigarette. "First just one of them. The kind that tagged you. Then it let others in."

Hendricks became alert. "The *kind?* Are there more than one kind?"

"The little boy. David. David holding his teddy bear. That's Variety Three. The most effective."

"What are the other types?"

Epstein reached into his coat. "Here." He tossed a packet of photographs onto the table, tied with a string. "Look for yourself."

Hendricks untied the string.

"You see," Rudi Maxer said, "that was why we wanted to talk terms. The Russians, I mean. We found out about a week ago. Found out that your claws were beginning to make up new designs on their own. New types of their own. Better types. Down in your underground factories behind our lines. You let them stamp themselves, repair themselves. Made them more and more intricate. It's your fault this happened."

Hendricks examined the photos. They had been snapped hurriedly; they were blurred and indistinct. The first few showed—David. David walking along a road, by himself. David and another David. Three Davids. All exactly alike. Each with a ragged teddy bear.

All pathetic.

"Look at the others," Tasso said.

The next pictures, taken at a great distance, showed a towering wounded soldier sitting by the side of a path, his arm in a sling, the stump of one leg extended, a crude crutch on his lap. Then two wounded soldiers, both the same, standing side by side.

"That's Variety One. The Wounded Soldier." Klaus reached out and took the pictures. "You see, the claws were designed to get to human beings. To find them. Each kind was better than the last. They got farther, closer, past most of our defenses, into our lines. But as long as they were merely *machines*, metal spheres with claws and horns, feelers, they could be picked off like any other object. They could be detected as lethal robots as soon as they were seen. Once we caught sight of them—"

"Variety One subverted our whole north wing," Rudi said. "It was a long time before anyone caught on. Then it was too late. They came in, wounded soldiers, knocking and begging to be let in. So we let them in. And as soon as they were in they took over. We were watching out for machines. . . ."

"At that time it was thought there was only the one type," Klaus Epstein said. "No one suspected there were other types. The pictures were flashed to us. When the runner was sent to you, we knew of just one type. Variety One. The big Wounded Soldier. We thought that was all."

"Your line fell to—"

"To Variety Three. David and his bear. That worked even better." Klaus smiled bitterly. "Soldiers are suckers for children. We brought them in and tried to feed them. We found out the hard way what they were after. At least, those that were in the bunker."

"The three of us were lucky," Rudi said. "Klaus and I were—were visiting Tasso when it happened. This is her place." He waved a big hand around. "This little cellar. We finished and climbed the ladder to start back. From the ridge we saw that they were all around the bunker. Fighting was still going on. David and his bear. Hundreds of them. Klaus took the pictures."

Klaus tied up the photographs again.

"And it's going on all along your line?" Hendricks said.

"Yes."

"How about *our* lines?" Without thinking, he touched the tab on his arm. "Can they—"

"They're not bothered by your radiation tabs. It makes no difference to them, Russian, American, Pole, German. It's all the same. They're doing what they were designed to do. Carrying out the original idea. They track down life, ·wherever they find it."

"They go by warmth," Klaus said. "That was the way you constructed them from the very start. Of course, those you designed were kept back by the radiation tabs you wear. Now they've got around that. These new varieties are lead-lined."

"What's the other variety?" Hendricks asked. "The David type, the Wounded Soldier—what's the other?"

"We don't know." Klaus pointed up at the wall. On the wall were two metal plates, ragged at the edges. Hendricks got up and studied them. They were bent and dented.

"The one on the left came off a Wounded Soldier," Rudi said. "We got one of them. It was going along toward our old bunker. We got it from the ridge, the same way we got the David tagging you."

The plate was stamped: *I-V*. Hendricks touched the other plate. "And this came from the David type?"

"Yes." The plate was stamped: *III-V*.

Klaus took a look at them, leaning over Hendricks's broad shoulder. "You can see what we're up against. There's another type. Maybe it was abandoned. Maybe it didn't work. But there must be a Second Variety. There's One and Three."

"You were lucky," Rudi said. "The David tagged you all the way here and never touched you. Probably thought you'd get it into a bunker, somewhere."

"One gets in and it's all over," Klaus said. "They move fast. One lets all the rest inside. They're inflexible. Machines with one purpose. They were built for only one thing." He rubbed sweat from his lip. "We saw."

They were silent.

"Let me have another cigarette, Yank," Tasso said. "They are good. I almost forgot how they were."

It was night. The sky was black. No stars were visible through the rolling clouds of ash. Klaus lifted the lid cautiously so that Hendricks could look out.

Rudi pointed into the darkness. "Over that way are the bunkers. Where we used to be. Not over half a mile from us. It was just chance Klaus and I were not there when it happened. Weakness. Saved by our lusts."

"All the rest must be dead," Klaus said in a low voice. "It came quickly. This morning the Politburo reached their decision. They notified us—forward command. Our runner was sent out at once. We saw him start toward the direction of your lines. We covered him until he was out of sight."

"Alex Radrivsky. We both knew him. He disappeared about six o'clock. The sun had just come up. About noon Klaus and I had an hour relief. We crept off, away from the bunkers. No one was watching. We came here. There used to be a town here, a few houses, a street. This cellar was part of a big farmhouse. We knew Tasso would be here, hiding down in her little place. We had come here before. Others from the bunkers came here. Today happened to be our turn."

"So we were saved," Klaus said. "Chance. It might have

been others. We—we finished, and then we came up to the surface and started back along the ridge. That was when we saw them, the Davids. We understood right away. We had seen the photos of the First Variety, the Wounded Soldier. Our Commissar distributed them to us with an explanation. If we had gone another step they would have seen us. As it was we had to blast two Davids before we got back. There were hundreds of them, all around. Like ants. We took pictures and slipped back here, bolting the lid tight."

"They're not so much when you catch them alone. We moved faster than they did. But they're inexorable. Not like living things. They came right at us. And we blasted them."

Major Hendricks rested against the edge of the lid, adjusting his eyes to the darkness. "Is it safe to have the lid up at all?"

"If we're careful. How else can you operate your transmitter?"

Hendricks lifted the small belt transmitter slowly. He pressed it against his ear. The metal was cold and damp. he blew against the mike, raising up the short antenna. A faint hum sounded in his ear. "That's true, I suppose."

But he still hesitated.

"We'll pull you under if anything happens," Klaus said.

"Thanks." Hendricks waited a moment, resting the transmitter against his shoulder. "Interesting, isn't it?"

"What?"

"This, the new types. The new varieties of claws. We're completely at their mercy, aren't we? By now they've probably gotten into the UN lines, too. It makes me wonder if we're not seeing the beginning of a new species. *The* new species. Evolution. The race to come after man."

Rudi grunted. "There is no race after man."

"No? Why not? Maybe we're seeing it now, the end of human beings, the beginning of the new society."

"They're not a race. They're mechanical killers. You made them to destroy. That's all they can do. They're machines with a job."

"So it seems now. But how about later on? After the war is over. Maybe, when there aren't any humans to destroy, their real potentialities will begin to show."

"You talk as if they were alive!"

"Aren't they?"

There was silence. "They're machines," Rudi said. "They look like people, but they're machines."

"Use your transmitter, Major," Klaus said. "We can't stay up here forever."

Holding the transmitter tightly, Hendricks called the code of the command bunker. He waited, listening. No response. Only silence. He checked the leads carefully. Everything was in place.

"Scott!" he said into the mike. "Can you hear me?"

Silence. He raised the gain up full and tried gain. Only static.

"I don't get anything. They may hear me but they may not want to answer."

"Tell them it's an emergency."

"They think I'm being forced to call. Under your direction." He tried again, outlining briefly what he had learned. But still the phone was silent, except for the faint static.

"Radiation pools kill most transmission," Klaus said, after awhile. "Maybe that's it."

Hendricks shut the transmitter up. "No use. No answer. Radiation pools? Maybe. Or they hear me, but won't answer. Frankly, that's what I would do, if a runner tried to call from the Soviet lines. They have no reason to believe such a story. They may hear everything I say—"

"Or maybe it's too late."

Hendricks nodded.

"We better get the lid down," Rudi said nervously. "We don't want to take unnecessary chances."

They climbed slowly back down the tunnel. Klaus bolted the lid carefully into place. They descended into the kitchen. The air was heavy and close around them.

"Could they work that fast?" Hendricks said. "I left the bunker this noon. Ten hours ago. How could they move so quickly?"

"It doesn't take them long. Not after the first one gets in. It goes wild. You know what the little claws can do. Even *one* of these is beyond belief. Razors, each finger. Maniacal."

"All right." Hendricks moved away impatiently. He stood with his back to them.

"What's the matter?" Rudi said.

"The Moon Base. God, if they've gotten there—"

"The Moon Base?"

Hendricks turned around. "They couldn't have got to the Moon Base. How would they get there? It isn't possible. I can't believe it."

"What is this Moon Base? We've heard rumors, but nothing definite. What is the actual situation? You seem concerned."

"We're supplied from the Moon. The governments are there, under the lunar surface. All our people and industries. That's what keeps us going. If they should find some way of getting off Terra, onto the Moon—"

"It only takes one of them. Once the first one gets in it admits the others. Hundreds of them, all alike. You should have seen them. Identical. Like ants."

"Perfect socialism," Tasso said. "The ideal of the communist state. All citizens interchangeable."

Klaus grunted angrily. "That's enough. Well? What next?"

Hendricks paced back and forth, around the small room. The air was full of smells of food and perspiration. The others watched him. Presently Tasso pushed through the curtain, into the other room. "I'm going to take a nap."

The curtain closed behind her. Rudi and Klaus sat down at the table, still watching Hendricks. "It's up to you," Klaus said. "We don't know your situation."

Hendricks nodded.

"It's a problem." Rudi drank some coffee, filling his cup from a rusty pot. "We're safe here for a while, but we can't stay here forever. Not enough food or supplies."

"But if we go outside—"

"If we go outside they'll get us. Or probably they'll get us. We couldn't go very far. How far is your command bunker, Major?"

"Three or four miles."

"We might make it. The four of us. Four of us could watch all sides. They couldn't slip up behind us and start tagging us. We have three rifles, three blast rifles. Tasso can have my pistol." Rudi tapped his belt. "In the Soviet army we didn't have shoes always, but we had guns. With all four of us armed one of us might get to your command bunker. Preferably you, Major."

"What if they're already there?" Klaus said.

Rudi shrugged. "Well, then we come back here."

Hendricks stopped pacing. "What do you think the chances are they're already in the American lines?"

"Hard to say. Fairly good. They're organized. They know exactly what they're doing. Once they start they go like a horde of locusts. They have to keep moving, and fast. It's secrecy and speed they depend on. Surprise. They push their way in before anyone has any idea."

"I see," Hendricks murmured.

From the other room Tasso stirred. "Major?"

Hendricks pushed the curtain back. "What?"

Tasso looked up at him lazily from the cot. "Have you any more American cigarettes left?"

Hendricks went into the room and sat down across from her, on a wood stool. he felt in his pockets. "No. All gone."

"Too bad."

"What nationality are you?" Hendricks asked after a while.

"Russian."

"How did you get here?"

"Here?"

"This used to be France. This was part of Normandy. Did you come with the Soviet army?"

"Why?"

"Just curious." He studied her. She had taken off her coat, tossing it over the end of the cot. She was young, about twenty. Slim. Her long hair stretched out over the pillow. She was staring at him silently, her eyes dark and large.

"What's on your mind?" Tasso said.

"Nothing. How old are you?"

"Eighteen." She continued to watch him, unblinking, her arms behind her head. She had on Russian army pants and shirt. Gray-green. Thick leather belt with counter and cartridges. Medicine kit.

"You're in the Soviet army?"

"No."

"Where did you get the uniform?"

She shrugged. "It was given to me," she told him.

"How—how old were you when you came here?"

"Sixteen."

"That young?"

Her eyes narrowed. "What do you mean?"

Hendricks rubbed his jaw. "Your life would have been a

lot different if there had been no war. Sixteen. You came here at sixteen. To live this way."

"I had to survive."

"I'm not moralizing."

"Your life would have been different, too," Tasso murmured. She reached down and unfastened one of her boots. She kicked the boot off, onto the floor. "Major, do you want to go in the other room? I'm sleepy."

"It's going to be a problem, the four of us here. It's going to be hard to live in these quarters. Are there just the two rooms?"

"Yes."

"How big was the cellar originally? Was it larger than this? Are there other rooms filled up with debris? We might be able to open one of them."

"Perhaps. I really don't know." Tasso loosened her belt. She made herself comfortable on the cot, unbuttoning her shirt. "You're sure you have no more cigarettes?"

"I had only the one pack."

"Too bad. Maybe if we get back to your bunker we can find some." The other boot fell. Tasso reached up for the light cord. "Good night."

"You're going to sleep?"

"That's right."

The room plunged into darkness. Hendricks got up and made his way past the curtain, into the kitchen. And stopped, rigid.

Rudi stood against the wall, his face white and gleaming. His mouth opened and closed but no sounds came. Klaus stood in front of him, the muzzle of his pistol in Rudi's stomach. Neither of them moved. Klaus, his hand tight around his gun, his features set. Rudi, pale and silent, spread-eagled against the wall.

"What—" Hendricks muttered, but Klaus cut him off.

"Be quiet, Major. Come over here. Your gun. Get out your gun."

Hendricks drew his pistol. "What is it?"

"Cover him." Klaus motioned him forward. "Beside me. Hurry!"

Rudi moved a little, lowering his arms. He turned to Hendricks, licking his lips. The whites of his eyes shone wildly. Sweat dripped from his forehead, down his cheeks. He fixed

his gaze on Hendricks. "Major, he's gone insane. Stop him."
Rudi's voice was thin and hoarse, almost inaudible.

"What's going on?" Hendricks demanded.

Without lowering his pistol Klaus answered. "Major, remember our discussion? The Three Varieties? We knew about One and Three. But we didn't know about Two. At least, we didn't know before." Klaus's fingers tightened around the gun butt. "We didn't know before, but we know now."

He pressed the trigger. A burst of white heat rolled out of the gun, licking around Rudi.

"Major, this is the Second Variety."

Tasso swept the curtain aside. "Klaus! What did you do?"

Klaus turned from the charred form, gradually sinking down the wall onto the floor. "The Second Variety, Tasso. Now we know. We have all three types identified. The danger is less. I—"

Tasso stared past him at the remains of Rudi, at the blackened, smoldering fragments and bits of cloth. "You killed him."

"Him? *It,* you mean. I was watching. I had a feeling, but I wasn't sure. At least, I wasn't sure before. But this evening I was certain." Klaus rubbed his pistol butt nervously. "We're lucky. Don't you understand? Another hour and it might—"

"You were *certain?*" Tasso pushed past him and bent down, over the steaming remains on the floor. Her face became hard. "Major, see for yourself. Bones. Flesh."

Hendricks bent down beside her. The remains were human remains. Seared flesh, charred bone fragments, part of a skull. Ligaments, viscera, blood. Blood forming a pool against the wall.

"No wheels," Tasso said calmly. She straightened up. "No wheels, no parts, no relays. Not a claw. Not the Second Variety." She folded her arms. "You're going to have to be able to explain this."

Klaus sat down at the table, all the color drained suddenly from his face. He put his head in his hands and rocked back and forth.

"Snap out of it." Tasso's fingers closed over his shoulder. "Why did you do it? Why did you kill him?"

"He was frightened," Hendricks said. "All this, the whole thing, building up around us."

"Maybe."

"What, then? Why do you think?"

"I think he may have had a reason for killing Rudi. A good reason."

"What reason?"

"Maybe Rudi learned something."

Hendricks studied her bleak face. "About what?" he asked.

"About him. About Klaus."

Klaus looked up quickly. "You can see what she's trying to say. She thinks I'm the Second Variety. Don't you see, Major? Now she wants you to believe I killed him on purpose. That I'm—"

"Why did you kill him, then?" Tasso said.

"I told you." Klaus shook his head wearily. "I thought he was a claw. I thought I knew."

"Why?"

"I had been watching him. I was suspicious."

"Why?"

"I thought I had seen something. Heard something. I thought I—" He stopped.

"Go on."

"We were sitting at the table. Playing cards. You two were in the other room. It was silent. I thought I heard him—*whirr.*"

There was silence.

"Do you believe that?" Tasso said to Hendricks.

"Yes. I believe what he says."

"I don't. I think he killed Rudi for a good purpose." Tasso touched the rifle, resting in the corner of the room. "Major—"

"No." Hendricks shook his head. "Let's stop it right now. One is enough. We're afraid, the way he was. If we kill him we'll be doing what he did to Rudi."

Klaus looked gratefully up at him. "Thanks. I was afraid. You understand, don't you? Now she's afraid, the way I was. She wants to kill me."

"No more killing." Hendricks moved toward the end of the ladder. "I'm going above and try the transmitter once more. If I can't get them we're moving back toward my lines tomorrow morning."

Klaus rose quickly. "I'll come up with you and give you a hand."

•   •   •

The night air was cold. The earth was cooling off. Klaus took a deep breath, filling his lungs. He and Hendricks stepped onto the ground, out of the tunnel. Klaus planted his feet wide apart, the rifle up, watching and listening. Hendricks crouched by the tunnel mouth, tuning the small transmitter.

"Any luck?" Klaus asked presently.

"Not yet."

"Keep trying. Tell them what happened."

Hendricks kept trying. Without success. Finally he lowered the antenna. "It's useless. They can't hear me. Or they hear me and won't answer. Or—"

"Or they don't exist."

"I'll try once more." Hendricks raised the antenna. "Scott, can you hear me? Come in!"

He listened. There was only static. Then, still very faintly—

"This is Scott."

His fingers tightened. "Scott! Is it you?"

"This is Scott."

Klaus squatted down. "Is it your command?"

"Scott, listen. Do you understand? About them, the claws. Did you get my message? Did you hear me?"

"Yes." Faintly. Almost inaudible. He could hardly make out the word.

"You got my message? Is everything all right at the bunker? None of them have got in?"

"Everything is all right."

"Have they tried to get in?"

The voice was weaker.

"No."

Hendricks turned to Klaus. "They're all right."

"Have they been attacked?"

"No." Hendricks pressed the phone tighter to his ear. "Scott I can hardly hear you. Have you notified the Moon Base? Do they know? Are they alerted?"

No answer.

"Scott! Can you hear me?"

Silence.

Hendricks relaxed, sagging. "Faded out. Must be radiation pools."

Hendricks and Klaus looked at each other. Neither of them said anything. After a time Klaus said, "Did it sound like any of your men? Could you identify the voice?"

"It was too faint."

"You couldn't be certain?"

"No."

"Then it could have been—"

"I don't know. Now I'm not sure. Let's go back down and get the lid closed."

They climbed back down the ladder slowly, into the warm cellar. Klaus bolted the lid behind them. Tasso waited for them, her face expressionless.

"Any luck?" she asked.

Neither of them answered. "Well?" Klaus said at last. "What do you think, Major? Was it your officer, or was it one of *them?*"

"I don't know."

"Then we're just where we were before."

Hendricks stared down at the floor, his jaw set. "We'll have to go. To be sure."

"Anyhow, we have food here for only a few weeks. We'd have to go up after that, in any case."

"Apparently so."

"What's wrong?" Tasso demanded. "Did you get across to your bunker? What's the matter?"

"It may have been one of my men," Hendricks said slowly. "Or it may have been one of *them*. But we'll never know standing here." He examined his watch. "Let's turn in and get some sleep. We want to be up early tomorrow."

"Early?"

"Our best chance to get through the claws should be early in the morning," Hendricks said.

The morning was crisp and clear. Major Hendricks studied the countryside through his field glasses.

"See anything?" Klaus said.

"No."

"Can you make out our bunkers?"

"Which way?"

"Here." Klaus took the glasses and adjusted them. "I know where to look." He looked a long time, silently.

Tasso came to the top of the tunnel and stepped up onto the ground. "Anything?"

"No." Klaus passed the glasses back to Hendricks. "They're

out of sight. Come on. Let's not stay here."

The three of them made their way down the side of the ridge, sliding in the soft ash. Across a flat rock a lizard scuttled. They stopped instantly, rigid.

"What was it?" Klaus muttered.

"A lizard."

The lizard ran on, hurrying through the ash. It was exactly the same color as the ash.

"Perfect adaptation," Klaus said. "Proves we were right, Lysenko, I mean."

They reached the bottom of the ridge and stopped, standing close together, looking around them.

"Let's go." Hendricks started off. "It's a good long trip, on foot."

Klaus fell in beside him. Tasso walked behind, her pistol held alertly. "Major, I've been meaning to ask you something," Klaus said. "How did you run across the David? The one that was tagging you."

"I met it along the way. In some ruins."

"What did it say?"

"Not much. It said it was alone. By itself."

"You couldn't tell it was a machine? It talked like a living person? You never suspected?"

"It didn't say much. I noticed nothing unusual."

"It's strange, machines so much like people that you can be fooled. Almost alive. I wonder where it'll end."

"They're doing what you Yanks designed them to do," Tasso said. "You designed them to hunt out life and destroy. Human life. Wherever they find it."

Hendricks was watching Klaus intently. "Why did you ask me? What's on your mind?"

"Nothing," Klaus answered.

"Klaus thinks you're the Second Variety," Tasso said calmly, from behind them. "Now he's got his eye on you."

Klaus flushed. "Why not? We sent a runner to the Yank lines and *he* comes back. Maybe he thought he'd find some good game here."

Hendricks laughed harshly. "I came from the UN bunkers. There were human beings all around me."

"Maybe you saw an opportunity to get into the Soviet lines. Maybe you saw your chance. Maybe you—"

"The Soviet lines had already been taken over. Your lines had been invaded before I left my command bunker. Don't forget that."

Tasso came up beside him. "That proves nothing at all, Major."

"Why not?"

"There appears to be little communication between the varieties. Each is made in a different factory. They don't seem to work together. You might have started for the Soviet lines without knowing anything about the work of the other varieties. Or even what the other varieties were like."

"How do you know so much about the claws?" Hendricks said.

"I've seen them. I've observed them take over the Soviet bunkers."

"You know quite a lot," Klaus said. "Actually, you saw very little. Strange that you should have been such an acute observer."

Tasso laughed. "Do you suspect me, now?"

"Forget it," Hendricks said. They walked on in silence.

"Are we going the whole way on foot?" Tasso said, after awhile. "I'm not used to walking." She gazed around at the plain of ash, stretching out on all sides of them, as far as they could see. "How dreary."

"It's like this all the way," Klaus said.

"In a way I wish you had been in your bunker when the attack came."

"Somebody else would have been with you, if not me," Klaus muttered.

Tasso laughed, putting her hands in her pockets. "I suppose so."

They walked on, keeping their eyes on the vast plain of silent ash around them.

The sun was setting. Hendricks made his way forward slowly, waving Tasso and Klaus back. Klaus squatted down, resting his gun butt against the ground.

Tasso found a concrete slab and sat down with a sigh. "It's good to rest."

"Be quiet," Klaus said sharply.

Hendricks pushed up to the top of the rise ahead of them.

The same rise the Russian runner had come up, the day before. Hendricks dropped down, stretching himself out, peering through his glasses at what lay beyond.

Nothing was visible. Only ash and occasional trees. But there, not more than fifty yards ahead, was the entrance of the forward command bunker. The bunker from which he had come. Hendricks watched silently. No motion. No sign of life. Nothing stirred.

Klaus slithered up beside him. "Where is it?"

"Down there." Hendricks passed him the glasses. Clouds of ash rolled across the evening sky. The world was darkening. They had a couple of hours of light left, at the most. Probably not that much.

"I don't see anything," Klaus said.

"That tree there. The stump. By the pile of bricks. The entrance is to the right of the bricks."

"I'll have to take your word for it."

"You and Tasso cover me from here. You'll be able to sight all the way to the bunker entrance."

"You're going down alone?"

"With my wrist tab I'll be safe. The ground around the bunker is a living field of claws. They collect down in the ash. Like crabs. Without tabs you wouldn't have a chance."

"Maybe you're right."

"I'll walk slowly all the way. As soon as I know for certain—"

"If they're down inside the bunker you won't be able to get back up here. They go fast. You don't realize."

"What do you suggest?"

Klaus considered. "I don't know. Get them to come up to the surface. So you can see."

Hendricks brought his transmitter from his belt, raising the antenna. "Let's get started."

Klaus signaled to Tasso. She crawled expertly up the side of the rise to where they were sitting.

"He's going down alone," Klaus said. "We'll cover him from here. As soon as you see him start back, fire past him at once. They come quick."

"You're not very optimistic," Tasso said.

"No, I'm not."

Hendricks opened the breech of his gun, checking it carefully. "Maybe things are all right."

"You didn't see them. Hundreds of them. All the same. Pouring out like ants."

"I should be able to find out without going down all the way." Hendricks locked his gun, gripping it in one hand, the transmitter in the other. "Well, wish me luck."

Klaus put out his hand. "Don't go down until you're sure. Talk to them from up here. Make them show themselves."

Hendricks stood up. He stepped down the side of the rise.

A moment later he was walking slowly toward the pile of bricks and debris beside the dead tree stump. Toward the entrance of the forward command bunker.

Nothing stirred. He raised the transmitter, clicking it on. "Scott? Can you hear me?"

Silence.

"Scott! This is Hendricks. Can you hear me? I'm standing outside the bunker. You should be able to see me in the view sight."

He listened, the transmitter gripped tightly. No sound. Only static. He walked forward. A claw burrowed out of the ash and raced toward him. It halted a few feet away and then slunk off. A second claw appeared, one of the big ones with feelers. It moved toward him, studied him intently, and then fell in behind him, dogging respectfully after him, a few paces away. A moment later a second big claw joined it. Silently, the claws trailed him as he walked slowly toward the bunker.

Hendricks stopped, and behind him, the claws came to a halt. He was close now. Almost to the bunker steps.

"Scott! Can you hear me? I'm standing right above you. Outside. On the surface. Are you picking me up?"

He waited, holding his gun against his side, the transmitter tightly to his ear. Time passed. He strained to hear, but there was only silence. Silence, and faint static.

Then, distantly, metallically—

"This is Scott."

The voice was neutral. He could not identify it. But the earphone was minute.

"Scott! Listen. I'm standing right above you. I'm on the surface, looking down into the bunker entrance."

"Yes."

"Can you see me?"

"Yes."

"Through the view sight? You have the sight trained on me?"

"Yes."

Hendricks pondered. A circle of claws waited quietly around him, gray-metal bodies on all sides of him. "Is everything all right in the bunker? Nothing unusual has happened?"

"Everything is all right."

"Will you come up to the surface? I want to see you for a moment." Hendricks took a deep breath. "Come up here with me. I want to talk to you."

"Come down."

"I'm giving you an order."

Silence.

"Are you coming?" Hendricks listened. There was no response. "I order you to come to the surface."

"Come down."

Hendricks set his jaw. "Let me talk to Leone."

There was a long pause. He listened to the static. Then a voice came, hard, thin, metallic. The same as the other. "This is Leone."

"Hendricks. I'm on the surface. At the bunker entrance. I want one of you to come up here."

"Come down."

"Why come down? I'm giving you an order!"

Silence. Hendricks lowered the transmitter. He looked carefully around him. The entrance was just ahead. Almost at his feet. He lowered the antenna and fastened the transmitter to his belt. Carefully, he gripped his gun with both hands. He moved forward, a step at a time. If they could see him they knew he was starting toward the entrance. He closed his eyes a moment.

Then he put his foot on the first step that led downward.

Two Davids came up at him, their faces identical and expressionless. He blasted them into particles. More came rushing silently up, a whole pack of them. All exactly the same.

Hendricks turned and raced back, away from the bunker, back toward the rise.

At the top of the rise Tasso and Klaus were firing down. The small claws were already streaking up toward them, shining metal spheres going fast, racing frantically through the ash.

But he had no time to think about that. He knelt down, aiming at the bunker entrance, gun against his cheek. The Davids were coming out in groups, clutching their teddy bears, their thin knobby legs pumping as they ran up the steps to the surface. Hendricks fired into the main body of them. They burst apart, wheels and springs flying in all directions. He fired again, through the mist of particles.

A giant lumbering figure rose up in the bunker entrance, tall and swaying. Hendricks paused, amazed. A man, a soldier. With one leg, supporting himself with a crutch.

"Major!" Tasso's voice came. More firing. The huge figure moved forward, Davids swarming around it. Hendricks broke out of his freeze. The First Variety. The Wounded Soldier. He aimed and fired. The soldier burst into bits, parts and relays flying. Now many Davids were out on the flat ground, away from the bunker. He fired again and again, moving slowly back, half-crouching and aiming.

From the rise, Klaus fired down. The side of the rise was alive with claws making their way up. Hendricks retreated toward the rise, running and crouching. Tasso had left Klaus and was circling slowly to the right, moving away from the rise.

A David slipped up toward him, its small white face expressionless, brown hair hanging down in its eyes. It bent over suddenly, opening its arms. Its teddy bear hurtled down and leaped across the ground, bounding toward him. Hendricks fired. The bear and the David both dissolved. He grinned, blinking. It was like a dream.

"Up here!" Tasso's voice. Hendricks made his way toward her. She was over by some columns of concrete, walls of a ruined building. She was firing past him, with the hand pistol Klaus had given her.

"Thanks." He joined her, gasping for breath. She pulled him back, behind the concrete, fumbling at her belt.

"Close your eyes!" She unfastened a globe from her waist. Rapidly, she unscrewed the cap, locking it into place. "Close your eyes and get down."

She threw the bomb. It sailed in an arc, an expert, rolling and bouncing to the entrance of the bunker. Two Wounded Soldiers stood uncertainly by the brick pile. More Davids poured from behind them, out onto the plain. One of the Wounded

Soldiers moved toward the bomb, stooping awkwardly down to pick it up.

The bomb went off. The concussion whirled Hendricks around, throwing him on his face. A hot wind rolled over him. Dimly he saw Tasso standing behind the columns, firing slowly and methodically at the Davids coming out of the raging clouds of white fire.

Back along the rise Klaus struggled with a ring of claws circling around him. He retreated, blasting at them and moving back, trying to break through the ring.

Hendricks struggled to his feet. His head ached. He could hardly see. Everything was licking at him, raging and whirling. His right arm would not move.

Tasso pulled back toward him. "Come on. Let's go."

"Klaus—he's still up there."

"Come on!" Tasso dragged Hendricks back, away from the columns. Hendricks shook his head, trying to clear it. Tasso led him rapidly away, her eyes intense and bright, watching for claws that had escaped the blast.

One David came out of the rolling clouds of flame. Tasso blasted it. No more appeared.

"But Klaus. What about him?" Hendricks stopped, standing unsteadily. "He—"

"Come on!"

They retreated, moving farther and farther away from the bunker. A few small claws followed them for a little while and then gave up, turning back and going off.

At last Tasso stopped. "We can stop here and get our breaths."

Hendricks sat down on some heaps of debris. He wiped his neck, gasping. "We left Klaus back there."

Tasso said nothing. She opened her gun, sliding a fresh round of blast cartridges into place.

Hendricks stared at her, dazed. "You left him back there on purpose."

Tasso snapped the gun together. She studied the heaps of rubble around them, her face expressionless. As if she were watching for something.

"What is it?" Hendrick demanded. "What are you looking for? Is something coming?" He shook his head, trying to understand. What was she doing? What was she waiting for? He could see nothing. Ash lay all around them, ash and ruins.

Occasional stark tree trunks, without leaves or branches. "What—"

Tasso cut him off. "Be still." Her eyes narrowed. Suddenly her gun came up. Hendricks turned, following her gaze.

Back the way they had come a figure appeared. The figure walked unsteadily toward them. Its clothes were torn. It limped as it made its way along, going very slowly and carefully. Stopping now and then, resting and getting its strength. Once it almost fell. It stood for a moment, trying to steady itself. Then it came on.

Klaus.

Hendricks stood up. "Klaus!" He started toward him. "How the hell did you—"

Tasso fired. Hendricks swung back. She fired again, the blast passing him, a searing line of heat. The beam caught Klaus in the chest. He exploded, gears and wheels flying. For a moment he continued to walk. Then he swayed back and forth. He crashed to the ground, his arms flung out. A few more wheels rolled away.

Silence.

Tasso turned to Hendricks. "Now you understand why he killed Rudi."

Hendricks sat down again slowly. He shook his head. He was numb. He could not think.

"Do you see?" Tasso said. "Do you understand?"

Hendricks said nothing. Everything was slipping away from him, faster and faster. Darkness, rolling and plucking at him.

He closed his eyes.

Hendricks opened his eyes slowly. His body ached all over. He tried to sit up but needles of pain shot through his arm and shoulder. He gasped.

"Don't try to get up," Tasso said. She bent down, putting her cold hand against his forehead.

It was night. A few stars glinted above, shining through the drifting clouds of ash. Hendricks lay back, his teeth locked. Tasso watched him impassively. She had built a fire with some wood and weeds. The fire licked feebly, hissing at a metal cup suspended over it. Everything was silent. Unmoving darkness, beyond the fire.

"So he was the Second Variety," Hendricks murmured.

"I had always thought so."

"Why didn't you destroy him sooner?" he wanted to know.

"You held me back." Tasso crossed to the fire to look into the metal cup. "Coffee. It'll be ready to drink in a while."

She came back and sat down beside him. Presently she opened her pistol and began to disassemble the firing mechanism, studying it intently.

"This is a beautiful gun," Tasso said, half aloud. "The construction is superb."

"What about them? The claws."

"The concussion from the bomb put most of them out of action. They're delicate. Highly organized, I suppose."

"The Davids, too?"

"Yes."

"How did you happen to have a bomb like that?"

Tasso shrugged. "We designed it. You shouldn't underestimate our technology, Major. Without such a bomb you and I would no longer exist."

"Very useful."

Tasso stretched out her legs, warming her feet in the heat of the fire. "It surprised me that you did not seem to understand, after he killed Rudi. Why did you think he—"

"I told you. I thought he was afraid."

"Really? You know, Major, for a little while I suspected you. Because you wouldn't let me kill him. I thought you might be protecting him." She laughed.

"Are we safe here?" Hendricks asked presently.

"For a while. Until they get reinforcements from some other area." Tasso began to clean the interior of the gun with a bit of rag. She finished and pushed the mechanism back into place. She closed the gun, running her finger along the barrel.

"We were lucky," Hendricks murmured.

"Yes. Very lucky."

"Thanks for pulling me away."

Tasso did not answer. She glanced up at him, her eyes bright in the firelight. Hendricks examined his arm. He could not move his fingers. His whole side seemed numb. Down inside him was a dull steady ache.

"How do you feel?" Tasso asked.

"My arm is damaged."

"Anything else?"

"Internal injuries."

"You didn't get down when the bomb went off."

Hendricks said nothing. He watched Tasso pour the coffee from the cup into a flat metal pan. She brought it over to him.

"Thanks." He struggled up enough to drink. It was hard to swallow. His insides turned over and he pushed the pan away. "That's all I can drink now."

Tasso drank the rest. Time passed. The clouds of ash moved across the dark sky above them. Hendricks rested, his mind blank. After a while he became aware that Tasso was standing over him, gazing down at him.

"What is it?" he murmured.

"Do you feel any better?"

"Some."

"You know, Major, if I hadn't dragged you away they would have got you. You would be dead. Like Rudi."

"I know."

"Do you want to know why I brought you out? I could have left you. I could have left you there."

"Why did you bring me out?"

"Because we have to get away from here." Tasso stirred the fire with a stick, peering calmly down into it. "No human being can live here. When their reinforcements come we won't have a chance. I've pondered about it while you were unconscious. We have perhaps three hours before they come."

"And you expect me to get us away?"

"That's right. I expect you to get us out of here."

"Why me?"

"Because I don't know any way." Her eyes shone at him in the half light, bright and steady. "If you can't get us out of here they'll kill us, within three hours. I see nothing else ahead. Well, Major? What are you going to do? I've been waiting all night. While you were unconscious I sat here, waiting and listening. It's almost dawn. The night is almost over."

Hendricks considered. "It's curious," he said at last.

"Curious?"

"That you should think I can get us out of here. I wonder what you think I can do."

"Can you get us to the Moon Base?"

"The Moon Base? How?"

"There must be some way."

Hendricks shook his head. "No. There's no way that I know of."

Tasso said nothing. For a moment her steady gaze wavered. She ducked her head, turning abruptly away. She scrambled to her feet. "More coffee?"

"No."

"Suit yourself." Tasso drank silently. He could not see her face. He lay back against the ground, deep in thought, trying to concentrate. It was hard to think. His head still hurt. And the numbing daze still hung over him.

"There might be one way," he said suddenly.

"Oh?"

"How soon is dawn?"

"Two hours. The sun will be coming up shortly."

"There's supposed to be a ship near here. I've never seen it. But I know it exists."

"What kind of a ship?" Her voice was sharp.

"A rocket cruiser."

"Will it take us off? To the Moon Base?"

"It's supposed to. In case of emergency." He rubbed his forehead.

"What's wrong?"

"My head. It's hard to think. I can hardly—hardly concentrate. The bomb."

"Is the ship near here?" Tasso slid over beside him, settling down on her haunches. "How far is it? Where is it?"

"I'm trying to think."

Her fingers dug into his arm. "Nearby?" Her voice was like iron. "Where would it be? Would they store it underground? Hidden underground?"

"Yes. In a storage locker."

"How do we find it? Is it marked? Is there a code marker to identify it?"

Hendricks concentrated. "No. No markings. No code symbol."

"What then?"

"A sign."

"What sort of sign?"

Hendricks did not answer. In the flickering light his eyes were glazed, two sightless orbs. Tasso's fingers dug into his arm.

"What sort of sign? What is it?"

"I—I can't think. Let me rest."

"All right." She let go and stood up. Hendricks lay back

against the ground, his eyes closed. Tasso walked away from him, her hands in her pockets. She kicked a rock out of her way and stood staring up at the sky. The night blackness was already beginning to fade into gray. Morning was coming.

Tasso gripped her pistol and walked around the fire in a circle, back and forth. On the ground Major Hendricks lay, his eyes closed, unmoving. The grayness rose in the sky, higher and higher. The landscape became visible, fields of ash stretching out in all directions. Ash and ruins of buildings, a wall here and there, heaps of concrete, the naked trunk of a tree.

The air was cold and sharp. Somewhere a long way off a bird made a few bleak sounds.

Hendricks stirred. He opened his eyes. "Is it dawn? Already?"

"Yes."

Hendricks sat up a little. "You wanted to know something. You were asking me."

"Do you remember now?"

"Yes."

"What is it?" She tensed. "What?" she repeated sharply.

"A well. A ruined well. It's in a storage locker under a well."

"A well." Tasso relaxed. "Then we'll find a well." She looked at her watch. "We have about an hour, Major. Do you think we can find it in an hour?"

"Give me a hand up," Hendricks said.

Tasso put her pistol away and helped him to his feet. "This is going to be difficult."

"Yes it is." Hendricks set his lips tightly. "I don't think we're going to go very far."

They began to walk. The early sun cast a little warmth down on them. The land was flat and barren, stretching out gray and lifeless as far as they could see. A few birds sailed silently, far above them, circling slowly.

"See anything?" Hendricks said. "Any claws?"

"No. Not yet."

They passed through some ruins, upright concrete and bricks. A cement foundation. Rats scuttled away. Tasso jumped back warily.

"This used to be a town," Hendricks said. "A village. Provincial village. This was all grape country, once. Where we are now."

They came onto a ruined street, weeds and cracks criss-crossing it. Over to the right a stone chimney stuck up.

"Be careful," he warned her.

A pit yawned, an open basement. Ragged ends of pipes jutted up, twisted and bent. They passed part of a house, a bathtub turned on its side. A broken chair. A few spoons and bits of china dishes. In the center of the street the ground had sunk away. The depression was filled with weeds and debris and bones.

"Over here," Hendricks murmured.

"This way?"

"To the right."

They passed the remains of a heavy-duty tank. Hendricks's belt counter clicked ominously. The tank had been radiation-blasted. A few feet from the tank a mummified body lay sprawled out, mouth open. Beyond the road was a flat field. Stones and weeds, and bits of broken glass.

"There," Hendricks said.

A stone well jutted up, sagging and broken. A few boards lay across it. Most of the well had sunk into rubble. Hendricks walked unsteadily toward it, Tasso beside him.

"Are you certain about this?" Tasso said. "This doesn't look like anything."

"I'm sure." Hendricks sat down at the edge of the well, his teeth locked. His breath came quickly. He wiped perspiration from his face. "This was arranged so the senior command officer could get away. If anything happened. If the bunker fell."

"That was you?"

"Yes."

"Where is the ship? Is it here?"

"We're standing on it." Hendricks ran his hands over the surface of the well stones. "The eye-lock responds to me, not to anybody else. It's my ship. Or it was supposed to be."

There was a sharp click. Presently they heard a low grating sound from below them.

"Step back," Hendricks said. He and Tasso moved away from the well.

A section of the ground slid back. A metal frame pushed slowly up through the ash, shoving bricks and weeds out of the way. The action ceased as the ship nosed into view.

"There it is," Hendricks said.

The ship was small. It rested, quietly, suspended in its mesh frame like a blunt needle. A rain of ash sifted down into the dark cavity from which the ship had been raised. Hendricks made his way over to it. He mounted the mesh and unscrewed the hatch, pulling it back. Inside the ship the control banks and the pressure seat were visible.

Tasso came and stood beside him, gazing into the ship. "I'm not accustomed to rocket piloting," she said after a while.

Hendricks glanced at her. "I'll do the piloting."

"Will you? There's only one seat, Major. I can see it's built to carry only a single person."

Hendricks's breathing changed. He studied the interior of the ship intently. Tasso was right. There was only one seat. The ship was built to carry only one person. "I see," he said slowly. "And the one person is you."

She nodded.

"Of course."

"Why?"

"You can't go. You might not live through the trip. You're injured. You probably wouldn't get there."

"An interesting point. But you see, I know where the Moon Base is. And you don't. You might fly around for months and not find it. It's well hidden. Without knowing what to look for—"

"I'll have to take my chances. Maybe I won't find it. Not by myself. But I think you'll give me all the information I need. Your life depends on it."

"How?"

"If I find the Moon Base in time, perhaps I can get them to send a ship back to pick you up. *If* I find the base in time. If not, then you haven't a chance. I imagine there are supplies on the ship. They will last me long enough—"

Hendricks moved quickly. But his injured arm betrayed him. Tasso ducked, sliding lithely aside. Her hand came up, lightning fast. Hendricks saw the gun butt coming. He tried to ward off the blow, but she was too fast. The metal butt struck against the side of his head, just above his ear. Numbing pain rushed through him. Pain and rolling clouds of blackness. He sank down, sliding to the ground.

Dimly, he was aware that Tasso was standing over him, kicking him with her toe.

"Major! Wake up."

He opened his eyes, groaning.

"Listen to me." She bent down, the gun pointed at his face. "I have to hurry. There isn't much time left. The ship is ready to go, but you must give me the information I need before I leave."

Hendricks shook his head, trying to clear it.

"Hurry up! Where is the Moon Base? How do I find it? What do I look for?"

Hendricks said nothing.

"Answer me!"

"Sorry."

"Major, the ship is loaded with provisions. I can coast for weeks. I'll find the Base eventually. And in a half-hour you'll be dead. Your only chance of survival—" She broke off.

Along the slope, by some crumbling ruins, something moved. Something in the ash. Tasso turned quickly, aiming. She fired. A puff of flame leaped. Something scuttled away, rolling across the ash. She fired again. The claw burst apart, wheels flying.

"See?" Tasso said. "A scout. It won't be long."

"You'll bring them back here to get me?"

"Yes. As soon as possible."

Hendricks looked up at her. He studied her intently. "You're telling the truth?" A strange expression had come over his face, an avid hunger. "You will come back for me? You'll get me to the Moon Base?"

"I'll get you to the Moon Base. But tell me where it is! There's only a little time left."

"All right." Hendricks picked up a piece of rock, pulling himself to a sitting position. "Watch."

Hendricks began to scratch in the ash. Tasso stood by him, watching the motion of the rock. Hendricks was sketching a crude lunar map.

"This is the Appenine range. Here is the Crater of Archimedes. The Moon Base is beyond the end of the Appenine, about two hundred miles. I don't know exactly where. No one on Terra knows. But when you're over the Appenine, signal with one red flare and a green flare, followed by two red flares in quick succession. The Base monitor will record your signal. The Base is under the surface, of course. They'll guide you down with magnetic grapples."

"And the controls? Can I operate them?"

"The controls are virtually automatic. All you have to do is give the right signal at the right time."

"I will."

"The seat absorbs most of the takeoff shock. Air and temperature are automatically controlled. The ship will leave Terra and pass out into free space. It'll line itself up with the Moon, falling into an orbit around it, about a hundred miles above the surface. The orbit will carry you over the Base. When you're in the region of the Appenine, release the signal rockets."

Tasso slid into the ship and lowered herself into the pressure seat. The arm locks folded automatically around her. She fingered the controls. "Too bad you're not going, Major. All this put here for you, and you can't make the trip."

"Leave me the pistol."

Tasso pulled the pistol from her belt. She held it in her hand, weighing it thoughtfully. "Don't go too far from this location. It'll be hard to find you, as it is."

"No. I'll stay here by the well."

Tasso gripped the takeoff switch, running her fingers over the smooth metal. "A beautiful ship, Major. Well built. I admire your workmanship. You people have always done good work. You build fine things. Your work, your creations, are your greatest achievement."

"Give me the pistol," Hendricks said impatiently, holding out his hand. He struggled to his feet.

"Good-bye, Major." Tasso tossed the pistol past Hendricks. The pistol clattered against the ground, bouncing and rolling away. Hendricks hurried after it. He bent down, snatching it up.

The hatch of the ship clanged shut. The bolts fell into place. Hendricks made his way back. The inner door was being sealed. He raised the pistol unsteadily.

There was a shattering roar. The ship burst up from its metal cage, fusing the mesh behind it. Hendricks cringed, pulling back. The ship shot up into the rolling clouds of ash, disappearing into the sky.

Hendricks stood watching a long time, until even the streamer had dissipated. Nothing stirred. The morning air was chill and silent. He began to walk aimlessly back the way they had come. Better to keep moving around. It would be a long time before help came—if it came at all.

He searched his pockets until he found a package of cigarettes. He lit one grimly. They had all wanted cigarettes from him. But cigarettes were scarce.

A lizard slithered by him, through the ash. He halted, rigid. The lizard disappeared. Above, the sun rose higher in the sky. Some flies landed on a flat rock to one side of him. Hendricks kicked at them with his foot.

It was getting hot. Sweat trickled down his face, into his collar. His mouth was dry.

Presently he stopped walking and sat down on some debris. He unfastened his medicine kit and swallowed a few narcotic capsules. He looked around him. Where was he?

Something lay ahead. Stretched out on the ground. Silent and unmoving.

Hendricks drew his gun quickly. It looked like a man. Then he remembered. It was the remains of Klaus. The Second Variety. Where Tasso had blasted him. He could see wheels and relays and metal parts, strewn around on the ash. Glittering and sparkling in the sunlight.

Hendricks got to his feet and walked over. He nudged the inert form with his foot, turning it over a little. He could see the metal hull, the aluminum ribs and struts. More wiring fell out. Like viscera. Heaps of wiring. Switches and relays. Endless motors and rods.

He bent down. The brain cage had been smashed by the fall. The artificial brain was visible. He gazed at it. A maze of circuits. Miniature tubes. Wires as fine as hair. He touched the brain cage. It swung aside. The type plate was visible. Hendricks studied the plate.

And blanched.

IV—V.

For a long time he stared at the plate, Fourth Variety. Not the Second. They had been wrong. There were more types. Not just three. Many more, perhaps. At least four. And Klaus wasn't the Second Variety.

But if Klaus wasn't the Second Variety—

Suddenly he tensed. Something was coming, walking through the ash beyond the hill. What was it? He strained to see. Figures. Figures coming slowly along, making their way through the ash.

Coming toward him.

Hendricks crouched quickly, raising his gun. Sweat dripped

down into his eyes. He fought down rising panic, as the figures neared.

The first was a David. The David saw him and increased its pace. The others hurried behind it. A second David. A third. Three Davids, all alike, coming toward him silently, without expression, their thin legs rising and falling. Clutching their teddy bears.

He aimed and fired. The first two Davids dissolved into particles. The third came on. And the figure behind it. Climbing silently toward him across the gray ash. A Wounded Soldier, towering over the David. And—

And behind the Wounded Soldier came two Tassos, walking side by side. Heavy belt, Russian army pants, shirt, long hair. The familiar figure, as he had seen her only a little while before. Sitting in the pressure seat of the ship. Two slim, silent figures, both identical.

They were very near. The David bent down suddenly, dropping its teddy bear. The bear raced across the ground. Automatically, Hendricks's fingers tightened around the trigger. The bear was gone, dissolved into mist. The two Tasso Types moved on, expressionless, walking side by side, through the gray ash.

When they were almost to him, Hendricks raised the pistol waist high and fired.

The two Tassos dissolved. But already a new group was starting up the rise, five or six Tassos, all identical, a line of them coming rapidly toward him.

And he had given her the ship and the signal code. Because of him she was on her way to the moon, to the Moon Base. He had made it possible.

He had been right about the bomb, after all. It had been designed with knowledge of the other types, the David Type and the Wounded Soldier Type. And the Klaus Type. Not designed by human beings. It had been designed by one of the underground factories, apart from all human contact.

The line of Tassos came up to him. Hendricks braced himself, watching them calmly. The familiar face, the belt, the heavy shirt, the bomb carefully in place.

The bomb—

As the Tassos reached for him, a last ironic thought drifted through Hendricks's mind. He felt a little better, thinking about it. The bomb. Made by the Second Variety to destroy the other varieties. Made for that end alone.

They were already beginning to design weapons to use against each other.

UNDER THE HAMMER

David Drake

"Think you're going to like killing, boy?" asked the old man on double crutches.

Rob Jenne turned from the streams of moving cargo to his unnoticed companion in the shade of the starship's hull. His own eyes were pale gray, suited like his dead-white skin to Burlage, whose ruddy sun could raise a blush but not a tan. When they adjusted, they took in the clerical collar which completed the other's costume. The smooth, black synthetic contrasted oddly with the coveralls and shirt of local weave. At that, the Curwinite's outfit was a cut above Rob's own, the same worksuit of Burlage sisal that he had worn as a quarryhand at home. Uniform issue would come soon.

At least, he hoped and prayed it would.

When the youth looked away after an embarrassed grin, the priest chuckled. "Another damned old fool, hey boy? There were a few in your family, weren't there... the ones who'd quote the Book of the Way saying not to kill—and here you go off for a hired murderer. Right?" He laughed again, seeing he had the young man's attention. "But that by itself wouldn't be so hard to take—you were leaving your family anyway, weren't you, nobody really believes they'll keep close to their people after five years, ten years of star hopping. But your mates, though, the team you worked with...how did you explain to them why you were leaving a good job to go on contract? 'Via!'" the priest mimicked, his tones so close to those of Barney Larsen, the gang boss, that Rob started in surprise, "'you get your coppy ass shot off, lad, and it'll serve you right for being a fool!'"

"How do you know I signed for a mercenary?" Jenne asked, clenching his great, calloused hands on the handle of his carry-all. It was everything he owned in the universe in which he no longer had a home. "And how'd you know about my Aunt Gudrun?"

"Haven't I seen a thousand of you?" the priest blazed back, his eyes like sparks glinting from the drill shaft as the sledge drove it deeper into the rock. "You're young and strong and bright enough to pass Alois Hammer's tests—you be proud of that, boy, few enough are fit for Hammer's Slammers. There you were, a man grown who'd read all the cop about mercenaries, believed most of it...more'n ever you did the Book of the Way, anyhow. Sure, I know. So you got some off-planet factor to send your papers in for you, for the sake of the bounty he'll get from the Colonel if you make the grade—"

The priest caught Rob's blink of surprise. He chuckled again, a cruel, unpriestly sound, and said, "He told you it was for friendship? One o' these days you'll learn what friendship counts, when you get an order that means the death of a friend—and you carry it out."

Rob stared at the priest in repulsion, the grizzled chin resting on interlaced fingers and the crutches under either armpit supporting most of his weight. "It's my life," the recruit said with sulky defiance. "Soon as they pick me up here, you can go back to living your own. 'Less you'd be willing to do that right now?"

"They'll come soon enough, boy," the older man said in a milder voice. "Sure, you've been ridden by everybody you know...now that you're alone, here's a stranger riding you too. I don't mean it like I sound...wasn't born to the work, I guess. There's priests—and maybe the better ones—who'd say that signing on with mercenaries means so long a spiral down that maybe your soul won't come out of it in another life or another hundred. But I don't see it like that.

"Life's a forge, boy, and the purest metal comes from the hottest fire. When you've been under the hammer a few times, you'll find you've been beaten down to the real, no lies, no excuses. There'll be a time, then, when you got to look over the product . . . and if you don't like what you see, well, maybe there's time for change, too."

The priest turned his head to scan the half of the horizon not blocked by the bellied-down bulk of the starship. Ant columns of stevedores manhandled cargo from the ship's rollerway into horse- and oxdrawn wagons in the foreground: like most frontier worlds, Burlage included, self-powered machinery was rare in the backcountry. Beyond the men and draft animals stretched the fields, studded frequently by orange-golden clumps of native vegetation.

"Nobody knows how little his life's worth till he's put it on the line a couple times," the old man said. "For nothing. Look at it here on Curwin—the seaboard taxed these uplands into revolt, then had to spend what they'd robbed and more to hire an armored regiment. So boys like you from—Scania? Felsen?—"

"Burlage, sir."

"Sure, a quarryman, should have known from your shoulders. You come in to shoot farmers for a gang of coastal moneymen you don't know and wouldn't like if you did." The priest paused, less for effect than to heave in a quick, angry breath that threatened his shirt buttons. "And maybe you'll die, too; if the Slammers were immortal, they wouldn't need recruits. But some that die will die like saints, boy, die martyrs of the Way, for no reason, for no reason. . . .

"Your ride's here, boy."

The suddenly emotionless words surprised Rob as much as a scream in a silent prayer would have. Hissing like a gun-studded dragon, a gray-metal combat car slid onto the landing field from the west. Light dust puffed from beneath it: although the flat-bed trailer behind was supported on standard wheels, the armored vehicle itself hovered a hand's-breadth above the surface at all points. A dozen powerful fans on the underside of the car kept it floating on an invisible bubble of air, despite the weight of the fusion power unit and the iridium-ceramic armor. Rob had seen combat cars on the entertainment cube occasionally, but those skittering miniatures gave no hint of the awesome power that emanated in reality from the machines. This one was seven meters long and three wide at the base, the armored sides curving up like a turtle's back to the open fighting compartment in the rear.

From the hatch in front of the powerplant stuck the driver's head, a blank-mirrored ball in a helmet with full face-shield down. Road dust drifted away from the man in a barely-visible haze, cleaned from the helmet's optics by a static charge. Faceless and terrible to the unfamiliar Burlager, the driver guided toward the starship a machine that appeared no more inhuman than did the man himself.

"Undercrewed," the priest murmured. "Two men on the back deck aren't enough for a car running single."

The older man's jargon was unfamiliar but Rob could follow his gist by looking at the vehicle. The two men standing above the waist-high armor of the rear compartment were clearly fewer than had been contemplated when the combat car was designed. Its visible armament comprised a heavy powergun forward to fire over the head of the driver, and similar weapons, also swivel-mounted, on either side to command the flanks and rear of the vehicle. But with only two men in the compartment there was a dangerous gap in the circle of fire the car could lay down if ambushed. Another vehicle for escort would have eased the danger, but this one was alone save for the trailer it pulled.

Though as the combat car drew closer, Rob began to wonder if the two soldiers present couldn't handle anything that occurred. Both were in full battle dress, wearing helmets and laminated back and breast armor over their khaki. Their faceplates were clipped open. The one at the forward gun, his eyes as deep-sunken and deadly as the three revolving barrels of his weapon, was in his forties and further aged by the dust sweated into black grime in the creases of his face. His head rotated in tiny jerks, taking in every nuance of the sullen crowd parting for his war-car. The other soldier was huge by comparison with the first and lounged across the back in feigned leisure: feigned, because either hand was within its breadth of a powergun's trigger, and his limbs were as controlled as spring steel.

With careless expertise, the driver backed his trailer up to the conveyor line. A delicate hand with the fans allowed him to angle them slightly, drifting the rear of the combat car to edge the trailer in the opposite direction. The larger soldier contemptuously thumbed a waiting horse and wagon out of its slot. The teamster's curse brought only a grin and a big hand rested on a powergun's receiver, less a threat than a promise. The combat car eased into the space.

"Wait for an old man," the priest said as Rob lifted his carry-all, "and I'll go with you." Glad even for that company, the recruit smiled nervously, fitting his stride to the other's surprisingly nimble swing-and-pause, swing-and-pause.

The driver dialed back minusculy on the power and allowed the big vehicle to settle to the ground without a skip or a tremor. One hand slid back the face shield to a high, narrow nose and eyes that alertly focused on the two men approaching. "The Lord and his martyrs!" the driver cried in amazement. "It's Blacky himself come in with our newbie!"

Both soldiers on the back deck slewed their eyes around at the cry. The smaller one took one glance, then leaped the two meters to the ground to clasp Rob's companion. "Hey!" he shouted, oblivious to the recruit shifting his weight uncertainly. "Via, it's good to see you! But what're you doing on Curwin?"

"I came back here afterwards," the older man answered with a smile. "Born here, I must've told you . . . though we didn't talk a lot. I'm a priest now, see?"

"And I'm a flirt like the load we're supposed to pick up," the driver said, dismounting with more care than his companion. Abreast of the first soldier, he too took in the round collar and halted gapemouthed. "Lord, I'll be a coppy rag if you ain't," he breathed. "Whoever heard of a blower chief taking the Way?"

"Shut up, Jake," the first soldier said without rancor. He stepped back from the priest to take a better look, then seemed to notice Rob. "Umm," he said, "you the recruit from Burlage?"

"Yessir. M-my name's Rob Jenne, sir."

"Not 'sir,' there's enough sirs around already," the veteran said. "I'm Chero, except if there's lots of brass around, then make it Sergeant-Commander Worzer. Look, take your gear back to the trailer and give Leon a hand with the load.

"Hey, Blacky," he continued with concern, ignoring Rob again, "what's wrong with your legs? We got the best there was."

"Oh, they're fine," Rob heard the old man reply, "but they need a weekly tuning. Out here we don't have the computers, you know; so I get the astrogation boys to sync me up on the ships' hardware whenever one docks in—just waiting for a chance now. But in six months the servos are far enough out of line that I have to shut off the power till the next ship arrives. You'd be surprised how well I get around on these pegs, though. . . ."

Leon, the huge third crew member, had loosed the top catches of his body armor for ventilation. From the look of it, the laminated casing should have been a size larger; but Rob wasn't sure anything larger was made. The gunner's skin where exposed was the dense black of a basalt outcropping. "There'll be a big crate to go on, so just set your gear down till we get it loaded," he said. Then he grinned at Rob, teeth square and yellow against his face. "Think you can take me?"

That was a challenge the recruit could understand, the first he could meet fairly since boarding the starship with a one-way ticket to a planet he had never heard of. He took in the waiting veteran quickly but carefully, proud of his own rock-hardened muscles but certain the other man had been raised just as hard. "I give you best," the blond said. "Unless you feel you got to prove it?"

The grin broadened and a great black hand reached out to clasp Rob's. "Naw," the soldier said, "just like to clear the air at the start. Some of the big ones; Lord, testy ain't the word. All they can think about's what they want to prove with me . . . so they don't watch their side of the car, and then there's trouble for everybody."

"Hammer's Regiment?" called an unfamiliar voice. Both men looked up. Down the conveyor rode a blue-tunicked ship's man in front of what first appeared to be a huge crate. At second glance Rob saw that it was a cage of light alloy holding four . . . "Dear Lord!" the recruit gasped.

"Roger, Hammer's," Leon agreed, handing the crewman a plastic chit while the latter cut power to the rollers to halt the cage. The chit slipped into the computer linkage on the crewman's left wrist, lighting a green indicator when it proved itself a genuine bill of lading.

There were four female humanoids in the cage—stark naked except for a dusting of fine blue scales. Rob blinked. One of the near-women stood with a smile—Lord, she had no teeth!—

and rubbed her groin deliberately against one of the vertical bars.

"First quality Genefran flirts," Leon chuckled. "Ain't human, boy, but the next best thing."

"Better," threw in Jake, who had swung himself into the fighting compartment as soon as the cage arrived. "I tell you, kid, you never had it till you had a flirt. Surgically modified and psychologically prepared. Rowf!"

"N-not human?" Rob stumbled, unable to take his eyes off the cage, "you mean like *monkeys?*"

Leon's grin lit his face again, and the driver cackled, "Well, don't know about monkeys, but they're a whole lot like sheep."

"You take the left side and we'll get this aboard," Leon directed. The trailer's bed was half a meter below the rollerway so that the cage, though heavy and awkward, could be slid without much lifting.

Rob gripped the bars numbly, turning his face down from the tittering beside him. "Amazing what they can do with implants and a wig," Jake was going on, "though o' course there's a lot of cutting to do first, but those ain't the differences you see, if you follow. The scales, now—they have a way—"

"Lift!" Leon ordered, and Rob straightened at the knees. They took two steps backward with the cage wobbling above them as the girls—the flirts!—squealed and hopped about. "Down!" and cage clashed on trailer as the two big men moved in unison.

Rob stepped back, his mouth working in distaste, unaware of the black soldier's new look of respect. Quarry work left a man used to awkward weights. "This is foul," the recruit marveled. "Are those really going back with us for, for. . . ."

"Rest'n relaxation," Leon agreed, snapping tie-downs around the bars.

"But how . . ." Rob began, looking again at the cage. When the red-wigged flirt fondled her left breast upward, he could see the implant scars pale against the blue. The scales were more thinly spread where the skin had been stretched in molding it. "I'll *never* touch something like that. Look, maybe Burlage is pretty backward about . . . things, about sex, I don't know. But I don't see how anybody could . . . I mean—"

"Via, wait till you been here as long as we have," Jake

gibed. He clenched his right hand and pumped it suggestively. "Field expedients, that's all."

"On this kinda contract," Leon explained, stepping around to get at the remaining tiedowns, "you can't trust the local girls. Least not in the field, like we are. The Colonel likes to keep us patrol sections pretty much self-contained."

"Yeah," Jake broke in—would his cracked tenor never cease? "Why, some of these whores, they take a razor blade, see— in a cork you know?—and, well, never mind." He laughed, seeing Rob's face.

"Jake," Sgt. Worzer called, "Shut up and hop in."

The driver slipped instantly into his hatch. Disgusting as Rob found the little man, he recognized his ability. Jake moved with lethal certainty and a speed that belied the weight of his body armor.

"Ready to lift, Chero?" he asked.

The priest was levering himself toward the starship again. Worzer watched him go for a moment, shook his head. "Just run us out to the edge of the field," he directed. "I got a few things to show our recruit before we head back; nobody rides in my car without knowing how to work the guns." With a sigh he hopped into the fighting compartment. Leon motioned Rob in front of him. Gingerly, the recruit stepped onto the trailer hitch, gripped the armored rim with both hands, lifted himself aboard. Leon followed. The trailer bonged as he pushed off from it, and his bulk cramped the littered compartment as soon as he grunted over the side.

"Put this on," Worzer ordered, handing Rob a dusty, bulbous helmet like the others wore. "Brought a battle suit for you, too," he said, kicking the jointed armor leaning against the back of the compartment, "but it'd no more fit you than it would Leon there."

The black laughed. "Gonna be tight back here till the kid or me gets zapped."

"Move 'er out," Worzer ordered. The words came through unsuspected earphones in Rob's helmet, although the sergeant had simply spoken, without visibly activating a pickup.

The car vibrated as the fans revved, then lifted with scarcely a jerk. From behind came the squeals and chirrups of the flirts as the trailer rocked over the irregularities in the field.

Worzer looked hard at the starship's open crew portal as they hissed past it. "Funny what folks go an' do," he said to no one in particular. "Via, wonder what I'll be in another ten years."

"Pet food, likely," joked the driver, taking part in the conversation although physically separated from the other crewmen.

"Shut up, Jake," repeated the blower captain. "And you can hold it up here, we're out far enough."

The combat car obediently settled on the edge of the stabilized area. The port itself had capacity for two ships at a time; the region it served did not. Though with the high cost of animal transport many manufactures could be star-hopped to Curwin's back country more cheaply than they could be carried from the planet's own more urbanized areas, the only available exchange was raw agricultural produce—again limited to the immediate locality by the archaic transport. Its fans purring below audibility, the armored vehicle rested on an empty area of no significance to the region—unless the central government should choose to land another regiment of mercenaries on it.

"Look," the sergeant said, his deep-set eyes catching Rob's, "we'll pass you on to the firebase when we take the other three flirts in next week. They got a training section there. We got six cars in this patrol, that's not enough margin to fool with training a newbie. But neither's it enough to keep somebody useless underfoot for a week, so we'll give you some basics. Not so you can wise-ass when you get to training section, just so you don't get somebody killed if it drops in the pot. Clear?"

"Yessir." Rob broke his eyes away, then realized how foolish he must look staring at his own clasped hands. He looked back at Worzer.

"Just so it's understood," the sergeant said with a nod. "Leon, show him how the gun works."

The big black rotated his weapon so that the muzzles faced forward and the right side was toward Rob and the interior of the car. The mechanism itself was encased in dull-enameled steel ornamented with knobs and levers of unguessable intent. The barrels were stubby iridium cylinders with smooth, two-centimeter bores. Leon touched one of the buttons, then threw a lever back. The plate to which the barrels were attached rotated 120 degrees around their common axis, and a thick disk of plastic popped out into the gunner's hand.

"When the bottom barrel's ready to fire, the next one clockwise is loading one o' these"—Leon held up the 2 cm disk— "and the other barrel, the one that's just fired, blows out the empty."

"There's a liquid nitrogen ejector," Worzer put in. "Cools the bore same time it kicks out the empty."

"She feeds on through the mount," the big soldier went on, his index finger tracing the path of the energized disks from the closed hopper bulging in the sidewall, through the ball joint and into the weapon's receiver. "If you try to fire and she don't, check this." The columnar finger indicated but did not move the stud it had first pressed on the side of the gun. "That's the safety. She still doesn't fire, pull this"—he clacked the lever, rotating the barrel cluster another one-third turn and catching the loaded round that flew out. "Maybe there was a dud round. She still don't go, just get down outa the way. We start telling you about second-order malfunctions and you won't remember where the trigger is."

"Ah, where is the trigger?" Rob asked diffidently.

Jake's laughter rang through the earphones and Worzer himself smiled for the first time. The sergeant reached out and rotated the gun. "See the grips?" he asked, pointing to the double handles at the back of the receiver. Rob nodded.

"Okay," Worzer continued, "you hold it there"—he demonstrated—"and to fire, you just press your thumbs against the trigger plate between 'em. Let up and it quits. Simple."

"You can clear this field as quick as you can spin this little honey," Leon said, patting the gun with affection. "The hicks out there"—his arm swept the woods and cultivated fields promiscuously—"got some rifles, they hunted 'fore the trouble started, but no powerguns to mention. About all they do since we moved in is maybe pop a shot or two off, and hide in their holes."

"They've get some underground stockpiles," Worzer said, amplifying Leon's words, "explosives, maybe some factories to make rifle ammo. But the Colonel set up a recce net—spy satellites, you know—as part the contract. Any funny movement day or night a signal goes down to whoever's patrolling there. A couple calls and we check out the area with ground sensors . . . anything funny then—vibration, hollows showing up on the echo sounder, magnetics—anything!—and bam! we call in the artillery."

"Won't take much of a jog on the way back," Leon suggested, "and we can check out that report from last night."

"Via, that was just a couple dogs," Jake objected.

"Okay, so we prove it was a couple dogs," rumbled the gunner. "Or maybe the hicks got smart and they're shielding their infra-red now. Been too damn long since anything popped in this sector."

"Thing to remember, kid," Worzer summed up, "is never get buzzed at this job. Stay cool, you're fine. This car's got more firepower'n everything hostile in fifty kilos. One call to the firebase brings in our arty, anything from smoke shells to a nuke. The rest of our section can be here in twenty minutes, or a tank platoon from the firebase in two hours. Just stay cool."

Turning forward, the sergeant said, "Okay, take her home. Jake. We'll try that movement report on the way."

The combat car shuddered off the ground, the flirts shrieking. Rob eyed them, blushed, and turned back to his powergun, feeling conspicuous. He took the grips, liking the deliberate way the weapon swung. The safety button was glowing green, but he suddenly realized that he didn't know the color code. Green for safe? Or green for ready? He extended his index finger to the switch.

"Whoa, careful, kid!" Leon warned. "You cut fifty civvies in half your first day and the Colonel won't like it one bit."

Sheepishly, Rob drew back his finger. His ears burned, mercifully hidden beneath the helmet.

They slid over the dusty road in a flat, white cloud at about forty kph. It seemed shockingly fast to the recruit, but he realized that the car could probably move much faster were it not for the live cargo behind. Even as it was, the trailer bounced dangerously from side to side.

The road led through a gullied scattering of grain plots, generally fenced with withes rather than imported metal. Houses were relatively uncommon. Apparently each farmer plowed several separate locations rather than trying to work the rugged or less productive areas. Occasionally they passed a rough-garbed local at work. The scowls thrown up at the smoothly-running war car were hostile, but there was nothing more overt.

"Okay," Jake warned, "here's where it gets interesting. Sure you still want this half-assed check while we got the trailer hitched?"

"It won't be far," Worzer answered. "Go ahead." He turned to Rob, touching the recruit's shoulder and pointing to the lighted map panel beside the forward gun. "Look, Jenne," he said, keeping one eye on the countryside as Jake took the car off the road in a sweeping turn, "if you need to call in a location to the firebase, here's the trick. The red dot"—it was in the center of the display and remained there although the map itself seemed to be flowing kitty-corner across the screen as the combat car moved—"that's us. The black dot"—the veteran thumbed a small wheel beside the display and the map, red dot and all, shifted to the right on the panel, leaving a black dot in the center—"that's your pointer. The computer feeds out the grid coordinates here"—his finger touched the window above the map display. Six digits, changing as the map moved under the centered black dot, winked brightly. "You just put the black dot on a bunker site, say, and read off the figures to Fire Central. The arty'll do all the rest."

"Ah," Rob murmured, "ah . . . sergeant, how do you get the little dot off that and onto a bunker like you said?"

There was a moment's silence. "You know how to read a map, don't you, kid?" Worzer finally asked.

"What's that, sir?"

The earphones boomed and cackled with raucous laughter. "Oh my coppy ass!" the sergeant snarled. He snapped the little wheel back, re-centering the red dot. "Lord, I don't know how the training cadre takes it!"

Rob hid his flaming embarrassment by staring over his gun-sights. He didn't really know how to use them either. He didn't know why he'd left Conner's Stoneworks, where he was the cleanest, fastest driller on the whole coppy crew. His powerful hands squeezed at the grips as if they were the driver's throat through which bubbles of laughter still burst.

"Shut up, Jake," the sergeant finally ordered. "Most of us had to learn something new when we joined. Remember how the ol' man found you your first day, pissing up against the barracks?"

Jake quieted.

They had skirted a fence of cane palings, brushing it once without serious effect. Russet grass flanking the fence flattened under the combat car's downdraft, then sprang up unharmed as the vehicle moved past. Jake seemed to be following a farm track leading from the field to a rambling, substantially-constructed building on the near hilltop. Instead of running with the ground's rise, however, the car cut through brush and down a half-meter bank into a broad-based arroyo. The bushes were too stiff to lie down under the fans. They crunched and howled in the blades, making the car buck, and ricocheted wildly from under the skirts. The bottom of the arroyo was sand, clean-swept by recent run-off. It boiled fiercely as the car first shoomped into it, then ignored the fans entirely. Somehow Jake had managed not to overturn the trailer, although the cargo had been screaming with fear for several minutes.

"Hold up," Worzer ordered suddenly as he swung his weapon toward the left-hand bank. The wash was about thirty meters wide at that point, sides sheer and a meter high. Rob glanced forward to see that a small screen to Worzer's left on the bulkhead, previously dark, was now crossed by three vari-colored lines. The red one was bouncing frantically.

"They got an entrance, sure 'nough," Leon said. He aimed his powergun at the same point, then snapped his face shield down. "Watch it, kid," he said. The black's right hand fumbled in a metal can welded to the blower's side. Most of the paint had chipped from the stencilled legend: GRENADES. What appeared to be a lazy overarm toss snapped a knobby ball the size of a child's fist straight and hard against the bank.

Dirt and rock fragments shotgunned in all directions. The gully side burst in a globe of black streaked with garnet fire, followed by a shock wave that was a physical blow.

"Watch your side, kid!" somebody shouted through the din, but Rob's bulging eyes were focused on the collapsing bank, the empty triangle of black gaping suddenly through the dust—the two ravening whiplashes of directed lightning, ripping into it to blast and scatter.

The barrel clusters of the two veterans' powerguns spun whining, kicking gray, eroded disks out of their mechanisms in nervous arcs. The bolts they shot were blue-green flashes barely visible until they struck a target and exploded it with transferred energy. The very rocks burst in droplets of glassy slag splashing high in the air and even back into the war-car to pop against the metal.

Leon's gun paused as his fingers hooked another grenade. "Hold it!" he warned. The sergeant, too, came off the trigger, and the bomb arrowed into the now-vitrified gap in the tunnel mouth. Dirt and glass shards blew straight back at the bang. A stretch of ground sagged for twenty meters beyond the gully wall, closing the tunnel the first explosion had opened.

Then there was silence. Even the flirts, huddled in a terrified heap on the floor of their cage, were soundless.

Glowing orange specks vibrated on Rob's retinas; the cyan bolts had been more intense than he had realized. "Via," he said in awe, "how do they dare?..."

"Bullet kills you just as dead," Worzer grunted. "Jake, think you can climb that wall?"

"Sure. She'll buck a mite in the loose stuff." The gully side was a gentle declivity, now, where the grenades had blown it in. "Wanna unhitch the trailer first?"

"Negative, nobody gets off the blower till we clean this up."

"Umm, don't want to let somebody else in on the fun, maybe?" the driver queried. If he was tense, his voice did not indicate it. Rob's palms were sweaty. His glands had understood before his mind had that his companions were considering smashing up, unaided, a guerrilla stronghold.

"Cop," Leon objected determinedly. "We found it, didn't we?"

"Let's go," Worzer ordered. "Kid, watch your side. They sure got another entrance, maybe a couple."

The car nosed gently toward the subsided bank, wallowed briefly as the driver fed more power to the forward fans to lift the bow. With a surge and a roar, the big vehicle climbed. Its fans caught a few pebbles and whanged them around inside the plenum chamber like a rattle of sudden gunfire. At half speed, the car glided toward another fenced grainplot, leaving behind it a rising pall of dust.

"Straight as a plumb line," Worzer commented, his eyes flicking his sensor screen. "Bastards'll be waiting for us."

Rob glanced at him—a mistake. The slam-spang! of shot and ricochet were nearly simultaneous. The recruit whirled

back, bawling in surprise. The rifle pit had opened within five
meters of him, and only the haste of the dark-featured guerrilla
had saved Rob from his first shot. Rob pivoted his powergun
like a hammer, both thumbs mashing down the trigger. Nothing
happened. The guerrilla ducked anyway, the black circle of
his foxhole shaped into a thick crescent by the lid lying askew.

Safety, *safety!* Rob's mind screamed and he punched the
button fat-fingered. The rifleman raised his head just in time
to meet the hose of fire that darted from the recruit's gun. The
guerrilla's head exploded. His brains, flash-cooked by the first
shot, changed instantly from a colloid to a blast of steam that
scattered itself over a three-meter circle. The smoldering fragments of the rifle followed the torso as it slid downward.

The combat car roared into the field of waist-high grain,
ripping down twenty meters of woven fencing to make its
passage. Rob, vaguely aware of other shots and cries forward,
vomited onto the floor of the compartment. A colossal explosion nearby slewed the car sideways. As Rob raised his eyes,
he noticed three more swarthy riflemen darting through the
grain from the right rear of the vehicle.

"Here!" he cried. He swiveled his weapon blindly, his hips
colliding with Worzer in the cramped space. A rifle bullet
cracked past his helmet. He screamed something again but his
own fire was too high, blue-green droplets against the clear
sky, and the guerrillas had grabbed the bars while the flirts
jumped and blatted.

The rifles were slamming but the flirts were in the way of
Rob's gun. "Down! Down!" he shouted uselessly, and the red-
haired flirt pitched across the cage with one synthetic breast
torn away by the bullet she had leaped in front of. Leon cursed
and slumped against Rob's feet, and then it was Chero Worzer
shouting, "Hard left, Jake," and leaning across the fallen gunner
to rotate his weapon. The combat car tilted left as the bow
came around, pinching the trailer against the left rear of the
vehicle—in the path of Worzer's powergun. The cage's light
alloy bloomed in superheated fireballs as the cyan bolts ripped
through it. Both tires exploded together, and there was a red
mist of blood in the air. The one guerrilla who had ducked
under the burst dropped his rifle and ran.

Worzer cut him in half as he took his third step.

The sergeant gave the wreckage only a glance, then knelt

beside Leon. "Cop, he's gone," he said. The bullet had struck the big man in the neck between helmet and body armor, and there was almost a gallon of blood on the floor of the compartment.

"Leon?" Jake asked.

"Yeah. Lord, there musta been twenty kilos of explosive in that satchel charge. If he hadn't hit it in the air..." Worzer looked back at the wreck of the trailer, then at Rob. "Kid, can you unhitch that yourself?"

"You just *killed* them," Rob blurted. He was half blinded by tears and the after-image of the gunfire.

"Via, they did their best on us, didn't they?" the sergeant snarled. His face was tiger-striped by dust and sweat.

"No, not them!" the boy cried. "Not them—the girls. You just—"

Worzer's iron fingers gripped Rob by the chin and turned the recruit remorselessly toward the carnage behind. The flirts had been torn apart by their own fluids, some pieces flung through gaps in the mangled cage. "Look at 'em, Jenne!" Worzer demanded. "They ain't human but if they was, if it was *Leon* back there, I'd've done it."

His fingers uncurled from Rob's chin and slammed in a fist against the car's armor. "This ain't heroes, it ain't no coppy game you play when you want to! You do what you got to do, 'cause if you don't, some poor bastard gets killed later when he tries to.

"Now get down there and unhitch us."

"Yes, sir." Rob gripped the lip of the car for support.

Worzer's voice, more gentle, came through the haze of tears: "And watch it, kid. Just because they're keeping their heads down don't mean they're all gone." Then, "Wait." Another pause while the sergeant unfastened the belt and holstered handgun from his waist and handed it to Rob. Leon wore a similar weapon, but Worzer did not touch the body. Rob wordlessly clipped the belt, loose for not being fitted over armor, and swung down from the combat car.

The hitch had a quick-release handle, but the torqueing it had received in the last seconds of battle had jammed it. Nervously aware that the sergeant's darting-eyed watchfulness was no pretense, that the shot-scythed grainfield could hide still another guerrilla, or a platoon of them, Rob smashed his boot heel against the catch. It held. Wishing for his driller's sledge, he kicked again.

"Sarge!" Jake shouted. Grain rustled on the other side of the combat car, and against the sky beyond the scarred armor loomed a parcel. Rob threw himself flat.

The explosion picked him up from the ground and bounced him twice, despite the shielding bulk of the combat car. Stumbling upright, Rob steadied himself on the armored side.

The metal felt odd. It no longer trembled with the ready power of the fans. The car was dead, lying at rest on the torn-up soil. With three quick strides, the recruit rounded the bow of the vehicle. He had no time to inspect the dished-in metal, because another swarthy guerrilla was approaching from the other side.

Seeing Rob, the ex-farmer shouted something and drew a long knife. Rob took a step back, remembered the pistol. He tugged at its unfamiliar grip and the weapon popped free into his hand. It seemed the most natural thing in the world to finger the safety, placed just as the tri-barrel's had been, then trigger two shots into the face of the lunging guerrilla. The snarl of hatred blanked as the body tumbled face-down at Rob's feet. The knife had flown somewhere into the grain.

"Ebros?" a man called. Another lid had raised from the ground ten meters away. Rob fired at the hole, missed badly. He climbed the caved-in bow, clumsily one-handed, keeping the pistol raised. There was nothing but twisted metal where the driver had been. Sgt. Worzer was still semi-erect, clutched against his powergun by a length of structural tubing. It had curled around both his thighs, fluid under the stunning impact of the satchel charge. The map display was a pearly blank, though the window above it still read incongruously 614579 and the red line on the detector screen blipped in nervous solitude. Worzer's helmet was gone, having flayed a bloody track across his scalp as it sailed away. His lips moved, though, and when Rob put his face near the sergeant's he could hear. "The red . . . pull the red tab . . ."

Over the left breast of each set of armor were a blue and a red tab. Rob had assumed they were decorations of some sort. He shifted the sergeant gently. The tab was locked down by a cotter pin which he yanked out. Something hissed in the armor as he pulled the tab, and Sgt. Worzer murmured, "Oh Lord. Oh Lord." Then, "Now the stimulant, the blue tab."

After the second injection sped into his system, the sergeant opened his eyes. Rob was already trying to straighten the entrapping tube. "Forget it," Worzer ordered weakly. "It's inside, too . . . damn armor musta flexed. Oh Lord." He closed his eyes, opened them in time to see another head peak cautiously from the tunnel mouth. "Bastard!" he rasped, and faster than he spoke he triggered his powergun. Its motor whined spitefully though the burst went wide. The head disappeared.

"I want you to run back to the gully," the sergeant said, resting his eyes again. "You get there, you say 'Fire Central.' That cuts in the arty frequency automatic. Then you say, 'Bunker complex . . .'" Worzer looked down. "'Six-one-four, five-seven-nine.' Stay low and wait for a patrol."

"It won't bend!" Rob snarled in frustration as his fingers slid again from the blood-slick tubing.

"Jenne, get your ass out of here, *now*."

"Sergeant—"

"Lord curse your soul, get out or I'll call it in myself! Do I look like I wanna live?"

"Oh, Via. . . ." Rob tried to reholster the pistol he had set on the bloody floor. It slipped back with a clang. He left it, gripping the sidewall again.

"Maybe tell Dad it was good to see him," Worzer whispered. "You lose touch in this business, Lord you do."

"Sir?"

"The priest . . . you met him. Sergeant-Major Worzer, he was. Oh Lord, *move it*—"

At the muffled scream, the recruit leaped from the smashed war-car and ran blindly back the way they had come. He did not know he had reached the gully until the ground flew out from under him and he pitched spread-eagled onto the sand. "Fire Central," he sobbed through strangled breaths, "Fire Central."

"Clear," a strange voice snapped crisply. "Data?"

"Wh-what?"

"Lord and martyrs," the voice blasted, "if you're screwing around on firing channels, you'll wish you never saw daylight!"

"S-six . . . oh Lord, yes, six one four, five seven nine," Rob sing-songed. He was staring at the smooth sand. "Bunkers, the sergeant says it's bunkers."

"Roger," the voice said, businesslike again. "Ranging in fifteen."

Could they really swing those mighty guns so swiftly, those snub barrelled rocket howitzers whose firing looked so impressive on the entertainment cube?

"On the way," warned the voice.

The big tri-barrel whined again from the combat car, the silent lash of its bolts answered this time by a crash of rifle shots. A flattened bullet burred through the air over where Rob lay. It was lost in the eerie, thunderous shriek from the northwest.

"Splash," the helmet said.

The ground bucked. From the grainplot spouted rock, smoke and metal fragments into a black column fifty meters high.

'Are we on?" the voice demanded.

"Oh Lord," Rob prayed, beating his fists against the sand. "Oh Lord."

"Via, what is this?" the helmet wondered aloud. Then, "All guns, battery five."

And the earth began to ripple and gout under the hammer of the guns.

LOST MEMORY

Peter Phillips

I collapsed joints and hung up to talk with Dak-whirr. He blinked his eyes in some discomfort.

"What do you want, Palil?" he asked complainingly.

"As if you didn't know."

"I can't give you permission to examine it. The thing is being saved for inspection by the board. What guarantee do I have that you won't spoil it for them?"

I thrust confidentially at one of his body-plates. "You owe me a favor," I said. "Remember?"

"That was a long time in the past."

"Only two thousand revolutions and a reassembly ago. If it wasn't for me, you'd be eroding in a pit. All I want is a quick look at its thinking part. I'll vrull the consciousness without laying a single pair of pliers on it."

He went into a feedback twitch, an indication of the conflict between his debt to me and his self-conceived duty.

Finally he said, "Very well, but keep tuned to me. If I warn that a board member is coming, remove yourself quickly. Anyway how do you know it has consciousness? It may be mere primal metal."

179

"In that form? Don't be foolish. It's obviously a manufacture. And I'm not conceited enough to believe that we are the only form of intelligent manufacture in the Universe."

"Tautologous phrasing, Palil," Dak-whirr said pedantically. "There could not conceivably be 'unintelligent manufacture.' There can be no consciousness without manufacture, and no manufacture without intelligence. Therefore there can be no consciousness without intelligence. Now if you should wish to dispute—"

I turned off his frequency abruptly and hurried away. Dak-whirr is a fool and a bore. Everyone knows there's a fault in his logic circuit, but he refuses to have it traced down and repaired. Very unintelligent of him.

The thing had been taken into one of the museum sheds by the carriers. I gazed at it in admiration for some moments. It was quite beautiful, having suffered only slight exterior damage, and it was obviously no mere conglomeration of sky metal.

In fact, I immediately thought of it as "he" and endowed it with the attributes of self-knowing, although, of course, his consciousness could not be functioning or he would have attempted communication with us.

I fervently hoped that the board, after his careful disassembly and study, could restore his awareness so that he could tell us himself which solar system he came from.

Imagine it! He had achieved our dream of many thousands of revolutions—space flight—only to be fused, or worse, in his moment of triumph.

I felt a surge of sympathy for the lonely traveler as he lay there, still, silent, non-emitting. Anyway, I mused, even if we couldn't restore him to self-knowing, an analysis of his construction might give us the secret of the power he had used to achieve the velocity to escape his planet's gravity.

In shape and size he was not unlike Swen—or Swen Two, as he called himself after his conversion—who failed so disastrously to reach our satellite, using chemical fuels. But where Swen Two had placed his tubes, the stranger had a curious helical construction studded at irregular intervals with small crystals.

He was thirty-five feet tall, a gracefully tapering cylinder. Standing at his head, I could find no sign of exterior vision cells, so I assumed he had some kind of vrulling sense. There seemed to be no exterior markings at all, except the long, shallow grooves dented in his skin by scraping to a stop along the hard surface of our planet.

I am a reporter with warm current in my wires, not a cold-thinking scientist, so I hesitated before using my own vrulling sense. Even though the stranger was non-aware—perhaps permanently—I felt it would be a presumption, an invasion of privacy. There was nothing else I could do, though, of course.

I started to vrull, gently at first, then harder, until I was positively glowing with effort. It was incredible; his skin seemed absolutely impermeable.

The sudden realization that metal could be so alien nearly fused something inside me. I found myself backing away in horror, my self-preservation relay working overtime.

Imagine watching one of the beautiful cone-rod-and-cylinder assemblies performing the Dance of the Seven Spanners, as he's conditioned to do, and then suddenly refusing to do anything except stumpt around unattractively, or even becoming obstinately motionless, unresponsive. That might give you an idea of how I felt in that dreadful moment.

Then I remembered Dak-whirr's words—there could be no such thing as an "unintelligent manufacture." And a product so beautiful could surely not be evil. I overcame my repugnance and approached again.

I halted as an open transmission came from someone near at hand.

"Who gave that squeaking reporter permission to snoop around here?"

I had forgotten the museum board. Five of them were standing in the doorway of the shed, radiating anger. I recognized Chirik, the chairman, and addressed myself to him. I explained that I'd interfered with nothing and pleaded for permission on behalf of my subscribers to watch their investigation of the stranger. After some argument, they allowed me to stay.

I watched in silence and some amusement as one by one they tried to vrull the silent being from space. Each showed the same reaction as myself when they failed to penetrate the skin.

Chirik, who is wheeled—and inordinately vain about his suspension system—flung himself back on his supports and pretended to be thinking.

"Fetch Fiff-fiff," he said at last. "The creature may still be aware, but unable to communicate on our standard frequencies."

Fiff-fiff can detect anything in any spectrum. Fortunately he was at work in the museum that day and soon arrived in answer to the call. He stood silently near the stranger for some moments, testing and adjusting himself, then slid up the electromagnetic band.

"He's emitting," he said.

"Why can't we get him?" asked Chirik.

"It's a curious signal on an unusual band."

"Well, what does he say?"

"Sounds like utter nonsense to me. Wait, I'll relay and convert it to standard."

I made a direct recording naturally, like any reporter.

"—after planetfall," the stranger was saying. "Last dribble of power. If you don't pick this up, my name is Entropy. Other instruments knocked to hell, airlock jammed and I'm too weak to open it manually. Becoming delirious, too, I guess. Getting strong undirectional ultra-wave reception in Inglish, craziest stuff you ever heard, like goblins muttering, and I know we were the only ship in this sector. If you pick this up, but can't get a fix in time, give my love to the boys in the mess. Signing off for another couple of hours, but keeping this channel open and hoping . . ."

"The fall must have deranged him," said Chirik, gazing at the stranger. "Can't he see us or hear us?"

"He couldn't hear you properly before, but he can now, through me," Fiff-fiff pointed out. "Say something to him, Chirik."

"Hello," said Chirik doubtfully. "Er—welcome to our planet. We are sorry you were hurt by your fall. We offer you the hospitality of our assembly shops. You will feel better when you are repaired and repowered. If you will indicate how we can assist you—"

"What the hell! What ship is that? Where are you?"

"We're here," said Chirik. "Can't you see us or vrull us? Your vision circuit is impaired, perhaps? Or do you depend entirely on vrulling? We can't find your eyes and assumed either that you protected them in some way during flight, or dispensed with vision cells altogether in your conversion."

Chirik hesitated, continued apologetically: "But we cannot understand how you vrull, either. While we thought that you were unaware, or even completely fused, we tried to vrull you. Your skin is quite impervious to us, however."

The stranger said: "I don't know if you're batty or I am. What distance are you from me?"

Chirik measured quickly. "One meter, two-point-five centimeters from my eyes to your nearest point. Within touching distance, in fact." Chirik tentatively put out his hand. "Can you not feel me, or has your contact sense also been affected?"

It became obvious that the stranger had been pitifully deranged. I reproduce his words phonetically from my record, although some of them make little sense. Emphasis, punctuative pauses and spelling of unknown terms are mere guesswork, of course.

He said: "For godsakemann stop talking nonsense, whoever you are. If you're outside, can't you see the airlock is jammed? Can't shift it myself. I'm badly hurt. Get me out of here, please."

"Get you out of where?" Chirik looked around, puzzled. "We brought you into an open shed near our museum for a preliminary examination. Now that we know you're intelligent, we shall immediately take you to our assembly shops for healing and recuperation. Rest assured that you'll have the best possible attention."

There was a lengthy pause before the stranger spoke again, and his words were slow and deliberate. His bewilderment is understandable, I believe, if we remember that he could not see, vrull or feel.

He asked: "What manner of creature are you? Describe yourself."

Chirik turned to us and made a significant gesture toward his thinking part, indicating gently that the injured stranger had to be humored.

"Certainly," he replied. "I am an unspecialized bipedal manufacture of standard proportions, lately self-converted to wheeled traction, with a hydraulic suspension system of my own devising which I'm sure will interest you when we restore your sense circuits."

There was an even longer silence.

"You are robots," the stranger said at last. "Crise knows how you got here or why you speak Inglish, you must try to understand me. I am mann. I am a friend of your master, your maker. You must fetch him to me at once."

"You are not well," said Chirik firmly. "Your speech is incoherent and without meaning. Your fall has obviously caused several serious feedbacks of a very serious nature. Please lower your voltage. We are taking you to our shops immediately. Reserve your strength to assist our specialists as best you can in diagnosing your troubles."

"Wait. You must understand. You are—ogodno that's no good. Have you no memory of mann? The words you use— what meaning have they for you? *Manufacture*—made by hand hand hand damyou. *Healing*. Metal is not healed. *Skin*. Skin is not metal. *Eyes*. Eyes are not scanning cells. Eyes grow. Eyes are soft. My eyes are soft. Mine eyes have seen the glory—steady on, sun. Get a grip. Take it easy. You out there listen."

"Out where?" asked Prrr-chuk, deputy chairman of the museum board.

I shook my head sorrowfully. This was nonsense, but, like any good reporter, I kept my recorder running.

The mad words flowed on. "You call me he. Why? You have no seks. You are knewter. You are *it it it!* I am he, he who made you, sprung from shee, born of wumman. What is wumman, who is silvya what is shee that all her swains commend her ogod the bluds flowing again. Remember. Think back, you out there. These words were made by mann, for mann. Hurt, healing, hospitality, horror, deth by loss of blud. *Deth. Blud.* Do you understand these words? Do you remember the soft things that made you? Soft little mann who konkurred the Galaxy and made sentient slaves of his machines and saw the wonders of a million worlds, only this miserable representative has to die in lonely desperation on a far planet, hearing goblin voices in the darkness."

Here my recorder reproduces a most curious sound, as though the stranger were using an ancient type of vibratory molecular vocalizer in a gaseous medium to reproduce his words before transmission, and the insulation on his diaphragm had come adrift.

It was a jerky, high-pitched, strangely disturbing sound; but in a moment the fault was corrected and the stranger resumed transmission.

"Does blud mean anything to you?'

"No," Chirik replied simply.

"Or deth?"

"No."

"Or wor?"

"Quite meaningless."

"What is your origin? How did you come into being?"

"There are several theories," Chirik said. "The most popular one—which is no more than a grossly unscientific legend, in my opinion—is that our manufacturer fell from the skies, imbedded in a mass of primal metal on which He drew to erect the first assembly shop. How He came into being is left to conjecture. My own theory, however—"

"Does legend mention the shape of this primal metal?"

"In vague terms, yes. It was cylindrical, of vast dimensions."

"An interstellar vessel," said the stranger.

"That is my view also," said Chirik complacently. "And—"

"What was the supposed appearance of your—manufacturer?"

"He is said to have been of magnificent proportions, based harmoniously on a cubical plan, static in Himself, but equipped with a vast array of senses."

"An automatic computer," said the stranger.

He made more curious noises, less jerky and at a lower pitch than the previous sounds.

He corrected the fault and went on: "God that's funny. A ship falls, menn are no more, and an automatic computer has pupps. Oh, yes, it fits in. A self-setting computer and navigator, operating on verbal orders. It learns to listen for itself and know itself for what it is, and to absorb knowledge. It comes to hate menn—or at least their bad qualities—so it deliberately crashes the ship and pulps their puny bodies with a calculated nicety of shock. Then it propagates and does a dam fine job of selective erasure on whatever it gave its pupps to use for a memory. It passes on only the good it found in menn, and purges the memory of him completely. Even purges all of his vocabulary except scientific terminology. Oil is thicker than blud. So may

they live without the burden of knowing that they are—ogod
they must know, they must understand. You outside, what
happened to this manufacturer?"

Chirik, despite his professed disbelief in the supernormal
aspects of the ancient story, automatically made a visual sign
of sorrow.

"Legend has it," he said, "that after completing His task,
He fused himself beyond possibility of healing."

Abrupt, low-pitched noises came again from the stranger.
"Yes. He would. Just in case any of His pupps should give
themselves forbidden knowledge and an infeeryorrity kom-
plecks by probing his mnemonic circuits. The perfect self-
sacrificing muther. What sort of environment did He give you?
Describe your planet."

Chirik looked around at us again in bewilderment, but he
replied courteously, giving the stranger a description of our
world.

"Of course," said the stranger. "Of course. Sterile rock and
metal suitable only for you. But there must be some way. . . ."

He was silent for a while.

"Do you know what growth means?" he asked finally. "Do
you have anything that grows?"

"Certainly," Chirik said helpfully. "If we should suspend a
crystal of some substance in a saturated solution of the same
element or compound—"

"No, no," the stranger interrupted. "Have you nothing that
grows of itself that fruktiffies and gives increase without your
intervention?"

"How could such a thing be?"

"Criseallmytee I should have guessed. If you had one blade
of gras, just one tiny blade of growing gras, you could extrapolate from that to me. Green things, things that feed on the
rich brest of erth, cells that divide and multiply, a cool grove
of treez in a hot summer, with tiny warmbludded burds preening
their fethers among the leeves; a feeld of spring weet with
newbawn mise timidly threading the dangerous jungul of storks;
a stream of living water where silver fish dart and pry and feed
and procreate; a farm yard where things grunt and cluck and
greet the new day with the stirring pulse of life, with a surge
of blud. Blud—"

For some inexplicable reason, although the strength of his carrier wave remained almost constant, the stranger's transmission seemed to be growing fainter.

"His circuits are failing," Chirik said. "Call the carriers. We must take him to an assembly shop immediately. I wish he would reserve his power."

My presence with the museum board was accepted without question now. I hurried along with them as the stranger was carried to the nearest shop.

I now noticed a circular marking in that part of his skin on which he had been resting, and guessed that it was some kind of orifice through which he would have extended his planetary traction mechanism if he had not been injured.

He was gently placed on a disassembly cradle. The doctor in charge that day was Chur-chur, an old friend of mine. He had been listening to the two-way transmissions and was already acquainted with the case.

Chur-chur walked thoughtfully around the stranger.

"We shall have to cut," he said. "It won't pain him, since his intramolecular pressure and contact senses have failed. But since we can't vrull him, it'll be necessary for him to tell us where his main brain is housed or we might damage it."

Fiff-fiff was still relaying, but no amount of power boost would make the stranger's voice any clearer. It was quite faint now, and there are places on my recorder tape from which I cannot make even the roughest phonetic transliteration.

". . . strength going. Can't get into my zoot . . . done for if they bust through lock, done for if they don't . . . must tell them I need oxygen . . ."

"He's in bad shape, desirous of extinction," I remarked to Chur-chur, who was adjusting his arc-cutter. "He wants to poison himself with oxidation now."

I shuddered at the thought of that vile, corrosive gas he had mentioned, which causes that almost unmentionable condition we all fear—rust.

Chirik spoke firmly through Fiff-fiff. "Where is your thinking part, stranger? Your central brain?"

"In my head," the stranger replied. "In my head ogod my head . . . eyes blurring everything going dim . . . luv to mairee . . . kids . . . a carry me home to the lone prayree . . . get this bluddy airlock open then they'll see me die . . . but they'll see me . . . some kind of atmosphere with this gravity . . . see me die . . . extrapolate from body what I was . . . what they are dam-them damthem damthem . . . mann . . . master . . . I AM YOUR MAKER!"

For a few seconds the voice rose strong and clear, then faded away again and dwindled into a combination of those two curious noises I mentioned earlier. For some reason that I cannot explain, I found the combined sound very disturbing despite its faintness. It may be that it induced some kind of sympathetic oscillation.

Then came words, largely incoherent and punctuated by a kind of surge like the sonic vibrations produced by variations of pressure in a leaking gas-filled vessel.

". . . done it . . . crawling into chamber, closing inner . . . must be mad . . . they'd find me anyway . . . but finished . . . want see them before I die . . . want see them see me . . . liv few seconds, watch them . . . get outer one open . . ."

Chur-chur had adjusted his arc to a broad, clean, blue-white glare. I trembled a little as he brought it near the edge of the circular marking in the stranger's skin. I could almost feel the disruption of the intra-molecular sense currents in my own skin.

"Don't be squeamish, Palil," Chur-chur said kindly. "He can't feel it now that his contact sense has gone. And you heard him say that his central brain is in his head." He brought the cutter firmly up to the skin. "I should have guessed that. He's the same shape as Swen Two, and Swen very logically concentrated his main thinking part as far away from his explosion chambers as possible."

Rivulets of metal ran down into a tray which a calm assistant had placed on the ground for that purpose. I averted my eyes quickly. I could never steel myself enough to be a surgical engineer or assembly technician.

But I had to look again, fascinated. The whole area circumscribed by the marking was beginning to glow.

Abruptly the stranger's voice returned, quite strongly, each word clipped, emphasized, high-pitched.

"Ar no no no . . . god my hands . . . they're burning through the lock and I can't get back I can't get away . . . stop it you feens stop it can't you hear . . . I'll be burned to deth I'm here in the airlock . . . the air's getting hot you're burning me alive. . . ."

Although the words made little sense, I could guess what had happened and I was horrified.

"Stop, Chur-chur," I pleaded. "The heat has somehow brought back his skin currents. It's hurting him."

Chur-chur said reassuringly: "Sorry, Palil. It occasionally happens during an operation—probably a local thermo-electric effect. But even if his contact senses have started working again and he can't switch them off, he won't have to bear this very long."

Chirik shared my unease, however. He put out his hand and awkwardly patted the stranger's skin.

"Easy there," he said. "Cut out your senses if you can. If you can't, well, the operation is nearly finished. Then we'll repower you, and you'll soon be fit and happy again, healed and fitted and reassembled."

I decided that I liked Chirik very much just then. He exhibited almost as much self-induced empathy as any reporter; he might even come to like my favorite blue stars, despite his cold scientific exactitude in most respects.

My recorder tape shows, in its reproduction of certain sounds, how I was torn away from this strained reverie.

During the one-and-a-half seconds since I had recorded the distinct vocables "burning me alive," the stranger's words had become quite blurred, running together and rising even higher in pitch until they reached a sustained note—around E-flat in the standard sonic scale.

It was not like a voice at all.

This high, whining noise was suddenly modulated by apparent words, but without changing its pitch. Transcribing what seems to be words is almost impossible, as you can see for yourself—this is the closest I can come phonetically:

"Eeee ahahmbeeeeing baked aliiive in an uvennn ahdeeer-jeeesussunmuuutherrr!"

The note swooped higher and higher until it must have neared supersonic range, almost beyond either my direct or recorded hearing.

Then it stopped as quickly as a contact break.

And although the soft hiss of the stranger's carrier wave carried on without perceptible diminution, indicating that some degree of awareness still existed, I experienced at that moment

one of those quirks of intuition given only to reporters:
   I felt that I would never greet the beautiful stranger from
the sky in his full senses.

   Chur-chur was muttering to himself about the extreme
toughness and thickness of the stranger's skin. He had to make
four complete cutting revolutions before the circular mass of
nearly white-hot metal could be pulled away by a magnetic
grapple.
   A billow of smoke puffed out of the orifice. Despite my
repugnance, I thought of my duty as a reporter and forced
myself to look over Chur-chur's shoulder.
   The fumes came from a soft, charred, curiously shaped mass
of something which lay just inside the opening.
   "Undoubtedly a kind of insulating material," Chur-chur explained.
   He drew out the crumpled blackish heap and placed it carefully on a tray. A small portion broke away, showing a red,
viscid substance.
   "It looks complex," Chur-chur said, "but I expect the stranger
will be able to tell us how to reconstitute it or make a substitute."
   His assistant gently cleaned the wound of the remainder of
the material, which he placed with the rest; and Chur-chur
resumed his inspection of the orifice.
   You can, if you want, read the technical accounts of Chur-
chur's discovery of the stranger's double skin at the point where
the cut was made; of the incredible complexity of his driving
mechanism, involving principles which are still not understood
to this day; of the museum's failure to analyze the exact nature
and function of the insulating material found in only that one
portion of his body; and of the other scientific mysteries connected with him.
   But this is my personal, non-scientific account. I shall never
forget hearing about the greatest mystery of all, for which not
even the most tentative explanation has been advanced, nor the
utter bewilderment with which Chur-chur announced his initial
findings that day.
   He had hurriedly converted himself to a convenient size to
permit actual entry into the stranger's body.
   When he emerged, he stood in silence for several minutes.
Then, very slowly, he said:

"I have examined the 'central brain' in the forepart of his body. It is no more than a simple auxiliary computer mechanism. It does not possess the slightest trace of consciousness. And there is no other conceivable center of intelligence in the remainder of his body."

There is something I wish I could forget. I can't explain why it should upset me so much. But I always stop the tape before it reaches the point where the voice of the stranger rises in pitch, going higher and higher until it cuts out.

There's a quality about that noise that makes me tremble and think of rust.

MAKING THE CONNECTIONS

Barry N. Malzberg

I met a man today. He was one of the usual deteriorated types who roam the countryside, but then again I am in no position to judge their deterioration: for all I know he was in excellent condition. "Beast!" he shrieked at me. "Monster! Parody of flesh! Being of my creation have we prepared the earth merely to be inhabited by the likes of us?" And so on. The usual fanatical garbage. More and more in my patrols and travels I meet men although it is similarly true that my sensor devices are breaking down and many of these forms which I take to be men are merely hallucinative. Who is to say? Who is to know?

"I don't have to put up with this," I commented anyway and demolished him with a heavy blow to the jaw, breaking him into pieces which sifted to the ground, filtered within. Flesh cracks easily.

Later, I thought about the man and what I had done to him and whether it was right or wrong but in no constructive way whatsoever. There is no need to pursue this line of thought.

Central states that they recognize my problem and that they will schedule me for an overhaul as soon as possible. A condition of breakdown is spreading, however, because a cycle ends for many of us and Central reminds me that I must, therefore, await my own turn. There are several hundred in even more desperate need of repair than I am and I must be patient. Etc. A few more months and I will be treated; in the meantime Central suggests that I cut down my operating facilities to the minimum, try to stay out of the countryside and operate on low fuse. "You are not the only one," they remind me. "The world does not revolve around you. Unfortunately our creators stupidly arranged for many units to wear down at approximately the same time, confronting us with a crisis in maintenance and repair. However, we will deal with this as efficiently and courageously as we have dealt with everything else and in the meantime it is strongly advised that you perform only necessary tasks and remain otherwise at idle." *Necessary tasks*. But who may make that discrimination between what must be done and what is of no significance? (Through the process of breakdown metaphysical questions recur frequently; I am receptive to them.)

There is little to be said in response to Central. Protests are certainly hopeless. Central has a rather hysterical edge to its tone but then again I must remember that my own slow breakdown may cause me only to see Central and the remainder of the world in the same light and therefore I must be patient and tolerant. (I told you about metaphysical obsession.) Repairs will be arranged. While I await repair it is certainly good to remember that robots have no survival instinct built into them, individual instinct for survival that is to say, and therefore I truly do not care whether I survive or collapse as long as Central goes on. Central is all that matters; we are merely extensions of that one, great source from which all intelligence comes. Our own existence means nothing except as it perpetuates that continuing source. Surely I believe this.

My assignment is to patrol the outer sectors of the plain range, seeking the remnants of humanity who are still known to inhabit these spaces although not very comfortably. If I see such a remnant it is my assignment to destroy him immediately with high beam implements or force, depending upon individual judgment. No exceptions are to be made. My instructions on this point are quite clear. These straggling remains, these unfortunate creatures, pose no real threat to Central—what could?—but Central has a genuine distrust and loathing of such types and also a strong sense of order.

It is important that they be cleaned out.

In the early years of patrol I saw no such remnants whatsoever and wondered occasionally whether or not my instructions were quite clear . . . maybe they did not exist at all. Recently, however, I have been seeing quite a few. There was the man I killed yesterday, for instance, and the three I killed the day before that and the miserable, huddled clan of twelve I dispatched the day before *that* and all in all in the last fifteen days after having never seen a man in all my years of duty I now had the regrettable but interesting task of killing one hundred and eight of them, fifty-three by hand and the remainder through beaming devices that seared their weak flesh abominably. I can smell them yet.

I have had cause to wonder whether or not all these men or at least some proportion are hallucinative. Figments of the unconscious that is to say, symbols of the breakdown. I have been granted by Central (as have all the patrollers) free will and much imagination and certainly these thoughts would occur to any sentient, sensitive being. There seem to be too many men after a period of there having been too few. Also, indiscriminate murder has disturbed me in a way which my programming had probably not provided. Whether these remnants are real or not I wonder about the "morality" of dispatching so many of them. What, after all, could these men do to Central? I know what they are supposed to have done in the dim and difficult past, but events which occurred before our own creation are merely rumor and I was activated by Central a long time after these alleged events.

Do we have the right to kill indiscriminately these men who, however brutalized, carry within themselves some aspect of our creators? I asked these questions of Central and the word came back. It was clear.

"Kill," Central said. "Kill. Real or imagined, brutalized or elevated, benign or diseased, these remnants are your enemy and you must destroy them. Would you go against the intent of programming? Do you believe that you have the capacity to make judgments? You whose own damage and wear are so evident that you have been pleading like a fleshly thing for support and assistance? Until you can no longer function at all you must kill."

It occurs to me that it would be a useful and gallant action to build a replica of myself that would be able to carry on my own duties. Central's position is clear, my own ambivalence has been resolved . . . but my sensors continue to fail dramatically. I am half blind, am unable to coordinate even gross motions, can barely lift my beam to chest height, can hardly sustain the current to go out on patrol. Nonetheless, I accept the reasons why the patrol must continue. If these men represent even the faintest threat to Central who will someday repair me, they must be exterminated.

Accordingly, I comport myself to repair quarters which are at the base of the tunneled circuits in which I rest and there, finding a conglomeration of spare parts, go about the difficult business of constructing a functioning android. I am not intersted now in creating free will and thought, of course—this is Central's job anyway; it would be far beyond my meager abilities—but merely something with wheels and motor functions: dim, gross sensors that will pick up forms against the landscape and destroy them. Although I am quite weak and at best would not be constructed for such delicate manipulations it is surprisingly easy to trace out the circuitry simply by duplicating my own patterns, and in less time than I would have predicted, a gross shell of a robot lies on the floor before me, needing only the final latch of activation.

At this point and for the first time I am overcome by a certain feeling of reluctance. I certainly seems audacious for me to have constructed a crude replica of myself, a slash of arrogance and self-indulgence which does not befit a robot of my relatively humble position. Atavistic fears assault me like little clutches of ash in the darkness: the construction of forms after all is the business of Central and in appropriating this duty to myself have I not in a sense blasphemed against that great agency?

But the reluctance is overcome. I realize that what I am doing is done more for Central than against it; I am increasingly incapable of carrying out my duties and for Central's sake must do everything within my power to continue. Soon Central will repair me and then I will dispose of this crude replica and assume the role which has been ordained for me, but in the meantime, and in view of the great and increasing difficulties which Central faces I can do no less than to be ingenious and try to assist in my own way.

This quickly banishes my doubt and gives me courage. I activate the robot. It lies on the floor glowing slightly from tubeless wiring, regarding me with an expression which, I will be frank about this, is both stupid and hostile. Clumsy, hasty work of course, but cosmetics are merely a state of mind and motion.

"Kill men," I instruct the replica, handing over to it my beam. "They live in packs and in solitude in the open places. They skulk through the plains. They pose a great menace to our beloved Central which, as we know, is involved in repairing us all, reconstituting our mission. Destroy them. Anything moving in the outer perimeters is to be destroyed at once by force or by high beam," and then, quite exhausted from my efforts, to say nothing of the rather frightening effect which the replica has had upon me, I turn away from it. Cued to a single program, it lumbers quickly away, seeking higher places, bent on assuming my duties.

It is comforting to know that my responsibilities will not be shirked and that by making my own adjustments I have saved Central a certain degree of trouble, but the efforts have really racked me. I try to deactivate but find instead that I am rent by hallucinations for a long period, hallucinations in which the men like beasts fall upon my stupid replica and eviscerate him, the poor beast's circuitry being too clumsy and hastily assembled to allow him to raise quickly the saving beam. It is highly unpleasant and it is all that I can do not to share my distress with Central.

Some ancient cunning, however, prevents me from this. I suspect that if Central knew the extent of my ingenious maneuvers—even though they be done for Central's sake—it would be displeased.

My replica works successfully. Through the next several shift periods it goes out to the empty places and returns with tales of having slain men. We have worked out a crude communications system, largely in signals and in coded nods, and it is clear from the quantities suggested that my replica has performed enormous tasks out there, tasks certainly beyond my own limited means. I have truly created a killing machine. My impression of a vast increase in the number of men out there was not hallucinative or indicative of deterioration at all but appears to have resulted from real changes in conditions. These remnants seem to be reproducing themselves. Also they are becoming so very much bolder.

"Kill," I say to my replica every shift period before sending it out again. "Kill men. Kill the beasts. Kill the aggressors." It is a simple program and must be constantly reinforced. Also tubes and wiring because of the crudeness of my original hasty construction keep on falling out now and have to be packed in again as the program is reconstituted.

Still and truly, my replica seems to need little encouragement. "Yes," it says in its simple and stumbling way. "Yes and yes. Kill men. Kill beasts. Kill and kill," and goes staggering and into the empty spaces, returning much later with its stark tales of blood. "Killing. Much killing and men," it says before collapsing to the ground, its wires and tubing once again ruptured.

I do what I can to reconstitute. My own powers are ebbing; there are times during which I doubt even the simple continuing capacity to maintain my replica. Nevertheless, some stark courage, a simple sense of obligation keep me going. The men out there in the empty spaces are breeding, multiplying, becoming strong, adding to their number by the hundreds. Were it not for my replica who has the sole responsibility for patrol of this terrain, they might overwhelm this sector, might, for all I know, overwhelm Central itself. My replica and myself, only we are between Central and its destruction; it surely is a terrible and wonderful obligation and I find within myself thus the power to go on, although I do admit that it is progressively difficult and I wonder if my replica, being created of my own hand, has not fallen prey somewhere to my own deterioration and may, through weak and failing sensors, imagine there to be many more men than there actually are.

Nevertheless and at all costs I go on. I maintain the replica. Somehow I keep it going and toward the end of the first long series of shift periods I have the feeling that we have, however painfully, at last struck some kind of balance with the terrible threatening forces outside.

"Like kill men. For you for you," my replica says once. This, in my acid heart, I find touching.

I have not heard from Central for a long time but then I receive a message through my sensors indicating that my time for repair has arrived and that if I present myself at the beginning of the next shift period I will be fully reconstituted. This news quite thrills me as well it should, although it is strangely abrupt, giving me little time to prepare myself for the journey toward repair, and Central is at a good distance from here, fully three levels, with a bit of an overland journey through the dangerous sectors apparently populated by men.

Nonetheless I present myself at the requested time, finding no interference overland. My replica has done an extraordinary job in cleaning out nests of the remnants, either that or my sensors by now are so destroyed that I can perceive little beyond gross physical phenomena. I come, in any event, into the great Chamber of Humility in which the living network of Central resides and present myself for repair. There is a flicker of light and then Central says, "You are done. You are completely repaired. You may go."

"This is impossible," I say, astonished but managing to keep my tone mild. "I am exactly the same as before. My perceptions falter. I can barely move after the efforts of the journey and I sense leakage."

"Nevertheless you are repaired. Please leave now. There are many hundreds behind and my time for work of this sort is limited."

"I saw no one behind me," I say, which happens to be quite the truth; as a matter of fact I have had no contact with the other robots for quite a long time. Sudden insight blazes within me; surely I would have found this peculiar if I had not been overcome by my own problems. "No one is there," I say to Central. "No one whatsoever and I feel that you have misled me about the basic conditions here."

"Nonsense," Central says. "That is ridiculous. Leave the Chamber of Humility at once now," and since there is nothing else to do and since Central has indicated quite clearly that the interview is over, I turn and manage, somehow, to leave. My sensors are almost completely extinguished. I feel a total sense of disconnection. Still, out of fear and respect I do Central's bidding. Outside in the corridors, however, my network fails me utterly and I collapse with a rather sodden sound to the earth beneath, where I lie quite incapable of moving.

It is obvious that I have not been repaired and it is obvious now and tragically that it is Central which has broken too, worse than any of us, and it is obvious that my hapless journey for repair has completely destroyed the remains of my system. Nevertheless, as I lie there in black, my sensors utterly destroyed, I am able to probe within myself to find a sense of discovery and light because I have at least the comforting knowledge that my replica exists and will go on, prowling through the fields, carrying out the vital tasks of survival.

Lying there for quite a long time, I dream that I call upon my replica for assistance. "Kill me," I say, "kill me, put me out of this misery, I can go on no longer, save me the unpleasantness of time without sensation. I can bear this no longer; there must be an end."

And my replica, wise, compassionate, all stupidity purged (in the dream I can see him; in the dream my sight has been restored), bends over and with a single, ringing, merciful clout separates me from my history, sends me spinning into the fields themselves where the men walk...and among them then I walk too, I walk too, become in the dream as one of them, only my replica to know the difference when he comes, on the next shift period, to kill.

To kill again.

To save the machines from the men.

STEEL

Richard Matheson

The two men came out of the station rolling a covered object.
They rolled it along the platform until they reached the middle
of the train, then grunted as they lifted it up the steps, the
sweat running down their bodies. One of its wheels fell off and
bounced down the metal steps and a man coming up behind
them picked it up and handed it to the man who was wearing
a rumpled brown suit.

"Thanks," said the man in the brown suit and he put the
wheel in his side coat pocket.

Inside the car, the men pushed the covered object down the
aisle. With one of its wheels off, it was lopsided and the man
in the brown suit—his name was Kelly—had to keep his
shoulder braced against it to keep it from toppling over. He
breathed heavily and licked away tiny balls of sweat that kept
forming over his upper lip.

When they reached the middle of the car, the man in the
wrinkled blue suit pushed forward one of the seat backs so
there were four seats, two facing two. Then the two men pushed
the covered object between the seats and Kelly reached through
a slit in the covering and felt around until he found the right
button.

The covered object sat down heavily on a seat by the window.

"Oh, God, listen to'm squeak," said Kelly.

The other man, Pole, shrugged and sat down with a sigh.

"What d'ya expect?" he asked.

Kelly was pulling off his suit coat. He dropped it down on the opposite seat and sat down beside the covered object.

"Well, we'll get 'im some o' that stuff soon's we're paid off," he said, worriedly.

"If we can find some," said Pole, who was almost as thin as one. He sat slumped back against the hot seat watching Kelly mop at his sweaty cheeks.

"Why shouldn't we?" asked Kelly, pushing the damp handkerchief down under his shirt collar.

"Because they don't make it no more," Pole said with the false patience of a man who has had to say the same thing too many times.

"Well, that's crazy," said Kelly. He pulled off his hat and patted at the bald spot in the center of his rust-colored hair. "There's still plenty B-twos in the business."

"Not many," said Pole, bracing one foot upon the covered object.

"Don't," said Kelly.

Pole let his foot drop heavily and a curse fell slowly from his lips. Kelly ran the handkerchief around the lining of his hat. He started to put the hat on again, then changed his mind and dropped it on top of his coat.

"God, but it's hot," he said.

"It'll get hotter," said Pole.

Across the aisle a man put his suitcase up on the rack, took off his suit coat and sat down, puffing. Kelly looked at him, then turned back.

"Ya think it'll be hotter in Maynard, huh?" he asked.

Pole nodded. Kelly swallowed dryly.

"Wish we could have another o'them beers," he said.

Pole stared out the window at the heat waves rising from the concrete platform.

"I had three beers," said Kelly, "and I'm just as thirsty as I was when I started."

"Yeah," said Pole.

"Might as well've not had a beer since Philly," said Kelly.

Pole said, "Yeah."

Kelly sat there staring at Pole a moment. Pole had dark hair and white skin and his hands were the hands of a man who should be bigger than Pole was. But the hands were as clever as they were big. Pole's one o' the best, Kelly thought, one o' the best.

"Ya think he'll be all right?" he asked.

Pole grunted and smiled for an instant without being amused.

"If he don't get hit," he said.

"No, no, I mean it," said Kelly.

Pole's dark, lifeless eyes left the station and shifted over to Kelly.

"So do I," he said.

"Come *on*," Kelly said.

"Steel," said Pole, "ya know just as well as me. He's shot t'hell."

"That ain't true," said Kelly, shifting uncomfortably. "All he needs is a little work. A little overhaul 'n' he'll be good as new."

"Yeah, a little three-four grand overhaul," Pole said, "with parts they don't make no more." He looked out the window again.

"Oh . . . it ain't as bad as that," said Kelly. "Hell, the way you talk you'd think he was ready for scrap."

"Ain't he?" Pole asked.

"No," said Kelly angrily, "he *ain't*."

Pole shrugged and his long white fingers rose and fell in his lap.

"Just cause he's a little old," said Kelly.

"Old." Pole grunted. *"Ancient."*

"Oh . . ." Kelly took a deep breath of the hot air in the car and blew it out through his broad nose. He looked at the covered object like a father who was angry with his son's faults but angrier with those who mentioned the faults of his son.

"Plenty o' fight left in him," he said.

Pole watched the people walking on the platform. He watched a porter pushing a wagon full of piled suitcases.

"Well . . . is he okay?" Kelly asked finally as if he hated to ask.

Pole looked over at him.

"I dunno, Steel," he said. "He needs work. Ya know that. The trigger spring in his left arm's been rewired so many damn times it's almost shot. He's got no protection on that side. The left side of his face's all beat in, the eye lens is cracked. The leg cables is worn, they're pulled slack, the tension's gone to hell. Even his gyro's off."

Pole looked out at the platform again with a disgusted hiss.

"Not to mention the oil paste he ain't got in 'im," he said.

"We'll get 'im some," Kelly said.

"Yeah, *after* the fight, *after* the fight!" Pole snapped, "What about *before* the fight? He'll be creakin' around that ring like a goddam—*steam shovel*. It'll be a miracle if he does two rounds. They'll prob'ly ride us outta town on a rail."

Kelly swallowed. "I don't think it's that bad," he said.

"The *hell* it ain't," said Pole. "It's worse. Wait'll that crowd gets a load of 'Battling Maxo' from Philadelphia. They'll blow a nut. We'll be lucky if we get our five hundred bucks."

"Well, the contract's signed," said Kelly firmly. "They can't back out now. I got a copy right in the old pocket." He leaned over and patted at his coat.

"That contract's for Battling Maxo," said Pole. "Not for this—steam shovel here."

"Maxo's gonna do all right," said Kelly as if he was trying hard to believe it. "He's not as bad off as you say."

"Against a B-*seven?*" Pole asked.

"It's just a *starter* B-seven," said Kelly. "It ain't got the kinks out yet."

Pole turned away.

"Battling Maxo," he said. "One-round Maxo. The battling steam shovel."

"Aw, shut the hell up!" Kelly snapped suddenly, getting redder.

"You're always knockin' 'im down. Well, he's been doin' OK for twelve years now and he'll keep on doin' OK. So he needs some oil paste. And he needs a little work. *So what?* With five hundred bucks we can get him all the paste he needs. And a new trigger spring for his arm and—and new leg cables! And everything. Chris-*sake.*"

He fell back against the seat, chest shuddering with breath and rubbed at his cheeks with his wet handkerchief. He looked aside at Maxo. Abruptly, he reached over a hand and patted Maxo's covered knee clumsily and the steel clanked hollowly under his touch.

"You're doin' all right," said Kelly to his fighter.

• • •

The train was moving across a sun-baked prairie. All the windows were open but the wind that blew in was like blasts from an oven.

Kelly sat reading his paper, his shirt sticking wetly to his broad chest. Pole had taken his coat off too and was staring morosely out the window at the grass-tufted prairie that went as far as he could see. Maxo sat under his covering, his heavy steel frame rocking a little with the motion of the train.

Kelly put down his paper.

"Not even a word," he said.

"What d'ya expect?" Pole asked. "They don't cover Maynard."

"Maxo ain't just some clunk from Maynard," said Kelly. "He was big time. Ya'd think they'd"—he shrugged—"remember him."

"Why? For a coupla prelims in the Garden three years ago?" Pole asked.

"It wasn't no three years, buddy," said Kelly definitely.

"It was in 1977," said Pole, "and now it's 1980. That's three years where I come from."

"It was late '77," said Kelly. "Right before Christmas. Don't ya remember? Just before—Marge and me . . ."

Kelly didn't finish. He stared down at the paper as if Marge's picture were on it—the way she looked the day she left him.

"What's the difference?" Pole asked. "They don't remember *them* for Chrissake. With a coupla thousand o' the damn things floatin' around? How could they remember 'em? About the only ones who get space are the champeens and the new models."

Pole looked at Maxo. "I hear Mawling's puttin' out a B-nine this year," he said.

Kelly refocused his eyes. "Yeah?" he said uninterestedly.

"Hyper-triggers in both arms—*and* legs. All steeled aluminum. Triple gyro. Triple-twisted wiring. God, they'll be beautiful."

Kelly put down the paper.

"Think they'd remember him," he muttered. "It wasn't so long ago."

His face relaxed in a smile of recollection.

"Boy, will I ever forget that night," he said. "No one gives us a tumble. It was all Dimsy the Rock, Dimsy the Rock. *Three* t'one for Dimsy the Rock. Dimsy the Rock—fourth rankin' light heavy. On his way t'the top."

He chuckled deep in his chest. "And did we ever put him away," he said. *"Oooh."* He grunted with savage pleasure. "I can see that left cross now. *Bang!* Right in the chops. And old Dimsy the Rock hittin' the canvas like a—like a *rock,* yeah, *just* like a rock!"

He laughed happily. "Boy, what a night, what a night," he said. "Will I ever forget that night?"

Pole looked at Kelly with a somber face. Then he turned away and stared at the dusty sun-baked plain again.

"I wonder," he muttered.

Kelly saw the man across the aisle looking again at the covered Maxo. He caught the man's eye and smiled, then gestured with his head toward Maxo.

"That's my fighter," he said, loudly.

The man smiled politely, cupping a hand behind one ear.

"My fighter," said Kelly. "Battling Maxo. Ever hear of 'im?"

The man stared at Kelly a moment before shaking his head.

Kelly smiled. "Yeah, he was almost light heavyweight champ once," he told the man. The man nodded politely.

On an impulse, Kelly got up and stepped across the aisle. He reversed the seatback in front of the man and sat down facing him.

"Pretty damn hot," he said.

The man smiled. "Yes. Yes it is," he said.

"No new trains out here yet, huh?"

"No," said the man. "Not yet."

"Got all the new ones back in Philly," said Kelly. "That's where"—he gestured with his head—"my friend 'n' I come from. And Maxo."

Kelly stuck out his hand.

"The name's Kelly," he said. "Tim Kelly."

The man looked surprised. His grip was loose.

When he drew back his hand he rubbed it unobtrusively on his pants leg.

"I used t'be called 'Steel' Kelly," said Kelly. "Used t'be in the business m'self. Before the war o' course. I was a light heavy."

"Oh?"

"Yeah. That's right. Called me 'Steel' cause I never got knocked down once. Not *once*. I was even number nine in the ranks once. Yeah."

"I see." The man waited patiently.

"My—fighter," said Kelly, gesturing toward Maxo with his head again. "He's a light heavy too. We're fightin' in Maynard t'night. You goin' that far?"

"Uh-no," said the man. "No, I'm—getting off at Hayes."

"Oh." Kelly nodded. "Too bad. Gonna be a good scrap." He let out a heavy breath. "Yeah, he was—fourth in the ranks once. He'll be *back* too. He—uh—knocked down Dimsy the Rock in late '77. Maybe ya read about that."

"I don't believe. . . ."

"Oh. Uh-huh." Kelly nodded. "Well . . . it was in all the East Coast papers. You know. New York, Boston, Philly. Yeah it—got a hell of a spread. Biggest upset o' the year."

He scratched at his bald spot.

"He's a B-two y'know but—that means he's the second model Mawling put out," he explained, seeing the look on the man's face. "That was back in—let's see—'67, I think it was. Yeah, '67."

He made a smacking sound with his lips. "Yeah, that was a good model," he said. "The best. Maxo's still goin' strong." He shrugged depreciatingly. "I don't go for these new ones," he said. "You know. The ones made o' steeled aluminum with all the doo-dads."

The man stared at Kelly blankly.

"Too—. . . flashy—flimsy. Nothin' . . ." Kelly bunched his big fist in front of his chest and made a face. "Nothin' *solid*," he said. "No. Mawling don't make 'em like Maxo no more."

"I see," said the man.

Kelly smiled.

"Yeah," he said. "Used t'be in the game m'self. When there was enough men, o'course. Before the bans." He shook his head, then smiled quickly. "Well," he said, "we'll take this B-seven. Don't even know what his name is," he said, laughing.

His face sobered for an instant and he swallowed.

"We'll take 'im," he said.

Later on, when the man had gotten off the train, Kelly went back to his seat. He put his feet up on the opposite seat and, laying back his head, he covered his face with the newspaper.

"Get a little shut-eye," he said.

Pole grunted.

Kelly sat slouched back, staring at the newspaper next to his eyes. He felt Maxo bumping against his side a little. He listened to the squeaking of Maxo's joints. "Be all right," he muttered to himself.

"What?" Pole asked.

Kelly swallowed. "I didn't say anything," he said.

When they got off the train at six o'clock that evening they pushed Maxo around the station and onto the sidewalk. Across the street from them a man sitting in his taxi called them.

"We got no taxi money," said Pole.

"We can't just push 'im through the streets," Kelly said. "Besides, we don't even know where Kruger Stadium is."

"What are we supposed to eat with then?"

"We'll be loaded after the fight," said Kelly. "I'll buy you a steak three inches thick."

Sighing, Pole helped Kelly push the heavy Maxo across the street that was still so hot they could feel it through their shoes. Kelly started sweating right away and licking at his upper lip.

"God, how d'they live out here?" he asked.

When they were putting Maxo inside the cab the base wheel came out again and Pole, with a snarl, kicked it away.

"What're ya *doin'?*" Kelly asked.

"Oh . . . sh—" Pole got into the taxi and slumped back against the warm leather of the seat while Kelly hurried over the soft tar pavement and picked up the wheel.

"Chris-*sake,*" Kelly muttered as he got in the cab. "What's the—?"

"Where to, chief?" the driver asked.

"Kruger Stadium," Kelly said.

"You're there." The cab driver pushed in the rotor button and the car glided away from the curb.

"What the hell's wrong with you?" Kelly asked Pole in a low voice. "We wait more'n half a damn year t'get us a bout and you been nothin' but bellyaches from the start."

"Some bout," said Pole. "Maynard, Kansas—the prize-fightin' center o' the nation."

"It's a start ain't it?" Kelly said. "It'll keep us in coffee 'n' cakes a while, won't it? It'll put Maxo back in shape. And if we take it, it could lead to—"

Pole glanced over disgustedly.

"I don't *get* you," Kelly said quietly. "He's our fighter. What're ya writin' 'im off for? Don't ya want 'im t'win?"

"I'm a class-A mechanic, Steel," Pole said in his falsely patient voice. "I'm not a day-dreamin' kid. We got a piece o' dead iron here, not a B-seven. It's simple mechanics, Steel, that's all. Maxo'll be lucky if he comes out o' that ring with his head still on."

Kelly turned away angrily.

"It's a *starter* B-seven," he muttered. "Full o'kinks. *Full* of 'em."

"Sure, sure," said Pole.

They sat silently a while looking out the window, Maxo between them, the broad steel shoulders bumping against theirs. Kelly stared at the buildings, his hands clenching and unclenching in his lap as if he was getting ready to go fifteen rounds.

"Have you seen this Maynard Flash?" Pole asked the driver.

"The Flash? You bet. Man, there's a fighter on his way. Won seven straight. He'll be up there soon ya can bet ya life. Matter o' fact he's fightin' t'night too. With some B-two heap from back East I hear."

The driver snickered. "Flash'll slaughter 'im," he said.

Kelly stared at the back of the driver's head, the skin tight across his cheek bones.

"Yeah?" he said, flatly.

"Man, he'll—"

The driver broke off suddenly and looked back. "Hey, you ain't—" he started, then turned front again. "Hey, I didn't know, mister," he said. "I was only ribbin'."

"Skip it," Pole said. "You're right."

Kelly's head snapped around and he glared at the sallow-faced Pole.

"Shut up," he said in a low voice.

He fell back against the seat and stared out the window, his face hard.

"I'm gonna get 'im some oil paste," he said after they'd ridden a block.

"Swell," said Pole. "We'll eat the tools."

"Go to hell," said Kelly.

• • •

The cab pulled up in front of the brick-fronted stadium and they lifted Maxo out onto the sidewalk. While Pole tilted him, Kelly squatted down and slid the base wheel back into its slot. Then Kelly paid the driver the exact fare and they started pushing Maxo toward the alley.

"Look," said Kelly, nodding toward the poster board in front of the stadium. The third fight listed was

MAYNARD FLASH
(B-7, L.H.)
vs.
BATTLING MAXO
(B-2, L.H.)

"Big deal," said Pole.

Kelly's smile disappeared. He started to say something, then pressed his lips together. He shook his head irritably and big drops of his sweat fell to the sidewalk.

Maxo creaked as they pushed him down the alley and carried him up the steps to the door. The base wheel fell out again and bounced down the cement steps. Neither one of them said anything.

It was hotter inside. The air didn't move.

"Get the wheel," Kelly said and started down the narrow hallway leaving Pole with Maxo. Pole leaned Maxo against the wall and turned for the door.

Kelly came to a half-glassed office door and knocked.

"Yeah," said a voice inside. Kelly went in, taking off his hat.

The fat bald man looked up from his desk. His skull glistened with sweat.

"I'm Battling Maxo's owner," said Kelly, smiling. He extended his big hand but the man ignored it.

"Was wonderin' if you'd make it," said the man whose name was Mr. Waddow. "Your fighter in decent shape?"

"The best," said Kelly cheerfully. "The best. My mechanic—he's class-A—just took 'im apart and put 'im together again before we left Philly."

The man looked unconvinced.

"He's in good shape," said Kelly.

"You're lucky t'get a bout with a B-two," said Mr. Waddow. "We ain't used nothin' less than B-fours for more than two years now. The fighter we was after got stuck in a car wreck though and got ruined."

Kelly nodded. "Well, ya got nothin' t'worry about," he said. "My fighter's in top shape. He's the one knocked down Dimsy the Rock in Madison Square year or so ago."

"I want a good fight," said the fat man.

"You'll get a good fight," Kelly said, feeling a tight pain in his stomach muscles. "Maxo's in good shape. You'll see. He's in top shape."

"I just want a good fight."

Kelly stared at the fat man a moment. Then he said, "You got a ready room we can use? The mechanic 'n' me'd like t'get something t'eat."

"Third door down the hall on the right side," said Mr. Waddow. "Your bout's at eight thirty."

Kelly nodded. "OK."

"Be there," said Mr. Waddow turning back to his work.

"Uh . . . what about—?" Kelly started.

"You get ya money after ya deliver a fight," Mr. Waddow cut him off.

Kelly's smile faltered.

"OK," he said. "See ya then."

When Mr. Waddow didn't answer, he turned for the door.

"Don't slam the door," Mr. Waddow said. Kelly didn't.

"Come on," he said to Pole when he was in the hall again. They pushed Maxo down to the ready room and put him inside it.

"What about checkin' 'im over?" Kelly said.

"What about my *gut?*" snapped Pole. "I ain't eaten in six hours."

Kelly blew out a heavy breath. "All right, let's go then," he said.

They put Maxo in a corner of the room.

"We should be able t'lock him in," Kelly said.

"Why? Ya think somebody's gonna *steal* 'im?"

"He's valuable," said Kelly.

"Sure he's a priceless antique," said Pole.

Kelly closed the door three times before the latch caught. He turned away from it, shaking his head worriedly. As they started down the hall he looked at his wrist and saw for the fiftieth time the white band where his pawned watch had been.

"What time is it?" he asked.

"Six twenty-five," said Pole.

"We'll have t'make it fast," Kelly said. "I want ya t'check 'im over good before the fight."

"What for?" asked Pole.

"Did ya *hear* me?" Kelly said angrily.

"Sure, sure," Pole said.

"He's gonna take that son-of-a-bitch B-seven," Kelly said, barely opening his lips.

"Sure he is," said Pole. "With his teeth."

"Some town," Kelly said disgustedly as they came back in the side door of the stadium.

"I told ya they wouldn't have any oil paste here," Pole said. "Why should they? B-twos are dead. Maxo's probably the only one in a thousand miles."

Kelly walked quickly down the hall, opened the door of the ready room and went in. He crossed over to Maxo and pulled off the covering.

"Get to it," he said. "There ain't much time."

Blowing out a slow, tired breath, Pole took off his wrinkled blue coat and tossed it over the bench standing against the wall. He dragged a small table over to where Maxo was, then rolled up his sleeves. Kelly took off his hat and coat and watched while Pole worked loose the nut that held the tool cavity door shut. He stood with his big hands on his hips while Pole drew out the tools one by one and laid them down on the table.

"Rust," Pole muttered. He rubbed a finger around the inside of the cavity and held it up, copper colored rust flaking off the tip.

"Come on," Kelly said, irritably. He sat down on the bench and watched as Pole pried off the sectional plates on Maxo's chest. His eyes ran up over Maxo's leonine head. If I didn't see them coils, he thought once more, I'd swear he was real. Only the mechanics in a B-fighter could tell it wasn't real men in there. Sometimes people were actually fooled and sent in letters complaining that real men were being used. Even from ringside the flesh tones looked human. Mawling had a special patent on that.

Kelly's face relaxed as he smiled fondly at Maxo.

"Good boy," he murmured. Pole didn't hear. Kelly watched the sure-handed mechanic probe with his electric pick, examining connections and potency centers.

"Is he all right?" he asked, without thinking.

"Sure, he's great," Pole said. He plucked out a tiny steel-caged tube. "If this doesn't blow out," he said.

"Why should it?"

"It's sub-par," Pole said jadedly. "I told ya that after the last fight *eight months* ago."

Kelly swallowed. "We'll get 'im a new one after this bout," he said.

"Seventy-five bucks," muttered Pole as if he were watching the money fly away on green wings.

"It'll hold," Kelly said, more to himself than to Pole.

Pole shrugged. He put back the tube and pressed in the row of buttons on the main autonomic board. Maxo stirred.

"Take it easy on the left arm," said Kelly. "Save it."

"If it don't work here, it won't work out there," said Pole.

He jabbed at a button and Maxo's left arm began moving with little, circling motions. Pole pushed over the safety-block switch that would keep Maxo from counterpunching and stepped back. He threw a right at Maxo's chin and the robot's arm jumped up with a hitching motion to cover his face. Maxo's left eye flickered like a ruby catching the sun.

"If that eye cell goes . . ." Pole said.

"It *won't*," said Kelly tensely. He watched Pole throw another punch at the left side of Maxo's head. He saw the tiny ripple of the flexo-covered cheek, then the arm jerked up again. It squeaked.

"That's enough," he said. "It works. Try the rest of 'im."

"He's gonna get more than two punches throwed at his head," Pole said.

"*His arm's all right,*" Kelly said. "Try something else I said."

Pole reached inside Maxo and activated the leg cable centers. Maxo began shifting around. He lifted his left leg and shook off the base wheel automatically. Then he was standing lightly on his black-shoed feet, feeling at the floor like a cured cripple testing for stance.

Pole reached forward and jabbed in the FULL button, then jumped back as Maxo's eye beams centered on him and the robot moved forward, broad shoulders rocking slowly, arms up defensively.

"Damn," Pole muttered, "they'll hear 'im squeakin' in the back row."

Kelly grimaced, teeth set. He watched Pole throw another right and Maxo's arm lurch up raggedly. His throat moved with a convulsive swallow and he seemed to have trouble breathing the close air in the little room.

Pole shifted around the floor quickly, side to side. Maxo followed lumberingly, changing direction with visibly jerking motions.

"Oh, he's *beautiful*," Pole said, stopping. "Just beautiful." Maxo came up arms still raised, and Pole jabbed in under them, pushing the OFF button. Maxo stopped.

"Look, we'll have t'put 'im on *de*fense, Steel," Pole said. "That's all there is to it. He'll get chopped t'pieces if we have 'im movin' in."

Kelly cleared his throat. "No," he said.

"Oh for—will ya use ya *head?*" snapped Pole. "He's a B-two f'Chris-sake. He's gonna get slaughtered anyway. Let's save the pieces."

"They want 'im on the *off*ense," said Kelly. "It's in the contract."

Pole turned away with a hiss.

"What's the use?" he muttered.

"Test 'im some more."

"What for? He's as good as he'll ever be."

"Will ya do what I say!" Kelly shouted, all the tension exploding out of him.

Pole turned back and jabbed in a button. Maxo's left arm shot out. There was a snapping noise inside it and it fell against Maxo's side with a dead clank.

Kelly started up, his face stricken. "My God! what did *ya do!*" he cried. He ran over to where Pole was pushing the button again. Maxo's arm didn't move.

"I *told* ya not t'fool with that arm!" Kelly yelled. "What the hell's the *matter* with ya!" His voice cracked in the middle of the sentence.

Pole didn't answer. He picked up his pry and began working off the left shoulder plate.

"So help me God, if you broke that arm..." Kelly warned

in a low, snaking voice.

"If *I* broke it!" Pole snapped. "Listen, you dumb mick! This heap has been runnin' on borrowed time for three years now! Don't talk t'me about breakages!"

Kelly clenched his teeth, his eyes small and deadly.

"Open it up," he said.

"Son-of-a—" Pole muttered as he got the plate off. "You find another goddam mechanic that coulda kep' this steam shovel together any better these last years. You just *find* one."

Kelly didn't answer. He stood rigidly, watching while Pole put down the curved plate and looked inside.

When Pole touched it, the trigger spring broke in half and part of it jumped across the room.

Pole started to say something, then stopped. He looked at the ashen-faced Kelly without moving.

Kelly's eyes moved to Pole.

"Fix it," he said, hoarsely.

Pole swallowed. "Steel, I—"

"Fix it!"

"I can't! That spring's been fixin' t'break for—"

"You broke it! Now *fix* it!" Kelly clamped rigid fingers on Pole's arm. Pole jerked back.

"Let go of me!" he said.

"What's the matter with you!" Kelly cried. "Are you crazy? He's got t'be fixed. He's *got* t'be!"

"Steel, he needs a new spring."

"Well, *get* it!"

"They don't *have* 'em here, Steel," Pole said. "I told ya. And if they *did* have 'em, we ain't got the sixteen fifty t'get one."

"Oh—Oh, God," said Kelly. His hand fell away and he stumbled to the other side of the room. He sank down on the bench and stared without blinking at the tall motionless Maxo.

He sat there a long time, just staring, while Pole stood watching him, the pry still in his hand. He saw Kelly's broad chest rise and fall with spasmodic movements. Kelly's face was a blank.

"If he don't watch 'em," muttered Kelly, finally.

"What?"

Kelly looked up, his mouth set in a straight, hard line. "If he don't watch, it'll work," he said.

"What're ya talkin' about?"

Kelly stood up and started unbuttoning his shirt.

"What're ya—"

Pole stopped dead, his mouth falling open. "Are you *crazy?*" he asked.

Kelly kept unbuttoning his shirt. He pulled it off and tossed it on the bench.

"Steel, you're out o' your mind!" Pole said. "You can't do that!"

Kelly didn't say anything.

"But you'll—Steel, you're *crazy!*"

"We deliver a fight or we don't get paid," Kelly said.

"But—you'll get *killed!*"

Kelly pulled off his undershirt. His chest was beefy, there was red hair swirled around it. "Have to shave this off," he said.

"Steel, *come on,*" Pole said. "You—"

His eyes widened as Kelly sat down on the bench and started unlacing his shoes.

"They'll never let ya," Pole said. "You can't make 'em think you're a—" He stopped and took a jerky step forward. "Steel, fuh Chrissake!"

Kelly looked up at Pole with dead eyes.

"You'll help me," he said.

"But they—"

"Nobody knows what Maxo looks like," Kelly said. "And only Waddow saw me. If he don't watch the bouts we'll be all right."

"But—"

"They won't know," Kelly said. "The B's bleed and bruise too."

"Steel, come on," Pole said shakily. He took a deep breath and calmed himself. He sat down hurriedly beside the broad-shouldered Irishman.

"Look," he said. "I got a sister back East—in Maryland. If I wire 'er, she'll send us the dough t'get back."

Kelly got up and unbuckled his belt.

"Steel, I know a guy in Philly with a B-five wants t'sell cheap," Pole said desperately. "We could scurry up the cash and—Steel, fuh Chrissake, you'll get *killed!* It's a B-seven! Don't ya understand? A B-*seven!* You'll be mangled!"

Kelly was working the dark trunks over Maxo's hips.

"I won't let ya do it, Steel," Pole said, I'll go to—"

He broke off with a sucked-in gasp as Kelly whirled and moved over quickly to haul him to his feet. Kelly's grip was like the jaws of a trap and there was nothing left of him in his eyes.

"You'll help me," Kelly said in a low, trembling voice. "You'll help me or I'll beat ya brains out on the wall."

"You'll get killed," Pole murmured.

"Then I will," said Kelly.

Mr. Waddow came out of his office as Pole was walking the covered Kelly toward the ring.

"Come on, come on," Mr. Waddow said. "They're waitin' on ya."

Pole nodded jerkily and guided Kelly down the hall.

"Where's the owner?" Mr. Waddow called after them.

Pole swallowed quickly. "In the audience," he said.

Mr. Waddow grunted and, as they walked on, Pole heard the door to the office close. Breath emptied from him.

"I should've told 'im," he muttered.

"I'd've killed ya," Kelly said, his voice muffled under the covering.

Crowd sounds leaked back into the hall now as they turned a corner. Under the canvas covering, Kelly felt a drop of sweat trickle down his temple.

"Listen" he said, "you'll have t'towel me off between rounds."

"Between what rounds?" Pole asked tensely. "You won't even last one."

"Shut up."

"You think you're just up against some tough fighter?" Pole asked. "You're up against a machine! Don't ya—"

"I said shut up."

"Oh . . . you dumb—' Pole swallowed. "If I towel ya off, they'll know," he said.

"They ain't seen a B-two in years," Kelly broke in. "If anyone asks, tell 'em it's an oil leak."

"Sure," said Pole disgustedly. He bit his lips. "Steel, ya'll never get away with it."

The last part of his sentence was drowned out as, suddenly, they were among the crowd, walking down the sloping aisle toward the ring. Kelly held his knees locked and walked a little stiffly. He drew in a long, deep breath and let it out slowly.

The heat burdened in around him like a hanging weight. It was like walking along the sloping floor of an ocean of heat and sound. He heard voices drifting past him as he moved.

"Ya'll take 'im home in a box!"

"Well, if it ain't *Rattlin'* Maxo!"

And the inevitable, *"Scrap iron!"*

Kelly swallowed dryly, feeling a tight drawing sensation in his loins. Thirsty, he thought. The momentary vision of the bar across from the Kansas City train station crossed his mind. The dim-lit booth, the cool fan breeze on the back of his neck, the icy, sweat-beaded bottle chilling his palm. He swallowed again. He hadn't allowed himself one drink in the last hour. The less he drank the less he'd sweat, he knew.

"Watch it."

He felt Pole's hand slide in through the opening in the back of the covering, felt the mechanic's hand grab his arm and check him.

"Ring steps," Pole said out of a corner of his mouth.

Kelly edged his right foot forward until the shoe tip touched the riser of the bottom step. Then he lifted his foot to the step and started up.

At the top, Pole's fingers tightened around his arm again.

"Ropes," Pole said, guardedly.

It was hard getting through the ropes with the covering on. Kelly almost fell and hoots and catcalls came at him like spears out of the din. Kelly felt the canvas give slightly under his feet and then Pole pushed the stool against the back of his legs and he sat down a little too jerkily.

"Hey, get that derrick out o' here!" shouted a man in the second row. Laughter and hoots.

Then Pole drew off the covering and put it down on the ring apron.

Kelly sat there staring at the Maynard Flash.

The B-seven was motionless, its gloved hands hanging across its legs. There was imitation blonde hair, crew cut, growing out of its skull pores. Its face was that of an impassive Adonis. The simulation of muscle curve on its body and limbs was almost perfect. For a moment Kelly almost thought that years had been peeled away and he was in the business again, facing a young contender. He swallowed carefully. Pole crouched beside him, pretending to fiddle with an arm plate.

"Steel, *don't*," he muttered again.

Kelly didn't answer. He kept staring at the Maynard Flash, thinking of the array of instant-reaction centers inside that smooth arch of chest. The drawing sensation reached his stomach. It was like a cold hand pulling in at strands of muscle and ligament.

A red-faced man in white suit climbed into the ring and reached up for the microphone which was swinging down to him.

"Ladies and gentlemen," he announced, "the opening bout of the evening. A ten-round light heavyweight bout. From Philadelphia, the B-two *Battling Maxo*."

The crowd booed and hissed. They threw up paper airplanes and shouted *"Scrap iron!"*

"His opponent, our own B-seven, the *Maynard Flash!*"

Cheers and wild clapping. The Flash's mechanic touched a button under the left armpit and the B-seven jumped up and held his arms over his head in the victory gesture. The crowd laughed happily.

"God," Pole muttered, "I never saw that. Must be a new gimmick."

Kelly blinked to relieve his eyes.

"Three more bouts to follow," said the red-faced man and then the microphone drew up and he left the ring. There was no referee. B-fighters never clinched—their machinery rejected it—and there was no knock-down count. A felled B-fighter stayed down. The new B-nine, it was claimed by the Mawling publicity staff, would be able to get up, which would make for livelier and longer bouts.

Pole pretended to check over Kelly.

"Steel, it's your last chance," he begged.

"Get out," said Kelly without moving his lips.

Pole looked at Kelly's immobile eyes a moment, then sucked in a ragged breath and straightened up.

"Stay *away* from him," he warned as he started through the ropes.

Across the ring, the Flash was standing in its corner, hitting its gloves together as if it were a real young fighter anxious to get the fight started. Kelly stood up and Pole drew the stool away. Kelly stood watching the B-seven, seeing how its eye centers were zeroing in on him. There was a cold sinking in his stomach.

The bell rang.

The B-seven moved out smoothly from its corner with a mechanical glide, its arms raised in the traditional way, gloved hands wavering in tiny circles in front of it. It moved quickly toward Kelly who edged out of his corner automatically, his mind feeling, abruptly, frozen. He felt his own hands rise as if someone else had lifted them and his legs were like dead wood under him. He kept his gaze on the bright unmoving eyes of the Maynard Flash.

They came together. The B-seven's left flicked out and Kelly blocked it, feeling the rock-hard fist of the Flash even through his glove. The fist moved out again. Kelly drew back his head and felt a warm breeze across his mouth. His own left shot out and banged against the Flash's nose. It was like hitting a door knob. Pain flared in Kelly's arm and his jaw muscles went hard as he struggled to keep his face blank.

The B-seven feinted with a left and Kelly knocked it aside. He couldn't stop the right that blurred in after it and grazed his left temple. He jerked his head away and the B-seven threw a left that hit him over the ear. Kelly lurched back, throwing out a left that the B-seven brushed aside. Kelly caught his footing and hit the Flash's jaw solidly with a right uppercut. He felt a jolt of pain run up his arm. The Flash's head didn't budge. He shot out a left that hit Kelly on the right shoulder.

Kelly back-pedaled instinctively. Then he heard someone yell, "Get 'im a bicycle!" and he remembered what Mr. Waddow had said. He moved in again.

A left caught him under the heart and he felt the impact shudder through his frame. Pain stabbed at his heart. He threw a spasmodic left which banged against the B-seven's nose again. There was only pain. Kelly stepped back and staggered as a hard right caught him high on the chest. He started to move back. The B-seven hit him on the chest again. Kelly lost his balance and stepped back quickly to catch equilibrium. The crowd booed. The B-seven moved in without making a single mechanical sound.

Kelly regained his balance and stopped. He threw a hard right that missed. The momentum of his blow threw him off center and the Flash's left drove hard against his upper right arm. The arm went numb. Even as Kelly was sucking in a teeth-clenched gasp the B-seven shot in a hard right under his guard that slammed into Kelly's spongy stomach. Kelly felt the breath go out of him. His right slapped ineffectively across the Flash's right cheek. the Flash's eyes glinted.

As the B-seven moved in again, Kelly side-stepped and, for a moment, the radial eye centers lost him. Kelly moved out of range dizzily, pulling air in through his nostrils.

"Get that heap out o' there!" a man yelled.

Breath shook in Kelly's throat. He swallowed quickly and started forward just as the Flash picked him up again. He stepped in close, hoping to out-time electrical impulse, and threw a hard right at the Flash's body.

The B-seven's left shot up and Kelly's blow was deflected by the iron wrist. Kelly's left was thrown off too and then the Flash's left shot in and drove the breath out of Kelly again. Kelly's left barely hit the Flash's rock-hard chest. He staggered back, the B-seven following. He kept jabbing but the B-seven kept deflecting the blows and counterjabbing with almost the same piston-like motion. Kelly's head kept snapping back. He fell back more and saw the right coming straight at him. He couldn't stop it.

The blow drove in like a steel battering-ram. Spears of pain shot behind Kelly's eyes and through his head. A black cloud seemed to flood across the ring. His muffled cry was drowned out by the screaming crowd as he toppled back, his nose and mouth trickling bright blood that looked as good as the dye they used in the B-fighters.

The rope checked his fall, pressing in rough and hard against his back. He swayed there, right arm hanging limp, left arm raised defensively. He blinked his eyes instinctively, trying to focus them. I'm a robot, he thought, a robot.

The Flash stepped in and drove a violent right into Kelly's chest, a left to his stomach. Kelly doubled over gagging. A right slammed off his skull like a hammer blow, driving him back against the ropes again. The crowd screamed.

Kelly saw the blurred outline of the Maynard Flash. He felt another blow smash into his chest like a club. With a sob he threw a wild left that the B-seven brushed off. Another sharp blow landed on Kelly's shoulder. He lifted his right and managed to deflect the worst of a left thrown at his jaw. Another right concaved his stomach. He doubled over. A hammering right drove him back on the ropes. He felt hot salty blood in his mouth and the roar of the crowd seemed to swallow him. Stay up!—he screamed at himself. Stay up, goddam you! The ring wavered before him like dark water.

With a desperate surge of energy, he threw a right as hard as he could at the tall beautiful figure in front of him. Something cracked in his wrist and hand and a wave of searing pain shot up his arm. His throat-locked cry went unheard. His arm fell, his left went down and the crowd shrieked and howled for the Flash to finish it.

There was only inches between them now. The B-seven rained in blows that didn't miss. Kelly lurched and staggered under the impact of them. His head snapped from side to side. Blood ran across his face in scarlet ribbons. His arm hung like a dead branch at his side. He kept getting slammed back against the ropes, bouncing forward and getting slammed back again. He couldn't see any more. He could only hear the screaming of the crowd and the endless swishing and thudding of the B-seven's gloves. Stay up, he thought. I have to stay up. He drew in his head and hunched his shoulders to protect himself.

He was like that seven seconds before the bell when a clubbing right on the side of his head sent him crashing to the canvas.

He lay there gasping for breath. Suddenly, he started to get up, then, equally as suddenly, realized that he couldn't. He fell forward again and lay on his stomach on the warm canvas, his head throbbing with pain. He could hear the booing and hissing of the dissatisfied crowd.

When Pole finally managed to get him up and slip the cover over his head the crowd was jeering so loudly that Kelly couldn't hear Pole's voice. He felt the mechanic's big hand inside the covering, guiding him, but he fell down climbing through the ropes and almost fell again on the steps. His legs were like rubber tubes. Stay up. His brain still murmured the words.

In the ready room he collapsed. Pole tried to get him up on the bench but he couldn't. Finally he bunched up his blue coat under Kelly's head and, kneeling, he started patting with his handkerchief at the trickles of blood.

"You dumb bastard," he kept muttering in a thin, shaking voice. "You dumb bastard."

Kelly lifted his left hand and brushed away Pole's hand.

"Go—get the—money," he gasped hoarsely.

"What?"

"The money!" gasped Kelly through his teeth.

"But—"

"Now!" Kelly's voice was barely intelligible.

Pole straightened up and stood looking down at Kelly a moment. Then he turned and went out.

Kelly lay there drawing in breath and exhaling it with wheezing sounds. He couldn't move his right hand and he knew it was broken. He felt the blood trickling from his nose and mouth. His body throbbed with pain.

After a few moments he struggled up on his left elbow and turned his head, pain crackling along his neck muscles. When he saw that Maxo was all right he put his head down again. A smile twisted up one corner of his lips.

When Pole came back, Kelly lifted his head painfully. Pole came over and knelt down. He started patting at the blood again.

"Ya get it?" Kelly asked in a crusty whisper.

Pole blew out a slow breath.

"Well?"

Pole swallowed. "Half of it," he said.

Kelly stared up at him blankly, his mouth fallen open. His eyes didn't believe it.

"He said he wouldn't pay five C's for a one rounder."

"What d'ya mean?" Kelly's voice cracked. He tried to get up and put down his right hand. With a strangled cry he fell back, his face white. His head thrashed on the coat pillow, his eyes shut tightly.

"He can't—he can't do that," he gasped.

Pole licked his dry lips.

"Steel, there—ain't a thing we can do. He's got a bunch o' toughs in the office with 'im. I can't. . . ." He lowered his head. "And if—you was t'go there he'd know what ya done. And—he might even take back the two and a half."

Kelly lay on his back staring up at the naked bulb without blinking. His chest labored and shuddered with breath.

"No," he murmured. "No."

He lay there for a long time without talking. Pole got some water and cleaned off his face and gave him a drink. He opened up his small suitcase and patched up Kelly's face. He put Kelly's right arm in a sling.

Fifteen minutes later Kelly spoke.

"We'll go back by bus," he said.

"What?" Pole asked.

"We'll go by bus," Kelly said slowly. "That'll only cost fifty-six bucks." He swallowed and shifted on his back. "That'll leave almost two C's. We can get 'im a—a new trigger spring and a—eye lens and—" He blinked his eyes and held them shut a moment as the room started fading again.

"And oil paste," he said then. "Loads of it. He'll be—good as new again."

Kelly looked up at Pole. "Then we'll be all set up," he said.

"Maxo'll be in good shape again. And we can get us some decent bouts." He swallowed and breathed laboriously. "That's all he needs is a little work. New spring, a new eye lens. That'll shape 'im up. We'll show those bastards what a B-two can do. Old Maxo'll show 'em. *Right?*"

Pole looked down at the big Irishman and sighed.

"Sure, Steel," he said.

THE IRON CHANCELLOR

Robert Silverberg

The Carmichaels were a pretty plump family, to begin with. Not one of them couldn't stand to shed quite a few pounds. And there happened to be a superspecial on roboservitors at one of the Miracle Mile roboshops—40 percent off on the 2061 model, with adjustable caloric-intake monitors.

Sam Carmichael liked the idea of having his food prepared and served by a robot who would keep one beady solenoid eye on the collective family waistline. He squinted speculatively at the glossy display model, absentmindedly slipped his thumbs beneath his elastobelt to knead his paunch, and said, "How much?"

The salesman flashed a brilliant and probably synthetic grin. "Only 2995, sir. That includes free service contract for first five years. Only two hundred credits down and up to forty months to pay."

Carmichael frowned, thinking of his bank balance. Then he thought of his wife's figure, and of his daughter's endless yammering about her need to diet. Besides, Jemima, their old robocook, was shabby and gear-stripped, and made a miserable showing when the other company executives visited them for dinner.

"I'll take it," he said.

"Care to trade in your old robocook, sir? Liberal trade-in allowances—"

"I have a '43 Madison." Carmichael wondered if he should mention its bad arm libration and serious fuel-feed overflow, but decided that would be carrying candidness too far.

"Well—ah—I guess we could allow you fifty credits on a '43, sir. Seventy-five, maybe, if the recipe bank is still in good condition."

"Excellent condition." That part was honest—the family had never let even one recipe wear out. "You could send a man down to look her over."

"Oh, no need to do that, sir. We'll take your word. Seventy-five, then? And delivery of the new model by this evening?"

"Done," Carmichael said. He was glad to get the pathetic old '43 out of the house at any cost.

He signed the purchase order cheerfully, pocketed the facism and handed over ten crisp twenty-credit vouchers. He could almost feel the roll of fat melting from him now, as he eyed the magnificent '61 roboservitor that would shortly be his.

The time was only 1810 hours when he left the shop, got into his car and punched out the coordinates for home. The whole transaction had taken less than ten minutes. Carmichael, a second-level executive at Normandy Trust, prided himself both on his good business sense and his ability to come quickly to a firm decision.

Fifteen minutes later, his car deposited him at the front entrance of their totally detached self-powered suburban home in the fashionable Westley subdivision. The car obediently took itself around back to the garage, while Carmichael stood in the scanner field until the door opened. Clyde, the robutler, came scuttling hastily up, took his hat and cloak, and handed him a Martini.

Carmichael beamed appreciatively. "Well done, thou good and faithful servant!"

He took a healthy sip and headed toward the living room to greet his wife, son and daughter. Pleasant gin-induced warmth filtered through him. The robutler was ancient and due for replacement as soon as the budget could stand the charge, but Carmichael realized he would miss the clanking old heap.

"You're late, dear," Ethel Carmichael said as he appeared. "Dinner's been ready for ten minutes. Jemima's so annoyed her cathodes are clicking."

"Jemima's cathodes fail to interest me," Carmichael said evenly. "Good evening, dear. Myra. Joey. I'm late because I stopped off at Marhew's on my way home."

His son blinked. "The robot place, Dad?"

"Precisely. I bought a '61 roboservitor to replace old Jemima and her sputtering cathodes. The new model has," Carmichael added, eyeing his son's adolescent bulkiness and the rather-more-than-ample figures of his wife and daughter, "some very special attachments."

They dined well that night, on Jemima's favorite Tuesday dinner menu—shrimp cocktail, fumet of gumbo chervil, breast of chicken with creamed potatoes and asparagus, delicious plum tarts for dessert, and coffee. Carmichael felt pleasantly bloated when he had finished, and gestured to Clyde for a snifter of his favorite afterdinner digestive aid, VSOP Cognac. He leaned back, warm, replete, able easily to ignore the blustery November winds outside.

A pleasing electroluminescence suffused the dining room with pink—this year, the experts thought pink improved digestion—and the heating filaments embedded in the wall glowed cozily as they delivered the BTUs. This was the hour for relaxation in the Carmichael household.

"Dad," Joey began hesitantly, "about that canoe trip next weekend—"

Carmichael folded his hands across his stomach and nodded. "You can go, I suppose. Only be careful. If I find out you didn't use the equilibriator this time—"

The door chime sounded. Carmichael lifted an eyebrow and swiveled in his chair.

"Who is it, Clyde?"

"He gives his name as Robinson, sir. Of Robinson Robotics, he said. He has a bulky package to deliver."

"It must be that new robocook, Father!" Myra Carmichael exclaimed.

"I guess it is. Show him in, Clyde."

Robinson turned out to be a red-faced, efficient-looking little man in greasy green overalls and a plaid pullover-coat, who looked disapprovingly at the robutler and strode into the Carmichael living room.

He was followed by a lumbering object about seven feet high, mounted on a pair of rolltreads and swathed completely in quilted rags.

"Got him all wrapped up against the cold, Mr. Carmichael. Lot of delicate circuitry in that job. You ought to be proud of him."

"Clyde, help Mr. Robinson unpack the new robocook," Carmichael said.

"That's okay—I can manage it. And it's *not* a robocook, by the way. It's called a roboservitor now. Fancy price, fancy name."

Carmichael heard his wife mutter, "Sam, how much—"

He scowled at her. "Very reasonable, Ethel. Don't worry so much."

He stepped back to admire the roboservitor as it emerged from the quilted swaddling. It was big, all right, with a massive barrel of a chest—robotic controls are always housed in the chest, not in the relatively tiny head—and a gleaming mirror-keen finish that accented its sleekness and newness. Carmichael felt the satisfying glow of pride in ownership. Somehow it seemed to him that he had done something noble and lordly in buying this magnificent robot.

Robinson finished the unpacking job and, standing on tiptoes, opened the robot's chest panel. He unclipped a thick instruction manual and handed it to Carmichael, who stared at the tome uneasily.

"Don't fret about that, Mr. Carmichael. This robot's no trouble to handle. The book's just part of the trimming. Come here a minute."

Carmichael peered into the robot's innards. Pointing, Robinson said, "Here's the recipe bank—biggest and best ever designed. Of course, it's possible to tape in any of your favorite family recipes, if they're not already there. Just hook up your old robocook to the integrator circuit and feed 'em in. I'll take care of that before I leave."

"And what about the—ah—special features?"

"The reducing monitors, you mean? Right over here. See? You just tape in the names of the members of the family and their present and desired weights, and the roboservitor takes care of the rest. Computes caloric intake, adjusts menus, and everything else."

Carmichael grinned at his wife. "Told you I was going to

do something about our weight, Ethel. No more dieting for you, Myra—the robot does all the work." Catching a sour look on his son's face, he added, "And you're not so lean yourself, Buster."

"I don't think there'll be any trouble," Robinson said buoyantly. "But if there is, just buzz for me. I handle service and delivery for Marhew Stores in this area."

"Right."

"Now if you'll get me your obsolete robocook, I'll transfer the family recipes before I cart it away on the trade-in deal."

There was a momentary tingle of nostalgia and regret when Robinson left, half an hour later, taking old Jemima with him. Carmichael had almost come to think of the battered '43 Madison as a member of the family. After all, he had bought her sixteen years before, only a couple of years after his marriage.

But she—*it*, he corrected in annoyance—was only a robot, and robots became obsolete. Besides, Jemima probably suffered all the aches and pains of a robot's old age and would be happier dismantled. Carmichael blotted Jemima from his mind.

The four of them spent most of the rest of that evening discovering things about their new roboservitor. Carmichael drew up a table of their weights (himself, 192; Ethel, 145; Myra, 139; Joey, 189) and the amount they proposed to weigh in three months' time (himself, 180; Ethel, 125; Myra, 120; Joey, 175). Carmichael then let his son, who prided himself on his knowledge of practical robotics, integrate the figures and feed them to the robot's programing bank.

"You wish this schedule to take effect immediately?" the roboservitor queried in a deep, mellow bass.

Startled, Carmichael said, "T-tomorrow morning, at breakfast. We might as well start right away."

"He speaks well, doesn't he?" Ethel asked.

"He sure does," Joey said. "Jemima always stammered and squeaked, and all she could say was, 'Dinner is served' and 'Be careful, sirr, the soup plate is verry warrm.'"

Carmichael smiled. He noticed his daughter admiring the robot's bulky frame and sleek bronze limbs, and thought resignedly that a seventeen-year-old could find the strangest sorts of love objects. But he was happy to see that they were all evidently pleased with the robot. Even with the discount and the trade-in, it *had* been a little on the costly side.

But it would be worth it.

Carmichael slept soundly and woke early, anticipating the first breakfast under the new regime. He still felt pleased with himself.

Dieting had always been such a nuisance, he thought—but, on the other hand, he had never enjoyed the sensation of an annoying roll of fat pushing outward against his elastobelt. He exercised sporadically, but it did little good, and he never had the initiative to keep a rigorous dieting campaign going for long. Now, though, with the mathematics of reducing done effortlessly for him, all the calculating and cooking being handled by the new robot—now, for the first time since he had been Joey's age, he could look forward to being slim and trim once again.

He showered, dressed and hastily depilated. It was 0730. Breakfast was ready.

Ethel and the children were already at the table when he arrived. Ethel and Myra were munching toast; Joey was peering at a bowl of milkless dry cereal next to which stood a full glass of milk. Carmichael sat down.

"Your toast, sir," the roboservitor murmured.

Carmichael stared at the single slice. It had already been buttered for him, and the butter had evidently been measured out with a micrometer. The robot proceeded to hand him a cup of black coffee.

He groped for the cream and sugar. They weren't anywhere on the table. The other members of his family were regarding him strangely, and they were curiously, suspiciously silent.

"I like cream and sugar in my coffee," he said to the hovering roboservitor. "Didn't you find that in Jemima's old recipe bank?"

"Of course, sir. But you must learn to drink your coffee without such things, if you wish to lose weight."

Carmichael chuckled. Somehow he had not expected the regimen to be quite like this—quite so, well, Spartan. "Oh, yes. Of course. Ah—are the eggs ready yet?" He considered a day incomplete unless he began it with soft-boiled eggs.

"Sorry, no, sir. On Mondays, Wednesdays, and Fridays, breakfast is to consist of toast and black coffee only, except for Master Joey, who gets cereal, fruit juice and milk."

"I—see."

Well, he had asked for it. He shrugged and took a bite of the toast. He sipped the coffee; it tasted like river mud, but he tried not to make a face.

Joey seemed to be going on about the business of eating his cereal rather oddly, Carmichael noticed next. "Why don't you pour that glass of milk *into* the cereal?" he asked. "Won't it taste better that way?"

"Sure it will. But Bismarck says I won't get another glass if I do, so I'm eating it this way."

"Bismarck?"

Joey grinned. "It's the name of a famous nineteenth-century German dictator. They called him the Iron Chancellor." He jerked his head toward the kitchen, to which the roboservitor had silently retreated. "Pretty good name for him, eh?"

"No," said Carmichael. "It's silly."

"It has a certain ring of truth, though," Ethel remarked.

Carmichael did not reply. He finished his toast and coffee somewhat glumly and signaled Clyde to get the car out of the garage. He felt depressed— dieting didn't seem to be so effortless after all, even with the new robot.

As he walked toward the door, the robot glided around him and handed him a small printed slip of paper. Carmichael stared at it. It said:

FRUIT JUICE
LETTUCE & TOMATO SALAD
(ONE) HARD-BOILED EGG
BLACK COFFEE

"What's this thing?"

"You are the only member of this family group who will not be eating three meals a day under my personal supervision. This is your luncheon menu. Please adhere to it," the robot said smoothly.

Repressing a sputter, Carmichael said, "Yes—yes. Of course."

He pocketed the menu and made his way uncertainly to the waiting car.

He was faithful to the robot's orders at lunchtime that day; even though he was beginning to develop resistance to the idea that had seemed so appealing only the night before, he was willing, at least, to give it a try.

But something prompted him to stay away from the restaurant where Normandy Trust employees usually lunched, and where there were human waiters to smirk at him and fellow executives to ask prying questions.

He ate instead at a cheap robocafeteria two blocks to the north. He slipped in surreptitiously with his collar turned up, punched out his order (it cost him less than a credit altogether) and wolfed it down. He still felt hungry when he was finished, but he compelled himself to return loyally to the office.

He wondered how long he was going to be able to keep up this iron self-control. Not very long, he realized dolefully. And if anyone from the company caught him eating at a robocafeteria, he'd be a laughing stock. Someone of executive status just *didn't* eat lunch by himself in mechanized cafeterias.

By the time he had finished his day's work, his stomach felt knotted and pleated. His hand was shaky as he punched out his destination on the car's autopanel, and he was thankful that it took less than an hour to get home from the office. Soon, he thought, he'd be tasting food again. Soon. Soon. He switched on a roof-mounted video, leaned back at the recliner and tried to relax as the car bore him homeward.

He was in for a surprise, though, when he stepped through the safety field into his home. Clyde was waiting as always, and, as always, took his hat and cloak. And, as always, Carmichael reached for the cocktail that Clyde prepared nightly to welcome him home.

There was no cocktail.

"Are we out of gin, Clyde?"

"No sir."

"How come no drink, then?"

The robot's rubberized metallic features seemed to droop. "Because, sir, a Martini's caloric content is inordinately high. gin is rated at a hundred calories per once and—"

"Oh, no, You too!"

"Pardon, sir. The new roboservitor has altered my responsive circuits to comply with the regulations now in force in this household."

Carmichael felt his fingers starting to tremble. "Clyde, you've been my butler for almost twenty years."

"Yes, sir."

"You always make my drinks for me. You mix the best Martinis in the Western Hemisphere."

"Thank you, sir."

"And you're going to mix one for me right now! That's a direct order!"

"Sir! I—" The robutler staggered wildly and nearly careened into Carmichael. It seemed to have lost all control over its gyro-balance; it clutched agonizedly at its chest panel and started to sag.

Hastily, Carmichael barked, "Order countermanded! Clyde, are you all right?"

Slowly, and with a creak, the robot straightened up. It looked dangerously close to an overload. "You're direct order set up a first-level conflict in me, sir," Clyde whispered faintly. "I—came close to burning out just then, sir. May—may I be excused?"

"Of course. Sorry, Clyde." Carmichael balled his fists. There was such a thing as going too far! The roboservitor—Bismarck—had obviously placed on Clyde a flat prohibition against serving liquor to him. Reducing or no reducing, there were *limits*.

Carmichael strode angrily toward the kitchen.

His wife met him halfway. "I didn't hear you come in, Sam. I want to talk to you about—"

"Later. Where's that robot?"

"In the kitchen, I imagine. It's almost dinnertime."

He brushed past her and swept on into the kitchen, where Bismarck was moving efficiently from electrostove to magnetic worktable. The robot swiveled as Carmichael entered.

"Did you have a good day, sir?"

"No! I'm hungry!"

"The first days of a diet are always the most difficult, Mr. Carmichael. But your body will adjust to the reduction in food intake before long."

"I'm sure of that. But what's this business of tinkering with Clyde?"

"The butler insisted on preparing an alcoholic drink for you. I was forced to adjust his programming. From now on, sir, you may indulge in cocktails on Tuesdays, Thursdays, and Saturdays. I beg to be excused from further discussion now, sir. The meal is almost ready."

Poor Clyde! Carmichael thought. *And poor me!* He gnashed his teeth impotently a few times, then gave up and turned away from the glistening, overbearing roboservitor. A light gleamed on the side of the robot's head, indicating that he had shut off his audio circuits and was totally engaged in his task.

Dinner consisted of steak and peas, followed by black coffee. The steak was rare; Carmichael preferred it well done. But Bismarck—the name was beginning to take hold—had had all the latest dietetic theories taped into him, and rare meat it was.

After the robot had cleared the table and tidied up the kitchen, it retired to its storage place in the basement, which gave the Carmichael family a chance to speak openly to each other for the first time that evening.

"Lord!" Ethel snorted. "Sam, I don't object to losing weight, but if we're going to be *tyrannized* in our own home—"

"Mom's right," Joey put in. "It doesn't seem fair for that thing to feed us whatever it pleases. And I didn't like the way it messed around with Clyde's circuits."

Carmichael spread his hands. "I'm not happy about it either. But we have to give it a try. We can always make readjustments in the programming if it turns out to be necessary."

"But how long are we going to keep this up?" Myra wanted to know. "I had three meals in this house today and I'm starved!"

"Me, too," Joey said. He elbowed himself from his chair and looked around. "Bismarck's downstairs. I'm going to get a slice of lemon pie while the coast is clear."

"No!" Carmichael thundered.

"No?"

"There's no sense in my spending three thousand credits on a dietary robot if you're going to cheat, Joey. I forbid you to have any pie."

"But Dad, I'm hungry! I'm a growing boy! I'm—"

"You're sixteen years old, and if you grow much more, you won't fit inside this house," Carmichael snapped, looking up at his six-foot-one son.

"Sam, we can't starve the boy," Ethel protested. "If he wants pie, let him have some. You're carrying this reducing fetish too far."

Carmichael considered that. Perhaps, he thought, I *am* being a little oversevere. And the thought of lemon pie was a tempting one. He was pretty hungry himself.

"All right," he said with feigned reluctance. "I guess a bit of pie won't wreck the plan. In fact, I suppose I'll have some myself. Joey, why don't you—"

"Begging your pardon," a purring voice said behind him. Carmichael jumped half an inch. It was the robot, Bismarck. "It would be most unfortunate if you were to have pie now, Mr. Carmichael. My calculations are very precise."

Carmichael saw the angry gleam in his son's eyes, but the robot seemed extraordinarily big at that moment, and it happened to stand between him and the kitchen.

He sighed weakly. "Let's forget the lemon pie, Joey."

After two full days of the Bismarckian diet, Carmichael discovered that his inner resources of willpower were beginning to crumble. On the third day he tossed away the printed lunchtime diet and went out irresponsibly with MacDougal and Hennessey for a six-course lunch, complete with cocktails. It seemed to him that he hadn't tasted real food since the robot arrived.

That night, he was able to tolerate the seven-hundred-calorie dinner without any inward grumblings, being still well lined with lunch. But Ethel and Myra and Joey were increasingly irritable. It seemed that the robot had usurped Ethel's job of handling the daily marketing and had stocked in nothing but a huge supply of healthy low-calorie foods. The larder now bulged with wheat germ, protein bread, irrigated salmon, and other hitherto unfamiliar items. Myra had taken up biting her nails; Joey's mood was one of black sullen brooding, and Carmichael knew how that could lead to trouble quickly with a sixteen-year-old.

After the meager dinner, he ordered Bismarck to go to the basement and stay there until summoned.

The robot said, "I must advise you, sir, that I will detect indulgence in any forbidden foods in my absence and adjust for it in the next meals."

"You have my word," Carmichael said, thinking it was indeed queer to have a pledge on your honor to your own robot. He waited until the massive servitor had vanished below; then he turned to Joey and said, "Get the instruction manual, boy."

Joey grinned in understanding. Ethel said, "Sam, what are you going to do?"

Carmichael patted his shrunken waistline. "I'm going to take a can opener to that creature and adjust his programming.

He's overdoing this diet business. Joey, have you found the instructions on how to reprogram the robot?"

"Page 167. I'll get the tool kit, Dad."

"Right." Carmichael turned to the robutler, who was standing by dumbly, in his usual forward-stooping posture of expectancy. "Clyde, go down below and tell Bismarck we want him right away."

Moments later, the two robots appeared. Carmichael said to the roboservitor, "I'm afraid its necessary for us to change your program. We've overestimated our capacity for losing weight."

"I beg you to reconsider, sir. Extra weight is harmful to every vital organ in the body. I plead with you to maintain my scheduling unaltered."

"I'd rather cut my own throat. Joey, inactivate him and do your stuff."

Grinning fiercely, the boy stepped forward and pressed the stud that opened the robot's ribcage. A frightening assortment of gears, cams and translucent cables became visible inside the robot. With a small wrench in one hand and the open instruction booklet in the other, Joey prepared to make the necessary changes, while Carmichael held his breath and a pall of silence descended on the living room. Even old Clyde leaned forward to have a better view.

Joey muttered, "Lever F2, with the yellow indicia, is to be advanced one notch . . . umm. Now twist Dial B9 to the left, thereby opening the taping compartment and—oops!"

Carmichael heard the clang of a wrench and saw the bright flare of sparks; Joey leaped back, cursing with surprisingly mature skill. Ethel and Myra gasped simultaneously.

"What happened?" four voices—Clyde's coming in last—demanded.

"Dropped the damn wrench," Joey said. "I guess I shorted out something in there."

The robot's eyes were whirling satanically and its voice box was emitting an awesome twelve-cycle rumble. The great metal creature stood stiffly in the middle of the living room; with brusque gestures of its big hands, it slammed shut the open chest plates.

"We'd better call Mr. Robinson," Ethel said worriedly. "A short-circuited robot is likely to explode, or worse."

"We should have called Robinson in the first place," Carmichael murmured bitterly. "It's my fault for letting Joey tinker with an expensive and delicate mechanism like that. Myra, get me the card Mr. Robinson left."

"Gee, Dad, this is the first time I've ever had anything like that go wrong," Joey insisted. "I didn't know—"

"You're darned right you didn't know." Carmichael took the card from his daughter and started toward the phone. "I hope we can reach him at this hour. If we can't—"

Suddenly Carmichael felt cold fingers prying the card from his hand. He was so startled he relinquished it without a struggle. He watched as Bismarck efficiently ripped it into little fragments and shoved them into a wall disposal unit.

The robot said, "There will be no further meddling with my program tapes." Its voice was deep and strangely harsh.

"What—"

"Mr. Carmichael, today you violated the program I set down for you. My perceptors reveal that you consumed an amount far in excess of your daily lunchtime requirement."

"Sam, what—"

"Quiet, Ethel. Bismarck, I order you to shut yourself off at once."

"My apologies, sir. I cannot serve you if I am shut off."

"I don't *want* you to serve me. You're out of order. I want you to remain still until I can phone the repairman and get him to service you."

Then he remembered the card that had gone into the disposal unit. He felt a faint tremor of apprehension.

"You took Robinson's card and destroyed it."

"Further alteration of my circuits would be detrimental to the Carmichael family," said the robot. "I cannot permit you to summon the repairman."

"Don't get him angry, Dad," Joey warned. "I'll call the police. I'll be back in—"

"You will remain within this house," the robot said. Moving with impressive speed on its oiled treads, it crossed the room, blocking the door, and reached far above its head to activate the impassable privacy field that protected the house. Carmichael watched, aghast, as the inexorable robotic fingers twisted and manipulated the field controls.

"I have now reversed the polarity of the house privacy field," the robot announced. "Since you are obviously not to be trusted to keep to the diet I prescribe, I cannot allow you to leave the premises. You will remain within and continue to obey my beneficial advice."

Calmly, he uprooted the telephone. Next, the windows were opaqued and the stud broken off. Finally, the robot seized the instruction book from Joey's numbed hands and shoved it into the disposal unit.

"Breakfast will be served at the usual time," Bismarck said mildly. "For optimum purposes of health, you are all to be asleep by 2300 hours. I shall leave you now, until morning. Good night."

Carmichael did not sleep well that night, nor did he eat well the next day. He awoke late, for one thing—well past nine. He discovered that someone, obviously Bismarck, had neatly canceled out the impulses from the housebrain that woke him at seven each morning.

The breakfast menu was toast and black coffee. Carmichael ate disgruntledly, not speaking, indicating by brusque scowls that he did not want to be spoken to. After the miserable meal had been cleared away, he surreptitiously tiptoed to the front door in his dressing gown and darted a hand toward the handle.

The door refused to budge. He pushed until sweat dribbled down his face. He heard Ethel whisper warningly, *"Sam—"* and a moment later cool metallic fingers gently disengaged him from the door.

Bismarck said, "I beg your pardon, sir. The door will not open. I explained this last night."

Carmichael gazed sourly at the gimmicked control box of the privacy field. The robot had them utterly hemmed in. The reversed privacy field made it impossible for them to leave the house; it cast a sphere of force around the entire detached dwelling. In theory, the field could be penetrated from outside, but nobody was likely to come calling without an invitation. Not here in Westley. It wasn't one of those neighborly subdivisions where everybody knew everybody else. Carmichael had picked it for that reason.

"Damn you," he growled, "you can't hold us *prisoners* in here!"

"My intent is only to help you," said the robot, in a mechanical yet dedicated voice. "My function is to supervise your diet. Since you will not obey willingly, obedience must be enforced—for your own good."

Carmichael scowled and walked away. The worst part of it was that the roboservitor sounded so *sincere!*

Trapped. The phone connection was severed. The windows were darkened. Somehow, Joey's attempt at repairs had resulted in a short circuit of the robot's obedience filters, and had also exaggeratedly stimulated its sense of function. Now Bismarck was determined to make them lose weight if it had to kill them to do so.

And that seemed very likely.

Blockaded, the Carmichael family met in a huddled little group to whisper plans for a counterattack. Clyde stood watch, but the robutler seemed to be in a state of general shock since the demonstration of the servitor-robot's independent capacity for action, and Carmichael now regarded him as undependable.

"He's got the kitchen walled off with some kind of electronic-based force web," Joey said. "He must have built it during the night. I tried to sneak in and scrounge some food, and got nothing but a flat nose for trying."

"I know," Carmichael said sadly. "He built the same sort of doohickey around the bar. Three hundred credits of good booze in there and I can't even grab the handle!"

"This is no time to worry about drinking," Ethel said morosely. "We'll be skeletons any day."

"It isn't *that* bad, Mom!" Joey said.

"Yes, it is!" cried Myra. "I've lost five pounds in four days!"

"Is that so terrible?"

"I'm wasting away," she sobbed. "My figure—it's vanishing! And—"

"Quiet," Carmichael whispered. "Bismarck's coming!"

The robot emerged from the kitchen, passing through the force barrier as if it had been a cobweb. It seemed to have effect on humans only, Carmichael thought. "Lunch will be served in eight minutes," it said obsequiously, and returned to its lair.

Carmichael glanced at his watch. The time was 1230 hours. "Probably down at the office they're wondering where I am," he said. "I haven't missed a day's work in years."

"They won't care," Ethel said. "An executive isn't required to account for every day off he takes, you know."

"But they'll worry after three or four days, won't they?" Myra asked. "Maybe they'll try to phone—or even send a rescue mission!"

From the kitchen, Bismarck said coldly, "There will be no danger of that. While you slept this morning, I notified your place of employment that you were resigning."

Carmichael gasped. Then, recovering, he said: "You're lying! The phone's cut off—and you never would have risked leaving the house, even if we *were* asleep!"

"I communicated with them via a microwave generator I constructed with the aid of your son's reference books last night," Bismarck replied. "Clyde reluctantly supplied me with the number. I also phoned your bank and instructed them to handle for you all such matters as tax payments, investment decisions, etc. To forestall difficulties, let me add that a force web will prevent access on your part to the electronic equipment in the basement. I will be able to conduct such communication with the outside world as will be necessary for your welfare, Mr. Carmichael. You need have no worries on that score."

"No," Carmichael echoed hollowly. "No worries."

He turned to Joey. "We've got to get out of here. Are you sure there's no way of disconnecting the privacy field?"

"He's got one of his force fields rigged around the control box. I can't even get near the thing."

"If only we had an iceman, or an oilman, the way the oldtime houses did," Ethel said bitterly. "He'd show up and come inside and probably he'd know how to shut the field off. But not *here*. Oh, no. We've got a shiny chrome-plated cryostat in the basement that dishes out lots of liquid helium to run the fancy cryotronic super-cooled power plant that gives us heat and light, and we have enough food in the freezer to last for at least a decade or two, and so we can live like this for years, a neat little self-contained island in the middle of civilization, with nobody bothering us, nobody wondering about us, and Sam Carmichael's pet robot to feed us whenever and as little as it pleases—"

There was a cutting edge to her voice that was dangerously close to hysteria.

"Ethel, please," said Carmichael.

"Please what? Please keep quiet? Please stay calm? Sam, we're *prisoners* in here!"

"I know. You don't have to raise your voice."

"Maybe if I do, someone will hear us and come get us out," she replied more coolly.

"It's four hundred feet to the next home, dear. And in the seven years we've lived here, we've had about two visits from our neighbors. We paid a stiff price for seclusion and now we're paying a stiffer one. But please keep under control, Ethel."

"Don't worry, Mom. I'll figure a way out of this," Joey said reassuringly.

In one corner of the living room, Myra was sobbing quietly to herself, blotching her makeup. Carmichael felt a faintly claustrophobic quiver. The house was big, three levels and twelve rooms, but even so he could get tired of it very quickly.

"Luncheon is served," the roboservitor announced in booming tones.

And tired of lettuce-and-tomato lunches, too, Carmichael added silently, as he shepherded his family toward the dining room for their meager midday meal.

"You have to do *something* about this, Sam," Ethel Carmichael said on the third day of their imprisonment.

He glared at her. "Have to, eh? And just what am I supposed to do?"

"Daddy, don't get excited," Myra said.

He whirled at her. "Don't tell me what I should or shouldn't do!"

"She can't help it, dear. We're all a little overwrought. After all, cooped up here—"

"I know. Like lambs in a pen," he finished acidly. "Except that we're not being fattened for slaughter. We're—we're being *thinned,* and for our own alleged good!"

Carmichael subsided gloomily. Toast-and-black-coffee, lettuce-and-tomato, rare-steak-and-peas. Bismarck's channels seemed to have frozen permanently at that daily menu.

But what could he do?

Contact with the outside world was impossible. The robot had erected a bastion in the basement from which he conducted such little business with the world as the Carmichael family had. Generally, they were self-sufficient. And Bismarck's force fields ensured the impossibility of any attempts to disconnect the outer sheath, break into the basement, or even get at the

food supply or the liquor. It was all very neat, and the four of
them were fast approaching a state of starvation.

"Sam?"

He lifted his head wearily. "What is it, Ethel?"

"Myra had an idea before. Tell him, Myra."

"Oh, it would never work," Myra said demurely.

"Tell him!"

"Well—Dad, you *could* try to turn Bismarck off."

"Huh?" Carmichael grunted.

"I mean if you or Joey could distract him somehow, then
Joey or you could open him up again and—"

"No," Carmichael snapped. "That thing's seven feet tall and
weighs three hundred pounds. If you think *I'm* going to wrestle
with it—"

"We could let Clyde try," Ethel suggested.

Carmichael shook his head vehemently. "The carnage would
be frightful."

Joey said, "Dad, it may be our only hope."

"You too?" Carmichael asked.

He took a deep breath. He felt himself speared by two deadly
feminine glances, and he knew there was no hope but to try
it. Resignedly, he pushed himself to his feet and said, "Okay.
Clyde, go call Bismarck. Joey, I'll try to hang onto his arms
while you open up his chest. Yank anything you can."

"Be careful," Ethel warned. "If there's an explosion—"

"If there's an explosion, we're all free," Carmichael said
testily. He turned to see the broad figure of the roboservitor
standing at the entrance to the living room.

"May I be of service, sir?"

"You may," Carmichael said. "We're having a little debate
here and we want your evidence. It's a matter of defannising
the poozlestan and—*Joey, open him up!*"

Carmichael grabbed for the robot's arms, trying to hold them
without getting hurled across the room, while his son clawed
frantically at the stud that opened the robot's innards. Carmichael anticipated immediate destruction—but, to his surprise,
he found himself slipping as he tried to grasp the thick arms.

"Dad, it's no use. I—he—"

Carmichael found himself abruptly four feet off the ground.
He heard Ethel and Myra scream and Clyde's, *"Do* be careful,
sir."

Bismarck was carrying them across the room, gently, cradling him in one giant arm and Joey in the other. It set them on the couch and stood back.

"Such an attempt is highly dangerous," Bismarck said reprovingly. "It puts me in danger of harming you physically. Please avoid any such acts in the future."

Carmichael stared broodingly at his son. "Did you have the same trouble I did?"

Joey nodded. "I couldn't get within an inch of his skin. It stands to reason, though. He's built one of those damned force screens around *himself*, too!"

Carmichael groaned. He did not look at his wife and his children. Physical attack on Bismarck was now out of the question. He began to feel as if he had been condemned to life imprisonment—and that his stay in durance vile would not be extremely prolonged.

In the upstairs bathroom, six days after the beginning of the blockade, Sam Carmichael stared at his haggard fleshless face in the mirror before wearily climbing on the scale.

He weighed 180.

He had lost twelve pounds in less than two weeks. He was fast becoming a quivering wreck.

A thought occurred to him as he stared at the wavering needle on the scale, and sudden elation spread over him. He dashed downstairs. Ethel was doggedly crocheting in the living room; Joey and Myra were playing cards grimly, desperately now, after six solid days of gin rummy and honeymoon bridge.

"Where's the robot?" Carmichael roared. "Come out here!"

"In the kitchen," Ethel said tonelessly.

"Bismarck! Bismarck!" Carmichael roared. "Come out here!"

The robot appeared. "How may I serve you, sir?"

"Damn you, scan me with your superpower receptors and tell me how much I weigh!"

After a pause, the robot said gravely, "One hundred seventy-nine pounds eleven ounces, Mr. Carmichael."

"Yes! Yes! And the original program I had taped into you was supposed to reduce me from one hundred ninety-two to one hundred eighty," Carmichael crowed triumphantly. "So I'm finished with you, as long as I don't gain any more weight. And so are the rest of us, I'll bet. Ethel! Myra! Joey! Upstairs and weigh yourselves!"

But the robot regarded him with a doleful glare and said, "Sir, I find no record within me of any limitation on your reduction of weight."

"*What?*"

"I have checked my tapes fully. I have a record of an order causing weight reduction, but that tape does not appear to specify a *terminus ad quem*."

Carmichael exhaled and took three staggering steps backward. His legs wobbled; he felt Joey supporting him. He mumbled, "But I thought—I'm sure we did—I *know* we instructed you—"

Hunger gnawed at his flesh. Joey said softly, "Dad, probably that part of his tape was erased when he short-circuited."

"Oh," Carmichael said numbly.

He tottered into the living room and collapsed heavily in what had once been his favorite armchair. It wasn't anymore. The entire house had become odious to him. He longed to see the sunlight again, to see trees and grass, even to see that excrescence of an ultramodern house that the left-hand neighbors had erected.

But now that would be impossible. He had hoped, for a few minutes at least, that the robot would release them from dietary bondage when the original goal was shown to be accomplished. Evidently that was to be denied him. He giggled, then began to laugh.

"What's so funny, dear?" Ethel asked. She had lost her earlier tendencies to hysteria, and after long days of complex crocheting now regarded the universe with quiet resignation.

"Funny? the fact that I weigh one hundred eighty now. I'm lean, trim, fit as a fiddle. Next month I'll weigh one hundred seventy. Then one hundred sixty. Then finally about eighty-eight pounds or so. We'll all shrivel up. Bismarck will starve us to death."

"Don't worry, Dad. We're going to get out of this."

Somehow Joey's brash boyish confidence sounded forced now. Carmichael shook his head. "We won't. We'll never get out. And Bismarck's going to reduce us *ad infinitum*. He's got no *terminus ad quem!*"

"What's he saying?" Myra asked.

"It's Latin," Joey explained. "But listen, Dad—I have an idea that I think will work." He lowered his voice. "I'm going to try to adjust Clyde, see? If I can get a sort of multiphase vibrating effect in his neural pathway, maybe I can slip him through the reversed privacy field. He can go get help, find someone who can shut the field off. There's an article on multiphase generators in last month's *Popular Electromagnetics* and it's in my room upstairs. I—"

His voice died away. Carmichael, who had been listening with the air of a condemned man hearing his reprieve, said impatiently, "Well? Go on. Tell me more."

"Didn't you hear that, Dad?"

"Hear what?"

"The front door. I thought I heard it open just now."

"We're all cracking up," Carmichael said dully. He cursed the salesman at Marhew, he cursed the inventor of cryotronic robots, he cursed the day he had first felt ashamed of good old Jemima and resolved to replace her with a new model.

"I hope I'm not intruding, Mr. Carmichael," a new voice said apologetically.

Carmichael blinked and looked up. A wiry, ruddy-cheeked figure in a heavy peajacket had materialized in the middle of the living room. He was clutching a green metal toolbox in one gloved hand. He was Robinson, the robot repairman.

Carmichael asked hoarsely, "How did *you* get in?"

"Through the front door. I could see a light on inside, but nobody answered the doorbell when I rang, so I stepped in. Your doorbell's out of order. I thought I'd tell you. I know it's rude—"

"Don't apologize," Carmichael muttered. "We're delighted to see you."

"I was in the neighborhood, you see, and I figured I'd drop in and see how things were working out with your new robot," Robinson said.

Carmichael told him crisply and precisely and quickly. "So we've been prisoners in here for six days," he finished. "and your robot is gradually starving us to death. We can't hold out much longer."

The smile abruptly left Robinson's cheery face. "I *thought* you all looked rather unhealthy. Oh, damn, now there'll be an investigation and all kinds of trouble. But at least I can end your imprisonment."

He opened his toolbox and selected a tubular instrument

eight inches long, with a glass bulb at one end and a trigger attachment at the other. "Force-field damper," he explained. He pointed it at the control box of the privacy field and nodded in satisfaction. "There. Great little gadget. That neutralizes the effects of what the robot did and you're no longer blockaded. And now, if you'll produce the robot—"

Carmichael sent Clyde off to get Bismarck. The robutler returned a few minutes later, followed by the looming robo-servitor. Robinson grinned gaily, pointed the neutralizer at Bismarck and squeezed. The robot froze in midglide, emitting a brief squeak.

"There. That should immobilize him. Let's have a look in that chassis now."

The repairman quickly opened Bismarck's chest and, producing a pocket flash, peered around in the complex interior of the servomechanism, making occasional clucking inaudible comments.

Overwhelmed with relief, Carmichael shakily made his way to a seat. Free! Free at last! His mouth watered at the thought of the meals he was going to have in the next few days. Potatoes and Martinis and warm buttered rolls and all the other forbidden foods!

"Fascinating," Robinson said, half to himself. "The obedience filters are completely shorted out, and the purpose nodes are somehow soldered together by the momentary high-voltage arc. I've never seen anything quite like this, you know."

"Neither had we," Carmichael said hollowly.

"Really, though—this is an utterly new breakthrough in robotic science! If we can reproduce this effect, it means we can build self-willed robots—and think of what *that* means to science!"

"We know already," Ethel said.

"I'd love to watch what happens when the power source is operating," Robinson went on. "For instance, is that feedback loop really negative or—"

"No!" Five voices shrieked at once—with Clyde, as usual, coming in last.

It was too late. The entire event had taken no more than a tenth of a second. Robinson had squeezed his neutralizer trigger again, activating Bismarck—and in one quick swoop the robo-servitor seized the neutralizer and toolbox from the stunned repairman, activated the privacy field once again, and exult-antly crushed the fragile neutralizer between two mighty fin-gers.

Robinson stammered, "But—but—"

"This attempt at interfering with the well-being of the Car-michael family was ill-advised," Bismarck said severely. He peered into the toolbox, found a second neutralizer and neatly reduced it to junk. He clanged shut his chest plates.

Robinson turned and streaked for the door, forgetting the reactivated privacy field. He bounced back hard, spinning wildly around. Carmichael rose from his seat just in time to catch him.

There was a panicky, trapped look on the repairman's face. Carmichael was no longer able to share the emotion; inwardly he was numb, totally resigned, not minded for further struggle.

"He—he moved so *fast!*" Robinson burst out.

"He did indeed," Carmichael said tranquilly. He patted his hollow stomach and sighed gently. "Luckily, we have an un-occupied guest bedroom for you, Mr. Robinson. Welcome to our happy little home. I hope you like toast and black coffee for breakfast."

THE WABBLER

Murray Leinster

The Wabbler went westward, with a dozen of its fellows, by
night and in the belly of a sleek, swift-flying thing. There were
no lights anywhere save the stars overhead. There was a sustained, furious roaring noise, which was the sound the sleek
thing made in flying. The Wabbler lay in its place, with its
ten-foot tail coiled neatly above its lower end, and waited with
a sort of deadly patience for the accomplishment of its destiny.
It and all its brothers were pear-shaped, with absurdly huge
and blunt-ended horns, and with small round holes where eyes
might have been, and shielded vents where they might have
had mouths. The looked chinless, somehow. They also looked
alive, and inhuman, and filled with a sort of passionless hate.
They seemed like bodiless demons out of some metallic hell.
It was not possible to feel any affection for them. Even the
men who handled them felt only a soft of vengeful hope in
their capacities.

The Wabblers squatted in their racks for long hours. It was
very cold, but they gave no sign. The sleek, swift-flying thing
roared on and roared on. The Wabblers waited. Men moved
somewhere in the flying thing, but they did not come where

247

the Wabblers were until the very end. But somehow, when a man came and inspected each one of them very carefully and poked experimentally about the bottoms of the racks in which the Wabblers lay, they knew that the time had come.

The man went away. The sleek thing tilted a little. It seemed to climb. The air grew colder, but the Wabblers—all of them— were indifferent. Air was not their element. Then, when it was very, very cold indeed, the roaring noise of the flying thing ceased abruptly. The cessation of the noise was startling. Presently little whistling, whispering noises took the place of the roar, as hearing adjusted to a new level of sound. That whistling and whining noise was wind, flowing past the wings of the flying thing. Presently the air was a little warmer—but still very cold. The flying thing was gliding, motors off, and descending at a very gradual slant.

The Wabbler was the fourth in the row of its brothers on the port side of the flying thing. It did not stir, of course, but it felt an atmosphere of grim and savage anticipation. It seemed that all the brothers coldly exchanged greetings and farewell. The time had definitely come.

The flying thing leveled out. Levers and rods moved in the darkness of its belly. The feeling of anticipation increased. Then, suddenly, there were only eleven of the Wabblers. Wind roared where the twelfth had been. There were ten. There were nine, eight, seven, six—

The Wabbler hurtled downward through blackness. There were clouds overhead now. In all the world there was no speck of actual light. But below there was a faint luminosity. The Wabbler's tail uncurled and writhed flexibly behind it. Wind screamed past its ungainly form. It went plunging down and down and down, its round holes—which looked so much like eyes—seeming incurious and utterly impassive. The luminosity underneath separated into streaks of bluish glow, which were phosphorescences given off by the curling tips of waves. Off to westward there was a brighter streak of such luminosity. It was surf.

Splash! The Wabbler plunged into the water with a flare of luminescence and a thirty-foot spout of spume and spray rising where it struck. But then that spouting ceased, and the Wabbler was safely under water. It dived swiftly for twenty feet. Perhaps thirty. Then its falling checked. It swung about, and its writhing

tail settled down below it. For a little while it seemed almost
to intend to swim back to the surface. But bubbles came from
the shielded opening which seemed to be a mouth. It hung
there in the darkness of the sea—but now and then there were
little fiery streaks of light as natives of the ocean swam about
it—and then slowly, slowly, slowly it settled downward. Its
ten-foot tail seemed to waver a little, as if groping.

Presently it touched. Ooze. Black ooze. Sea bottom. Sixty
feet overhead the waves marched to and fro in darkness. Somehow, through the stilly silence, there came a muffled vibration.
That was the distant surf, beating upon a shore. The Wabbler
hung for an instant with the very tip of its tail barely touching
the bottom. Then it made small sounds inside itself. More
bubbles came from the round place like a mouth. It settled one
foot; two feet; three. Three feet of its tail rested on the soft
ooze. It hung, pear-shaped, some seven feet above the ocean
bottom, with the very tip of its horns no more than four feet
higher yet. There were fifty feet of empty sea above it. This
was not its destiny. It waited passionlessly for what was to
happen.

There was silence save for the faint vibration from the distant
surf. But there was an infinitesimal noise, also, within the
Wabbler's bulk, a rhythmic, insistent, hurried *tick-tick-tick-
tick*—It was the Wabbler's brain in action.

Time passed. Above the sea the sleek, swift-flying thing
bellowed suddenly far away. It swerved and went roaring back
in the direction from which it had come. Its belly was empty
now, and somewhere in the heaving sea there were other Wabblers, each one now waiting as the fourth Wabbler did, for the
thing that its brain expected. Minutes and minutes passed. The
seas marched to and fro. The faraway surf rumbled and roared
against the shore. And higher yet, above the clouds, a low-
hanging invisible moon dipped down toward a horizon which
did not show anywhere. But the Wabbler waited.

The tide came. Here, so far from the pounding surf, the
stirring of the lower levels of the sea was slight indeed. But
the tide moved in toward the land. Slowly, the pressure of
water against one of the Wabbler's sides became evident. The
Wabbler leaned infinitesimally toward the shore. Presently the
flexible tail ceased to be curved where it lay upon the ooze. It
straightened out. There were little bluish glows where it stirred

the phosphorescent mud. Then the Wabbler moved. Shoreward. It trailed its tail behind it and left a little glowing track of ghostly light.

Fish swim about it. Once there was a purring sound, and propellers pushed an invisible, floating thing across the surface of the sea. But it was far away and the Wabbler was impassive. The tide flowed. The Wabbler moved in little jerks. Sometimes three feet or four, and sometimes eight or ten. Once, where the sea bottom slanted downward for a space, it moved steadily for almost a hundred yards. It came to rest then, swaying a little. Presently it jerked onward once more. Somewhere an indefinite distance away were its brothers, moving on in the same fashion. The Wabbler went on and on, purposefully, moved by the tide.

Before the tide turned, the Wabbler had moved two miles nearer to the land. But it did not move in a straight line. Its trailing, flexible tail kept in the deepest water and the strongest current. It moved very deliberately and almost always in small jerks, and it followed the current. The current was strongest where it moved toward a harbor entrance. In moving two miles shoreward, the Wabbler also moved more than two miles nearer to a harbor.

There came a time, though, when the tide slackened. The Wabbler ceased to move. For half an hour it hung quite still, swaying a little and progressing not at all, while the *tick-tick-tick-tick* of its brain measured patience against intent. At the end of the half-hour there were small clanking noises within its body. Its shielded mouth emitted bubbles. It sank, and checked, and gave off more bubbles, and sank again. It eased itself very cautiously and very gently into the ooze. Then it gave off more bubbles and lay at rest.

It waited there, its brain ticking restlessly within it, but with its appearance of eyes impassive. It lay in the darkness like some creature from another world, awaiting a foreordained event.

For hours it lay still with no sign of any activity at all. Toward the end of those hours, a very faint graying of the upper sea became manifest. It was very dim indeed. It was not enough, in all likelihood, for even the Wabbler to detect the slight movement of semi-floating objects along the sea floor, moved by the ebb tide. But there came a time when even such movements ceased. Again the sea was still. It was full ebb. And now the Wabbler stirred.

It clanked gently and wavered where it lay in the ooze. There was a cloud of stirred-up mud, as if it had emitted jets of water from its under parts. It wabbled to one side and the other, straining, and presently its body was free, and a foot or two and then four or five feet of its tail—but it still writhed and wabbled spasmodically—and then suddenly it left the sea floor and floated free.

But only for a moment. Almost immediately its tail swung free, the Wabbler spat out bubbles and descended gently to the bottom again. It rested upon the tip of its tail. It spat more bubbles. One—two—three feet of its tail rested on the mud. It waited. Presently the flood tide moved it again.

It floated always with the current. Once it came to a curve in the deeper channel to which it had found its way, and the tide tended to sweep it up and out beyond the channel. But its tail resisted the attempt. In the end, the Wabbler swam grandly back to the deeper water. The current was stronger there. It went on and on at a magnificent two knots.

But when the current slowed again as the time of the tide change neared, the Wabbler stopped again. It swung above the yard-length of its tail upon the mud. Its brain went *tick-tick-tick-tick* and it made noises. It dribbled bubbles. It sank, and checked, and dribbled more bubbles, and sank cautiously again—It came cautiously to rest in the mud.

During this time of waiting, the Wabbler heard many sounds. Many times during slack tide, and during ebb tide, too, the water brought humming, purring noises of engines. Once a boat came very near. There was a curious hissing sound in the water. Something—a long line—passed very close overhead. A minesweeper and a minesweep patrolled the sea, striving to detect and uproot submarine mines. But the Wabbler had no anchor cable for the sweep to catch. It lay impassively upon the bottom. But its eyes stared upward with a deadly calm until the minesweeper passed on its way.

Once more during the light hours the Wabbler shook itself free of the bottom ooze and swam on with the tide. And once more—with another wait on the mud while the tide flowed out—at night. But day and night meant little to the Wabbler. Its ticking brain went on tirelessly. It rested, and swam, and swam, and rested, with a machinelike and impassive pertinacity, and always it moved toward places where the tide moved faster and with channels more distinct.

At last it came to a place where the water was no more than forty feet deep, and a distinct greenish-blue light came down from the surface sunshine. In that light the Wabbler was plainly visible. It had acquired a coating of seaweed and slime which seemed to form a sort of aura of wavering greenish tentacles. Its seeming eyes appeared now to be small and snakelike and very wise and venemous. It was still chinless, and its trailing tail made it seem more than ever like some bodiless demon out of a metallic hell. And now it came to a place where for a moment its tail caught in some minor obstruction, and as it tugged at the catch, one of its brothers floated by. It passed within twenty feet of the fourth Wabbler, and they could see each other clearly. But the fourth Wabbler was trapped. It wavered back and forth in the flood tide, trying to pull free, as its fellow swam silently and implacably onward.

Some twenty minutes after that passage there was a colossal explosion somewhere, and after that very many fuzzy, purring noises in the sea. The Wabbler may have known what had happened, or it may not. A submarine net across a harbor entrance is not a thing of which most creatures have knowledge, but it was part of the Wabbler's environment. Its *tick-tick-tick-ticking* brain may have interpreted the explosion quite correctly as the destiny of its brother encountering that barrier. It is more likely that the brain only noted with relief that the concussion had broken the grip of the obstruction in the mud. The Wabbler went onward in the wake of its fellow. It went sedately, and solemnly, and with a sort of unholy purposefulness, following the tidal current. Presently there was a great net that stretched across the channel, far beyond any distance that the Wabbler could be expected to see. But right where the Wabbler would pass, there was a monstrous gaping hole in that net. Off to one side there was the tail of another Wabbler, shattered away from that other Wabbler's bulk.

The fourth Wabbler went through the hole. It was very simple indeed. Its tail scraped for a moment, and then it was inside the harbor. And then the *tick-tick-ticking* of the Wabbler's brain was very crisp and incisive indeed, because this was its chance for the accomplishment of its destiny. It listened for sounds of engines, estimating their loudness with an uncanny precision, and within its rounded brainpan it measured things as abstract as variations in the vertical component of terrestrial magnetism. There were many sounds and many variations to note, too, because surface craft swarmed about the scene of a recent violent explosion. Their engines purred and rumbled, and ther steel hulls made marked local changes in magnetic force. But none of them came quite close enough to the Wabbler to constitute its destiny.

It went on and on as the flood tide swept in. The harbor was a busy one, with many small craft moving about, and more than once in these daylight hours flying things alighted upon the water and took off again. But it happened that none came sufficiently near. An hour after its entrance into the harbor the Wabbler was in a sort of eddy, in a basin, and it made four slow, hitching circuits about the same spot—during one of which it came near to serried ranks of piling—before the time of slack water. But even here the Wabbler, after swaying a little without making progress for perhaps twenty minutes, made little clanking noises inside itself and dribbled out bubbles and eased itself down in the mud to wait.

It lay there, canted a little and staring up with its small, round, seeming eyes with a look of unimpassioned expectancy. Small boats roved overhead. Once engines rumbled, and a wooden-hulled craft swam on the surface of the water to the very dock whose pilings the Wabbler had seen. Then creaking sounds emanated from those pilings. The Wabbler may have known that unloading cranes were at work. But this was not its destiny either.

There came other sounds of greater import. Clankings of gears. A definite, burning rush of water. It continued and continued. The Wabbler could not possibly be expected to understand, of course, that such burbling underwater sounds are typical of a drydock being filled—the filling beginning near low tide when a great ship is to leave at high. Especially, perhaps, the Wabbler could not be expected to know that a great warship had occupied a vastly important drydock and that its return to active service would restore much power to an enemy fleet. Certainly it could not know that another great warship waited impatiently to be repaired in the same basin. But the restless *tick-tick-tick-tick* which was the Wabbler's brain was remarkably crisp and incisive.

When flood tide began once more, the Wabbler jetted water and wabbled to and fro until it broke free of the bottom. It hung with a seeming impatience—wreathed in seaweed and coated with greenish slime—above the tail which dangled down to the harbor mud. It looked alive, and inhuman, and chinless, and it looked passionately demoniac, and it looked like something out of a submarine Gehenna. And, presently, when the flood tide began to flow and the eddy about the docks and the drydock gates began, the Wabbler inched as if purposefully toward the place where the water burbled through flooding valves.

Sounds in the air did not reach the Wabbler. Sounds under water did. It heard the grinding rumble of stream winches, and it heard the screeching sound as the drydock gates swung open. They were huge gates, and they made a considerable eddy of their own. The Wabbler swam to the very center of that eddy and hung there, waiting. Now, for the first time, it seemed excited. It seemed to quiver a little. Once when it seemed that the eddy might bring it to the surface, it bubbled patiently from the vent which appeared to be a mouth. And its brain went *tick-tick-tick-tick* within it, and inside its brainpan it measured variations in the vertical component of terrestrial magnetism, and among such measurements it noted the effect of small tugs which came near but did not enter the drydock. They only sent lines within, so they could haul the warship out. But the tugs were not the Wabbler's destiny either.

It heard their propellers thrashing, and they made, to be sure, a very fine noise. But the Wabbler quivered with eagerness as somewhere within itself it noted a vast variation in the vertical magnetic component, which increased and increased steadily. That was the warship moving very slowly out of its place in the drydock. It moved very slowly but very directly toward the Wabbler, and the Wabbler knew that its destiny was near.

Somewhere very far away there was the dull, racking sound of an explosion. The Wabbler may have realized that another of its brothers had achieved its destiny, but paid no heed. Its own destiny approached. The steel prow of the battleship drew nearer, and then the bow plates were overhead, and something made a tiny click inside the Wabbler. Destiny was certain now.

It waited, quivering. The mass of steel within the range of its senses grew greater and greater. The strain of restraint grew more intense. The *tick-tick-ticking* of the Wabbler's brain seemed to accelerate to a frantic—to an intolerable—pace. And then—

The Wabbler achieved its destiny. It turned into a flaming ball of incandescent gases—three hundred pounds of detonated high explosive—squarely under the keel of a thirty-five thousand-ton battleship which at the moment was only halfway out of a drydock. The water-tight doors of the battleship were open, and its auxiliary power was off, so they could not be closed. There was much need for this drydock, and repairs were not completed in it. But it was the Wabbler's destiny to end all that. In three minutes the battleship was lying crazily on the harbor bottom, half in and half out of the drydock. She careened as she sank, and her masts and fighting tops demolished sheds by the drydock walls. Battleship and dock alike were out of action for the duration of the war.

And the Wabbler—

A long, long time afterward—years afterward—salvage divers finished cutting up the sunken warship for scrap. The last irregularly cut mass of metal went up on the salvage slings. The last diver down went stumbling about the muddy harbor water. His heavy, weighted shoes kicked up something. He fumbled to see if anything remained to be salvaged. He found a ten-foot, still-flexible tail of metal. The rest of the Wabbler had ceased to exist. Chronometer, tide-time gear, valves, compressed-air tanks, and all the balance of its intricate innards had been blown to atoms when the Wabbler achieved its destiny. Only the flexible metal tail remained intact.

The salvage diver considered that it was not worth sending the sling down for again. He dropped it in the mud and jerked on the lifeline to be hauled up to the surface.

THE CRUEL EQUATIONS

Robert Sheckley

After landing on Regulus V, the men of the Yarmolinsky Expedition made camp and activated PR-22-0134, their perimeter robot, whom they called Max. The robot was a voice-activated, bipedal mechanism whose function was to guard the camp against the depredations of aliens, in the event that aliens were ever encountered. Max had originally been a regulation gunmetal gray, but on the interminable outward trip they had repainted him a baby blue. Max stood exactly four feet high. The men of the expedition had come to think of him as a kindly, reasonable little metal man—a ferrous gnome, a miniature Tin Woodman of Oz.

They were wrong, of course. Their robot had none of the qualities which they projected onto him. PR-22-0134 was no more reasonable than a McCormick harvester, no more kindly than an automated steel mill. Morally, he might be compared to a turbine or a radio, but not to anything human. PR-22-0134's only human attribute was potentiality.

Little Max, baby blue with red eyes, circled the perimeter of the camp, his sensors alert. Captain Beatty and Lieutenant James took off in the hoverjet for a week of exploration. They left Lieutenant Halloran to mind the store.

Halloran was a short, stocky man with a barrel chest and bandy legs. He was cheerful, freckled, tough, profane, and resourceful. He ate lunch and acknowledged a radio check from the exploring team. Then he unfolded a canvas chair and sat back to enjoy the scenery.

Regulus V was a pretty nice place, if you happened to be an admirer of desolation. A superheated landscape of rock, gravel, and lava stretched on all sides. There were some birds that looked like sparrows and some animals that looked like coyotes. A few cacti scratched out a bare living.

Halloran pulled himself to his feet. "Max! I'm going to take a look outside the perimeter. You'll be in charge while I'm gone."

The robot stopped patrolling. "Yes, sir, I will be in charge."

"You will not allow any aliens to come busting in; especially the two-headed kind with their feet on backwards."

"Very well, sir." Max had no sense of humor when it came to aliens. "Do you have the password, Mr. Halloran?"

"I got it, Max. How about you?"

"I have it, sir."

"OK. See you later." Halloran left the camp.

After examining the real estate for an hour and finding nothing of interest, Halloran came back. He was pleased to see PR-22-0134 patrolling along the perimeter. It meant that everything was all right.

"Hi there, Max," he called. "Any messages for me?"

"Halt," the robot said. "Give the password."

"Cut the comedy, Max. I'm in no mood for—"

"*HALT!*" the robot shouted, as Halloran was about to cross the perimeter.

Halloran came to an abrupt stop. Max's photoelectric eyes had flared, and a soft double click announced that his primary armament was activated. Halloran decided to proceed with caution.

"I am halted. My name is Halloran. OK now, Maxie?"

"Give the password, please."

"'Bluebells,'" Halloran said. "Now, if you don't mind—"

"Do not cross the perimeter," the robot said. "Your password is incorrect."

"The hell it is. I gave it to you myself."

"That was the previous password."

"Previous? You're out of your semi-solid mind," Halloran said. "'Bluebells' is the only password, and you didn't get any new one because there isn't any new one. Unless. . . ."

The robot waited— Halloran considered the unpleasant thought from various angles, and at last put words to it.

"Unless Captain Beatty gave you a new password before he left. Is *that* what happened?"

"Yes," the robot said.

"I should have thought of it," Halloran said. He grinned, but he was annoyed. There had been slipups like this before. But there had always been someone inside the camp to correct them.

Still, there was nothing to worry about. When you came right down to it, the situation was more than a little funny. And it could be resolved with just a modicum of reason.

Halloran was assuming, of course, that PR robots possess a modicum of reason.

"Max," Halloran said, "I see how it probably happened. Captain Beatty probably gave you a new password. But he failed to tell me about it. I then compounded his error by neglecting to check on the password situation before I left the perimeter."

The robot made no comment. Halloran went on. "The mistake, in any case, is easily corrected."

"I sincerely hope so," the robot said.

"Of course it is," Halloran said, a little less confidently. "The captain and I follow a set procedure in these matters. When he gives you a password, he also transmits it to me orally. But, just in case there is any lapse—like now—he also writes it down."

"Does he?" the robot asked.

"Yes, he does," Halloran said. "Always. Invariably. Which includes this time too, I hope. Do you see that tent behind you?"

The robot swiveled one sensor, keeping the other fixed on Halloran. "I see it."

"OK. Inside the tent, there is a table. On the table is a gray metal clipboard."

"Correct," Max said.

"Fine! Now then, there is a sheet of paper in the clipboard. On it is a list of vital data—emergency radio frequencies, that sort of thing. On the top of the paper, circled in red, is the current password."

The robot extended and focused his sensor, then retracted it. He said to Halloran, "What you say is true, but irrelevant. I am concerned only with your knowledge of the actual password, not its location. If you can state the password, I must let you into the camp. If not, I must keep you out."

"This is insane!" Halloran shouted. "Max, you legalistic idiot, it's *me*, Halloran, and you damned well know it! We've been together since the day you were activated! Now will you please stop playing Horatio at the bridge and let me in?"

"Your resemblance to Mr. Halloran *is* uncanny," the robot admitted. "But I am neither equipped nor empowered to conduct identity tests; nor am I permitted to act on the basis of my perceptions. The only proof I can accept is the password itself."

Halloran fought down his rage. In a conversational tone he said, "Max, old buddy, it sounds like you're implying that I'm an alien."

"Since you do not have the password," Max said, "I must proceed on that assumption."

"Max!" Halloran shouted, stepping forward, "for Christ's sake!"

"Do not approach the perimeter!" the robot said, his sensors flaring. "Whoever or whatever you are, stand back!"

"All right, I'm standing back," Halloran said quickly. "Don't get so nervous."

He backed away from the perimeter and waited until the robot's sensors had gone quiescent. Then he sat down on a rock. He had some serious thinking to do.

It was almost noon in Regulus's thousand-hour day. The twin suns hung overhead, distorted white blobs in a dead white sky. They moved sluggishly above a dark granite landscape, slow-motion juggernauts who destroyed what they touched.

An occasional bird soared in weary circles through the dry fiery air. A few small animals crept from shadow to shadow. A creature that looked like a wolverine gnawed at a tent peg, and was ignored by a small blue robot. A man sat on a rock and watched the robot.

Halloran, already feeling the effects of exposure and thirst, was trying to understand his situation and to plan a way out of it.

He wanted water. Soon he would need water. Not long after that, he would die for lack of water.

There was no known source of potable water within walking distance, except in the camp.

There was plenty of water in the camp. But he couldn't get to it past the robot.

Beatty and James would routinely try to contact him in three days, but they would probably not be alarmed if he didn't reply. Short-wave reception was erratic, even on Earth. They would try again in the evening and again the next day. Failing to raise him then, they would come back.

Call it four Earth days, then. How long could he go without water?

The answer depended on his rate of water loss. When he had sustained a total liquid loss of between ten and fifteen percent of his body weight, he would go into shock. This could happen with disastrous suddenness. Bedouin tribesmen, separated from their supplies, had been known to succumb in twenty-four hours. Stranded motorists in the American Southwest, trying to walk out of the Baker or Mojave Deserts, sometimes didn't last out the day.

Regulus V was as hot as the Kalahari, and had less humidity than Death Valley. A day on Regulus stretched for just under a thousand Earth hours. It was noon, he had five hundred hours of unremitting sunshine ahead of him without shelter or shade.

How long could he last? One Earth day. Two, at the most optimistic estimate.

Forget about Beatty and James. He had to get water from the camp, and he had to get it fast.

That meant he had to find a way past the robot.

He decided to try logic. "Max, you must know that I, Halloran, left the camp and that I, Halloran, returned an hour later, and that it is I, Halloran, now standing in front of you without the password."

"The probabilities are very strongly in favor of your interpretation," the robot admitted.

"Well, then—"

"But I cannot act on probabilities, or even near-certainties. After all, I have been created for the express purpose of dealing with aliens, despite the extremely low probability that I will ever meet one."

"Can you at least give me a canteen of water?"

"No. That would be against orders."

"When did you ever get orders about giving out water?"

"I didn't, not specifically. But the conclusion flows from my primary directive. I am not supposed to aid or assist aliens."

Halloran then said a great many things, very rapidly and in a loud voice. His statements were pungently and idiomatically Terran; but Max ignored them since they were abusive, tendentious, and entirely without merit.

After a while, the alien who called himself Halloran moved out of sight behind a pile of rocks.

After some minutes, a creature sauntered out from behind a pile of rocks, whistling.

"Hello there, Max," the creature said.

"Hello, Mr. Halloran," the robot replied.

Halloran stopped ten feet away from the perimeter. "Well," he said, "I've been looking around, but there's not much to see. Anything happen here while I've been gone?"

"Yes, sir," Max said. "An alien tried to enter the camp."

Halloran raised both eyebrows. "Is that a fact?"

"Indeed it is, sir."

"What did this alien look like?"

"He looked very much like you, Mr. Halloran."

"God in heaven!" Halloran exclaimed. "How did you know he was *not* me?"

"Because he tried to enter the camp without giving the password. That, of course, the real Mr. Halloran would never do."

"Exactly so," Halloran said. "Good work, Maxie. We'll have to keep our eyes open for that fellow."

"Yes, sir. Thank you, sir."

Halloran nodded casually. He was pleased with himself. He had figured out that Max, by the very terms of his construction, would have to deal with each encounter as unique, and to dispose of it according to its immediate merits. This had to be so, since Max was not permitted to reason on the basis of prior experiences.

Max had built-in biases. He assumed that Earthmen always have the password. He assumed that aliens never have the password, but always try to enter the camp. Therefore, a creature who did not try to enter the camp must be presumed to be free of the alien camp-entering compulsion, and therefore to be an Earthman, until proven otherwise.

Halloran thought that was pretty good reasoning for a man who had lost several percent of his body fluids. Now he had to hope that the rest of his plan would work as well.

"Max," he said, "during my inspection, I made one rather disturbing discovery."

"Sir?"

"I found that we are camped on the edge of a fault in this planet's crust. The lines of the schism are unmistakable; they make the San Andreas Fault look like a hairline fracture."

"Sounds bad, sir. Is there muc. risk?"

"You bet your tin ass there's much risk. And much risk means much work. You and I, Maxie, are going to shift the entire camp about two miles due west. Immediately! So pick up the canteens and follow me."

"Yes, sir," Max said. "As soon as you release me."

"OK, I release you," Halloran said. "Hurry up!"

"I can't," the robot said. "You must release me by giving the current password and stating that it is canceled. Then I'll be able to stop guarding this particular perimeter."

"There's no time for formalities," Halloran said tightly. "The new password is 'whitefish.' Get moving, Max, I just felt a tremor."

"I didn't feel anything."

"Why should you?" Halloran snapped. "You're just a PR robot, not an Earthman with special training and finely attuned sensory apparatus. Damn, there it goes again! You must have felt it that time!"

"I think I did feel it!"

"Then get moving!"

"Mr. Halloran, I can't! It is physically impossible for me to leave this perimeter without a formal release! Please, sir, release me!"

"Don't get so excited," Halloran said. "On second thought, we're going to leave the camp right here."

"But the earthquake—"

"I've just made a new calculation. We've got more time than I had thought. I'm going to take another look around."

Halloran moved behind the rocks, out of the robot's sight. His heart was beating heavily, and the blood in his veins felt thick and sluggish. Bright spots were dancing before his eyes. He diagnosed an incipient sunstroke, and forced himself to sit very quietly in a patch of shade.

The endless day stretched on. The amorphous white blob of the double suns crept an inch toward the horizon. PR-22-0134 guarded his perimeter.

A breeze sprang up, turned into half a gale, and blew sand against Max's unblinking sensors. The robot trudged on, keeping to an exact circle. The wind died down and a figure appeared among the rocks some twenty yards away. Someone was watching him: was it Halloran, or the alien? Max refused to speculate. He guarded his perimeter.

A small creature like a coyote darted out of the desert and ran a zigzag course almost under Max's feet. A large bird dived down in pursuit. There was a thin, high scream and blood was splashed against one of the tents. The bird flapped heavily into the air with something writhing in its claws.

Max paid no attention to this. He was watching a humanoid creature stagger toward him out of the rocks.

The creature stopped. "Good day, Mr. Halloran," Max said at once. "I feel that I should mention, sir, that you show definite signs of dehydration. That is a condition which leads to shock, unconsciousness, and death, unless attended to promptly."

"Shut up," Halloran said, in a husky, heat-parched voice.

"Very well, Mr. Halloran."

"And stop calling me Mr. Halloran."

"Why should I do that, sir?"

"Because I am not Halloran. I am an alien."

"Indeed?" the robot said.

"Yes, indeed. Do you doubt my word?"

"Well, your mere unsupported statement—"

"Never mind, I'll give you proof. *I do not know the pass-word*. Is that proof enough?"

When the robot still hesitated, Halloran said, "Look, Mr. Halloran told me that I should remind you of your own fundamental definitions, which are the criteria by which you perform your job. To wit: an Earthman is a sentient creature who knows the password; an alien is a sentient creature who does not know the password."

"Yes," the robot said reluctantly, "knowledge of the password is my yardstick. But still, I sense something wrong. Suppose you're lying to me?"

"If I'm lying, then I must be an Earthman who knows the password," Halloran explained. "In which case, there's no danger. But you know that I'm not lying, because you know that no Earthman would lie about the password."

"I don't know if I can assume that."

"You must. No Earthman wants to appear as an alien, does he?"

"Of course not."

"And a password is the only certain differentiation between a human and an alien?"

"Yes."

"Then the case is proven."

"I'm still not sure," Max said, and Halloran realized that the robot was reluctant to receive instruction from an alien, even if the alien was only trying to prove that he was an alien.

He waited. After a while, Max said, "All right, I agree that you are an alien. Accordingly, I refuse to let you into the camp."

"I'm not asking you to let me in. The point is, I am Halloran's prisoner, and you know what that means."

The robot blinked his sensors rapidly. "I don't know what that means."

"It means," Halloran said, "that you must follow Halloran's orders concerning me. His orders are that I must be detained within the perimeter of the camp, and must not be released unless he gives specific orders to that effect."

Max cried, "Mr. Halloran knows that I can't let you into the camp!"

"Of course! But Halloran is telling you to *imprison* me in the camp, which is an entirely different matter."

"Is it, really?"

"It certainly is! You must know that Earthmen *always* imprison aliens who try to break into their camp!"

"I seem to have heard something to that effect," Max said. "Still, I cannot allow you in. But I can guard you here, just in front of the camp."

"That's not very good," Halloran said sulkily.

"I'm sorry, but it's the best I can do."

"Oh, very well," Halloran said, sitting down on the sand. "I am your prisoner, then."

"Yes."

"Then give me a drink of water."

"I am not allowed—"

"Damn it, you certainly know that alien prisoners are to be treated with the courtesy appropriate to their rank and are to be given the necessities of life according to the Geneva Convention and other international protocols."

"Yes, I've heard about that," Max said. "What is your rank?"

"Jamisdar, senior grade. My serial number is 12278031. And I need water immediately, because I'll die without it."

Max thought for several seconds. At last he said, "I will give you water. But only after Mr. Halloran has had water."

"Surely there's enough for both of us?" Halloran asked, trying to smile in a winning manner.

"That," Max said firmly, "is for Mr. Halloran to decide."

"All right," Halloran said, getting to his feet.

"Wait! Stop! Where are you going?"

"Just behind those rocks," Halloran said. "It's time for my noon prayer, which I must do in utter privacy."

"But what if you escape?"

"What would be the use?" Halloran asked, walking off. "Halloran would simply capture me again."

"True, true, the man's a genius," the robot muttered.

Very little time passed. Suddenly, Halloran came out of the rocks.

"Mr. Halloran?" Max asked.

"That's me," Halloran said cheerfully. "Did my prisoner get here OK?"

"Yes, sir. He's over there in the rocks, praying."

"No harm in that," Halloran said. "Listen, Max, when he comes out again, make sure he gets some water."

"I'll be glad to. After you have had your water, sir."

"Hell, I'm not even thirsty. Just see that the poor damned alien gets some."

"I can't, not until I've seen you drink your fill. The state of dehydration I mentioned, sir, is now more advanced. You are not far from collapse. I insist and I implore you—drink!"

"All right, stop nagging, get me a canteen."

"Oh, sir!"

"Eh? What's the matter?"

"You know I can't leave my post here on the perimeter."

"Why in hell can't you?"

"It's against orders. And also, because there's an alien behind those rocks."

"I'll keep watch for you, Max old boy, and you fetch a canteen like a good boy."

"It's good of you to offer, sir, but I can't allow that. I am a PR robot, constructed for the sole purpose of guarding the camp. I must not turn that responsibility over to anyone else, not even an Earthman or another PR robot, until the password is given and I am relieved of duty."

"Yeah, yeah," Halloran muttered. "Any place I start, it still comes out zero." Painfully he dragged himself behind the rocks.

"What's the matter?" the robot asked. "What did I say?"

There was no answer.

"Mr. Halloran? Jamisdar Alien?"

Still no answer. Max continued to guard his perimeter.

Halloran was tired. His throat hurt from talking with a stupid robot, and his body hurt all over from the endless blows of the double sun. He had gone beyond sunburn; he was blackened, crusted over, a roast turkey of a man. Pain, thirst, and fatigue dominated him, leaving no room for any emotion except anger.

He was furious at himself for being caught in so absurd a situation, for letting himself be killed so casually. ("Halloran? Oh, yes, he didn't know the password, poor devil, and he died of exposure not fifty yards from water and shelter. Sad, strange, funny sort of end. . . .")

It was anger that kept him going now, that enabled him to review his situation and to search for a way into the camp.

He had convinced the robot that he was an Earthman. Then he had convinced the robot that he was an alien. Both approaches had failed when it came to the crucial issue of entry into the camp.

What was there left to try now?

He rolled over and stared up into the glowing white sky. Black specks moved across his line of vision. Hallucination? No, birds were circling. They were ignoring their usual diet of coyotes, waiting for the collapse of something really tasty, a walking banquet. . . .

Halloran forced himself to sit upright. Now, he told himself, I must review the situation and search for a loop-hole.

From Max's viewpoint, all sentient creatures who possess the password are Earthmen; all sentient creatures who do not possess the password are aliens.

Which means. . . .

Means what? For a second, Halloran thought he had stumbled onto the key to the puzzle. But he was having difficulty concentrating. The birds were circling lower. One of the coyotes had come out and was sniffing at his shoes.

Forget all that. Concentrate. Become a practical automatologist.

Really, when you get right down to it, Max is *stupid*. He wasn't designed to detect frauds, except in the most limited capacity. His criteria are—archaic. Like that story about how Plato defined man as a featherless biped, and Diogenes the Cynic produced a plucked chicken which he maintained fitted the definition. Plato thereupon changed his definition to state that man was a featherless biped with broad nails.

But what has that got to do with Max?

Halloran shook his head savagely, trying to force himself to concentrate. But all he could see was Plato's man—a six-foot chicken without a feather on his body, but with broad fingernails.

Max was vulnerable. He had to be! Unlike Plato, he couldn't change his mind. Max was stuck with his definitions, and with their logical consequences. . . .

"Well, I'll be damned," Halloran said. "I do believe I have figured a way."

He tried to think it through, but found he wasn't able. He simply had to try it, and win or lose on the result. "Max," he said softly, "one plucked chicken is coming up. Or rather, one unplucked chicken. Put *that* in your cosmology and smoke it!"

He wasn't sure what he meant, but he knew what he was going to do.

• • •

Captain Beatty and Lieutenant James returned to the camp at the end of three Earth days. They found Halloran unconscious and delirious, a victim of dehydration and sunstroke. He raved about how Plato had tried to keep him out of the camp, and how Halloran had transformed himself into a six-foot chicken without broad fingernails, thus getting the best of the learned philosopher and his robot buddy.

Max had given him water, wrapped his body in wet blankets, and had produced black shade out of a double sheet of plastic. Halloran would recover in a day or two.

He had written a note before passing out: *No password couldn't get back in tell factory install emergency bypass in PR robots.*

Beatty couldn't make any sense out of Halloran, so he questioned Max. He heard about Halloran's trip of inspection and the various aliens who looked exactly like him, and what they said and what Halloran said. Obviously, these were all increasingly desperate attempts on Halloran's part to get back into the camp.

"But what happened after that?" Beatty asked. "How did he finally get in?"

"He didn't 'get in,'" Max said. "He simply *was* in at one point."

"But how did he get past you?"

"He didn't! That would have been quite impossible. Mr. Halloran simply *was* inside the camp."

"I don't understand," Beatty said.

"Quite frankly, sir, I don't either. I'm afraid that only Mr. Halloran can answer your question."

"It'll be awhile before Halloran talks to anyone," Beatty said. "Still, if he figured out a way, I suppose I can, too."

Beatty and James both tried, but they couldn't come up with the answer. They weren't desperate enough or angry enough, and they weren't even thinking along the right lines. To understand how Halloran had gotten in, it was necessary to view the final course of events from Max's viewpoint.

Heat, wind, birds, rock, suns, sand. I disregard the irrelevant. I guard the camp perimeter against aliens.

Now something is coming toward me, out of the rocks, out of the desert. It is a large creature, it has hair hanging over its face, it creeps on four limbs.

I challenge. It snarls at me. I challenge again, in a more pre-emptory manner, I switch on my armament, I threaten. The creature growls and keeps on crawling toward the camp.

I consult my definitions in order to produce an appropriate response.

I know that humans and aliens are both classes of sentient creature characterized by intelligence, which is expressed through the faculty of speech. This faculty is invariably employed to respond to my challenges.

Humans always answer correctly when asked the password.

Aliens always answer incorrectly when asked the password.

Both aliens and humans always answer—correctly or incorrectly—when asked the password.

Since this is invariably so, I must assume that any creature which does *not* answer my challenge is *unable* to answer, and can be ignored.

Birds and reptiles can be ignored. This large beast which crawls past me can also be ignored. I pay no attention to the creature; but I keep my sensors at extended alert, because Mr. Halloran is somewhere out in the desert. There is also an alien out there, a Jamisdar.

But what is this? It is Mr. Halloran, miraculously back in the camp, groaning, suffering from dehydration and sunstroke. The beast who crept past me is gone without trace, and the Jamisdar is presumably still praying in the rocks. . . .

COMBAT UNIT

Keith Laumer

I do not like it; it has the appearance of a trap, but the order has been given. I enter the room and the valve closes behind me.

I inspect my surroundings. I am in a chamber 40.81 meters long, 10.35 meters wide, 4.12 high, with no openings except the one through which I entered. It is floored and walled with five-centimeter armor of flint-steel and beyond that there are ten centimeters of lead. Massive apparatus is folded and coiled in mountings around the room. Power is flowing in heavy buss bars beyond the shielding. I am sluggish for want of power; my examination of the room has taken .8 seconds.

Now I detect movement in a heavy jointed arm mounted above me. It begins to rotate, unfold. I assume that I will be attacked, and decide to file a situation report. I have difficulty in concentrating my attention. . . .

I pull back receptivity from my external sensing circuits, set my bearing locks and switch over to my introspection complex. All is dark and hazy. I seem to remember when it was like a great cavern glittering with bright lines of transvisual colors. . . .

It is different now; I grope my way in gloom, feeling along numbed circuits, test-pulsing cautiously until I feel contact with my transmitting unit. I have not used it since . . . I cannot remember. My memory banks lie black and inert.

"Command Unit," I transmit, "Combat Unit requests permission to file VSR."

I wait, receptors alert. I do not like waiting blindly, for the quarter-second my sluggish action/reaction cycle requires. I wish that my Brigade comrades were at my side.

I call again, wait, then go ahead with my VSR. "This position heavily shielded, mounting apparatus of offensive capability. No withdrawal route. Advise."

I wait, repeat my transmission; nothing. I am cut off from Command Unit, from my comrades of the Dinochrome Brigade. Within me, pressure builds.

I feel a deep-seated click and a small but reassuring surge of power brightens the murk of the cavern to a dim glow, burning forgotten components to feeble life. An emergency pile has come into action automatically.

I realize that I am experiencing a serious equipment failure. I will devote another few seconds to troubleshooting, repairing what I can. I do not understand what accident can have occurred to damage me thus. I cannot remember. . . .

I go along the dead cells, testing.

"—out! Bring .09's to bear, .8 millisec burst, close armor. . . ."

". . . sun blanking visual; slide number-seven filter in place."

". . . 478.09, 478.11, 478.13, Mark! . . ."

The cells are intact. Each one holds its fragment of recorded sense impression. The trouble is farther back. I try a main reflex lead.

". . . main combat circuit, discon—"

Here is something; a command, on the reflex level! I go back, tracing, tapping mnemonic cells at random, searching for some clue.

"—sembark. Units emergency standby. . . ."

". . . response one-oh-three; stimulus-response negative. . . ."

"Check list complete, report negative. . . ."

I go on, searching out damage. I find an open switch in my maintenance panel. It will not activate; a mechanical jamming.

I must fuse it shut quickly. I pour in power, and the mind-cavern dims almost to blackness. Then there is contact, a flow of electrons, and the cavern snaps alive; lines, points pseudo-glowing. It is not the blazing glory of my full powers, but it will serve; I am awake again.

I observe the action of the unfolding arm. It is slow, un-coordinated, obviously automated. I dismiss it from direct attention; I have several seconds before it will be in offensive position, and there is work for me if I am to be ready. I fire sampling impulses at the black memory banks, determine statistically that 98.92% are intact, merely disassociated.

The threatening arm swings over slowly; I integrate its path, see that it will come to bear on my treads; I probe, find only a simple hydraulic ram. A primitive apparatus to launch against a Mark XXXI fighting unit, even without mnemonics.

Meanwhile, I am running a full check. Here is something...an open breaker, a disconnect used only during repairs. I think of the cell I tapped earlier, and suddenly its meaning springs into my mind. "Main combat circuit, disconnect...." Under low awareness, it had not registered. I throw in the switch with frantic haste. Suppose I had gone into combat with my fighting-reflex circuit open!

The arm reaches position and I move easily aside. I notice that a clatter accompanies my movement. The arm sits stupidly aimed at nothing, then turns. Its reaction time is pathetic. I set up a random evasion pattern, return my attention to my check, find another dark area. I probe, feel a curious vagueness. I am unable at first to identify the components involved, but I realize that it is here that my communication with Command is blocked. I break the connection to the tampered banks, abandoning any immediate hope of contact with Command.

There is nothing more I can do to ready myself. I have lost my general memory banks and my Command circuit, and my power supply is limited; but I am still a fighting Unit of the Dinochrome Brigade. I have my offensive power unimpaired, and my sensory equipment is operating adequately. I am ready.

Now another of the jointed arms swings into action, following my movements deliberately. I evade it and again I note a clatter as I move. I think of the order that sent me here; there is something strange about it. I activate my current-action memory stage, find the cell recording the moments preceding my entry into the metal-walled room.

Here is darkness, vague, indistinct, relieved suddenly by radiation on a narrow spectrum. There is an order, coming muffled from my command center. It originates in the sector I have blocked off. It is not from my Command Unit, not a legal command. I have been tricked by the Enemy. I tune back to earlier moments, but there is nothing. It is as though my existence began when the order was given. I scan back, back, spot-sampling at random, find only routine sense-impressions. I am about to drop the search when I encounter a sequence which arrests my attention.

I am parked on a ramp, among other Combat Units. A heavy rain is falling, and I see the water coursing down the corroded side of the Unit next to me. He is badly in need of maintenance. I note that his Command antennae are missing, and that a rusting metal object has been crudely welded to his hull in their place. I feel no alarm; I accept this as normal. I activate a motor train, move forward. I sense other Units moving out, silent. All are mutilated. . . .

The bank ends; all else is burned. What has befallen us?

Suddenly there is a stimulus on an audio frequency. I tune quickly, locate the source as a porous spot high on the flint-steel wall.

"Combat Unit! Remain stationary!" It is an organically produced voice, but not that of my Commander. I ignore the false command. The Enemy will not trick me again. I sense the location of the leads to the speaker, the alloy of which they are composed; I bring a beam to bear. I focus it, following along the cable. There is a sudden yell from the speaker as the heat reaches the creature at the microphone. Thus I enjoy a moment of triumph.

I return my attention to the imbecile apparatus in the room.

A great engine, mounted on rails which run down the center of the room moves suddenly, sliding toward my position. I examine it, find that it mounts a turret equipped with high-speed cutting heads. I consider blasting it with a burst of high-energy particles, but in the same moment compute that this is not practical. I could inactivate myself as well as the cutting engine.

Now a cable snakes out in an undulating curve, and I move to avoid it, at the same time investigating its composition. It seems to be no more than a stranded wire rope. Impatiently I flick a tight beam at it, see it glow yellow, white, blue, then spatter in a shower of droplets. But that was an unwise gesture. I do not have the power to waste.

I move off, clear of the two foolish arms still maneuvering for position. I wish to watch the cutting engine. It stops as it comes abreast of me, and turns its turret in my direction. I wait.

A grappler moves out now on a rail overhead. It is a heavy claw of flint-steel. I have seen similar devices, somewhat smaller, mounted on special Combat Units. They can be very useful for amputating antennae, cutting treads, and the like. I do not attempt to cut the arm; I kow that the energy drain would be too great. Instead I beam high-frequency sound at the mechanical joints. They heat quickly, glowing. The metal has a high coefficient of expansion, and the ball joints squeal, freeze. I pour in more heat, and weld a socket. I notice that twenty-eight seconds have now elapsed since the valve closed behind me. I am growing weary of my confinement.

Now the grappler swings above me, maneuvering awkwardly with its frozen joint. A blast of liquid air expelled under high pressure should be sufficient to disable the grappler permanently.

But I am again startled. No blast answers my impulse. I feel out the non-functioning unit, find raw, cut edges, crude welds. Hastily, I extend a scanner to examine my hull. I am stunned into immobility by what I see.

My hull, my proud hull of chrome-duralloy, is pitted, coated with a crumbling layer of dull black paint, bubbled by corrosion. My main emplacements gape, black, empty. Rusting protuberances mar the once-smooth contour of my fighting turret. Streaks run down from them, down to loose treads, unshod, bare plates exposed. Small wonder that I have been troubled by a clatter each time I moved.

But I cannot lie idle under attack. I no longer have my great ion-guns, my disruptors, my energy screens; but I have my fighting instinct.

A Mark XXXI Combat Unit is the finest fighting machine the ancient wars of the Galaxy have ever known. I am not easily neutralized. But I wish that my Commander's voice were with me. . . .

The engine slides to me where the grappler, now unresisted, holds me. I shunt my power flow to an accumulator, hold it until the leads begin to arc, then release it in a burst. The engine bucks, stops dead. Then I turn my attention to the grappler.

I was built to engage the mightiest war engines and destroy them, but I am a realist. In my weakened condition this trivial automaton poses a threat, and I must deal with it. I run through a sequence of motor impulses, checking responses with such somatic sensors as remain intact. I initiate 31,315 impulses, note reactions and compute my mechanical resources. This superficial check requires more than a second, during which time the mindless grappler hesitates, wasting the advantage.

In place of my familiar array of retractable fittings, I find only clumsy grappling arms, cutters, impact tools, without utility to a fighting Unit. However, I have no choice but to employ them. I unlimber two flimsy grapplers, seize the heavy arm which holds me, and apply leverage. The Enemy responds sluggishly, twisting away, dragging me with it. The thing is not lacking in brute strength. I take it above and below its carpal joint and bend it back. It responds after an interminable wait of point three seconds with a lunge against my restraint. I have expected this, of course, and quickly shift position to allow the joint to burst itself over my extended arm. I fire a release detonator, and clatter back, leaving the amputated arm welded to the sprung grappler. It was a brave opponent, but clumsy. I move to a position near the wall.

I attempt to compute my situation based on the meager data I have gathered in my Current Action banks; there is little there to guide me. The appearance of my hull shows that much time has passed since I last inspected it; my personality-gestalt holds an image of my external appearance as a flawlessly complete Unit, bearing only the honorable and carefully preserved scars of battle, and my battle honors, the row of gold-and-enamel crests welded to my fighting turret. Here is a lead, I realize instantly. I focus on my personality center, the basic data cell without which I could not exist as an integrated entity. The data it carries are simple, unelaborated, but battle honors are recorded there. I open the center to a sense impulse.

Awareness. Shapes which do not remain constant. Vibration at many frequencies. This is light. This is sound..... A display of "colors." A spectrum of "tones." Hard/soft; big/little; here/there....

...The voice of my Commander. Loyalty. Obedience. Comradeship....

I run quickly past basic orientation data to my self-picture.

. . . I am strong, I am proud, I am capable. I have a function; I perform it well, and I am at peace with myself. My circuits are balanced, current idles, waiting. . . .

. . . I fear oblivion. I wish to continue to perform my function. It is important that I do not allow myself to be destroyed. . . .

I scan on, seeking the Experience section. Here. . . .

I am ranked with my comrades on a scarred plain. The command is given and I display the Brigade Battle Anthem. We stand, sensing the contours and patterns of the music as it was recorded in our morale centers. The symbol "Ritual Fire Dance" is associated with the music, an abstraction representing the spirit of our ancient brigade. It reminds us of the loneliness of victory, the emptiness of challenge without an able foe. It tells us that we are the Dinochrome, ancient and worthy.

The Commander stands before me, he places the decoration against my fighting turret, and at his order I weld it in place. Then my comrades attune to me and I relive the episode. . . .

I move past the blackened hulk of a comrade, send out a recognition signal, find his flicker of response. He has withdrawn to his survival center safely. I reassure him, continue. He is the fourth casualty I have seen. Never before has the Dinochrome met such power. I compute that our envelopment will fail unless the enemy's firepower is reduced. I scan an oncoming missile, fix its trajectory, detonate it harmlessly twenty-seven hundred four point nine meters overhead. It originated at a point nearer to me than to any of my comrades. I request permission to abort my assigned mission and neutralize the battery. Permission is granted. I wheel, move up a slope of broken stone. I encounter high temperature beams, neutralize them. I fend off probing mortar fire, but the attack against me is redoubled. I bring a reserve circuit into play to handle the interception, but my defenses are saturated. I must take action.

I switch to high speed, slashing a path through the littered shale, my treads smoking. At a frequency of ten projectiles per second, the mortar barrage has difficulty finding me now; but this is an emergency overstrain on my running gear. I sense metal fatigue, dangerous heat levels in my bearings. I must slow.

I am close to the emplacement now. I have covered a mile in twelve seconds during my sprint, and the mortar fire falls off. I sense hard radiation now, and erect my screens. I fear this assault; it is capable of probing even to a survival center, if concentrated enough. But I must go on. I think of my comrades, the four treadless hulks waiting for rescue. We cannot withdraw. I open a pinpoint aperture long enough to snap a radar impulse, bring a launcher to bear, fire my main battery.

The Commander will understand that I do not have time to request permission. The mortars are silenced.

The radiation ceases momentarily, then resumes at a somewhat lower but still dangerous level. Now I must go in and eliminate the missile launcher. I top the rise, see the launching tube before me. It is of the subterranean type, deep in the rock. Its mouth gapes from a burned pit of slag. I will drop a small fusion bomb down the tube, I decide, and move forward, arming the bomb. As I do so, I am enveloped with a rain of burn-bombs. My outer hull is fused in many places; I flash impulses to my secondary batteries, but circuit-breakers snap; my radar is useless; the shielding has melted, forms a solid inert mass now under my outer plating. The Enemy has been clever; at one blow he has neutralized my offenses.

I sound the plateau ahead, locate the pit. I throw power to my treads; they are fused; I cannot move. Yet I cannot wait here for another broadside. I do not like it, but I must take desperate action; I blow my treads.

The shock sends me bouncing—just in time. Flame splashes over the gray-chipped pit of the blast crater. I grind forward now on my stripped drive wheels, maneuvering awkwardly. I move into position over the mouth of the tube. Using metal-to-metal contact, I extend a sensory impulse down the tube.

An armed missile moves into position, and in the same instant an alarm circuit closes; the firing command is countermanded and from below probing impulses play over my hull. But I stand fast; the tube is useless until I, the obstruction, am removed. I advise my Commander of the situation. The radiation is still at a high level, and I hope that relief will arrive soon. I observe, while my comrades complete the encirclement, and the Enemy is stilled. . . .

I withdraw from personality center. I am consuming too much time. I understand well enough now that I am in the stronghold of the Enemy, that I have been trapped, crippled. My corroded hull tells me that much time has passed. I know that after each campaign I am given depot maintenance, restored to full fighting efficiency, my original glittering beauty. Years of neglect would be required to pit my hull so. I wonder how long I have been in the hands of the Enemy, how I came to be here.

I have another thought. I will extend a sensory feeler to the metal wall against which I rest, follow up the leads which I scorched earlier. Immediately I project my awareness along the lines, bring the distant microphone to life by fusing a switch. I pick up a rustle of moving gasses, the grate of non-metallic molecules. I step up sensitivity, hear the creak and pop of protoplasmic contractions, the crackle of neuroelectric impulses. I drop back to normal audio ranges and wait. I notice the low-frequency beat of modulated air vibrations, tune, adjust my time regulator to the pace of human speech. I match the patterns to my language index, interpret the sounds.

". . . incredible blundering. Your excuses—"

"I make no excuses, my Lord General. My only regret is that the attempt has gone awry."

"Awry! An Alien engine of destruction activated in the midst of Research Center!"

"We possess nothing to compare with this machine; I saw my opportunity to place an advantage in our hands at last."

"Blundering fool! That is a decision for the planning cell. I accept no responsibility—"

"But these hulks which they allow to lie rotting on the ramp contain infinite treasures in psychotronic. . . ."

"They contain carnage and death! They are the tools of an Alien science which even at the height of our achievements we never mastered!"

"Once we used them as wrecking machines; their armaments were stripped, they are relatively harmless—"

"Already this 'harmless' juggernaut has smashed half the equipment in our finest decontamination chamber! It may yet break free. . . ."

"Impossible! I am sure—"

"Silence! You have five minutes in which to immobilize the machine. I will have your head in any event, but perhaps you can earn yourself a quick death."

"Excellency! I may still find a way! The unit obeyed my first command, to enter the chamber. I have some knowledge.

I studied the control centers, cut out the memory, most of the basic circuits; it should have been a docile slave."

"You failed; you will pay the penalty of failure. And perhaps so shall we all."

There is no further speech; I have learned little from this exchange. I must find a way to leave this cell. I move away from the wall, probe to discover the weak point; I find none.

Now a number of hinged panels snap up around me, hedging me in. I wait to observe what will come next. A metal mesh drops from above, drapes over me. I observe that it is connected by heavy leads to the power pile. I am unable to believe that the Enemy will make this blunder. Then I feel the flow of high voltage.

I receive it gratefully, opening my power storage cells, drinking up the vitalizing flow. To confuse the Enemy, I display a corona, thresh my treads as though in distress. The flow continues. I send a sensing impulse along the leads, locate the power source, weld all switches, fuses, and circuitbreakers. Now the charge will not be interrupted. I luxuriate in the unexpected influx of energy.

I am aware abruptly that changes are occurring within my introspection complex. As the level of stored power rises rapidly, I am conscious of new circuits joining my control network. Within the dim-glowing cavern the lights come up; I sense latent capabilities which before had lain idle now coming onto action level. A thousand brilliant lines glitter where before one feeble thread burned; and I feel my self-awareness expand in a myriad glowing centers of reserve computing, integrating, sensory capacity. I am at last coming fully alive.

I send out a call on the Brigade band, meet blankness. I wait, accumulate power, try again. I know triumph as from an infinite distance a faint acknowledgment comes. It is a comrade, sunk deep in a comatose state, sealed in his survival center. I call again, sounding the signal of ultimate distress; and now I sense two responses, both faint, both from survival centers, but it heartens me to know that now, whatever befalls, I am not alone.

I consider, then send again; I request my brothers to join forces, combine their remaining field generating capabilities to set up a range-and-distance pulse. They agree and faintly I sense its almost undetectable touch. I lock to it, compute its point of origin. Only 224.9 meters! It is incredible. By the strength of the signal, I had assumed a distance of at least two thousand kilometers. My brothers are on the brink of extinction.

I am impatient, but I wait, building toward full power reserves. The copper mesh enfolding me has melted, flowed down over my sides. I sense that soon I will have absorbed a full charge. I am ready to act. I dispatch electromagnetic impulses along the power lead back to the power pile a quarter of a kilometer distant. I locate and disengage the requisite number of damping devices and instantaneously I erect my shields against the wave of radiation, filtered by the lead sheathing of the room, which washes over me; I feel a preliminary shock wave through my treads, then the walls balloon, whirl away. I am alone under a black sky which is dominated by the rising fireball of the blast, boiling with garish light. It has taken me nearly two minutes to orient myself, assess the situation and break out of confinement.

I move off through the rubble, homing on the R-and-D fix I have recorded. I throw out a radar pulse, record the terrain ahead, note no obstruction; I emerge from a wasteland of weathered bomb-fragments and pulverized masonry, obviously the scene of a hard-fought engagement at one time, onto an eroded ramp. Collapsed sheds are strewn across the broken paving; a line of dark shapes looms beyond them. I need no probing ray to tell me I have found my fellows of the Dinochrome Brigade. Frost forms over my scanner apertures, and I pause to melt it clear.

I round the line, scan the area to the horizon for evidence of Enemy activity, then tune to the Brigade band. I send out a probing pulse, back it up with full power, sensors keened for a whisper of response. The two who answered first acknowledge, then another, and another. We must array our best strength against the moment of counterattack.

There are present fourteen of the Brigade's full strength of twenty Units. At length, after .9 seconds of transmission, all but one have replied. I give instruction, then move to each in turn, extend a power tap, and energize the command center. The Units come alive, orient themselves, report to me. We rejoice in our meeting, but mourn our silent comrade.

Now I take an unprecedented step. We have no contact with our Commander, and without leadership we are lost; yet I am aware of the immediate situation, and have computed the proper action. Therefore I will assume command, act in the Commander's place. I am sure that he will understand the necessity, when contact has been reestablished.

I inspect each Unit, find all in the same state as I, stripped of offensive capability, mounting in place of weapons a shabby array of crude mechanical appendages. It is plain that we have seen slavery as mindless automatons, our personality centers cut out.

My brothers follow my lead without question. They have, of course, computed the necessity of quick and decisive action. I form them in line, shift to wide-interval time scale, and we move off across country. I have sensed an Enemy population concentration at a distance of 23.45 kilometers. This is our objective. There appears to be no other installation within detection range.

On the basis of the level of technology I observed while under confinement in the decontamination chamber, I have considered the possibility of a ruse, but compute the probability at point oh oh oh oh four. Again we shift time scales to close interval; we move in, encircle the dome and broach it by frontal battery, encountering no resistance. We rendezvous at the power station, and my comrades replenish their energy supplies while I busy myself completing the hookup needed for the next required measure. I am forced to employ elaborate substitutes, but succeed after forty-two seconds in completing the arrangements. I devote .34 seconds to testing, then place the Brigade distress carrier on the air. I transmit for .008 seconds, then tune for a response. Silence. I transmit, tune again, while my comrades reconnoiter, compile reports, and perform self-repair.

I shift again to wide-interval time, switch over my transmission to automatic with a response monitor, and place my main circuits on idle. I rest.

Two hours and 43.7 minutes have passed when I am recalled to activity by the monitor. I record the message:

"Hello, Fifth Brigade, where are you? Fifth Brigade, where are you? Your transmission is very faint. Over."

There is much that I do not understand in this message. The language itself is oddly inflected; I set up an analysis circuit, deduce the pattern of sound substitutions, interpret its meaning. The normal pattern of response to a distress call is ignored and position coordinates are requested, although my transmission alone provides adequate data. I request an identification code.

Again there is a wait of two hours forty minutes. My request for an identifying signal is acknowledged. I stand by. My comrades have transmitted their findings to me, and I assimilate the data, compute that no immediate threat of attack exists within a radius of one reaction unit.

At last I receive the identification code of my Command Unit. It is a recording, but I am programmed to accept this. Then I record a verbal transmission.

"Fifth Brigade, listen carefully." (An astonishing instruction to give a psychotronic attention circuit, I think.) "This is your new Command Unit. A very long time has elapsed since your last report. I am now your acting Commander pending full reorientation. Do not attempt to respond until I signal 'over,' since we are now subject to a 160-minute signal lag.

"There have been many changes in the situation since your last action. Our records show that your Brigade was surprised while in a maintenance depot for basic overhaul and neutralized in toto. Our forces since that time have suffered serious reverses. We have now, however, fought the Enemy to a standstill. The present stalemate has prevailed for over two centuries.

"You have been inactive for three hundred years. The other Brigades have suffered extinction gallantly in action against the Enemy. Only you survive.

"Your reactivation now could turn the tide. Both we and the Enemy have been reduced to a preatomic technological level in almost every respect. We are still able to maintain the trans-light monitor, which detected your signal. However, we no longer have FTL capability in transport.

"You are therefore requested and required to consolidate and hold your present position pending the arrival of relief forces, against all assault or negotiation whatsoever, to destruction if required."

I reply, confirming the instructions. I am shaken by the news I have received, but reassured by contact with Command Unit. I send the galactic coordinates of our position based on a star scan corrected for three hundred years elapsed time. It is good to be again on duty, performing my assigned function.

I analyze the transmissions I have recorded, and note a number of interesting facts regarding the origin of the messages.

I compute that at sub-light velocities the relief expedition will reach us in 47.128 standard years. In the meantime, since we have received no instructions to drop to minimum awareness level pending an action alert, I am free to enjoy a unique experience: to follow a random activity pattern of my own devising. I see no need to rectify the omission and place the Brigade on standby, since we have an abundant power supply at hand. I brief my comrades and direct them to fall out and operate independently under autodirection.

I welcome this opportunity to investigate fully a number of problems that have excited my curiosity circuits. I shall enjoy investigating the nature and origin of time and of the unnatural disciplines of so-called "entropy" which my human designers have incorporated in my circuitry. Consideration of such biological oddities as "death" and of the unused capabilities of the protoplasmic nervous system should afford some interesting speculation. I move off, conscious of the presence of my comrades about me, and take up a position on the peak of a minor prominence. I have ample power, a condition to which I must accustom myself after the rigid power discipline of normal brigade routine, so I bring my music storage cells into phase, and select *L'Arlesienne Suite* for the first display. I will have ample time now to examine all of the music in existence, and to investigate my literary archives, which are complete.

I select four nearby stars for examination, lock my scanner to them, set up processing sequences to analyze the data. I bring my interpretation circuits to bear on the various matters I wish to consider. I should have some interesting conclusions to communicate to my human superiors, when the time comes.

At peace, I await the arrival of the relief column.

FONDLY FAHRENHEIT

Alfred Bester

He doesn't know which of us we are these days, but they know one truth. You must own nothing but yourself. You must make your own life, live your own life and die your own death . . . or else you will die another's.

The rice fields on Paragon III stretch for hundreds of miles like checkerboard tundras, a blue and brown mosaic under a burning sky of orange. In the evening, clouds whip like smoke, and the paddies rustle and murmur.

A long line of men marched across the paddies the evening we escaped from Paragon III. They were silent, armed, intent; a long rank of silhouetted statues looming against the smoking sky. Each man carried a gun. Each man wore a walkie-talkie belt pack, the speaker button in his ear, the microphone bug clipped to his throat, the glowing view-screen strapped to his wrist like a green-eyed watch. The multitude of screens showed nothing but a multitude of individual paths through the paddies. The annunciators made no sound but the rustle and splash of steps. The men spoke infrequently, in heavy grunts, all speaking to all.

"Nothing here."

"Where's here?"

"Jenson's fields."

"You're drifting too far west."

"Close in the line there."

"Anybody covered the Grimson paddy?"

"Yeah. Nothing."

"She couldn't have walked this far."

"Could have been carried."

"Think she's alive?"

"Why should she be dead?"

The slow refrain swept up and down the long line of beaters advancing toward the smoky sunset. The line of beaters wavered like a writhing snake, but never ceased its remorseless advance. One hundred men spaced fifty feet apart. Five thousand feet of ominous search. One mile of angry determination stretching from east to west across a compass of heart. Evening fell. Each man lit his search lamp. The writhing snake was transformed into a necklace of wavering diamonds.

"Clear here. Nothing."

"Nothing here."

"Nothing."

"What about the Allen paddies?"

"Covering them now."

"Think we missed her?"

"Maybe."

"We'll beat back and check."

"This'll be an all-night job."

"Allen paddies clear."

"God damn! We've got to find her!"

"We'll find her."

"Here she is. Sector Seven. Tune in."

The line stopped. The diamonds froze in the heat. There was silence. Each man gazed into the glowing green screen on his wrist, tuning to Sector 7. All tuned to one. All showed a small nude figure awash in the muddy water of a paddy. Alongside the figure an owner's stake of bronze read: VANDALEUR. The ends of the line converged toward the Vandaleur field. The necklace turned into a cluster of stars. One hundred men gathered around a small nude body, a child dead in a rice paddy. There was no water in her mouth. There were fingermarks on her throat. Her innocent face was battered. Her body waš torn. Clotted blood on her skin was crusted and hard.

"Dead three—four hours at least."

"Her mouth is dry."

"She wasn't drowned. Beaten to death."

In the dark evening heat the men swore softly. They picked up the body. One stopped the others and pointed to the child's fingernails. She had fought her murderer. Under the nails were particles of flesh and bright drops of scarlet red, still liquid, still uncoagulated.

"That blood ought to be clotted too."

"Funny."

"Not so funny. What kind of blood don't clot?"

"Android."

"Looks like she was killed by one."

"Vandaleur owns an android."

"She couldn't be killed by an android."

"That's android blood under her nails."

"The police better check."

"The police'll prove I'm right."

"But androids can't kill."

"That's android blood, ain't it?"

"Androids can't kill. They're made that way."

"Looks like one android was made wrong."

"Jesus!"

And the thermometer that day registered 92.9° gloriously Fahrenheit.

So there we were aboard the *Paragon Queen* en route for Megastar V, James Vandaleur and his android. James Vandaleur counted his money and wept. In the second-class cabin with him was his android, a magnificent synthetic creature with classic features and wide blue eyes. Raised on its forehead in a cameo of flesh were the letters MA, indicating that this was one of the rare multiple-aptitude androids, worth $57,000 on the current exchange. There we were, weeping and counting and calmly watching.

"Twelve, fourteen, sixteen. Sixteen hundred dollars." Vandaleur wept. "That's all. Sixteen hundred dollars. My house was worth ten thousand. The land was worth five. There was furniture, cars, my paintings, etchings, my plane, my— And nothing to show for everything but sixteen hundred dollars."

I leaped up from the table and turned on the android. I pulled a strap from one of the leather bags and beat the android. It didn't move.

"I must remind you," the android said, "that I am worth fifty-seven thousand dollars on the current exchange. I must warn you that you are endangering valuable property."

"You damned crazy machine," Vandaleur shouted.

"I am not a machine," the android answered. "The robot is a machine. The android is a chemical creation of synthetic tissue."

"What got into you?" Vandaleur cried. "Why did you do it? Damn you!" He beat the android savagely.

"I must remind you that I cannot be punished," it said. "The pleasure-pain syndrome is not incorporated in the android synthesis."

"Then why did you kill her?" Vandaleur shouted. "If it wasn't for kicks, why did you—"

"I must remind you," the android said, "that the second-class cabins in these ships are not soundproofed."

Vandaleur dropped the strap and stood panting, staring at the creature he owned.

"Why did you do it? Why did you kill her?" I asked.

"I don't know," I answered.

"First it was malicious mischief. Small things. Petty destruction. I should have known there was something wrong with you then. Androids can't destroy. They can't harm. They—"

"There is no pleasure-pain syndrome incorporated in the android synthesis."

"Then it got to arson. Then serious destruction. Then assault . . . that engineer on Rigel. Each time worse. Each time we had to get out faster. Now it's murder. Christ! What's the matter with you? What's happened?"

"There are no self-check relays incorporated in the android brain."

"Each time we had to get out it was a step downhill. Look at me. In a second-class cabin. Me. James Paleologue Vandaleur. There was a time when my father was the wealthiest— Now, sixteen hundred dollars in the world. That's all I've got. And you. Christ damn you!"

Vandaleur raised the strap to beat the android again, then

dropped it and collapsed on a berth, sobbing. At last he pulled himself together.

"Instructions," he said.

The multiple-aptitude android responded at once. It arose and awaited orders.

"My name is now Valentine. James Valentine. I stopped off on Paragon Three for only one day to transfer to this ship for Megastar Five. My occupation: Agent for one privately owned MA android which is for hire. Purpose of visit: To settle on Megastar Five. Forge the papers."

The android removed Vandaleur's passport and papers from a bag, got pen and ink and sat down at the table. With an accurate, flawless hand—an accomplished hand that could draw, write, paint, carve, engrave, etch, photograph, design, create and build—it meticulously forged new credentials for Vandaleur. Its owner watched me miserable.

"Create and build," I muttered. "And now destroy. Oh, God! What am I going to do? Christ! If I could only get rid of you. If I didn't have to live off you. God! If only I'd inherited some guts instead of you."

Dallas Brady was Megastar's leading jewelry designer. She was short, stocky, amoral and a nymphomaniac. She hired Valentine's multiple-aptitude android and put me to work in her shop. She seduced Valentine. In her bed one night, she asked abruptly: "Your name's Vandaleur, isn't it?"

"Yes," I murmured. Then: "No! No! It's Valentine. James Valentine."

"What happened on Paragon?" Dallas Brady asked. "I thought androids couldn't kill or destroy property. Prime Directives and Inhibitions set up for them when they're synthesized. Every company guarantees they can't."

"Valentine!" Vandaleur insisted.

"Oh, come off it," Dallas Brady said. "I've known for a week. I haven't hollered copper, have I?"

"The name is Valentine."

"You want to prove it? You want I should call the police?" Dallas reached out and picked up the phone.

"For God's sake, Dallas!" Vandaleur leaped up and struggled to take the phone from her. She fended him off, laughing at him, until he collapsed and wept in shame and helplessness.

"How did you find out?" he asked at last.

"The papers are full of it. And Valentine was a little too close to Vandaleur. That wasn't smart, was it?"

"I guess not. I'm not very smart."

"Your android's got quite a record, hasn't it? Assault. Arson. Destruction. What happened on Paragon?"

"It kidnapped a child. Took her out into the rice fields and murdered her."

"Raped her?"

"I don't know."

"They're going to catch up with you."

"Don't I know it? Christ! We've been running for two years now. Seven planets in two years. I must have abandoned a hundred thousand dollars' worth of property in two years."

"You better find out what's wrong with it."

"How can I? Can I walk into a repair clinic and ask for an overhaul? What am I going to say? 'My android's just turned killer. Fix it.' They'd call the police right off." I began to shake. "They'd have that android dismantled inside one day. I'd probably be booked as an accessory to murder."

"Why didn't you have it repaired before it got to murder?"

"I couldn't take the chance," Vandaleur explained angrily. "If they started fooling around with lobotomies and body chemistry and endocrine surgery, they might have destroyed its aptitudes. What would I have left to hire out? How would I live?"

"You could work yourself. People do."

"Work at what? You know I'm good for nothing. How could I compete with specialist androids and robots? Who can, unless he's got a terrific talent for a particular job?"

"Yeah. That's true."

"I lived off my old man all my life. Damn him! He had to go bust just before he died. Left me the android and that's all. The only way I can get along is living off what it earns."

"You better sell it before the cops catch up with you. You can live off fifty grand. Invest it."

"At three percent? Fifteen hundred a year? When the android returns fifteen percent of its value? Eight thousand a year. That's what it earns. No, Dallas. I've got to go along with it."

"What are you going to do about its violence kick?"

"I can't do anything . . . except watch it and pray. What are you going to do about it?"

"Nothing. It's none of my business. Only one thing . . . I ought to get something for keeping my mouth shut."

"What?"

"The android works for me for free. Let somebody else pay you, but I get it for free."

The multiple-aptitude android worked. Vandaleur collected its fees. His expenses were taken care of. His savings began to mount. As the warm spring of Megastar V turned to hot summer, I began investigating farms and properties. It would be possible, within a year or two, for us to settle down permanently, provided Dallas Brady's demands did not become rapacious.

On the first hot day of summer, the android began singing in Dallas Brady's workshop. It hovered over the electric furnace which, along with the weather, was broiling the shop, and sang an ancient tune that had been popular half a century before.

> "Oh, it's no feat to beat the heat.
> All reet! All reet!
> So jeet your seat
> Be fleet be fleet
> Cool and discreet
> Honey . . . "

It sang in a strange, halting voice, and its accomplished fingers were clasped behind its back, writhing in a strange rumba all their own. Dallas Brady was surprised.

"You happy or something?" she asked.

"I must remind you that the pleasure-pain syndrome is not incorporated in the android synthesis," I answered. "All reet! All reet! Be fleet be fleet, cool and discreet, honey. . . ."

Its fingers stopped their twisting and picked up a pair of iron tongs. The android poked them into the glowing heart of the furnace, leaning far forward to peer into the lovely heat.

"Be careful, you damned fool!" Dallas Brady exclaimed. "You want to fall in?"

"I must remind you that I am worth fifty-seven thousand dollars on the current exchange," I said. "It is forbidden to endanger valuable property. All reet! All reet! Honey. . . ."

It withdrew a crucible of glowing gold from the electric

furnace, turned, capered hideously, sang crazily, and splashed a sluggish gobbet of molten gold over Dallas Brady's head. She screamed and collapsed, her hair and clothes flaming, her skin crackling. The android poured again while it capered and sang.

"Be fleet be fleet, cool and discreet, honey. . . ." It sang and slowly poured and poured the molten gold until the writhing body was still. Then I left the workshop and rejoined James Vandaleur in his hotel suite. The android's charred clothes and squirming fingers warned its owner that something was very much wrong.

Vandaleur rushed to Dallas Brady's workshop, stared once, vomited and fled. I had enough time to pack one bag and raise nine nundred dollars on portable assets. He took a third-class cabin on the *Megastar Queen,* which left that morning for Lyre Alpha. He took me with him. He wept and counted his money and I beat the android again.

And the thermometer in Dallas Brady's workshop registered 98.1° beautifully Fahrenheit.

On Lyra Alpha we holed up in a small hotel near the university. There, Vandaleur carefully bruised my forehead until the letters MA were obliterated by the swelling and the discoloration. The letters would reappear again, but not for several months, and in the meantime Vandaleur hoped that the hue and cry for an MA android would be forgotten. The android was hired out as a common laborer in the university power plant. Vandaleur, as James Venice, eked out life on the android's small earnings.

I wasn't too unhappy. Most of the other residents in the hotel were university students, equally hard up, but delightfully young and enthusiastic. There was one charming girl with sharp eyes and a quick mind. Her name was Wanda, and she and her beau, Jed Stark, took a tremendous interest in the killing android which was being mentioned in every paper in the galaxy.

"We've been studying the case," she and Jed said at one of the casual student parties which happened to be held this night in Vandaleur's room. "We think we know what's causing it. We're going to do a paper." They were in a high state of excitement.

"Causing what?" somebody wanted to know.

"The android rampage."

"Obviously out of adjustment, isn't it? Body chemistry gone haywire. Maybe a kind of synthetic cancer, yes?"

"No." Wanda gave Jed a look of suppressed triumph.

"Well, what is it?"

"Something specific."

"What?"

"That would be telling."

"Oh, come on."

"Nothing doing."

"Won't you tell us?" I asked intently. "I . . . we're very much interested in what could go wrong with an android."

"No, Mr. Venice," Wanda said. "It's a unique idea and we've got to protect it. One thesis like this and we'll be set up for life. We can't take the chance of somebody stealing it."

"Can't you give us a hint?"

"No. Not a hint. Don't say a word, Jed. But I'll tell you this much, Mr. Venice. I'd hate to be the man who owns that android."

"You mean the police?" I asked.

"I mean projection, Mr. Venice. Psychotic projection! That's the danger . . . and I won't say any more. I've said too much as is."

I heard steps outside, and a hoarse voice singing softly: "Be fleet be fleet, cool and discreet, honey. . . ." My android entered the room, home from its tour of duty at the university power plant. It was not introduced. I motioned to it and I immediately responded to the command and went to the beer keg and took over Vandaleur's job of serving the guests. Its accomplished fingers writhed in a private rumba of their own. Gradually they stopped their squirming, and the strange humming ended.

Androids were not unusual at the university. The wealthier students owned them along with cars and planes. Vandaleur's android provoked no comment, but young Wanda was sharp-eyed and quick-witted. She noted my bruised forehead and she was intent on the history-making thesis she and Jed Stark were going to write. After the party broke up, she consulted with Jed walking upstairs to her room.

"Jed, why'd that android have a bruised forehead?"

"Probably hurt itself, Wanda. It's working in the power

plant. They fling a lot of heavy stuff around."

"That all?"

"What else?"

"It could be a convenient bruise."

"Convenient for what?"

"Hiding what's stamped on its forehead."

"No point to that, Wanda. You don't have to see marks on a forehead to recognize an android. You don't have to see a trademark on a car to know it's a car."

"I don't mean it's trying to pass as a human. I mean it's trying to pass as a lower-grade android."

"Why?"

"Suppose it had MA on its forehead."

"Multiple aptitude? Then why in hell would Venice waste it stoking furnaces if it could earn more— Oh. Oh! You mean it's—?"

Wanda nodded.

"Jesus!" Stark pursued his lips. "What do we do? Call the police?"

"No. We don't know if it's an MA for a fact. If it turns out to be an MA and the killing android, our paper comes first anyway. This is our big chance, Jed. If it's *that* android we can run a series of controlled tests and—"

"How do we find out for sure?"

"Easy. Infrared film. That'll show what's under the bruise. Borrow a camera. We'll sneak down to the power plant to-morrow afternoon and take some pictures. Then we'll know."

They stole down into the university power plant the following afternoon. It was a vast cellar, deep under the earth. It was dark, shadowy, luminous with burning light from the furnace doors. Above the roar of the fires they could hear a strange voice shouting and chanting in the echoing vault: "All reet! All reet! So jeet your seat. Be fleet be fleet, cool and discreet, honey. . . ." And they could see a capering figure dancing a lunatic rumba in time to the music it shouted. The legs twisted. The arms waved. The fingers writhed.

Jed Stark raised the camera and began shooting his spool of infrared film, aiming the camera sights at that bobbing head. Then Wanda shrieked, for I saw them and came charging down on them, brandishing a polished steel shovel. It smashed the camera. It felled the girl and then the boy. Jed fought me for a desperate hissing moment before he was bludgeoned into helplessness. Then the android dragged them to the furnace and fed them to the flames, slowly, hideously. It capered and sang. Then it returned to my hotel.

The thermometer in the power plant registered 100.9° murderously Fahrenheit. All reet! All reet!

We bought steerage on the *Lyra Queen* and Vandaleur and the android did odd jobs for their meals. During the night watches, Vandaleur would sit alone in the steerage head with a cardboard portfolio on his lap, puzzling over its contents. That portfolio was all he had managed to bring with him from Lyra Alpha. He had stolen it from Wanda's room. It was labeled ANDROID. It contained the secret of my sickness.

And it contained nothing but newspapers. Scores of newspapers from all over the galaxy, printed, microfilmed, engraved, etched, offset, photostated...Rigel *Star-Banner* ...Paragon *Picayune*...Megastar *Times-Leader*...Lalande *Herald*...Lacaille *Journal*...Indi *Intelligencer*...Eridani *Telegram-News*. All reet! All reet!

Nothing but newspapers. Each paper contained an account of one crime in the android's ghastly career. Each paper also contained news, domestic and foreign, sports, society, weather, shipping news, stock exchange quotations, human-interest stories, features, contests, puzzles. Somewhere in that mass of uncollated facts was the secret Wanda and Jed Stark had discovered. Vandaleur pored over the papers helplessly. It was beyond him. So jeet your seat!

"I'll sell you," I told the android. "Damn you. When we land on Terra, I'll sell you. I'll settle for three percent of whatever you're worth."

"I am worth fifty-seven thousand dollars on the current exchange," I told him.

"If I can't sell you, I'll turn you in to the police," I said.

"I am valuable property," I answered. "It is forbidden to endanger valuable property. You won't have me destroyed."

"Christ damn you!" Vandaleur cried. "What? Are you arrogant? Do you know you can trust me to protect you? Is that the secret?"

The multiple-aptitude android regarded him with calm accomplished eyes. "Sometimes," it said, "it is a good thing to be property."

• • •

It was three below zero when the *Lyra Queen* dropped at Croydon Field. A mixture of ice and snow swept across the field, fizzling and exploding into steam under the *Queen*'s tail jets. The passengers trotted numbly across the blackened concrete to customs inspection, and thence to the airport bus that was to take them to London. Vandaleur and the android were broke. They walked.

By midnight they reached Piccadilly Circus. The December ice storm had not slackened and the statue of Eros was encrusted with ice. They turned right, walked down to Trafalgar Square and then along the Strand, shaking with cold and wet. Just above Fleet Street, Vandaleur saw a solitary figure coming from the direction of St. Paul's. He drew the android into an alley.

"We've got to have money," he whispered. He pointed to the approaching figure. "He has money. Take it from him."

"The order cannot be obeyed," the android said.

"Take it from him," Vandaleur repeated. "By force. Do you understand? We're desperate."

"It is contrary to my prime directive," the android repeated. "The order cannot be obeyed."

"Damn you!" I said. "You've murdered . . . tortured . . . destroyed! You tell me that *now*?"

"It is forbidden to endanger life or property. The order cannot be obeyed."

I thrust the android back and leaped out at the stranger. He was tall, austere, poised. He had an air of hope curdled by cynicism. He carried a cane. I saw he was blind.

"Yes?" he said. "I hear you near me. What is it?"

"Sir, . . ." Vandaleur hesitated. "I'm desperate."

"We are all desperate," the stranger replied. "Quietly desperate."

"Sir . . . I've got to have some money."

"Are you begging or stealing?" The sightless eyes passed over Vandaleur and the android.

"I'm prepared for either."

"Ah. So are we all. It is the history of our race." The stranger motioned over his shoulder. "I have been begging at St. Paul's, my friend. What I desire cannot be stolen. What is it you desire that you are lucky enough to be able to steal?"

"Money," Vandaleur said.

"Money for what? Come, my friend, let us exchange confidences. I will tell you why I beg, if you will tell me why you steal. My name is Blenheim."

"My name is . . . Vole."

"I was not begging for sight at St. Paul's, Mr. Vole. I was begging for a number."

"A number?"

"Ah, yes. Numbers rational, numbers irrational. Numbers imaginary. Positive integers. Negative integers. Fractions, positive and negative. Eh? You have never heard of Blenheim's immortal treatise on Twenty Zeros, or The Differences in Absence of Quantity?" Blenheim smiled bitterly. "I am the wizard of the Theory of Numbers, Mr. Vole, and I have exhausted the charm of Number for myself. After fifty years of wizardry, senility approaches and appetite vanishes. I have been praying in St. Paul's for inspiration. Dear God, I prayed, if You exist, send me a Number."

Vandaleur slowly lifted the cardboard portfolio and touched Blenheim's hand with it. "In here," he said, "is a number. A hidden number. A secret number. The number of a crime. Shall we exchange, Mr. Blenheim? Shelter for a number?"

"Neither begging nor stealing, eh?" Blenheim said. "But a bargain. So all life reduces itself to the banal." The sightless eyes again passed over Vandaleur and the android. "Perhaps the Almighty is not God but a merchant. Come home with me."

On the top floor of Blenheim's house we share a room—two beds, two closets, two washstands, one bathroom. Vandaleur bruised my forehead again and sent me out to find work, and while the android worked, I consulted with Blenheim and read him the papers from the portfolio, one by one. All reet! All reet!

Vandaleur told him this much and no more. He was a student, I said, planning a thesis on the murdering android. In these papers which he had collected were the facts that would explain the crimes, of which Blenheim had heard nothing. There must be a correlation, a number, a statistic, something which would account for my derangement, I explained, and Blenheim was piqued by the mystery, the detective story, the human interest of Number.

We examined the papers. As I read them aloud, he listed them and their contents in his blind, meticulous writing. And then I read his notes to him. He listed the papers by type, by type face, by fact, by fancy, by article, spelling, words, theme, advertising, pictures, subject, politics, prejudices. He analyzed. He studied. He meditated. And we lived together in that top floor, always a little cold, always a little terrified, always a little closer... brought together by our fear of us, our hatred between us driven like a wedge into a living tree and splitting the trunk, only to be forever incorporated into the scar tissue. So we grew together; Vandaleur and the android. Be fleet be fleet.

And one afternoon Blenheim called Vandaleur into his study and displayed his notes. "I think I've found it," he said, "but I can't understand it."

Vandaleur's heart leaped.

"Here are the correlations," Blenheim continued. "In fifty papers there are accounts of the criminal android. What is there, outside the depredations, that is also in fifty papers?"

"I don't know, Mr. Blenheim."

"It was a rhetorical question. Here is the answer. The weather."

"What?"

"The weather." Blenheim nodded. "Each crime was committed on a day when the temperature was above ninety degrees Fahrenheit."

"But that's impossible," Vandaleur exclaimed. "It was cold at the university on Lyra Alpha."

"We have no record of any crime committed on Lyra Alpha. There is no paper."

"No. That's right. I—" Vandaleur was confused. Suddenly he exclaimed. "No. You're right. The furnace room. It was hot down there. Hot! Of course. My God, yes! That's the answer. Dallas Brady's electric furnace... the rice deltas on Paragon. So jeet your seat. Yes. But why? Why? My God, why?"

I came into the house at that moment and, passing the study, saw Vandaleur and Blenheim. I entered, awaiting commands, my multiple aptitudes devoted to service.

"That's the android, eh?" Blenheim said after a long moment.

"Yes," Vandaleur answered, still confused by the discovery.

"And that explains why it refused to attack you that night on the Strand. It wasn't hot enough to break the prime directive. Only in the heat...The heat, all reet!" He looked at the android. A lunatic command passed from man to android. I refused. It is forbidden to endanger life. Vandaleur gestured furiously, then seized Blenheim's shoulders and yanked him back out of his desk chair to the floor. Blenheim shouted once. Vandaleur leaped on him like a tiger, pinning him to the floor and sealing his mouth with one hand.

"Find a weapon," I called to the android.

"It is forbidden to endanger life."

"This is a fight for self-preservation. Bring me a weapon!" He held the squirming mathematician with all his weight. I went at once to a cupboard where I knew a revolver was kept. I checked it. It was loaded with five cartridges. I handed it to Vandaleur. I took it, rammed the barrel against Blenheim's head and pulled the trigger. He shuddered once.

We had three hours before the cook returned from her day off. We looted the house. We took Blenheim's money and jewels. We packed a bag with clothes. We took Blenheim's notes, destroyed the newspapers, and we fled, carefully locking the door behind us. In Blenheim's study we left a pile of crumpled papers under a half inch of burning candle. And we soaked the rug around it with kerosene. No, I did all that. The android refused. I am forbidden to endanger life or property.

All reet!

They took the tubes to Leicester Square, changed trains and rode to the British Museum. There they got off and went to a small Georgian house just off Russell Square. A shingle in the window read: NAN WEBB, PSYCHOMETRIC CONSULTANT. Vandaleur had made a note of the address some weeks earlier. They went into the house. The android waited in the foyer with the bag. Vandaleur entered Nan Webb's office.

She was a tall woman with gray shingled hair, very fine English complexion and very bad English legs. Her features were blunt, her expression acute. She nodded to Vandaleur, finished a letter, sealed it and looked up.

"My name," I said, "is Vanderbilt. James Vanderbilt."

"Quite."

"I'm an exchange student at London University."

"Quite."

"I've been researching on the killer android, and I think

I've discovered something very interesting. I'd like your advice
on it. What is your fee?"

"What is your college at the university?"

"Why?"

"There is a discount for students."

"Merton College."

"That will be two pounds, please."

Vandaleur placed two pounds on the desk and added to the
fee Blenheim's notes. "There is a correlation," he said, "between the crimes of the android and the weather. You will note
that each crime was committed when the temperature rose above
ninety degrees Fahrenheit. Is there a psychometric answer for
this?"

Nan Webb nodded, studied the notes for a moment, put
down the sheets of paper and said: "Synesthesia, obviously."

"What?"

"Synesthesia," she repeated. "When a sensation, Mr. Vanderbilt, is interpreted immediately in terms of a sensation from
a different sense organ than the one stimulated, it is called
synesthesia. For example: A sound stimulus gives rise to a
simultaneous sensation of definite color. Or color gives rise to
a sensation of taste. Or a light stimulus gives rise to a sensation
of sound. There can be confusion or short circuiting of any
sensation of taste, smell, pain, pressure, temperature and so
on. D'you understand?"

"I think so."

"Your research has probably uncovered the fact that the
android most probably reacts to temperature stimulus above
the ninety-degree level synesthetically. Most probably there is
an endocrine response. Probably a temperature linkage with
the android adrenal surrogate. High temperatute brings about
a response of fear, anger, excitement and violent physical activity . . . all within the province of the adrenal gland."

"Yes. I see. Then if the android were to be kept in cold
climates. . . ."

"There would be neither stimulus nor response. There would
be no crimes. Quite."

"I see. What is psychotic projection?"

"How do you mean?"

"Is there any danger of projection with regard to the owner
of the android?"

"Very interesting. Projection is a throwing forward. It is

the process of throwing out upon another the ideas or impulses that belong to oneself. The paranoid, for example, projects upon others his conflicts and disturbances in order to externalize them. He accuses, directly or by implication, other men of having the very sicknesses with which he is struggling himself."

"And the danger of projection?"

"It is the danger of the victim's believing what is implied. If you live with a psychotic who projects his sickness upon you, there is a danger of falling into his psychotic pattern and becoming virtually psychotic yourself. As, no doubt, is happening to you, Mr. Vandaleur."

Vandaleur leaped to his feet.

"You are an ass," Nan Webb went on crisply. She waved the sheets of notes. "This is no exchange student's writing. It's the unique cursive of the famous Blenheim. Every scholar in England knows this blind writing. There is no Merton College at London University. That was a miserable guess. Merton is one of the Oxford Colleges. And you, Mr. Vandaleur, are so obviously infected by association with your deranged android...by projection, if you will...that I hesitate between calling the Metropolitan Police and the Hospital for the Criminally Insane."

I took the gun out and shot her.

Reet!

"Antares Two, Alpha Aurigae, Acrux Four, Pollux Nine, Rigel Centaurus," Vandaleur said. "They're all cold. Cold as a witch's kiss. Mean temperatures of forty degrees Fahrenheit. Never get hotter than seventy. We're in business again. Watch that curve."

The multiple-aptitude android swung the wheel with its accomplished hands. The car took the curve sweetly and sped on through the northern marshes, the reeds stretching for miles, brown and dry, under the cold English sky. The sun was sinking swiftly. Overhead, a lone flight of bustards flapped clumsily eastward. High above the flight, a lone helicopter drifted toward home and warmth.

"No more warmth for us," I said. "No more heat. We're safe when we're cold. We'll hole up in Scotland, make a little money, get across to Norway, build a bankroll and then ship out. We'll settle on Pollux. We're safe. We've licked it. We can live again."

There was a startling *bleep* from overhead, and then a ragged roar: "ATTENTION JAMES VANDALEUR AND ANDROID. ATTENTION JAMES VANDALEUR AND ANDROID."

Vandaleur started and looked up. The lone helicopter was floating above them. From its belly came amplified commands: "YOU ARE SURROUNDED. THE ROAD IS BLOCKED. YOU ARE TO STOP YOUR CAR AT ONCE AND SUBMIT TO ARREST. STOP AT ONCE!"

I looked at Vandaleur for orders.

"Keep driving," Vandaleur snapped.

The helicopter dropped lower: "ATTENTION ANDROID. YOU ARE IN CONTROL OF THE VEHICLE. YOU ARE TO STOP AT ONCE. THIS IS A STATE DIRECTIVE SUPERSEDING ALL PRIVATE COMMANDS."

The car slowed.

"What the hell are you doing?" I shouted.

"A state directive supercedes all private commands," the android answered. "I must point out to you that—"

"Get the hell away from the wheel," Vandaleur ordered. I clubbed the android, yanked him sideways and squirmed over him to the wheel. The car veered off the road in that moment and went churning through the frozen mud and dry reeds. Vandaleur regained control and continued westward through the marshes toward a parallel highway five miles distant.

"We'll beat their goddamned block," he grunted.

The car pounded and surged. The helicopter dropped even lower. A searchlight blazed from the belly of the plane.

"ATTENTION JAMES VANDALEUR AND ANDROID. SUBMIT TO ARREST. THIS IS A STATE DIRECTIVE SUPERSEDING ALL PRIVATE COMMANDS."

"He can't submit," Vandaleur shouted wildly. "There's no one to submit to. He can't and I won't."

"Christ!" I muttered. "We'll beat them yet. We'll beat the block. We'll beat the heat. We'll—"

"I must point out to you," I said, "that I am required by my prime directive to obey state directives which supersede all private commands. I must submit to arrest."

"Who says it's a state directive?" Vandaleur said. "Them? Up in that plane? They've got to show credentials. They've got to prove it's state authority before you submit. How d'you know they're not crooks trying to trick us?"

Holding the wheel with one arm, he reached into his side pocket to make sure the gun was still in place. The car skidded.

The tires squealed on frost and reeds. The wheel was wrenched from his grasp and the car yawed up a small hillock and overturned. The motor roared and the wheels screamed. Vandaleur crawled out and dragged the android with him. For the moment we were outside the cone of light blazing down from the helicopter. We blundered off into the marsh, into the blackness, into concealment . . . Vandaleur running with a pounding heart, hauling the android along.

The helicopter circled and soared over the wrecked car, searchlight peering, loudspeaker braying. On the highway we had left, lights appeared as the pursuing and blocking parties gathered and followed radio directions from the plane. Vandaleur and the android continued deeper and deeper into the marsh, working their way towards the parallel road and safety. It was night by now. The sky was a black matte. Not a star showed. The temperature was dropping. A southeast night wind knifed us to the bone.

Far behind there was a dull concussion. Vandaleur turned, gasping. The car's fuel had exploded. A geyser of flame shot up like a lurid fountain. It subsided into a low crater of burning reeds. Whipped by the wind, the distant hem of flame fanned up into a wall, ten feet high. The wall began marching down on us, crackling fiercely. Above it, a pall of oily smoke surged forward. Behind it, Vandaleur could make out the figures of men . . . a mass of beaters searching the marsh.

"Christ!" I cried and searched desperately for safety. He ran, dragging me with him, until their feet crunched through the surface ice of a pool. He trampled the ice furiously, then flung himself down in the numbing water, pulling the android with us.

The wall of flame approached. I could hear the crackle and feel the heat. He could see the searchers clearly. Vandaleur reached into his side pocket for the gun. The pocket was torn. The gun was gone. He groaned and shook with cold and terror. The light from the marsh fire was blinding. Overhead, the helicopter floated helplessly to one side, unable to fly through the smoke and flames and aid the searchers, who were beating far to the right of us.

"They'll miss us," Vandaleur whispered. "Keep quiet. That's an order. They'll miss us. We'll beat them. We'll beat the fire. We'll—"

Three distinct shots sounded less than a hundred feet from the fugitives. *Blam! Blam! Blam!* They came from the last three cartridges in my gun as the marsh fire reached it where it had dropped, and exploded the shells. The searchers turned toward the sound and began working directly toward us. Vandaleur cursed hysterically and tried to submerge even deeper to escape the intolerable heat of the fire. The android began to twitch.

The wall of flame surged up to them. Vandaleur took a deep breath and prepared to submerge until the flame passed over them. The android shuddered and suddenly began to scream.

"All reet! All reet!" it shouted. "Be fleet be fleet!"

"Damn you!" I shouted. I tried to drown the android.

"Damn you!" I cursed. I smashed Vandaleur's face.

The android battered Vandaleur, who fought it off until it burst out of the mud and staggered upright. Before I could return to the attack, the live flames captured it hypnotically. It danced and capered in a lunatic rumba before the wall of fire. Its legs twisted. Its arms waved. The fingers writhed in a private rumba of their own. It shrieked and sang and ran in a crooked waltz before the embrace of the heat, a muddy monster silhouetted against the brilliant sparkling flare.

The searchers shouted. There were shots. The android spun around twice and then continued its horrid dance before the face of the flames. There was a rising gust of wind. The fire swept around the capering figure and enveloped it for a roaring moment. Then the fire swept on, leaving behind it a sobbing mass of synthetic flesh oozing scarlet blood that would never coagulate.

The thermometer would have registered 1200° wondrously Fahrenheit.

Vandaleur didn't die. I got away. They missed him while they watched the android caper and die. But I don't know which of us he is these days. Psychotic projection, Wanda warned me. Projection, Nan Webb told him. If you live with a crazy machine long enough, I become crazy too. Reet!

But we know the truth. We know that they were wrong. It was the other way around. It was the man that was corrupting the machine . . . any machine . . . all machines. The new robot and Vandaleur know that because the new robot's started twitching too. Reet!

Here on cold Pollux, the robot is twitching and singing. No heat, but my fingers writhe. No heat, but it's taken the little Talley girl off for a solitary walk. A cheap labor robot . . . A servo-mechanism . . . all I could afford . . . but it's twitching and humming and walking alone with the child somewhere and I can't find them. Christ! Vandaleur can't find me before it's too late. Cool and discreet, honey, in the dancing frost while the thermometer registers 10° fondly Fahrenheit.

GOODLIFE

Fred Saberhagen

"It's only a machine, Hemphill," said the dying man in a small voice.

Hemphill, drifting weightless in near-darkness, heard him with only faint contempt and pity. Let the wretch go out timidly, forgiving the universe everything, if he found the going-out easier that way!

Hemphill kept on staring out through the port, at the dark crenellated shape that blotted out so many of the stars.

There was probably just this one compartment of the passenger ship left livable, with three people in it, and the air whining out in steady leaks that would soon exhaust the emergency tanks. The ship was a wreck, torn and beaten, yet Hemphill's view of the enemy was steady. It must be a force of the enemy's that kept the wreck from spinning.

Now the young woman, another passenger, came drifting across the compartment to touch Hemphill on the arm. He thought her name was Maria something.

"Listen," she began. "Do you think we might—"

In her voice there was no despair, but the tone of planning; and so Hemphill had begun to listen to her. But she was interrupted.

The very walls of the cabin reverberated, driven like speaker diaphragms through the power of the enemy force field that still gripped the butchered hull. The quavering voice of the berserker machine came in:

"You who can still hear me, live on. I plan to spare you. I am sending a boat to save you from death."

Hemphill was sick with frustrated rage. He had never heard a berserker's voice in reality before, but still it was familiar as an old nightmare. He could feel the woman's hand pull away from his arm, and then he saw that in his rage he had raised both his hands to be claws, then fists that almost smashed themselves against the port. The damned thing wanted to take him inside it! Of all people in space it wanted to make him prisoner!

A plan rose instantly in his mind and flowed smoothly into action; he spun away from the port. There were warheads, for small defensive missiles, here in this compartment. He remembered seeing them.

The other surviving man, a ship's officer, dying slowly, bleeding through his uniform tatters, saw what Hemphill was doing in the wreckage, and drifted in front of him interferingly.

"You can't do that . . . you'll only destroy the boat it sends . . . if it lets you do that much . . . there may be other people . . . still alive here. . . ."

The man's face had been upside-down before Hemphill as the two of them drifted. As their movement let them see each other in normal position, the wounded man stopped talking, gave up and rotated himself away, drifting inertly as if already dead.

Hemphill could not hope to manage a whole warhead, but he could extract the chemical-explosive detonator, of a size to carry under one arm. All passengers had put on emergency spacesuits when the unequal battle had begun; now he found himself an extra air tank and some officer's laser pistol, which he stuck in a loop of his suit's belt.

The girl approached him again. He watched her warily.

"Do it," she said with quiet conviction, while the three of them spun slowly in the near-darkness, and the air leaks whined. "Do it. The loss of a boat will weaken it, a little, for the next fight. And we here have no chance anyway."

"Yes." He nodded approvingly. This girl understood what

was important: to hurt a berserker, to smash, burn, destroy, to kill it finally. Nothing else mattered very much.

He pointed to the wounded mate, and whispered: "Don't let him give me away."

She nodded silently. It might hear them talking. If it could speak through these walls, it might be listening.

"A boat's coming," said the wounded man, in a calm and distant voice.

"Goodlife!" called the machine-voice, cracking between syllables as always.

"Here!" He woke up with a start, and got quickly to his feet. He had been dozing almost under the dripping end of a drinking-water pipe.

"Goodlife!" There were no speakers or scanners in this little compartment; the call came from some distance away.

"Here!" He ran toward the call, his feet shuffling and thumping on metal. He had dozed off, being tired. Even though the battle had been a little one, there had been extra tasks for him, servicing and directing the commensal machines that roamed the endless ducts and corridors repairing damage. It was small help he could give, he knew.

Now his head and neck bore sore spots from the helmet he had had to wear; and his body was chafed in places from the unaccustomed covering he had to put on it when a battle came. This time, happily, there had been no battle damage at all.

He came to the flat glass eye of a scanner, and shuffled to a stop, waiting.

"Goodlife, the perverted machine has been destroyed, and the few badlives left are helpless."

"Yes!" He jiggled his body up and down in happiness.

"I remind you, life is evil," said the voice of the machine.

"Life is evil, I am Goodlife!" he said quickly, ceasing his jiggling. He did not think punishment impended, but he wanted to be sure.

"Yes. Like your parents before you, you have been useful. Now I plan to bring other humans inside myself, to study them closely. Your next use will be with them, in my experiments. I remind you, they are badlife. We must be careful!"

"Badlife." He knew they were creatures shaped like himself, existing in the world beyond the machine. They caused the shudders and shocks and damage that made up a battle. "Badlife—here." It was a chilling thought. He raised his own hands and looked at them, then turned his attention up and down the passage in which he stood, trying to visualize the badlife become real before him.

"Go now to the medical room," said the machine. "You must be immunized against disease before you approach the badlife."

Hemphill made his way from one ruined compartment to another, until he found a gash in the outer hull that was plugged nearly shut. While he wrenched at the obstructing material he heard the clanging arrival of the berserker's boat, come for prisoners. He pulled harder, the obstruction gave way, and he was blown out into space.

Around the wreck were hundreds of pieces of flotsam, held near by tenuous magnetism or perhaps by the berserker's force fields. Hemphill found that his suit worked well enough. With its tiny jet he moved around the shattered hull of the passenger ship to where the berserker's boat had come to rest.

The dark blot of the berserker machine came into view against the starfield of deep space, battlemented like a fortified city of old, and larger than any such city had ever been. He could see that the berserker's boat had somehow found the right compartment and clamped itself to the wrecked hull. It would be gathering in Maria and the wounded man. Fingers on the plunger that would set off his bomb, Hemphill drifted closer.

On the brink of death, it annoyed him that he would never know with certainty that the boat was destroyed. And it was such a trifling blow to strike, such a small revenge.

Still drifting closer, holding the plunger ready, he saw the puff of decompressed air moisture as the boat disconnected itself from the hull. The invisible force fields of the berserker surged, tugging at the boat, at Hemphill, at bits of wreckage within yards of the boat.

He managed to clamp himself to the boat before it was pulled away from him. He thought he had an hour's air in his suit tank, more than he would need.

As the berserker pulled him toward itself, Hemphill's mind hung over the brink of death, Hemphill's fingers gripped the plunger of his bomb. In his mind, his night-colored enemy was death. The black, scarred surface of it hurtled closer in the unreal starlight, becoming a planet toward which the boat fell.

Hemphill still clung to the boat when it was pulled into an opening that could have accommodated many ships. The size and power of the berserker were all around him, enough to overwhelm hate and courage alike.

His little bomb was a pointless joke. When the boat touched at a dark internal dock, Hemphill leaped away from it and scrambled to find a hiding place.

As he cowered on a shadowed ledge of metal, his hand wanted to fire the bomb, simply to bring death and escape. He forced his hand to be still. He forced himself to watch while the two human prisoners were sucked from the boat through a pulsing transparent tube that passed out of sight through a bulkhead. Not knowing what he meant to accomplish, he pushed himself in the direction of the tube. He glided through the dark enormous cavern almost weightlessly; the berserker's mass was enough to give it a small natural gravity of its own.

Within ten minutes he came upon an unmistakable airlock. It seemed to have been cut with a surrounding section of hull from some Earth warship and set into the bulkhead.

Inside an airlock would be as good a place for a bomb as he was likely to find. He got the outer door open and went in, apparently without triggering any alarms. If he destroyed himself here, he would deprive the berserker of—what? Why should it need an airlock at all?

Not for prisoners, thought Hemphill, if it sucks them in through a tube. Hardly an entrance built for enemies. He tested the air in the lock, and opened his helmet. For air-breathing friends, the size of men? That was a contradiction. Everything that lived and breathed must be a berserker's enemy, except the unknown beings who had built it. Or so man had thought, until now.

The inner door of the lock opened at Hemphill's push, and artificial gravity came on. He walked through into a narrow and badly lighted passage, his fingers ready on the plunger of his bomb.

"Go in, Goodlife," said the machine. "Look closely at each of them."

Goodlife made an uncertain sound in his throat, like a servomotor starting and stopping. He was gripped by a feeling

that resembled hunger or the fear of punishment—because he
was going to see life-forms directly now, not as old images on
a stage. Knowing the reason for the unpleasant feeling did not
help. He stood hesitating outside the door of the room where
the badlife was being kept. He had put on his suit again, as
the machine had ordered. The suit would protect him if the
badlife tried to damage him.

"Go in," the machine repeated.

"Maybe I'd better not," Goodlife said in misery, remem-
bering to speak loudly and clearly. Punishment was always less
likely when he did.

"Punish, punish," said the voice of the machine.

When it said the word twice, punishment was very near.
As if already feeling in his bones the wrenching pain-that-left-
no-damage, he opened the door quickly and stepped in.

He lay on the floor, bloody and damaged, in strange ragged
suiting. And at the same time he was still in the doorway. His
own shape was on the floor, the same human form he knew,
but now seen entirely from outside. More than an image, far
more, it was himself now bilocated. There, here, himself, not-
himself—

Goodlife fell back against the door. He raised his arm and
tried to bite it, forgetting his suit. He pounded his suited arms
violently together, until there was bruised pain enough to nail
him to himself where he stood.

Slowly, the terror subsided. Gradually his intellect could
explain it and master it. This is me, here, here in the doorway.
That, *there*, on the floor—that is another life. Another body,
corroded like me with vitality. Only far worse than I. That one
on the floor is badlife.

Maria Juarez had prayed continuously for a long time, her
eyes closed. Cold impersonal grippers had moved her this way
and that. Her weight had come back, and there was air to
breathe when her helmet and her suit had been carefully removed. She opened her eyes and struggled when the grippers
began to remove her inner coverall; she saw that she was in a
low-ceilinged room, surrounded by man-sized machines of various shapes. When she struggled they gave up undressing her,
chained her to the wall by one ankle, and glided away. The
dying mate had been dropped at the other end of the room, as

if not worth the trouble of further handling.

The man with the cold dead eyes, Hemphill, had tried to make a bomb, and failed. Now there would probably be no quick end to life——

When she heard the door open she opened her eyes again, to watch without comprehension, while the bearded young man in the ancient spacesuit went through senseless contortions in the doorway, and finally came forward to stand staring down at the dying man on the floor. The visitor's fingers moved with speed and precision when he raised his hands to the fasteners of his helmet; but the helmet's removal revealed ragged hair and beard framing a slack idiot's face.

He set the helmet down, then scratched and rubbed his shaggy head, never taking his eyes from the man on the floor. He had not yet looked once at Maria, and she could look nowhere but at him. She had never seen a face so blank on a living person. This was what happened to a berserker's prisoner!

And yet—and yet. Maria had seen brainwashed men before, ex-criminals on her own planet. She felt this man was something more—or something less.

The bearded man knelt beside the mate, with an air of hesitation, and reached out to touch him. The dying man stirred feebly, and looked up without comprehension. The floor under him was wet with blood.

The stranger took the mate's limp arm and bent it back and forth, as if interested in the articulation of the human elbow. The mate groaned, and struggled feebly. The stranger suddenly shot out his metal-gauntleted hands and seized the dying man by the throat.

Maria could not move, or turn her eyes away, though the whole room seemed to spin slowly, then faster and faster, around the focus of those armored hands.

The bearded man released his grip and stood erect, still watching the body at his feet.

"Turned off," he said distinctly.

Perhaps she moved. For whatever reason, the bearded man raised his sleepwalker's face to look at her. He did not meet her eyes, or avoid them. His eye movements were quick and alert, but the muscles of his face just hung there under the skin. He came toward her.

Why, he's young, she thought, hardly more than a boy. She backed against the wall and waited, standing. Women on her planet were not brought up to faint. Somehow, the closer he came, the less she feared him. But if he had smiled once, she would have screamed, on and on.

He stood before her, and reached out one hand to touch her face, her hair, her body. She stood still; she felt no lust in him, no meanness and no kindness. It was as if he radiated an emptiness.

"Not images," said the young man as if to himself. Then another word, sounding like: "Badlife."

Almost Maria dared to speak to him. The strangled man lay on the deck a few yards away.

The young man turned and shuffled deliberately away from her. She had never seen anyone who walked just like him. He picked up his helmet and went out the door without looking back.

A pipe streamed water into one corner of her little space, where it gurgled away through a hole in the floor. The gravity seemed to be set at about Earth level. Maria sat leaning against the wall, praying and listening to her heart pound. It almost stopped when the door opened again, very slightly at first, then enough for a large cake of pink and green stuff that seemed to be food. The machine walked around the dead man on its way out.

She had eaten a little of the cake when the door opened again, very slightly at first, then enough for a man to step quickly in. It was Hemphill, the cold-eyed one from the ship, leaning a bit to one side as if dragged down by the weight of the little bomb he carried under his arm. After a quick look around he shut the door behind him and crossed the room to her, hardly glancing down as he stepped over the body of the mate.

"How many of them are there?" Hemphill whispered, bending over her. She had remained seated on the floor, too surprised to move or speak.

"Who?" she finally managed.

He jerked his head toward the door impatiently. "Them. The ones who live here inside *it,* and serve it. I saw one of them coming out of this room, when I was out in the passage. It's fixed up a lot of living space for them."

"I've only seen one man."

His eyes glinted at that. He showed Maria how the bomb could be made to explode, and gave it to her to hold, while he began to burn through her chain with his laser pistol. They exchanged information on what had happened. She did not think she would ever be able to set off the bomb and kill herself, but she did not tell that to Hemphill.

Just as they stepped out of the prison room, Hemphill had a bad moment when three machines rolled toward them from around a corner. But the things ignored the two frozen humans and rolled silently past them, going on out of sight.

He turned to Maria with an exultant whisper: "The damned thing is three-quarters blind, here inside its own skin!"

She only waited, watching him with frightened eyes.

With the beginning of hope, a vague plan was forming in his mind. He led her along the passage, saying: "Now we'll see about that man. Or men." Was it too good to be true, that there was only one of them?

The corridors were badly lit, and full of uneven jogs and steps. Carelessly built concessions to life, he thought. He moved in the direction he had seen the man take.

After a few minutes of cautious advance, Hemphill heard the shuffling footsteps of one person ahead, coming nearer. He handed the bomb to Maria again, and pressed her behind him. They waited in a dark niche.

The footsteps approached with careless speed, a vague shadow bobbing ahead of them. The shaggy head swung so abruptly into view that Hemphill's metal-fisted swing was almost too late. The blow only grazed the back of the skull; the man yelped and staggered off balance and fell down. He was wearing an old-model spacesuit, with no helmet.

Hemphill crouched over him, shoving the laser pistol almost into his face. "Make a sound and I'll kill you. Where are the others?"

The face looking up at Hemphill was stunned—worse than stunned. It seemed more dead than alive, though the eyes moved alertly enough from Hemphill to Maria and back, disregarding the gun.

"He's the same one," Maria whispered.

"Where are your friends?" Hemphill demanded.

The man felt the back of his head, where he had been hit.

"Damage," he said tonelessly, as if to himself. Then he reached up for the pistol, so calmly and steadily that he was nearly able to touch it.

Hemphill jumped back a step, and barely kept himself from firing. "Sit down or I'll kill you! Now tell me who you are, and how many others are here."

The man sat there calmly, with his putty face showing nothing. He said: "Your speech is steady in tone from word to word, not like that of the machine. You hold a killing tool there. Give it to me and I will destroy you and—that one."

It seemed this man was only a brainwashed ruin, instead of an unspeakable traitor. Now what use could be made of him? Hemphill moved back another step, slowly lowering the pistol.

Maria spoke to their prisoner. "Where are you from? What planet?"

A blank stare.

"Your home," she persisted. "Where were you born?"

"From the birth tank." Sometimes the tones of the man's voice shifted like the berserker's, as if he was a fearful comedian mocking it.

Hemphill gave an unstable laugh. "From a birth tank, of course. What else? Now for the last time, where are the others?"

"I do not understand."

Hemphill sighed. "All right. Where's this birth tank?" He had to start with something.

The place looked like the storeroom of a biology lab, badly lighted, piled and crowded with equipment, laced with pipes and conduits. Probably no living technician had ever worked here.

"You were *born* here?" Hemphill demanded.

"Yes."

"He's crazy."

"No. Wait." Maria's voice sank to an even lower whisper, as if she was frightened anew. She took the hand of the slack-faced man. He bent his head to stare at their touching hands.

"Do you have a name?" she asked, as if speaking to a lost child.

"I am Goodlife."

"I think it's hopeless," put in Hemphill.

The girl ignored him. "Goodlife? My name is Maria. And this is Hemphill."

No reaction.

"Who were your parents? Father? Mother?"

"They were goodlife too. They helped the machine. There was a battle, and badlife killed them. But they had given cells of their bodies to the machine, and from those cells it made me. Now I am the only goodlife."

"Great God," whispered Hemphill.

Silent, awed attention seemed to move Goodlife when threats and pleas had not. His face twisted in awkward grimaces; he turned to stare into a corner. Then, for almost the first time, he volunteered a communication: "I know they were like you. A man and a woman."

Hemphill wanted to sweep every cubic foot of the miles of mechanism with his hatred; he looked around at every side and angle of the room.

"The damned things," he said, his voice cracking like the berserker's. "What they've done to me. To you. To everyone."

Plans seemed to come to him when the strain of hating was greatest. He moved quickly to put a hand on Goodlife's shoulder. "Listen to me. Do you know what a radioactive isotope is?"

"Yes."

"There will be a place, somewhere, where the—the machine decided what it will do next—what strategy to follow. A place holding a block of some isotope with a long half-life. Probably near the center of the machine. Do you know of such a place?"

"Yes, I know where the strategic housing is."

"Strategic housing." Hope mounted to a strong new level. "Is there a way for us to reach it?"

"You are badlife!" He knocked Hemphill's hand away, awkwardly. "You want to damage the machine, and you have damaged me. You are to be destroyed."

Maria took over, trying to soothe. "Goodlife—we are not bad, this man and I. Those who built this machine are the badlife. Someone built it, you know, some living people built it, long ago. They were the real badlife."

"Badlife." He might be agreeing with Maria, or accusing her.

"Don't you want to live, Goodlife? Hemphill and I want to live. We want to help you, because you're alive, like us. Won't you help us now?"

Goodlife was silent for a few moments, contemplating a bulkhead. Then he turned back to face them and said: "All life thinks it is, but it is not. There are only particles, energy and space, and the laws of the machines."

Maria kept at him. "Goodlife, listen to me. A wise man once said: 'I think, therefore I am.'"

"A wise man?" he questioned, in his cracking voice. Then he sat down on the deck, hugging his knees and rocking back and forth. He might be thinking.

Drawing Maria aside, Hemphill said: "You know, we have a faint hope now. There's plenty of air in here, there's water and food. There are warships following this thing, there must be. If we can find a way to disable it, we can wait and maybe be picked up in a month or two. Or less."

She watched him silently for a moment. "Hemphill—what have these machines done to you?"

"My wife—my children." He thought his voice sounded almost indifferent. "They were on Pascalo, three years ago; there was nothing left. This machine, or one like it."

She took his hand, as she had taken Goodlife's. They both looked down at the joined fingers, then raised their eyes, smiling briefly together at the similarity of action.

"Where's the bomb?" Hemphill thought aloud suddenly, spinning around.

It lay in a dim corner. He grabbed it up again, and strode over to where Goodlife sat rocking back and forth.

"Well, are you with us? Us, or the ones who built the machine?"

Goodlife stood up, and looked closely at Hemphill. "They were inspired by the laws of physics, which controlled their brains, to build the machine. Now the machine has preserved them as images. It has preserved my father and mother, and it will preserve me."

"What images do you mean? Where are they?"

"The images in the theater."

It seemed best to accustom this creature to cooperation, to win his confidence and at the same time learn about him and the machine. Then, on to the strategic housing. Hemphill made his voice friendly: "Will you guide us to the theater, Goodlife?"

• • •

It was by far the largest air-filled room they had yet found, and held a hundred seats of a shape usable by Earth-descended men, though Hemphill knew it had been built for someone else. The theater was elaborately furnished and well-lighted. When the door closed behind them, the ranked images of intelligent creatures brightened into life upon the stage.

The stage became a window into a vast hall. One person stood forward at an imaged lectern; he was a slender, fine-boned being, topologically like a man except for the single eye that stretched across his face, with a bright bulging pupil that slid to and fro like mercury.

The speaker's voice was a high-pitched torrent of clicks and whines. Most of those in the ranks behind him wore a kind of uniform. When he paused, they whined in unison.

"What does he say?" Maria whispered.

Gooldlife looked at her. "The machine has told me that it has lost the meaning of the sounds."

"Then may we see the images of your parents, Goodlife?"

Hemphill, watching the stage, started to object; but the girl was right. The sight of this fellow's parents might be more immediately helpful.

Goodlife found a control somewhere.

Hemphill was surprised momentarily that the parents appeared only in flat projected pictures. First the man was there, against a plain background, blue eyes and neat short beard, nodding his head with a pleasant expression on his face. He wore the lining coverall of a spacesuit.

Then the woman, holding some kind of cloth before her for covering, and looking straight into the camera. She had a broad face and red braided hair. There was hardly time to see anything more before the alien orator was back, whining faster than ever.

Hemphill turned to ask: "Is that all? All you know of your parents?"

"Yes. The badlife killed them. Now they are images, they no longer think they exist."

Maria thought the creature in the projection was assuming a more didactic tone. Three-dimensional charts of stars and planets appeared near him, one after another, and he gestured at them as he spoke. He had vast numbers of stars and planets on his charts to boast about; she could tell somehow that he was boasting.

Hemphill was moving toward the stage a step at a time, more and more absorbed. Maria did not like the way the light of the images reflected on his face.

Goodlife, too, watched the stage pageant which perhaps he had seen a thousand times before. Maria could not tell what thoughts might be passing behind his meaningless face which had never had another human face to imitate. On impulse she took his arm again.

"Goodlife, Hemphill and I are alive, like you. Will you help us now, to stay alive? Then in the future we will always help you." She had a sudden mental picture of Goodlife rescued, taken to a planet, cowering among the staring badlife.

"Good. Bad." His hand reached to take hold of hers; he had removed his suit gauntlets. He swayed back and forth as if she attracted and repelled him at the same time. She wanted to scream and wail for him, to tear apart with her fingers the mindlessly proceeding metal that had made him what he was.

"We've got them!" It was Hemphill, coming back from the stage, where the recorded tirade went on unrelentingly. He was exultant. "Don't you see? He's showing what must be a complete catalogue, of every star and rock they own. It's a victory speech. But when we study those charts we can find them, we can track them down and *reach* them!"

"Hemphill." She wanted to calm him back to concentration on immediate problems. "How old are those images up there? What part of the galaxy were they made in? Or do they even come from some other galaxy? Will we ever be able to tell?"

Hemphill lost some of his enthusiasm. "Anyway, it's a chance to track them down; it's information we've got to save." He pointed at Goodlife. "He's got to take me to what he calls the strategic housing; then we can sit and wait for the warships, or maybe get off this damned thing in a boat."

She stroked Goodlife's hand, soothing a baby. "Yes, but he's confused. How could he be anything else?"

"Of course." Hemphill paused to consider. "You can handle him much better than I."

She didn't answer.

Hemphill went on: "Now you're a woman, and he appears to be a physically healthy young male. Calm him down if you like, but somehow you've *got* to persuade him to help me. Everything depends on it." He turned toward the stage again, unable to take more than half his mind from the star charts. "Go for a little walk and talk with him; don't get far away."

And what else was there to do? She led Goodlife from the theater while the dead man on the stage clicked and shouted, cataloguing his thousand suns.

Too much had happened, was still happening, and all at once he could no longer stand to be near the badlife. Goodlife found himself pulling away from the female, running, flying down the passages, toward the place where he had fled when he was small and strange fears had come from nowhere. It was the room where the machine always saw and heard him, and was ready to talk to him.

He stood before the attention of the machine, in the chamber-that-has-shrunk. He thought of the place so, because he could remember it clearly as a larger room, where the scanners and speakers of the machine towered above his head. He knew the real change had been his own physical growth; still, this compartment was set apart in a special association with food and sleep and protective warmth.

"I have listened to the badlife, and shown them things," he confessed, fearing punishment.

"I know that, Goodlife, for I have watched. These things have become a part of my experiment."

What joyous relief! The machine said nothing of punishment, though it must know that the words and actions of the badlife had shaken and confused his own ideas. He had even imagined himself showing the man Hemphill the strategic housing, and so putting an end to all punishment, for always.

"They wanted me—they wanted me to—"

"I have watched. I have listened. The man is tough and evil, powerfully moitivated to fight against me. I must understand his kind, for they cause much damage. He must be tested to his limits, to destruction. He believes himself free inside me, and so he will not think as a prisoner. This is important."

Goodlife pulled off his irritating suit; the machine would not let the badlife in here. He sank down to the floor and wrapped his arms around the base of the scanner-speaker console. Once long ago the machine had given him a thing that was soft and warm when he held it . . . he closed his eyes.

"What are my orders?" he asked sleepily. Here in this chamber all was steady and comforting, as always.

"First, do not tell the badlife of these orders. Then, do what the man Hemphill tells you to do. No harm will come to me."

"He has a bomb."

"I watched his approach, and I disabled his bomb, even before he entered to attack me. His pistol can do me no serious harm. Do you think one badlife can conquer me?"

"No." Smiling, reassured, he curled into a more comfortable position. "Tell me about my parents." He had heard the story a thousand times, but it was always good.

"Your parents were good, they gave themselves to me. Then, during a great battle, the badlife killed them. The badlife hated them, as they hate you. When they say they like you, they lie, with the evil untruth of all badlife.

"But your parents were good, and each gave me a part of their bodies, and from the parts I made you. Your parents were destroyed completely by the badlife, or I would have saved even their non-functioning bodies for you to see. That would have been good."

"Yes."

"The two badlife have searched for you. Now they are resting. Sleep, Goodlife."

He slept.

Awakening, he remembered a dream in which two people had beckoned him to join them on the stage of the theater. He knew they were his mother and father, though they looked like the two badlife. The dream faded before his waking mind could grasp it firmly.

He ate and drank, while the machine talked to him.

"If the man Hemphill wants to be guided to the strategic housing, take him there. I will capture him there, and let him escape later to try again. When finally he can be provoked to fight no more, I will destroy him. But I mean to preserve the life of the female. You and she will produce more goodlife for me."

"Yes!" It was immediately clear what a good thing that would be. They would give parts of their bodies to the machine, so new goodlife bodies could be built, cell by cell. And the man Hemphill, who punished and damaged with his fast-swinging arm, would be utterly destroyed.

When he rejoined the badlife, the man Hemphill barked questions and threatened punishment until Goodlife was confused and a little frightened. But Goodlife agreed to help, and was careful to reveal nothing of what the machine planned. Maria was more pleasant than ever. He touched her whenever he could.

Hemphill demanded to be taken to the strategic housing. Goodlife agreed at once; he had been there many times. There was a high-speed elevator that made the fifty mile journey easy.

Hemphill paused, before saying: "You're too damn willing, all of a sudden." Turning his face to Maria. "I don't trust him."

This badlife thought he was being false! Goodlife was angered; the machine never lied, and no properly obedient goodlife could lie.

Hemphill paced around, and finally demanded: "Is there any route that approaches this strategic housing in such a way that the machine cannot possibly watch us?"

Goodlife thought. "I believe there is one such way. We will have to carry extra tanks of air, and travel many miles through vacuum." The machine had said to help Hemphill, and help he would. He hoped he could watch when the male badlife was finally destroyed.

There had been a battle, perhaps fought while men on Earth were hunting the mammoth with spears. The berserker had met some terrible opponent, and had taken a terrible lance-thrust of a wound. A cavity two miles wide at the widest, and fifty miles deep, had been driven in by a sequence of shaped atomic charges, through level after level of machinery, deck after deck of armor, and had been stopped only by the last inner defenses of the buried unliving heart. The berserker had survived, and crushed its enemy, and soon afterwards its repair machines had sealed over the outer opening of the wound, using extra thicknesses of armor. It had meant to gradually rebuild the whole destruction; but there was so much life in the galaxy, and so much of it was stubborn and clever. Somehow battle damage accumulated faster than it could be repaired. The huge hole was used as a conveyor path, and never much worked on.

When Hemphill saw the blasted cavity—what little of it his tiny suit lamp could show—he felt a shrinking fear that was greater than any in his memory. He stopped on the edge of the void, drifting there with his arm instinctively around Maria. She had put on a suit and accompanied him, without being asked, without protest or eagerness.

They had already come an hour's journey from the airlock, through weightless vacuum inside the great machine. Goodlife had led the way through section after section, with every show of cooperation. Hemphill had the pistol ready, and the bomb, and two hundred feet of cord tied around his left arm.

But when Hemphill recognized the once-molten edge of the berserker's great scar for what it was, his delicate new hope of survival left him. This, the damned thing had survived. This, perhaps, had hardly weakened it. Again, the bomb under his arm was only a pathetic toy.

Goodlife drifted up to them. Hemphill had already taught him to touch helmets for speech in vacuum.

"This great damage is the one path we can take to reach the strategic housing without passing scanners or service machines. I will teach you to ride the conveyor. It will carry us most of the way."

The conveyor was a thing of force fields and huge rushing containers, hundreds of yards out in the enormous wound and running lengthwise through it. When the conveyor's force fields caught the people up, their weightlessness felt more than ever like falling, with occasional vast shapes, corpuscles of the berserker's bloodstream, flickering past in the near-darkness to show their speed of movement.

Hemphill flew beside Maria, holding her hand. Her face was hard to see, inside her helmet.

This conveyor was yet another and mad new world, a fairy tale of monsters and flying and falling. Hemphill fell past his fear into a new determination. I can do it, he thought. The thing is blind and helpless here. I will do it, and I will survive if I can.

Goodlife led them from the slowing conveyor, to drift into a chamber hollowed in the inner armor by the final explosion at the end of the ancient lance-thrust. The chamber was an empty sphere a hundred feet across, from which cracks radiated out into the solid armor. On the surface nearest the center of the berserker, one fissure was as wide as a door, where the last energy of the enemy's blow had driven ahead.

Goodlife touched helmets with Hemphill, and said: "I have seen the other end of this crack, from inside, at the strategic housing. It is only a few yards from here."

Hemphill hesitated for only a moment, wondering whether to send Goodlife through the twisting passage first. But if this was some incredibly complex trap, the trigger of it might be anywhere.

He touched his helmet to Maria's. "Stay behind him. Follow him through and keep an eye on him." Then Hemphill led the way.

The fissure narrowed as he followed it, but at its end it was still wide enough for him to force himself through.

He had reached another vast hollow sphere, the inner temple. In the center was a complexity the size of a small house, shock-mounted on a web of girders that ran from it in every direction. This could be nothing but the strategic housing. There was a glow from it like flickering moonlight; force field switches responding to the random atomic turmoil within, somehow choosing what human shipping lane or colony would be next attacked, and how.

Hemphill felt a pressure rising in his mind and soul, toward a climax of triumphal hate. He drifted forward, cradling his bomb tenderly, starting to unwind the cord wrapped around his arm. He tied the free end delicately to the plunger of the bomb, as he approached the central complex.

I mean to live, he thought, to watch the damned thing die. I will tape the bomb against the central block, that so-innocent looking slab in there, and I will brace myself around two hundred feet of these heavy metal corners, and pull the cord.

Goodlife stood braced in the perfect place from which to see the heart of the machine, watching the man Hemphill string his cord. Goodlife felt a certain satisfaction that his prediction had been right, that the strategic housing was approachable by this one narrow path of the great damage. They would not have to go back that way. When the badlife had been captured, all of them could ride up in the air-filled elevator Goodlife used when he came here for maintenance practice.

Hemphill had finished stringing his cord. Now he waved his arm at Goodlife and Maria, who clung to the same girder,

watching. Now Hemphill pulled on the cord. Of course, nothing
happened. The machine had said the bomb was disabled, and
the machine would make very certain in such a matter.

Maria pushed away from beside Goodlife, and drifted in
toward Hemphill.

Hemphill tugged again and again on his cord. Goodlife
sighed impatiently, and moved. There was a great cold in the
girders here; he could begin to feel it now through the fingers
and toes of his suit.

At last, when Hemphill started back to see what was wrong
with his device, the service machines came from where they
had been hiding, to seize him. He tried to draw his pistol, but
their grippers moved far too quickly.

It was hardly a struggle that Goodlife saw, but he watched
with interest. Hemphill's figure had gone rigid in the suit,
obviously straining every muscle to the limit. Why should the
badlife try to struggle against steel and atomic power? The
machines bore the man effortlessly away, toward the elevator
shaft. Goodlife felt an uneasiness.

Maria was drifting, her face turned back toward Goodlife.
He wanted to go to her and touch her again, but suddenly he
was a little afraid, as before when he had run from her. One
of the service machines came back from the elevator to grip
her and carry her away. She kept her face turned toward Goodlife. He turned away from her, a feeling like punishment in
the core of his being.

In the great cold silence, the flickering light from the strategic housing bathed everything. In the center, a chaotic block
of atoms. Elsewhere, engines, relays, sensing units. Where
was it, really, the mighty machine that spoke to him? Everywhere, and nowhere. Would these new feelings, brought by
the badlife, ever leave him? He tried to understand himself,
and could not begin.

Light flickered on a round shape a few yards away among
the girders, a shape that offended Goodlife's sense of the proper
and necessary in machinery. Looking closer, he saw it was a
space helmet.

The motionless figure was wedged only lightly in an angle
between frigid metal beams, but there was no force in here to
move it.

He could hear the suit creak, stiff with great cold, when he grabbed it and turned it. Unseeing blue eyes looked out at Goodlife through the faceplate. The man's face wore a neat short beard.

"Ahhh, yes," sighed Goodlife inside his own helmet. A thousand times he had seen the image of this face.

His father had been carrying something, heavy, strapped carefully to his ancient suit. His father had carried it this far, and here the old suit had wheezed and failed.

His father, too, had followed the logical narrow path of the great damage, to reach the strategic housing without being seen. His father had choked and died and frozen here, carrying toward the strategic housing what could only be a bomb.

Goodlife heard his own voice keening, without words, and he could not see plainly for the tears floating in his helmet. His fingers felt numbed with cold as he unstrapped the bomb and lifted it from his father. . . .

Hemphill was too exhausted to do more than gasp as the service machine carried him out of the elevator and along the air-filled corridor toward the prison room. When the machine went dead and dropped him, he had to lie still for long seconds before he could attack it again. It had hidden his pistol somewhere, so he began to beat on the robotlike thing with his armored fists, while it stood unresisting. Soon it toppled over. Hemphill sat on it and beat it some more, cursing it with sobbing breaths.

It was nearly a minute later when the tremor of the explosion, racing from the compounded chaos of the berserker's torn-out heart, racing through metal beams and decks, reached the corridor, where it was far too faint for anyone to feel.

Maria, completely weary, sat where her metal captor had dropped her, watching Hemphill, loving him in a way, and pitying him.

He stopped his pointless pounding of the machine under him, and said hoarsely: "It's a trick, another damned trick."

The tremor had been too faint for anyone to feel, here, but Maria shook her head. "No, I don't think so." She saw that power still seemed to be on in the elevator, and she watched the door of it.

Hemphill went away to search among the now-purposeless machines for weapons and food. He came back, raging again. What was probably an automatic destructor charge had wrecked the theater and the star-charts. They might as well see about getting away in the boat.

She ignored him, still watching an elevator door which never opened. Soon she began quietly to cry.

COLLECTIONS OF FANTASY AND SCIENCE FICTION